The
Ultra
Thin
Man

The Ultra Thin Man

PATRICK SWENSON

TOR®

A Tom Doherty Associates Book

New York

THE ULTRA THIN MAN

Copyright © 2014 by Patrick Swenson

A Tor Book
Published by Tom Doherty Associates, LLC
175 Fifth Avenue
New York, NY 10010

www.tor-forge.com

Tor® is a registered trademark of Tom Doherty Associates, LLC.

The Library of Congress Cataloging-in-Publication Data is available
upon request.

ISBN 978-0-7653-3694-1 (hardcover)
ISBN 978-1-4668-2929-9 (e-book)

Tor books may be purchased for educational, business, or
promotional use. For information on bulk purchases, please contact
Macmillan Corporate and Premium Sales Department at 1-800-221-7945,
extension 5442, or write specialmarkets@macmillan.com.

First Edition: August 2014

Printed in the United States of America

0 9 8 7 6 5 4 3 2 1

To the most important people in my life—

Orion Avery, son of fire and light, and elf ruler,

*my mom JoAnn and my four brothers and four sisters,
who've never failed to support this lifelong dream of mine,*

*my mom Dorothy, my dad Marvin, and my dad Oscar,
whose loving memories keep me going, even now,*

and Nichollow V

Acknowledgments

I can't even begin to count the people in my life whose friendship and guidance helped make this book a reality. No writer truly writes alone.

First readers provided support and made suggestions to make this book better. Thank you, Jack Skillingstead, Brenda Cooper, Nicole Thomson, Orlyn Carney, and Michael Bishop for your willingness to look at early drafts. I am truly amazed by my friends. They have encouraged me in so many ways that I would not be the person or the writer I am today without them. I wish I had space to name every one. I'd be remiss if I didn't at least single out my very best friends: Barb and J. C. Hendee, Jack Skillingstead, and Mark Teppo. Thanks for your unconditional friendship.

Thanks to David Hartwell, my editor, who believed in me way back at the Clarion West Writers Workshop in 1986. Twenty-six years later, he bought this book, then whipped it into shape. It's no secret he's one of the most respected editors in the SF field. Thanks also to Marco Palmieri, who from the beginning kept me on the straight and narrow, and never tired of answering my questions.

I'd also like to thank my agent, Paul Lucas, who took a chance and represented the book. Those phone calls and e-mails at the beginning helped change everything. I breathe a little easier knowing he has my back.

To my mom, JoAnn, and my brothers and sisters—Marva Kay, Mike, Kathi Jo, Scott, Melanie, Lesliann, Paul, and Jim—thank you for believing in me. Extra kudos go to brother Paul, who came up with the title *The Ultra Thin Man* (even though we didn't know what it meant), and wrote some early chapters with me. Years passed and our lives got busy and we stopped writing it. A number of years ago, Paul graciously said "yes" when I asked if I could write the book on my own. Although some of his early chapters were cut, moved, or reimagined, some of his input remains. Thanks, bro. I hope you like how it all turned out.

I belonged to several writers groups for many years, including the Fairwood Writers, some of which saw early chapters of this book. I apologize if I forget anyone, but these writers gave the most years of valuable critiques and advice. Thanks to Tracy Moore, Kevin Kerr, David Herter, David Addleman, Leslie Clark, Honna Swenson, Renee Stern, Darragh Metzger, David Silas, John Pitts, Brenda Cooper, Allan Rouselle, and Harold Gross.

To every writing teacher I had who saw potential in my writing, my sincerest gratitude. To Mr. David Coburn, my high school English teacher: You may have never known it, but I was very influenced and inspired by your commitment to good writing. To the students I've taught during thirty-eight years in education—and there are a lot of you—thanks for listening and learning. If every student I ever taught bought one copy of the book, my publisher would be very happy.

My son, Orion, was not around when this book had its humble beginnings. Now, at age twelve, he's often nearby as I'm writing. Thanks, O, for your unending imagination and creative spirit. I love you.

The
Ultra
Thin
Man

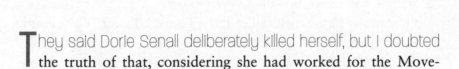

One

They said Dorie Senall deliberately killed herself, but I doubted the truth of that, considering she had worked for the Movement.

Seemed everything the Network Intelligence Organization dealt with on the eight worlds of the Union these days tied into the Movement. Three years ago, when my partner Alan Brindos and I decided to give up our private detective biz to contract with the NIO, we had no idea how much the Movement would change everything.

I sent an ENT to Danny Cadra; the electromagnetic niche-holo tracker left my office and searched for his location in the NIO building. It found him in Evidence, and the pulsing disc hovered within his vision until he acknowledged it with a flick of his hand. He looked more than annoyed, but that was the point of an ENT. My message projected directly into Cadra's visual cortex, instructing him to bring a holo-vid unit and the incident report to my office.

I nodded at him when he finally came in.

"Love those niche-holos," I said. As Movement Special Ops, I was authorized to send them.

"Yeah, of course you do," Cadra said, snapping a vid bullet into the unit. "Holo-recording, just sent through the slot from Ribon. It's Miss Senall's apartment in Venasaille."

Venasaille was the largest city on the colony planet Ribon. I had never been to Ribon, but figured I'd get there someday, when the timing was right.

"Okay." I walked back to my desk and let him place the vid

unit on top of it. About six inches square, it hummed like a tiny insect when he activated it; a newer model, something I never could have afforded for my own private eye business.

"You're going to love this," Cadra said.

I thought he meant the incident report—and maybe he meant that too—but it turned out he meant the quality of the holo-recording itself.

Cadra moved the chair in front of the desk out of the way, and I remained standing in the path of the projection. A 3-D slide with the routing list flipped up there first, with "Dave Crowell" at the top of the names, half of whom I didn't even know.

"It starts in Miss Senall's suite at the Tempest Tower," Cadra said. "That afternoon, on the balcony."

The vid itself lit up, and I was standing on the balcony, right behind Dorie Senall, who supposedly worked for the U.U. Mining Corporation. Standing beside her was our own NIO undercover agent, Jennifer Lisle, who had spent the last few months gathering evidence about Dorie's involvement in the Movement, including a possible working relationship with the terrorist Terl Plenko, leader of the whole goddamn thing. I jumped back a little, surprised at how real the two women looked standing there, locked in a kiss.

"A kiss?" I said to Cadra, who had come up beside me.

"Yeah, surprise, huh?"

Dorie and Jennifer were carbon copies of each other, but Dorie had long jet-black hair and brown eyes, while Jennifer had long blond hair and blue eyes. Pretty similar in height. Both slender, long-legged, and small-breasted.

The view twisted a bit, and I had a better look at Dorie, who smiled playfully.

"I'm going to lower the shield," Dorie said.

Jennifer, confused, said, "Okay."

The camera zoomed in on Dorie, focusing on a panel neatly inset into the wall of the balcony that she flipped up. She palmed the sensor and lowered the electromagnetic shield.

Dorie smiled, then leaned back precariously over the edge, a hundred floors up, letting the breeze blow across her arched back, whipping her black hair upward as though she were falling.

"Jesus," Jennifer said, "be *careful*."

The view shot out, spun, and rotated so quickly that I put my arms out to catch my balance. Soon I had a straight-down look at her death-defying move.

"Holy shit," I said.

"Marble camera," Cadra said. "Very small. Transparent. Mostly it stays near the ceilings, floats and positions itself for the best angles, zooms in and out. You've got to agree the definition is absolutely amazing. Nothing but the best for even our borrowed hounds."

I winced at the term. I was a minor player in the NIO, and some didn't much care about my contract status.

I glanced Cadra's way and watched him staring at the recording. "Did Lisle place the camera in the suite?"

"Yeah, when she arrived, set to record remotely the first time she spoke."

Cadra barely moved, his eyes locked on the vid, on the girls enjoying the night air. I wondered how many times he'd seen it.

A few minutes later, the girls moved back inside the suite. Dorie motioned her toward a brown leather couch. The painting on the wall behind it looked like a Vapelt, but it had to be a print. From what I could tell, the suite looked upscale, with dark wood floors, quality furniture and lighting, floor-to-ceiling bookcases, a video wall screen, that sort of thing. Certainly more suite than Dorie could afford on a U.U. Mining paycheck.

Dorie smiled and lay down with her head in Jennifer's lap. She ran her fingernails gently over Jennifer's stomach, bunching up the material of her blouse, then traced a line upward with her index finger between her breasts, to her neck and under her chin. Jennifer smiled, eyes closed.

Dorie inched Jennifer's blouse up a little and kissed her there on the belly. She looked up at Jennifer's face and said, "I want to share something with you."

The marble cam rolled right, caught Jennifer slowly opening her eyes. The definition was so remarkable I could even see flecks of gray in the blue irises.

"How would you like to be someone?" Dorie asked. "Someone with a hand in shaping the future of sentient life?"

Jennifer shook her head. "What are you talking about?"

Dorie got up from the couch so abruptly that I flinched. She shouted almost incoherently, "I'm talking about the fucking Movement!"

"Movement?" Jennifer asked, feigning ignorance.

"You know. Terl Plenko? Leader of the Movement?" Dorie smiled. "I hear he might come here to Ribon."

On Dorie's vid screen on the back wall of her suite's living room, U-ONE, the Union government network, showed the silhouette of a Union Ark as it sailed across black space, and due to the wonders of the NIO marble cam, I could even read the word ORGON flashing in the lower-right corner. Sloping arid hills below the Ark erupted in flames as invisible tongues licked from the Ark's guns. Viewers probably didn't know much about the small planet Orgon, a volatile colony where lawlessness sometimes necessitated the need for Union intervention, but it didn't matter. Televised broadcasts of Union raids brought high ratings.

Jennifer probably knew the stakes had gone up. She glanced at the camera, tucking blond hair behind her ears, as if to say to the surveillance team, "You getting all this?"

"How many people watched the vid live when this went down?" I asked as the cam rolled again, capturing the girls from an angle just above Dorie's vid screen.

"Just two. A Lieutenant Branson, and the captain there, Captain Rand."

Dorie paced the room, and the marble camera followed her from above, recording her movements as it repositioned. Dorie stopped in front of the vid screen, facing Jennifer, who had twisted around on the couch to watch. Dorie took out something red from a cubbyhole underneath the vid screen. Also, a glass tumbler filled with something.

"Cadra?" I asked, pointing at the screen.

He blinked, then said, "Oh. RuBy. And Scotch in the glass."

I nodded. RuBy was a drug from Helkunntanas. The alien substance was legal on most worlds, despite opposition against it. I noticed how expertly Dorie rolled the RuBy, its faceted surface pooling bloody light, some of the red dye trailing in the sweat of her palm.

She popped it into her mouth, chasing it with the Scotch in the tumbler, ice clacking. A shudder passed through her body, tightening her skin, the lines in her face. Her face seemed peaceful for a few moments—her jaw slack as she tilted her head back, eyes closed—but her fists closed into a tight ball, and her arms and legs shook.

She opened her eyes, smiled warmly. In the next moment, her feral nature slammed back and she exalted in the high, jumping and twisting for show, showing off her body. I jumped back as her movement brought her close to me. She said, "That's some good shit!"

She crept to the couch, grinning, slid onto Jennifer's lap. "You want some?" Jennifer shook her head. "No?" Dorie cupped Jennifer's breast, caressed her nipple through the flimsy material. "You want some of the action I'm offering you? The chance of a lifetime, girl of adventure." The camera zoomed in on Dorie; her eyes were lit up from the RuBy, damp hair falling dark over her face.

Jennifer tried to move. Dorie's body, bathed in sweat, held her down. The marble camera was damn good. Beads of RuBy-induced sweat glistened on Dorie's face. She forced her lips onto Jennifer's mouth. Jennifer pulled away. "Shit, Dorie! Take another pill. I'm not in the mood. Get *off.*"

Dorie drew back, scowling. Jennifer started to say something, and Dorie struck her hard. Before Jennifer could react, Dorie slapped her again. Blood speckled the white sofa cushion. The marble camera rolled, and I felt a bit dizzy with the sudden movement. Jennifer's head came up, blood smeared over her lips.

Dorie grabbed Jennifer's hair and gave it a vicious yank. "You'll do what I say and you'll like it." The marble cam zoomed in, catching the fear in Jennifer's eyes. Dorie opened her hand and caressed the hair she had just grabbed. Jennifer pressed the back of her wrist to her bloody lip.

I turned quickly to Cadra and said, "Was that an echo?"

"You hear it? That's what blew Lisle's cover. Watch."

It was as if it had taken a moment for Dorie to recognize the echo, her dialogue starting up.

"What?" Dorie said, turning around. "What the fuck is this?"

The marble cam seemed to know exactly where to focus its attention, coming in closer on Dorie's wall vid. The Orgon raid disappeared from the screen, replaced by Dorie's living room, her own image doubling her motions, as though U-ONE were a sponge sucking violence into the airwaves. She leaped off the couch. Jennifer, her view unobstructed, looked shocked.

I turned to Cadra. "Okay, how does something like that happen? Looping the holo-recording into her goddamn suite's vid screen?"

"Christ if I know. Some glitch."

Dorie hunted frantically around the suite, cursing. The camera followed her, and it was as if I were walking behind her. A *glitch*? Something like that didn't just happen; someone had betrayed Jennifer Lisle. Was it the Venasaille cop, Branson? The captain?

Suddenly Dorie had a blaster in her hand. Jennifer froze on the sofa, probably wondered where her team was. Not to mention who had sold her out and given Dorie a front-row seat for the surveillance footage.

The view rolled left.

Dorie strode toward the entryway, which happened to be straight at me, raising the blaster. I ducked out of the way as she raised the blaster higher, toward the ceiling. The camera caught her squinting as she triggered her weapon, the blaster's beam randomly boring holes in the walls and ceiling.

The view rolled left, right, halted. A blinding flash killed the holo and I defensively raised my hand to my face, startled.

"Lucky shot," Cadra said. "After that, Branson's backup team went in."

"Where were they?"

"Room next door. Miss Senall picked off two of them. Hold on."

Cadra reached into his jacket pocket and pulled out a second vid bullet.

"There's more?"

"Branson chucked a second marble cam in there as they stormed the suite."

Cadra ejected the first bullet and snapped in the second. I strode back to the middle of the room just as the new vid lit up around me.

Immediately, the camera zoomed in on Jennifer Lisle, who had started to run away from Dorie. The camera recorded the scene at a lower angle now, there being no pressing need for it to stay hidden near the ceiling. The camera must have sensed a change in Dorie's body position, for the view swiveled, catching Dorie as she turned away from the suite door and aimed at Jennifer—through me.

I tensed as she fired, the beam going through my midsection.

Looking behind me, I saw Jennifer go down with a hole burned through her leg; she cried out as she fell, clutching at the wound with her hand.

"Dorie turned and went after Jennifer at that moment?" I asked. "With more cops piling through the door?"

Cadra shrugged. "Doesn't make sense, I know."

"Weird."

"Gets weirder." He pointed at Dorie, who started to run toward the balcony. She ignored Jennifer sprawled on the carpet.

The Venasaille police were yelling at her to stop. The marble camera didn't bother with the police. It stayed on Dorie as she fired her blaster at the French doors that led to the balcony, ripping them apart. Pieces flew toward the marble cam, causing me to once again involuntarily duck.

"God*damn* it," I whispered, but I kept my eyes on Dorie's back as she ran through the ruined doors. The camera followed her, catching the very moment she stumbled. One cop's blaster had hit her in the leg. She hobbled forward toward the unshielded edge of the balcony.

Momentum carried her forward.

She pitched over the side and, unbelievably, the marble cam followed her. It was like some sort of virtual thrill ride. I dropped to my knees to steady myself, watching the unusual angle, my point of view following Dorie Senall as she fell one hundred floors. She had her blaster going, carving veins down the face of the Tempest Tower.

There was a moment when the pavement rose up to meet her, when it rushed into my own eyes, that I expected the marble camera to follow her the whole way, smashing itself onto the street, but it stopped several floors up and gave me a sickening view of Dorie Senall exploding on the sidewalk.

TWO

Alan Brindos arrived on the largest of all the Union worlds, Ribon, in the city of Venasaille, two days after Dorie Senall's death. The Network Intelligence Office superseded local authority whenever the Movement was involved, and seeing as Dave Crowell was the head of the Movement commission, Brindos had been sent to pull rank and get more information.

Brindos was on Ribon less than a day when things started to go to hell. The ride through the jump slot had been bad enough—Dave knew he hated spaceflight and field work both—but having to deal with the Venasaille police was worse, and what followed *that* was . . . well, beyond description.

Brindos missed the old days, when he and Dave Crowell worked on their own, solving the big cases. Okay, none of them had ever been that big. Well, except the Baron Rieser gig. The data forger had taken them on a wild chase around the Union until he disappeared from sight. Brindos, who had no family, liked the close relationship he had with Crowell, and this Movement contract kept them farther apart than he liked. Brindos had been a foster kid all his life, and he'd had quite enough of that not-knowing-where-he-was-going-to-be-next kind of thing.

Although Captain Sydney Rand of the Venasaille police department logged an official protest to the NIO office upon Brindos's arrival, as soon as he finished watching the holo-vid of Dorie's death, Brindos ordered an immediate neuro-chemical autopsy of her remains. Rand called in the coroner, pulling him away from dinner with his family, and he locked him in the morgue when he arrived a half hour later. Brindos had the results an hour after that.

The autopsy revealed psychosis in the form of paranoid schizo-phrenia, a condition made dangerous by Dorie's drug and alcohol intake. The lack of even solid circumstantial evidence supporting her alleged illegal recruiting scam, and now possible connections to Terl Plenko, meant either suspicions were unfounded, or she really knew what she was doing keeping them in the dark.

Because Dorie's history of pathological behavior kept him from separating her truths from her lies, and because all her references to the Movement were vague during the holo-recording to begin with—no *direct* admissions of association—Brindos was forced to look closer for hard evidence that would help justify a raid on Coral Moon.

Using the holo-recording, he had the police department's comput-ers map the spots Dorie's body, eyes, and posture pointed to during heightened moments of her conversations concerning the Movement. Her unconscious attention consistently focused on the area below the vid screen.

Lieutenant Branson brought Brindos to Dorie's suite and they checked it out. Brindos had assumed she'd been thinking about the RuBy, for that's where she'd rolled it, underneath the vid. When he shined his flashlight in the small cubbyhole, however, toward the very back, barely visible, he spotted something.

He motioned to Branson, and the lieutenant rummaged around in a plastic bag he'd brought with him. He came up with a small aerosol spritz, sprayed his left hand with a light latex polymer, and reached into the cubby. What he pulled out seemed inconsequential at first, a small metal sculpture, spherical in shape.

Branson turned it over a few times in his palm. "What's this?"

"Mortaline," Brindos said.

"What?"

"The metal it's made of. Very rare, and fucking expensive. Only found on Coral. The last major deposits of it were mined years ago, as far as I know, and they're now just cleaning up the smaller bits and pieces in the Rock Dome. Along with all the other failing mines, of course."

"A connection to Coral."

Brindos nodded as Branson handed the sculpture over. About the size of a grapefruit, it resembled a planet twisting out of shape, as though a man inside were struggling to break out. A closer look, however, revealed that the black metal's etchings included subtle forms on the surface, a sea of writhing bodies, what seemed like thousands. Each had a different face, and yet I could see the eyes of every face etched into the sculpture, and they seemed alive with torment.

Like the rest of Dorie's apartment, this valuable piece of art—albeit *disturbing* art—was more than she could afford. He wondered if it had been a gift. He figured everything in this apartment had been a gift. From the Movement.

"DNA?" Brindos asked.

Branson nodded and pulled out a sequencer from the bag. He passed it over the black mortaline. "Miss Senall's DNA," he said, checking the readout. He waited some more. "Also, DNA of the artist, looks like. All over the crevices of the sculpture's surface." He looked up suddenly, a smile on his face. "A perfect match."

"Match to whom?"

Branson passed the sequencer. Coded DNA strands on the left, photo on the right. An old photo, not very flattering, of a First Clan Helk.

Helks.

Humans regarded the *other* nonhuman race in the Union, the orange-haired Memors, almost as saints. The Memors discovered Earth and offered their jump-slot technology. It gave Earth access to known habitable worlds that could be used as colonies.

Helks, on the other hand, found by humans twenty years later in 2060, were gigantic and not as highly regarded. Brindos had never been to Helkunntanas and had no desire to go; most humans couldn't stand the heat, and very few liked the idea of walking around surrounded on all sides by giants. A Fourth Clan Helk you could talk to without feeling terribly inadequate, but that was it. A light fur covered their broad bodies, and they had legs like small tree trunks, and long arms that rippled with muscle. Their heads were hairless, the skin dark and leathery due to the desert climate of their homeworld. When you met a Helk, you took in its size, its sad eyes, the rows of sharp teeth, then decided whether to say hello or run like hell.

Helks and humans didn't always trust each other, or play nice. It had become a growing concern even before Terl Plenko's Movement. Humans started calling them Hulks, a colloquial expression that carried with it a pointedly negative connotation. Truth to tell, the name fit, if nothing else, because of the aliens' immense size.

Clans were based on size and social class, although a certain amount of crossover was allowed depending on upward mobility. First Clan was the largest of four clans. And this First Clan Helk on Branson's sequencer was one of the largest Brindos knew.

The Helk peering out from the DNA sequencer was the Movement of Worlds leader, Terl Plenko.

"Goddamn." Brindos pulled out his code card, the NIO agent super tool that allowed them direct communication with the agency brass, other agents, and the DataNet, and had more hidden gadgets than any civilian comm card. It was a little bigger than an old-fashioned paper business card, just as thin, and flexible, covered with flash membranes and tiny nodes. His finger whispered along the comm node, and he sent a message to Dave Crowell at the New York office a few seconds later, giving him a go-ahead to alert the director and President Nguyen to raid Coral Moon.

Over twenty small domes on Coral made the moon habitable, conditions imitating Ribon enough so colonists could live and work there. Mining on Coral had been big business, but most of the desired minerals had been mined out, and times were tough.

The NIO had hoped Dorie would raise the stakes on a tenuous friendship with Jennifer by offering a one-way ticket to Coral Moon, a suspected Movement outpost, making it sound like some holiday. Ribon officials had believed Dorie's dismissal a month earlier from U.U. Mining Corporation had been a cover so she could run illegal recruits past customs to the outpost on Coral.

Crowell acknowledged Brindos and decided to send a message straight to Union President Richard Nguyen's chief of staff. President Nguyen authorized three Arks for a raid on Coral Moon. It was unknown if the Movement had ships that could match even one Union Ark, but four Ribon days after Dorie's death, three Arks arrived through the jump slot, armed for battle. They found the moon abandoned, its mass so ravaged by deep core explosives that officials feared it might become unstable in its orbit. As a precautionary measure, Ribon Provincial ordered evacuations of Ribon colonists, command and civilian, loading them onto transport ships, then sending them through the jump slot to a classified location, at some refugee camp on one of the other Union worlds. The transports ran continuously, and after two days, the Arks arrived. After completing a detailed analysis of Coral, the Ark captains okayed a request from Provincial to load as many refugees as they could fit aboard their ships, then jumped home.

Brindos reviewed the survey photos of Coral's surface while the evacuation procedures continued, and found the evidence striking. Structures on Coral's surface had been blasted and melted beyond recognition, particularly around the area called the Rock Dome, where much of Coral's mining took place. All that, coupled with the moon's missing mass, intentionally removed by explosives not sanctioned for mining, demonstrated evidence of an actual firepower higher than previously thought.

An hour after the Arks left the system, a final, cataclysmic explosion on Coral's far side lit up the sky. Specifics of the explosion and the harrowing results didn't come through until much later, but only a few Transworld Transport jump vessels managed to reach the system in time to attempt a rescue of more Ribon colonists. Brindos had already boarded a specially designated TWT vessel, *Gateshead,* loaded with politicians, dignitaries, and scientists, the last ones out of there.

Brindos sat across the aisle from Grahlst Tah'lah, a Memor scientist assigned to the *Gateshead*. They had been discussing the grim news.

"The explosion wasn't nuclear?" Brindos asked the Memor.

"Even that wouldn't have been enough to cause the damage," Grahlst Tah'lah said, his orange hair tied back in a tight knot.

"What's the Science Consortium say about this? Is that their opinion as well?"

The Memor pursed thick, pale lips. "The five from the Consortium have been quiet about the possibilities."

"Have you heard from them at all since this happened?"

"No. It is . . . disconcerting."

"Okay, so if not nukes, what the hell blew up Coral?"

"Rumors are spreading regarding some sort of antimatter disruption."

"*Anti*matter?"

"It is improbable, of course. The amount of antimatter needed to cause an explosion of that magnitude has never before been created, let alone collected without mishap."

Brindos had heard as much. Heard that the amount of antimatter humans had created in the past hundred years might light up a small colony town for about a minute and a half.

"What's going to happen to Ribon?" Brindos asked.

"Coral didn't fragment completely, but its orbit, now compromised, puts it in the path of Ribon. In a few days, Ribon's atmosphere and gravitation will shatter what is left of the small moon, and pieces will orbit Ribon. Soon, the planet will have Saturn-like rings."

"A number of fragments will reach Ribon itself, won't they?" he asked.

Grahlst Tah'lah nodded and looked at him across the aisle. "Some have already entered the atmosphere. Without time to prepare for a calamity as destructive as this, the damage will be devastating, reaching worldwide in hours. The resulting gamma rays from the antimatter weapon will certainly alter the chemistry of living things still on Ribon. Although Coral absorbed much of the rays, and others dispersed into space, it won't be known how much of the electromagnetic wave will find its way to Ribon."

"And for those people not evacuated in time?"

"It will make no difference. Ribon will intersect the moon's orbit and some of Coral's larger fragments will slam into it. Shockwaves from the impacts will cause worldwide earthquakes, awakening dormant volcanoes and triggering massive tidal waves. Dust clouds will blanket the planet. Ash will fall from the sky."

Dear God, Brindos thought. Ribon would know nothing but darkness for months. Plants would die. Animals would die.

Colonists would die.

Sickened, Brindos barely made it in time to the *Gateshead*'s tiny lavatory and threw up. He had an idea how horrific the loss of life and damage would be. His heart thumped in his chest, and anger rose inside, making him shake. Even with the Arks, even with the transport jumps, only a fraction of Ribon's population was moved off-planet.

He staggered back to his seat, barely able to walk. Grahlst Tah'lah left him alone.

How could this have happened? Was it deliberate? Had Plenko killed this moon without regard for the inhabitants of Ribon? How had he found the destructive means needed to pull off this despicable act of terrorism?

Brindos stared out the window of the *Gateshead,* the last emergency Transworld Transport. Now he could see the pieces of Coral quite clearly. The *Gateshead* was out in far orbit, having just departed Swan Station. All remaining evacuation ships had passed through the jump slot hours before.

Moments before they jumped, he watched some of the remnants of Coral drop away into Ribon's atmosphere like pebbles disappearing into fog. A million Ribon colonists were dying. It was the worst thing he had ever seen in his life.

He wept.

Brindos visited Jennifer Lisle at Sacred Mercy Hospital in New York when he returned. They'd treated her on Ribon, then shipped her off to Earth just before Coral's high dive. She told him mostly what he already knew from her report, but added a few extra details.

Dorie had first met Jennifer in Celine's, a cafe in Venasaille where Jennifer had spent evenings watching the ice melt in her Scotch. Talking to Jennifer in person, without the distance provided by the holo-recording, Brindos felt a little uneasy. She was attractive the way a pretty librarian seems sexy with her glasses off. Withdrawn, aloof, skeptical of everything. She'd been disturbed by Dorie, and on more than one occasion had told her to fuck off. But that had only kept Dorie coming on to her. Jennifer had a job to do, and maybe she succeeded in winning over Dorie because of her earlier denials. Jennifer kept mostly to the script given to her by the Network Intelligence Office's top officials, but she figured a little improvising wouldn't hurt.

What Dorie lacked in charm, she made up for in persistence. Dorie wanted Jennifer, and as time wore on, her confidence grew and Jennifer's guard eased, revealing a sexual curiosity. A few days after the initial meeting in Celine's, they ended up in Dorie's suite. Brindos asked her about the holo-recording looping into the suite's vid unit, wondering if she had any enemies, anyone who might've wanted to see her cover blown. She didn't know, but it had definitely unnerved her.

Brindos thanked Jennifer, wished her a speedy recovery, and flew back to New York to work out the kinks this goddamn trip had inflicted on him. He wanted to forget the whole mission, but figured he hadn't heard the last of the whole affair. Of Dorie Senall, of Coral and of Ribon, of Terl Plenko, and of the Movement.

Sure enough, a week later, at NIO headquarters in New York, Brindos was put back to work.

He met Crowell in his temporary cubicle on the twenty-eighth floor, the same floor his own cubicle was on, the same floor as Director Timothy James's office and Assistant Director Aaron Bardsley. Only the size and poshness of the offices changed. Offices ringed the floor, and the cubicles of many NIO agents sat in the middle hub. It was evening, and most of the offices were dark, agents and staff at home.

Crowell was a big man, maybe 250 pounds, all muscle, a product of his strict five-times-a-week weight workout. Brindos wouldn't have wanted to run into him in a dark alley. More than once Brindos had been happy he was on his side. Crowell had fifty pounds on Brindos and, at age thirty, was five years younger. Stubble darkened his face—the beginnings of a beard that matched his dark brown hair. He never grew out a beard, though. His brown eyes could cut through you with a glance.

"After Ribon," Crowell said from behind his desk, "probably the last thing you want to do is hop on a transport to Temonus, but I need you to follow up on the lead I've been given on Tony Koch."

"Koch?"

Crowell nodded. "If one of Terl Plenko's cronies is on Temonus as has been reported, maybe Plenko himself is over there. Frankly, it's probably a dead end. That's why I thought of you. You can stay a couple of extra weeks. You're due for a vacation."

"Look," Brindos said, "I may be due, but *you* need the vacation. Have the square boys in the round office been putting the spurs to you because of Coral? Because you went over James's head?"

"They gave me a choice between getting my nuts crunched in a vise or letting Nguyen throw darts at my ass."

"Right," Brindos said. "What you tell them?"

"I told them to save it for Plenko, that I'd have him for them within a year."

"Liar."

"Yeah, well those inflatable Plenko Halloween costumes are real lifelike, and I've got one that's just your size."

"Great. I'll stay here and terrorize New York while *you* go to Temonus and sip aqua vitae out of some coconut with a toothpick umbrella."

Crowell leaned back in his chair and sighed. "Not that easy, Alan. You're going. Your itinerary and ticket info's been synched to your code card. Connection to Florida tomorrow morning, then shuttle to Egret Station. Transworld Transport to Solan Station, Temonus. Leaves tomorrow night."

Brindos eyed his code card, saw the notification pulse green, popping up as a new node on the membrane. He wished it would disappear.

Crowell reached into his desk drawer. "Oh, yeah." He rummaged around for a moment. "Reading material."

He passed a flashroll to Brindos. It was extra large, as big as an antique paper scroll, because it was a *National Geographic,* which demanded increased node circuitry and flash memory to accommodate the graphic-heavy publication. Crowell was the only person he knew who would've preferred a paper edition, but no periodical had even bothered with that kind of nostalgia for decades.

Along the skin of the rolled-up flashmag, the magazine's yellow square logo pulsed. Brushing it with his finger brought up a preview holo of the front cover, the words NATIONAL GEOGRAPHIC in block letters next to the logo, with a subhead: CELEBRATING 225 YEARS. A beautiful shot of some green wetlands filled the holo block. The headline: "Temonus, the Union's New Frontier." From last month, June 2113.

Crowell pointed at the flashmag. "I've marked an article for you to look at, and left some of my own notes in there. I want you to read it and let me know what you think once you get to Temonus."

"Okay."

"Looks beautiful, Alan," Crowell said, closing his drawer and leaning back in his chair. "I wish I could go with you, I really do."

"The fuck you do." He didn't believe him for a second. Crowell didn't get out of the office. Besides, if given a choice, he wouldn't pick Temonus. It would be Aryell, where he'd left behind Cara Landry. He'd fallen hard for her right after they'd contracted with the NIO.

"I'm looking further into this Dorie Senall thing. If you find any connections, I want to know."

"Fine." Brindos knew he wasn't getting out of this one, as much as he'd hoped Crowell might change his mind.

"Koch is your priority," Crowell said. "Remember, if you *do* find him, call me. But keep your distance. Like Plenko, he's a Helk, First Clan, big as they come."

When Brindos got home to his apartment around eleven o'clock, he powered up his code card, and in the semidark of his apartment, the flash membrane lit up with a burst that made him look away a moment. With a swish of his finger he brought up the mission folder with the details of the assignment. Crowell had written "Optay Ecret-say" across the holo image of the folder. Crowell, always the joker, not one to follow NIO protocols, or at least not very seriously.

Brindos thanked Crowell for generally keeping him in his cubicle and out of Director James's sights by sending low-profile ops, nothing strenuous. *He knows me too well.* One of the reasons Brindos didn't particularly care for contract work was the travel. Space flight was a reasonably safe bet now, but he hated it. It wasn't about safety, or claustrophobia, or uncomfortable differences in gravity, it was just boring. He'd been in enough solar systems to make Galileo pee his pants, but the thrill went out of it. Space was one big black boring void, and most of the worlds in it were poison to humans.

Crowell had found his way to Timothy James's good graces and grabbed major administration duties. Administration choked Brindos, but Crowell was adept at cutting through red tape. He loved everything about the Union of Worlds, particularly its mix of new and old. You found that curious mix not only on Earth, but also the colony planets of Orgon, Barnard's, Ribon, Temonus, and Aryell. Things were a little different on the two nonhuman worlds of Helkunntanas and Memory, of course. Crowell loved antiques and memorabilia; he longed for the old days, but they were days he had never lived through, only read about, or heard stories about.

Time to find out what Temonus had to offer. Older civilizations throughout the Network had yet to pay much attention to the young Union colony, and information, even within intelligence circles, was scarce.

Brindos caught the shuttle to Egret in time to make his connection with Transworld Transport Flight #135 through the jump slot to Temonus. With time to burn, he sat back in his private flight cubicle and took out the *National Geographic*. Brindos unlocked and unrolled the flashmag, the full digital image of the front cover filling the membrane. He stretched and pulled, the nanocircuitry adjusting, expanding the view, then he thumbed the contents node.

Crowell had already digitally dog-eared the magazine, penning questions and observations in the margins. One note said, "Cross-reference my appendix, node six, about this, which explains in detail what we know of the device. If you get a chance, take the guided tour and send me a T-shirt."

He was referring to a double-page spread with the heading "Weather Perfect." The text read: "Temonus may be young as colonies go, but the advances in weather control technology are making the other worlds of the Union take notice. An engineering marvel known as the Transcontinental Conduit, a spiderweb-thin filament, stretches across the tiny continent of Ghal, held by six towers, each a half mile high, and five hundred feet in diameter. From Tower One in East City, it whistles over plains and valleys as blue as the liquor Temonus is famous for. It stretches over the Micro region, a network of over a thousand small lakes. The Conduit passes over Midwest City skies, continuing to the coast, where it ties off at Tower Six in West City.

"The Conduit—invented by the Science Consortium, and endorsed by Union President Nguyen—was completed a year ago despite early objections from the Temonus provincial government, which had concerns about environmental impact studies left undone. Reports of early tests were encouraging and quieted most skeptics. Because of its classified status, the Conduit is not open to the public, and it is protected by a high-alert security grid and hot zone."

Crowell had been joking then, about the guided tour. But Brindos did wonder if he might find a T-shirt to bring back.

The photos, he suspected, didn't do the massive structure justice. He whisked across several of the included graphics of the circular towers, pulling them up in holo from the main membrane to get a closer look. The towers were a glossy black, almost featureless, except for some handholds, outer ladders, and opaqued windows that ran up and down its surface. Even as a graphic, Tower One exuded an almost menacing presence, towering over East City. Almost invisible to the eye, the thin wire stretched across the city out of the frame of the graphic to where it connected to Tower Two, far out of sight.

On the facing page was a photo of five scientists: two humans, a Helk, and a Memor. Brindos expanded this and zoomed in on them.

The caption below read: "The Science Consortium. Five of the Union's brightest minds are behind the Conduit and the cutting-edge weather control technology."

And where was the Consortium now? No one had heard from them since before the Coral Moon disaster.

He let his finger hover over the Memor in the graphic, who stood tall and stiff next to the Helk. Her orange hair was bright and long in stark contrast to the bald Helk; the short, thick brown hair of one human; and the thinning gray hair of the other. A text bubble coalesced above her with a quote.

"This is an exciting development in meteorological progress," Lorway said. "We're literally changing the landscape of Temonus and making it a better world."

Lorway. Brindos had heard of her. A female Memor of note, considering most Memor females did not reach any level of importance. During mating, most Memors morphed male, but those rarer occasions when Memors intersexually assigned themselves female, they were bonded to multiple males, their surnames stripped. Lorway was rumored to be bonded to just one male. More often, Memor females were bonded to a dozen males, or more.

So the Transcontinental Conduit was a collaborative effort.

Brindos nodded to himself as he looked at the Memor's face. She seemed uncomfortable, large, puffy lips locked in a hard smile. Quite the accomplishment to get the Memors signed on to something like this. The technology of the Memors, the creators of the jump slots, could be stunningly breathtaking, although many of the advancements the Memors kept to themselves.

There were also rumors about their enhanced memory capabilities, and their notion of shared memory, which enabled them to excel at Union conference tables and mediation hearings. And yet, most Memors stayed out of the limelight. They didn't venture far from planet Memory.

The Memor planet had strikingly beautiful cities. Brindos had been there once, before the NIO contract, on a chase of data forger Baren Rieser. Buildings bloomed from the surface like trees, tall and formidable, but aesthetically pleasing with their glass exteriors and brushed, hand-carved stones. The air was a bit thin for humans, but breathable without breathing aids. Memors certainly didn't like Earth's hyper-oxygenated atmosphere—probably another reason they preferred to stay home. But in fact, their whole world was beautiful. For as long as the Memors had been on their planet—thousands of years—it felt like a new colony world, the waters pure and unpolluted, skies blue and pristine.

Brindos flicked the photo of the Science Consortium members back to the membrane and kept looking at the Temonus article, but found nothing else about the Conduit and how it actually *controlled* the weather; the staff writers had decided to enhance the unique graphics with a minimum of text. But he found the cross-reference node Crowell had placed on the article, a tiny red square that outlined the letters "CF." He pushed it and it took him to Crowell's note:

"This is what I could scrounge up on what the NIO knows regarding the Conduit. The Science Consortium applied for the usual patents and permissions, commissioned impact studies [although all not completed as you know, resulting in early opposition—concern mostly about the wetlands], passed stringent QC checks from the Union and provincial governments, and received the blessings of the intelligence community—NIO, Kenn, and MSA—after confirming no danger of military or terrorist capabilites. The wire connects the six towers as an array of transmitters to push, from the tower caps, artificially created high-frequency waves amplified from Temonus's existing electromagnetic field, which occurs between the surface and the ionosphere, creating what scientists on Earth call Schumann resonances. [This tech is nothing new, Alan, around for hundreds of years. Memors snapped it into a usable interface, however, with a way to harness the energy and inject it into the ionosphere about ninety miles up, without the need for chemical seeding.]"

Brindos thumbed a node to continue.

"The Conduit itself helps generate the massive energy needed, as much as six million watts. The end result: a purposeful pushing of ionized water particles upward, causing the ionosphere to extend outward, thereby causing the stratosphere to fill in the space. Temonus's jet stream reroutable. Cloud formations and plumes controllable. [Again, not new tech, but the Memors shared the methods to perfect it.]"

Crowell's note ended there, and he was thankful. He didn't need to know much more about the Conduit than that. He rolled the flashmag and put it away, then returned to the mission folder on his code card. Crowell's earlier folder message, obviously placed there with a data-timed command, now said, "Still Optay Ecretsay."

Time to dig into the Koch matter.

Nearly a day later, Earth time, ten thousand kilometers out from Temonus, the planet showed up on the monitor in his flight cubicle. The pictures in the magazine had displayed Temonus's natural beauty to full advantage, and indeed, from up here, it looked very Earth-like.

From five hundred kilometers up on Solan Station, however, while awaiting transfer to the surface in the lounge, nothing but vast patches of blue made the planet look like an impossible ball of water in the vacuum of space. Temonus had very few land masses. Cloud formations across the southern pole gave the planet a nice little smile.

He closed his eyes a moment, reverent, remembering Ribon and the horrors visited upon it by Coral.

He didn't remember falling asleep, but a call to board the shuttle to the surface awakened him. Wearily, travelers channeled into the umbilical tube that connected to the drop shuttle. Under their arms they carried coats they'd had no need of, tired now of the weather-controlled metal environments, all dreaming of rain and wind, the natural light of a sky.

Brindos watched Temonus turning below them, the Republic of Ghal slipping slowly by. He staggered down to the drop shuttle like a man heading for bed.

Three

A few days after shipping off Alan Brindos to Temonus, I decided to walk to the NIO headquarters. The New York afternoon beat down on me as I walked, a haze nearly obscuring the sun; still, it was summer, and damn hot. It never got this hot in Seattle, and even now, three years after closing the detective agency, I missed the gray days of drizzle. I loosened my tie and shirt collar and gazed up and down Wall Street, which was nearly deserted. Not much remained of the original business district that had once made New York the hub of late-twentieth- and early-twenty-first-century America.

We were forced into the future upon discovery of two alien races. This got things moving away from Earth in speedy fashion because the first aliens, the Memors, stumbled upon us in 2040 and gave us jump slots and interstellar travel. *Here's tech that will change the future of your meager lives and fuck up your learning curve big time. Have fun, kids.*

A decade later, humans colonized the worlds of the Union, and a decade after that they discovered Helkunntanas, the home of the ugliest and meanest species known to God above. The Exchange and most investment firms moved out to the other seven planets of the Union to more effectively profit from the mass of humanity that had spread throughout the galaxy. By 2063, just fifty years ago, the New York business district had been reduced to a shadow of its former glory.

I avoided the slideway, as did most people. I was certain it would slip a cog and throw me.

A few blocks from NIO headquarters, I routed a call on my code card to my mom at her lake place in Montana. I did my best to check up on her regularly, but I didn't always do such a good job of it.

Mom had never been the same after Dad left—or disappeared, I guess—when I was sixteen. He was presumed dead, drowned in the lake, but no body had been found. Mom had stayed at the family home on Flathead Lake and told me not to worry about her, but I knew it was getting harder for her as the years piled on. The cold of winter didn't help matters, but she never wanted to go somewhere warm, even though I'd offered to help.

Mom's words came to me all in a rush. "David? Where are you? Are you in town?"

"No, Mom, I'm in New York. Just saying hello."

"When are you coming, David? I would've liked to have seen you for your thirtieth birthday. Or any day, you know. I've not seen you in a while."

Hadn't seen her in a year, at least.

"Soon, Mom. After this mess is done."

"The Movement thing?"

"Yeah."

She didn't say anything, but I could sense her disappointment. She knew as well as I did that the Movement thing might go on a long time.

"The marina still running?" I asked. The Hammond Marina had been a family business. Mom had sold it after Dad disappeared, not wanting to deal with the hassle of upkeep. My memory of it was hazy at best.

"I think so," Mom said. "But I don't get out of the house much, other than to go down to the shore and enjoy the sun when it manages to come out."

I came upon four kids playing Stickman near an overflowing Dumpster. One boy, not more than seven, banged a rhythm on the metal Dumpster with a piece of rusted metal, and it was loud.

Oddly enough, I didn't have any memories of a happy childhood, playing kid games, running around the lake place with friends.

"I'm headed in to work," I said, "so I'll have to let you go."

"What's that noise, David?"

"Just some kids. I'll talk again soon. Love you."

"Good-bye, David. Love you too."

The banging intensified as I put away the code card, the boy's eyes closed in concentration. Other kids skipped along elaborate chalk diagrams of circles, squares, and triangles marked with the individual letters of "Stickman." Stickman glorified the popular comic flashbook superhero of the same name. I'd casually read a few issues of *Stickman* on a personal DataNet visor, and I knew the basics of the street game. As they moved along the diagram in no apparent pattern, the kids chanted together:

Stickman, Stickman, coming to our house,
Save the day! Save the day!
O save us from that louse!
The Movement's here and Plenko's near,
His revolution made;
But never fear, Stickman's here,
O don't you be afraid!

The object of the game was to capture and execute Stickman's archenemy, Terl Plenko, the leader of the Movement of Worlds. The kids glanced over at me, but they didn't seem frightened of me. None of them really understood the implications of Terl Plenko's revolution. Did anyone? Why, other than for personal power, was he enticing worlds to break away from the Union, a government he pronounced corrupt and immoral?

I left the kids behind and turned left onto Williams Street. The massive towers of New York, stained with oil and corrosion, jutted high into the overcast sky like giant mystic runes. Waterfalls trickled from rusted sculptures. For a brief moment, a break in the clouds brought out the sun, and the spray of water droplets created weak rainbows in the hazy sunlight.

A moment later, a terrific rumble Dopplered above, sending a tremor through the cracked pavement under my feet. Union assault planes, hunting for Terl Plenko. I looked up but couldn't see them. No one had spotted a Movement vessel for months, but every time something bad happened on Earth, Plenko was said to be the cause, and the Union dispatched assault planes to chase him down. Perhaps he was such a useful demon that the Union couldn't do without him, but what he'd done to Ribon and Coral made me sick to my stomach.

The NIO knew Plenko had left Earth. What were the assault planes chasing, then? Shadows? The Movement had stretched to nearly every world in the Union, reaching out to the colonies, preaching independence. Here on Earth, Plenko's Movement seemed to have lost steam.

My duties to the NIO kept me on Earth, and I hadn't minded that for a long time, but lately I'd felt the need to escape.

Those who had left Earth for the worlds of the Union dreamed of coming back one day, but I just wanted a break. I would not stay on Earth forever; the NIO contract wouldn't last forever, and Mom would understand. My heart yearned for a different planet.

Aryell. Older than Temonus by a little, but small, and more of a backwater planet, a tourist spot. Home of the Flaming Sea and the best snow in the Union. I'd had just one assignment there, three years ago, just before Alan and I decided to contract with the NIO. I met Cara there. I sort of fell in love with her, but never really told her.

When the NIO pulled me back to New York, I left her behind.

The moment I entered the NIO headquarters, an ENT accosted me. "Shit," I mumbled, shying away from the flashing niche-holo. I was supposed to dish these out, not receive them.

I swiped at it with my hand and read the message from NIO Assistant Director Aaron Bardsley for a briefing. Well, *this* was going to be fun. Bardsley was quite the strait-laced boss, and didn't put up with my jokes and good-natured ribbing. He would grill me about my recent decisions regarding the Movement, I figured, passing his thoughts up the datawell to Director James, but I had a few items I wanted to discuss with him as well, including the discovery of some key DataNet files about Terl Plenko.

On my floor, one from the top, I made my way through the

maze of cubicles to the offices behind them. Mary Blair, the assistant director's secretary, showed me the way, just in case I'd forgotten, and after I slipped through the double doors, she closed them behind me.

Bardsley's suite made his office a home away from home, suitable for week-long stays if the need arose, as it often did. During my first few years with the NIO, we had very little contact, only bumping into each other for NIO briefings, but he was my number-one contact these days.

Timothy James, however, was a different story. I saw him rarely. I didn't like him much. Most agents didn't. We sometimes called him Tim Jim, or Timmy Jimmy. He had moved up quickly in the NIO ranks—too quickly for my liking. But President Nguyen liked him, and to be fair, James had proved more than competent.

He'd been director for seven years, appointed during Union President Richard Nguyen's third term in office.

Because everything seemed to be about the Movement these days, I saw Bardsley a lot here in his office suite. Spacious, most definitely, with sleeping quarters and a bathroom smart-rigged into the floor plan, available with a push of a button. In the corner of the office next to the entryway, a bar and lounge area stood at the ready. The window behind his desk, which took up the entire back wall, looked out over the New York skyline. The thick black carpet felt like a sponge as I crossed the room to the director's desk.

I wondered what James's suite must look like.

Bardsley greeted me with a nod and an outstretched hand. He'd turned sixty a week before but he looked older, his gray hair sparse, his dark brown eyes all business, no pleasure. His thin frame was tightly wrapped in a custom-tailored black suit jacket that made him look like an undertaker. Matched the carpet, anyway. I wasn't dressed for a funeral, but thoughts of my own demise came to mind when I saw Bardsley's face, which looked like the front holo of the *Times,* all bad news, but controlled in neat columns. Without a word, he motioned me to a chair next to his desk. A see-through cube on the front edge of the desk contained a blue and gold fluidic mass that budded, twisted, and elongated through the nano-slurry inside that controlled it.

"You sent Brindos to Temonus," he said.

I pulled my attention from the cube and looked at him. So much for pleasantries. It sounded like an accusation, and I wondered where he would go with this. "I did."

He leaned back and crossed his arms. "For Plenko?"

"For Koch, actually," I said, getting the gist of it now. A little light shed on why I was here. "He probably won't turn up, so I told Alan to take some vacation time."

Bardsley stared at me, his eyes hard obsidian. He was thinking hard about something else, not Alan Brindos and where I sent him.

"Why did you go over my head and contact President Nguyen about Coral?"

That *wasn't* what I expected him to ask, but I had a snap answer for him. "I decided the severity of the situation demanded quick action, and you were not available."

"I wasn't?"

"No, you were out of the building."

"Did you try to call me? Or—God forbid you'd ever think of this—the director?"

A lump formed in my throat and I scratched at the stubble on my chin that suddenly decided to sweat and itch. "No, sir. Again, I felt the need to—"

He waved off my response, apparently satisfied, but I knew better. "Director's been hard enough to get a hold of lately. But was I unavailable when you decided to send Brindos to Temonus?"

I didn't answer. Sure, I'd sent Alan without telling James, but then again, it *was* my right as Movement Ops Director. Why was he so concerned about this?

Why did I feel put off?

Bardsley smiled. "I'm sure you felt it was necessary to act quickly there too?"

It wasn't even the same thing, but I kept quiet about that. Instead, I brought up those DataNet files. "I found some information on Plenko while prepping files on Koch for Alan's code card. Seems Director James knew where Plenko was and commissioned agents to tail him a few months ago." And you didn't tell your Ops Director about it, I added silently.

Bardsley looked away, shuffled some papers. I clenched my teeth, then looked down at the carpet. It wasn't any fun not being able to crack a joke.

"We did put a tail on him," Bardsley said, frowning, though from the *way* he said it, he might as well have said, "Just what the hell are you doing?"

Good question. Hell, I didn't know that I was really *doing* anything.

"Plenko's done plenty of world hopping," Bardsley said. "He's Transworld Transport's best customer. We found names on passenger lists three or four dozen times during the past year that later turned out to be aliases."

I shook my head. "The tail didn't last long because agents lost him a few months ago. No help from TWT. Why the hell is he flying TWT instead of his own private shuttles?"

"Sliding in unnoticed as a passenger on authorized TWT flights *is* quite the trick," Bardsley said with a frown.

"How could TWT miss him? I could name a dozen worlds Plenko's been to in the past year alone, compliments of TWT, and that's not counting the ones rumors say he visited."

"Like Coral."

He was fishing now, trying to get me to say something about the debacle at Coral that he didn't already know. Bardsley had sent Jennifer Lisle there a month earlier to check out the leads he'd sniffed out, and Alan found the proof. Like I knew anything else that would make him feel better about losing Ribon, and the moon that had caused the devastation.

The loss of life on Coral and Ribon had sent shivers down the spine of the Union. As large as Ribon was, it would never recover fully from the disaster. The pure callousness of Plenko's interference there was inexcusable and most of the provincial world governments, and their citizens, had denounced the attacks. The economic downturn that had crippled the Exchange on every world had caused widespread panic. Now, just a short while later, cries for Terl Plenko's head had lessened, and the voices in favor of his primary objective—independence—had gained momentum.

I said, "Whether Plenko visited Coral in person or not, I don't know, but he was involved in it."

"So you're sniffing around Temonus for the same reasons," Bardsley said. "Leads. Hunches."

Oh, yeah, now I remembered what I was doing. Detective work. "Yes, sir."

He tapped lightly on his desk a moment, seemingly staring at the wall behind me. "Where's this leading?"

I decided just to let it come out. I leaned forward in my chair. "Director James canceled the tail, but Plenko was seen a few days ago on Temonus, in Midwest City."

Bardsley pursed his lips. "Curious. Koch *and* Plenko on Temonus. Your best guess: Why would Plenko be on Temonus?"

I had no definitive answer for him, but I made my guess. "The Movement's activities here on Earth have become a low priority. They've relocated their base of operations. Earth could be a front, a way to establish Plenko's name and give him power to gather recruits. This woman Alan checked out on Ribon, the one who preferred to fall one hundred floors to her death than surrender to the assault team? She was smuggling workers past customs to Coral, recruiting for the Movement."

"Dorie Senall."

"You knew her?"

He shook his head. "But I read the reports. I have to finish this up. What do you want me to do?"

I stood and backed away from the desk a little, still facing Bardsley. Some space away from him, some height over him. "Alan Brindos is looking for Tony Koch, of course, but I'd like to give the matter of Terl Plenko priority. If there's a remote possibility of the Movement's ringleader being there—"

"Yes, well, at least you're asking this time," Bardsley said, interrupting me. "Have you heard from Brindos?"

"Not yet."

"He better be careful. Plenko is extremely dangerous, especially if cornered."

No kidding. Plenko, a First Clan Helk, was big enough to take on several of NIO's best men without breaking a sweat. Tony Koch was a Helk too, though born and raised on Earth. Helks often took human names for business purposes, but Plenko had kept his Helk name.

"I want you to stay close, Crowell," he said, "and in my sights. Nguyen wants you close. Brindos is on his own, and he can report in as necessary."

"If he runs into trouble, a transport can jump his way," I said, hinting.

"I doubt it would do any good. It would take a transport a few days to queue through the jump slot, and the director is not recommending the president send out any Arks without probable cause." He stood abruptly. "Let me know what you find out."

"Yes, sir," I said.

"The Movement clearly has an interest in Temonus. Rumors of Temonus's secession from the Union of Worlds are increasing. Certain Temonus senators are trying to bring it to a vote. If it doesn't happen, then what? The Movement's terrorist atrocities on Coral and Ribon prove they could just as easily do something drastic to provoke Temonus to break away."

Something less drastic, I hoped, than destroying the world. Blowing up the planets the Movement wanted to win over to their cause didn't exactly make sense. I paused, trying to decide how to phrase my next question to the director. So far this morning, Bardsley had been relaxed, even during my reports about Koch and Plenko. I had considered not bringing up the subject about sending Alan to Temonus, because I knew how anything dealing with the Movement made his blood pressure soar, and I was obviously in enough hot water already.

"Sir," I began, "has President Nguyen been notified of Plenko's disappearance? Union assault planes are chasing his shadow all over the city."

Bardsley nodded, but now his voice took on a reproving tone. "We'll inform the president, but remember, just because Plenko's not around doesn't mean the Movement's gone with him."

Four

Crowell's information pointed Alan Brindos to Midwest City, so he spent three days there chasing the Koch lead until it dried up like a trickle in the desert.

He stepped outside the Orion Hotel to watch the sun go down. A farewell ribbon of fire glowed orange on the western horizon, and the low dome of the sky gave up its midnight blue and changed to black. A hollow hum that modulated pitch every few seconds made him look up. The Transcontinental Conduit was above him somewhere, and maybe that's what the humming was coming from. He had checked and there were no tours, as he'd thought. The Orion's gift shop had some T-shirts though. The humming got him thinking about the weather and Crowell's note about how the damn thing worked. It was impressive, he had to admit.

He kept staring into the cold night sky. Truth to tell, anything could be causing that noise. Anything. Brindos felt his calm, peaceful mood slipping away as he went back inside.

Joseph, the hotel concierge, gave him a nod as he walked past him into the lobby. Right now Joseph knew Brindos by an alias, Dexter Roberts. *I'm good at being someone other than myself,* he thought. His whole family had been killed during a freak flash flood in New Mexico when he was eight years old. He was visiting his granddad in Phoenix when it happened. Granddad passed away three years later, and Brindos was shuttled back and forth between foster homes for the next half-dozen years. He had so many last names he had almost forgotten his real one.

Brindos acknowledged Joseph with a wave. Should he order room service or go out to eat? Such were the demands lately on his mental powers. He snagged a newspaper flashroll of the *Midwest City Tribune* from the front desk and headed for a bank of ten elevators that fanned out across the far side of the lobby. Their mirrored surfaces reflected a panoramic view of the Orion's interior, his approaching image a shivery spot of black swimming in a chrome sea. The elevator bank's ability to morph his image so profoundly startled him every time he approached. He chose elevator number three—or maybe it chose him.

An ad slogan for a product he couldn't even remember went through his head: *You don't have to believe in the subliminal. It believes in you.*

The soft pulse of the lounge act off the main lobby fell abruptly silent when the elevator swallowed Brindos whole. A slight G-force hit him in the knees, signaling the ascent. Circles of light burst quickly up the panel in front of him, illuminating the number of each floor that dropped away. There were no buttons to press. Sensors read the room number from the key in his pocket, or he could have used voice commands to go to a floor other than his own. Some of the more ancient elevators back on Earth still had the buttons anyway, to give you the illusion that you had at least an iota of control over your life.

By the time evening had fallen on his fourth day in Midwest City, Brindos had decided Crowell had been right about Temonus. Dead end on Koch. Looked like he'd be able to enjoy a little vacation time after all. Then it would be back to the safety of his desk in New York.

He retired early to his room and turned the vid on with the sound turned down. A sunset blazed on the wall screen, and a bloodred streak cast a hellish light over everything. Superimposed in the lower right of the screen were the words LIVE: NEAR EAST CITY. He plopped down in a chair, but tensed and moved to the edge of the seat as he recognized the vid images.

A ship had crashed. He twisted the newspaper flashroll tighter in his hand, the red blinking node reminding him he hadn't unrolled it yet. An inferno filled the screen, then the camera angle shifted slightly, and the glowing remnants of an interstellar cruiser came into view. The surrounding plain burned out of control; pieces of fuselage were scattered far into the distance. He saw a few bodies too, but the network did a good job keeping the auto-cam focused elsewhere. Shivering, he felt the magnitude of the disaster even through the vid screen.

The auto-cam robot, impervious to the heat, provided the striking images as it sailed over the burning landscape, quickly approaching the carrier. It slipped into one of the burning sections searching for carnage, heat moving like liquid before the lens. Special enhancement straightened out the shimmering forms, but there was still little to see, everything twisted beyond recognition. The auto-cam pivoted, peering through a gaping rent in the hull. Off in the distance, a piece of the wreckage as big as a city block burned.

Brindos leaned back and rubbed his temples, trying to take it all in.

Something moved in the flames. He saw it even as the auto-cam picked up on it, enhancing that area of the screen. It was a servo-robot, coming into focus as the auto-cam moved in. The large machine lumbered erratically through the melting fuselage. Had it been aboard the cruiser before the crash? It left the fuselage and continued its jerky waltz across the open plain, fire and smoke trickling from its metal skin. Brindos moved forward in his chair again, fascinated by the obviously malfunctioning servo-robot. Its sensor panel filled the screen as the auto-cam zoomed in on it. Gauges and probes, all twisted and black, resembled a stoic cartoon face concealing the madness coursing through its heat-fused circuits. Then the screen went white, a flash, dimming down to the soft arc of airborne debris, a shadow quickly moving toward the auto-cam. Brindos instinctively jerked back as the screen went blank.

He sat limp in his chair, staring at static. The newspaper slipped to the floor, and when he picked it up and unlocked it with his thumb, the node flashed green, and the thin membrane shimmered to life with the front page image of the *Tribune*. The headline, in its tall bold-faced type, announced "The Movement Is Here."

Brindos thumbed the upper right-hand corner, and the membrane came out of low-power mode and brightened, transforming instantly to sharp-edged black-and-white text and full-color images. He looked closer at the lead article, flicked it, pulled, and stretched the flash for a larger image. What the headline really said was "The Moment Is Here." A senator from Northern Ghal, Bill Ralton, had made a little speech the previous morning. He had boldly suggested that the colony petition the Union of Worlds for independence. A holo-recording of the senator speaking from the floor in the House ran continuously, looping every five seconds: Ralton, raising his arm in a gesture of leadership, clenching his fist, bringing it down, gripping the sides of the podium with both hands, leaning closer to the camera. Apparently, Senator Ralton impressed the other representatives, for quite a number of them came forward to endorse the proposal. Perhaps the headline *should* have read "The Movement Is Here."

Somewhere between the televised disaster and the *Tribune* headline, any thoughts of a post-mission, relaxing holiday disappeared. He looked at the vid again, which still showed static. Did no one at the station know what had happened? He turned it off and stared at the blank wall screen for a long time. He mulled over all he knew about the Movement and Temonus, which wasn't much, and he could make no sense out of any of it.

Brindos woke up the next morning, still in the chair, and didn't have a clue what time he'd fallen asleep.

He reset the newspaper for the morning edition, waited a moment for it to download and, as expected, found the story on the front page, the headline reading "Death Toll Rises from Cruiser and Conduit Disaster."

Appparently, the cruiser had carried crews and supplies en route to the terminals outside East City. This was a Class-A carrier, strictly prohibited from coming near terminals within urban zoning.

A fail-safe tracking system supposedly prevented air traffic from colliding with the Transcontinental Conduit, but, for reasons unknown, the carrier steered into it anyway, stretching it. The errant carrier pulled over Tower One and dragged it for twenty kilometers, plowing through residential areas of East City until it finally embedded itself in the East City reservoir like a grapple hook, holding the Conduit taut. Incredibly, the filament still held. The Conduit cut through the advancing hull of the ship, and the ship fragmented onto the plains below.

Brindos received news snippets on his code card as word of the disaster reached the rest of the Union worlds. Casualties included over five hundred dead, several thousand injured, and thousands more evacuated from the immediate area. Officials expected the number of the dead to rise to nearly a thousand. Tower Two on the outskirts of the city had survived intact, as had the other four towers across Ghal, but the Conduit, still relatively taut, now had to be tagged with flourescent markers in the areas of East City where the public could come into contact with it. Experts were unclear whether the temporary disruption of the Conduit's operation might have an effect on weather patterns.

It was time for him to go to East City and see it all for himself.

Brindos approached the front entrance of the hotel and stopped at the desk of the concierge, but it wasn't Joseph standing there. It was a skinny man whose name tag said CECIL.

"Excuse me," Brindos said. Cecil looked up with a smile. "I need the next shuttle to East City—"

"I'm sorry, you can't go. All passage to and from East City has been canceled."

"I *need* to go."

"Everyone has to go, needs to go. Let me tell you," he said, "this isn't my job. They hired me to be a management trainee, not this, this—ah, here it is." He pulled out a sheet of paper from the pile on his desk and practically threw it at Brindos.

Getting away from Cecil, he read the announcement. No ground transportation. Flights to East City canceled. No one allowed near the disaster site. Everything a mess, total chaos and havoc.

Brindos found Joseph standing outside the front doors. The light of day was muted due to heavy cloud cover, rain threatening. Across the street from the Orion, a competing hotel, the Glitz, still had its chasing-lights marquee announcing free meals and cocktails, automated sleep systems, and 20 percent off anything in the adjoining emporium.

Earlier, Joseph had complained about the "glitz" of the Glitz. "Like a bad neighbor moving in," he said. He also talked about the old days on Earth, during better times. Brindos approached him now and the concierge smiled.

"You ever get time off?" Brindos asked him. "Sleep?"

"Mr. Roberts, good morning. An old man like me, I take all the hours they give me. Did I tell you about the Tigers?" he asked.

"Call me Dexter." Brindos smiled back, remembering an earlier discussion about major league parks, night baseball, hot dogs, beer, and open air. Joseph had mentioned the Yankees, but not the Tigers. "You lived in Detroit?"

"Oh, yes. Grew up there. For a while, I lived in New York, and I saw a few Yankees games as a young man. When I went back to Detroit, I went to thirty games a year. The Tigers rarely won, but so what?"

"I never saw a big league game," Brindos admitted. "They were all closed down by the time I was old enough."

"Goddamn open space laws. Without the major sports arenas . . . well, that basically did in all of professional sports. That's part of why I left."

"A few teams still operate and play in smaller parks. There's a Tigers team still playing at a high school field. Nothing like the old days, though."

"Got that right," he mumbled.

"Anyway, remember you said if I needed anything, to see you?"

"What you need?"

"Cab ride to the airport. Cecil says I can't get there."

Joseph snorted, walked to the street, and hailed a cab with his hotel datacard. Within two minutes, the automated cab rolled up to the front doors of the Orion.

"Joe," Brindos said with a smile, "if you're ever back on Earth, tickets to any baseball game we can find are on me."

"You're on. Anything you need, you see me, like I said. I've bypassed a few lockouts and downloaded the airport into the cab's travel routine. Just one of the many perks allowed a hotel concierge like myself." He winked. "It'll get you there, Mr. Roberts."

"Dexter. Please. Thanks, Joe."

Brindos got in the back of the cab, said "M.W.C. Airport" to the voice box between the seats, and off it went. As the cab rolled out of the business district and through an area of fairly new, no-frills, low-income housing projects, Brindos noticed the clean, sparse appearance of the neighborhoods. The windswept concrete streets and boxlike structures reminded him of an industrial park. Other street traffic had been diverted to smaller arterials, but the cab had no problem bypassing the programming.

Arriving at the terminal, he headed inside, got his bearings, and eventually found the TWT desk. A fellow wearing tortoiseshell glasses and an expensive suit stood behind a holo-DataNet board. As Brindos approached, the board winked out and the man smiled politely.

"East City, please," Brindos said.

"I'm sorry, sir, no flights to East City."

"No, no, the press shuttle."

The man smiled broadly, told Brindos that colony officials had scheduled the flight to East City in a half hour, then asked for identification. Goddamn, he hated this kind of thing. Crowell owed him big time. He gave him a name and showed his code card, which now, thanks to the appropriate data from the NIO, looked like a press card from Interworld Press Service, one Dexter Morrison. Plenty of other off-world reporters were stranded here, and Brindos was unlikely to attract unwanted attention.

Ten minutes later he was on the press shuttle. He snoozed during most of the flight. On the final approach to East City, a soft, automated ping woke him. Brindos looked out his window down onto East City at what looked like a dry riverbed cutting a wide swath through heavily built-up areas of the city. As he gathered his wits, Brindos realized he was looking at the drag path of Tower One.

From his bird's-eye view the massive tower sat at a tilt on the far horizon of the city. In the foreground, as the shuttle sank down onto East City, sides of buildings, whole city blocks in fact, had been completely destroyed. The areas most heavily affected appeared to be more of the same residential housing projects he'd seen just a few hours earlier in Midwest City. Streetlights sputtered on as daylight faded. The shuttle swung in for its landing, and as they passed over the airport—well out of the disaster area—Brindos noticed that, contrary to what Cecil had told him, it looked untouched by the disaster.

Shortly after landing, he found himself sitting in an airport cafe called the Temonus Trolley, waiting for the promised tour of the crash site. The place was packed and he ended up taking the last open table. The menu offered American West Coast cuisine as well as local vegetarian fare and some Helk specialties. He doubted the Helk food was authentic, so far away from Helkunntanas, so he played it safe when the order board holoed in front of him and ordered the California burger.

A reporter asked if he could sit with him and he nodded. "Dexter Morrison," Brindos said, using his Interworld Press alias.

"Melok."

Brindos raised his eyebrows.

"Just Melok," he said, smiling. He ordered a patty melt, then tapped the holo a few times to request extra grilled onions, and Swiss cheese instead of cheddar. It looked like he could use it. He was so skinny, Brindos thought he might drift away at any moment. His name seemed familiar, and when he asked him about it, he said he was a reporter from a Midwest City Helk paper, *Cal Gaz*, which loosely translated meant *The Monitor*.

"Maybe you've seen my name there," he said.

"Not likely. Never read that paper. And it's Helk, right? They let human reporters on staff at a Helk paper?"

"Sometimes. I'm the only one at the moment," he said. "It's a bit intimidating being around all those Helks, but the pay's good. Where you from, Dex? You mind I call you Dex?"

"Call me what you like. New York. I came here on vacation."

"And then the disaster puts you right into reporter mode."

"For now, until I can get myself home. They can't ground flights forever, right?"

"People are under the impression the airport has been damaged," he said.

"Seems to be all right."

"The airport is shut down, Dexter, that's a fact. But rumor says the Conduit was sabotaged. And so flights canceled, safety and security reasons."

Brindos looked down at his coffee. He picked it up and took a sip, looking at Melok over the rim. "Sabotage? Really?"

"But then there's the official government stance."

That much Brindos knew from the paper. "The need for a thorough recheck of all aerial tracking and guidance systems before the resumption of normal air traffic."

Melok smiled. "Was that word for word? Because that was good."

Their food came via a servo-robot a bit later, and Brindos let Melok grab the plates off the serving tray. The servo-robot said "Enjoy" in a nasal twang and scooted off. Brindos dug into the California burger, suddenly starving.

Playing the part of an off-world reporter, he felt safe continuing to talk about the Conduit. "Why would someone sabotage it?"

"It controls the weather," Melok said quickly.

"Sure, I know that much. Snazzy tech. Is it working?"

"I don't know. I've not really looked into it much. It alters weather patterns somehow, but it's difficult to measure over the short term. Rainfall in the farm belt is down this season, for whatever it's worth."

"You know that the Science Consortium designed it?"

"Sure."

"But who runs it?"

"Don't know. Why do you want to know?"

"I'd like to talk to someone about it."

"Don't know." Melok took another bite of his sandwich.

"You don't know if I can talk to someone?" Brindos said, trying to refocus the reporter's attention. Melok's disjointed manner was putting him off a little.

"I don't know who runs it now. The Consortium still? Maybe?"

What Brindos really wanted to ask him for was a connection between the Conduit disaster, Temonus's possible secession from the Union, and the Movement. Now *that* would've been a bombshell to drop on Melok.

"Is there anyone on this world who *does* know about it?" Brindos asked.

Melok chased his food down with the rest of his coffee. He smiled. "We may seem a little backward to you, Dex, who no doubt has traveled much and experienced many exotic and modern worlds. We may seem"—he paused, staring away, twirling a French fry in the air, searching for the right words—"passive. But, I assure you that at least *I* am curious about the Conduit and this disaster. I wouldn't be here otherwise."

Brindos finished his burger, pushed his plate toward the middle of the table, and said, "Sorry, forget it."

He waved it off. "Hey, Dex, look, no worries." He leaned in toward Brindos. "It's the Movement, you know?"

Oh, yeah, he knew.

"Plenko's got everyone running scared," Melok said. "He's a menace. I'm sure he's behind the Conduit mishap, but I'm not sure how I approach it at *Cal Gaz*. Publisher's being very difficult about any piece that puts Helks in a bad light."

He gave Brindos his card—an actual paper one—and said to look him up if he found out anything interesting and he'd do the same.

Yeah, right. First chance he got.

Brindos put his card in his pocket without looking at it.

A quick briefing before the tour started turned out to be short and uninformative. The information available to the press revealed little: names of the deceased (a partial list); name of the carrier involved in the wreck, the *Exeter*; and names of the captain and crew. Evacuation zones. A plea for monetary aid. No official information about the cause of the catastrophe, but the gathered reporters did get a more detailed description of the events.

If the *Exeter* incident was sabotage, or an act of terrorism cour-
tesy of the Movement, it hadn't worked; these people seemed as
terrorized as a napping gorilla after a full meal. Brindos sensed an
apathetic attitude about the recent disaster. You never knew what
lay beneath the surface, but these people just didn't seem appropri-
ately upset, never mind primed for a revolution.

They took Brindos and the others out to the crash site immediately after the briefing. He would've played real reporter and talked
to other sources about what was really going on, but only other
reporters scrambled around the ruins, taking vids and pictures of
the area, trying to stay out of the way of the emergency workers
doing their jobs. Like Midwest City, the older sections of East City
were no more than fifteen years old; the white prefab buildings
looked as new as the day they were put up. City officials had closed
all roads leading into the disaster area to all but emergency vehicles,
but they allowed the press to inspect the damage on foot. The street
was residential, more tenements, but the absence of activity gave
Brindos the impression they were unoccupied, the people evacuated
somewhere away from the destruction.

This neighborhood near the reservoir stood in the shadow of
the displaced Tower One. Brindos saw it looming ahead of him like
an obsidian giant bending over the tops of the quiet streets, its pin-
nacle shrouded by clouds.

He walked to the street's modified ending, a valley of fresh earth
a kilometer across. Buildings on either side of him, sheared off at
mid-structure, dangled their internal ligaments over the precipice.
Up and down the wide brown gap, crews worked diligently, but he
wasn't sure whether they were trying to restore the giant device to
working order, or salvage what they could of it.

Brindos toured the area the best he could the next half hour,
then the press shuttle left East City. The ride back to Midwest City
was quiet. Melok sat three rows up from him on the press shuttle
and Brindos wondered if the reporter would figure out his angle for
a story in *Cal Gaz*.

After he got back to the Orion Hotel, Brindos's code card

beeped with a message from Crowell outlining his meeting with Aaron Bardlsey. Brindos acknowledged it, briefing him on his visit to East City, and said he'd give the matter of Terl Plenko top priority as requested. His hunch now was that Plenko and Koch were both alive and well on Temonus.

awoke at nine in the morning the day after my meeting with Assistant Director Bardsley. It was my day off, but I didn't think I'd even make it out of my studio apartment. I hadn't worked out in the gym for several days and it was pissing me off. I rubbed my eyes, turned over, and recalled mornings on Aryell with Cara sitting on the corner of her bed, wearing one of my white T-shirts and nothing else. She would hold her arms over her head and move side to side, stretching, auburn hair flowing across her back. Turn and look at me from under her long lashes. Smile. Brush her hair back off her forehead and curl it behind her ear.

She never knew how much I cared for her. Figured, I'm sure, that I was this man of mystery who engaged in an off-world affair the length of my stay on Aryell, but that I'd soon be on my way.

I blinked and rubbed my eyes. I flashed a moment on an image of Cara at her house in Kimson City on Aryell. I wondered if whatever had once brought us together had tried to work its magic again, thoughts of her coming to me like the perceived passion I'd left behind. Could've just been stress at work. Why hadn't I even written to her?

I sat there a good fifteen minutes, eyeing the bottle of good Temonus whiskey on the nightstand, the kind of whiskey everyone talked about and everyone spent too much money on to get. Me included. I'd spent half a week's pay last night, wanting a good stiff drink. It was still unopened.

I called Mom, told her I was doing fine, asked how she was do-

THE ULTRA THIN MAN

ing, same routine. Always after calling, I felt guilty. I wanted to see her more often. She had fewer friends now than I did when I was a kid, and that was saying a lot. She'd never quite gotten over losing Dad.

Why *was* the whiskey still unopened?

My code card chimed on the nightstand. I glanced over there, groaned, and stood. I grabbed my robe off the floor and walked over. I wondered if Brindos had information for me about Koch or Plenko. I slipped the robe on as I picked up the card.

The message was not from Brindos.

An unregistered. Everything froze inside me. A message with no point of origin, no ID, no reply protocol. What we called a one-way, illegal as hell. I could hardly move, shocked by the impossibility of it. Due to strict coding and powerful blocking nanoware, this kind of message never popped up on an NIO agent's code card. And yet here it was. The note that shimmered onto my screen was short:

Floor 13. 2 pm. Your life is in danger. I have urgent information for you. —Gray

The thirteenth floor?

The unregistered couldn't have meant Floor 13 of the NIO building because there *was* no Floor 13, thanks in part to a nod to an old superstition. So what the hell did Floor 13 mean? Was it a place or a project name? I sure as hell didn't know who Gray was, or what he—or she—would want to see me about. The common-sense part of me screamed setup, but the curious-as-all-hell side, the one that didn't get out much, couldn't pass up the intrigue.

What kind of urgent information could an unregistered possibly have for me?

I got dressed—suit, jacket, blaster—everything I'd throw on when going to work on a normal day. I spent the next thirty minutes charging my finger capacitors, even though I had never used them before. I hadn't wanted them, but they were forced upon me, government-issue. A mandatory surgical procedure had given me the ability to discharge a hell of a shock, one cap in each pointer finger, enough to put someone out. They might come in handy after all. I had to make allowances for this whole thing being a setup, even though I had no idea where to look for Floor 13.

Floor 13 or not, the NIO building was where I needed to go. So much for the Temonus whiskey. So much for my day off.

On my way to the NIO offices I checked my code card, but nothing new turned up from the global data searches I'd set up earlier to research Conduit day-to-day operations. I'd asked fellow agents to take a peek around as well, see if I was missing something obvious. Nothing.

A few blocks from the NIO building I remembered Floor 13.

It came as a memory, or maybe a flash of insight. I don't know *why,* but I peered to my right, down an alley. In the distance was a building that could've taken up an entire city block. I must have passed that alley a hundred times on that very same street, maybe even looked down that alley a dozen times, but why would I have noticed a distant, somewhat run-down building, with FLOOR 13 stamped near its roof line in big block letters?

I ran most of the way. Ten minutes later, I got there, and as I stared at the Floor 13 letters on the side of the building I realized the place had been some kind of dance club. I had a vague recollection about it. Floor 13. Abandoned now, looked like, as many buildings were. A narrow building, thirteen floors.

I expected the double-door entrance to be locked, chained, or both, but it was wide open. Christ. I drew the blaster from my suit jacket.

I slid inside and the elevator was right in front of me. Just a smidgen of light seeped into the room from the double doors, but I could tell the whole bottom floor was abandoned. A lot of garbage littered the floor, but I couldn't tell what most of it was in the low light.

Twelve more floors in this building, but I doubted there was such a thing as a grand tour. At this point I was only interested in number thirteen.

I called the elevator and stood poised, blaster raised and ready.

The doors opened right away and I saw nothing in the elevator's darkness. I walked in. The 1 button cast the only light inside, and it gave just enough light to pick out the 13 button. I pushed it and the elevator rose. I expected a noisy ride, neglected machinery and all that, but it ran smooth and quiet.

Okay. I'd figured out Floor 13. Now what about this goddamn Gray?

The elevator slowed to a stop and the doors opened. My blaster still raised, I stepped out into silence.

The hairs on the back of my neck stood up. No one was in sight. Feeling terribly exposed, I swept my blaster side to side, up, back down, but I couldn't see anything. No tables, chairs, shelves, no carpet, not even a disco ball. The place was nearly dark except for the glow of a few safety spots creating scattered pools of light. This didn't look like my kind of place. What kind of music had they played here?

I wondered why it had closed, and how long it had been closed.

The elevator door clicked shut behind me. I inched toward the nearest pool of light, my footsteps echoing in the open space.

"That's close enough," a deep voice said from somewhere in front of me. I stopped a few steps away from the pool of light, surprised by the loudness of the words. The voice sounded low and guttural, almost like a growl, but I couldn't see him.

"Gray?" My voice echoed off the bare walls. "A little more light on the subject would be nice. How do you expect me to dance—"

"Shut up, Crowell," came the voice. "Drop the blaster."

Got my name right, so at least I was in the right place. I waited, but just for a moment. I edged a little closer to the light, testing him. If he said something else, I might be able to pinpoint his location, get off a wild shot. Not good odds though.

I heard the click of a weapon readied.

I stopped, held the blaster above my head a moment, then crouched down and placed it on the floor.

"Kick it into the light," the gruff voice said.

I straightened and did so, my nerves all jumbled up now. "Gray? Is that your name?" I looked around slowly, but still couldn't make out where he might be. "What am I doing here?"

"I'm warning you about your own agency."

"The NIO. Really."

"You need to get away from here."

"I don't—"

"I've been inside the NIO DataNet," the voice said.

"You can't have been in the DataNet unless you're NIO. Are you?"

"I've had access to a DataNet level deep in the NIO basement. You know what that is, of course."

I did know. And it was impossible. "Even I don't have clearance for that. There's no way—"

"The ultra thin level is not for anyone's eyes except the top NIO hierarchy."

"Ultra thin level. You're kidding, right?"

"You and Alan Brindos are being traced."

My stomach flipped a few times, and I took a moment to look around me. Was this really the only other person here in this abandoned dance club?

"Let me see you. Who *are* you?"

"I'm Gray. Your life is in danger. The NIO cannot be trusted. Because of the Movement, which you are investigating, increased funding has gone to the NIO and to the Science Consortium."

"Science Consortium. Five Union scientists. I'd say that's common knowledge."

"You sent Brindos to Temonus," Gray said, seemingly ignoring me. "You should *not* have."

"It was my right as—"

"You told him to investigate the Transcontinental Conduit."

I wondered how he knew all this. "And?"

"A lot of the funding is tied to it."

"The Science Consortium designed it. Do you read *National Geographic*?"

"It is so much bigger than that."

"In what way?"

"Temonus. Ribon. Coral. Aryell. Something bigger than the Movement."

"Bigger than—" I snorted. Laughed. But in my mind, I thought of Cara. She was on Aryell, and now this Gray was telling me it was involved in something bigger than the Movement.

"The NIO has traces on Plenko and his aliases," Gray said. "Tony Koch, Tom Knox, Tam Chinkno. This commission came from Director Timothy James."

Tony Koch wasn't Plenko's right-hand man? He *was* a Plenko alias? "Koch, an alias? Tom Knox too? Knox was supposedly an alias for Tony Koch."

I was familiar enough, too with the Chinkno alias. These Helk names gave me a headache.

Gray said, "Depends on how you look at it. There's also a trace on Dorie Senall."

"A trace on a dead woman? The NIO must have recalled that trace by now. If she hadn't taken her high dive from her Venasaille tower, her name would mean little."

"You're wrong about that."

"And a trace on me. And Brindos."

"Yes."

I tried to follow what he was saying. Did he really know anything, or was he himself some sort of Movement crackpot?

"Why should I trust anything you say?" I asked. "Do you even know what an NIO trace involves?"

"With an NIO trace on you, at the very least, a tracking program has wormed into your code card and interfaced with an NIO monitoring cobweb. The only way to counteract a cobweb of that variety is jump-slot travel."

All true. How did he *know* all this?

"This is why you must leave, and leave now," he said. "The NIO will arrest you on suspicion of treason when you return to your office."

I glared in the direction of Gray's voice.

"I'm going to bet you have a way to confirm the trace," he said.

I did. What Timothy James or Aaron Bardsley didn't know was that Brindos had done some reprogramming of our code cards. Tampering with them was enough to get us fired from the NIO itself, but we had managed to install various subroutines that could give us information other agents might not have access to.

I ran one of our own tracking programs, one of the most illegal applications available on the Net. It hadn't occurred to either Brindos or me to look, but now that I did, it became obvious within minutes that Gray was telling the truth. A monitoring cobweb had been uploaded onto my code card, and not too long ago. A few days.

"Helk snot," I whispered. I could read between the lines. I was in trouble, as Gray was telling me, and that trouble was coming from the NIO higher-ups.

"You shouldn't have sent Brindos to Temonus," Gray said. "Now you're apart and it's not going to be easy for you two."

"Please—how do you know all this?"

"I can't tell you more. There's a chance I've said too much. I honestly don't know where your loyalties lie. Or Brindos's."

"Our loyalties? What the hell—"

"You'll have to chance going to Aryell on your own."

"Aryell. Why Aryell?" Although I wanted nothing more than to go to Aryell. To see Cara.

"You can communicate with Brindos safely once you've arrived. If you send something before then, it will need strict coding. I imagine you have other . . . unique . . . applications on your code card that will allow you to do that."

"You can't just tell me where—"

"You *have* to go to Aryell."

"Why won't you let me see you? What's the big mystery?"

"I have to shoot you now."

Shit. I didn't hesitate. I didn't know this Gray, so it wasn't hard to let self-preservation and reflexes kick in. I turned, ran into the darkness, and dove for the ground. A weapon discharged, and a flash hit the wall in front of me, lighting the floor a split second, long enough for Gray to find me and discharge the weapon again. An energy pulse hit me square in the back.

The elevator appeared for a brief moment in the light, and I had a glimpse of its doors opening as the pain raced through me, the muscles in my body seizing up into tight knots. Then I blacked out.

* * *

I woke and immediately wished for a hangover. Better to suffer that than the needles piercing my brain and the muscle spasms moving up and down my quivering body.

Why the hell had Gray warned me before shooting?

I sat up and tried to shake the fog from my head. I scanned the room and found I had been left where I had fallen, room still dark but for the safety lights, no other movement around me.

But something was different.

In the circle of light on the floor nearest to me lay a privacy visor, the telltale silver mask glistening.

An NIO privacy visor, a sensitive piece of equipment that just didn't get passed around the office.

A blinking green light on its side signaled a connection to the DataNet. A moment later I thought to check for my blaster and code card. Gray had put the blaster back in my suit jacket. A check of my hands told me my finger caps still had power. I pulled out the code card, and a red bubble pulsed like a beating heart on the screen.

Gray had fried the close-ops comm unit. So much for trying to contact anyone in the nearby NIO building. He didn't trust me, and now he wanted to see what I'd do, not being able to contact the NIO, was that it?

The time display running in the bottom corner of the code card told me I'd been out cold ten minutes. I assumed Gray had taken the elevator and left.

Why had he warned me, then shot me? Why leave me with my weapons and a visor connected to the DataNet? I bent down and picked up the visor and thought a moment. No one had ever died or been seriously injured tapping into a privacy visor. Still, I shivered, feeling myself unravel a little more. I could call the elevator again, wait for it, take the visor to my office. Or straight to Bardsley. Or James. But suddenly I wasn't sure how safe my office would be.

A tracking cobweb, he'd said. A trace on us by the same organization I worked for.

I took a deep breath and placed the mask over my eyes. It was light in weight, translucent, and flexible. Like a blindfold, the privacy visor blocked out the light as its edges sealed and conformed to my head. This wasn't my visor, but they were one-size-fits-all.

The screen shimmered to life. An already loaded DataNet page appeared in front of my eyes. Gray had managed an anonymous login.

It contained an order from Timothy James for my arrest.

Gray—if that was who I was really dealing with—had led me this far. Did the NIO have ties to the Movement and Temonus politics? They had an *interest* in it, but did it go deeper? The Transcontinental Conduit tied in somehow too. Someone—probably James—had authorized the extra funding to the Science Consortium's Conduit research after the thing was built. Why?

I had virtually no access to any of this sensitive information, this ultra thin level, whatever the hell that was.

We'd been set up. The goddamn NIO was waiting to sacrifice Alan goat and Dave goat. Could I explain the NIO's involvement with the Movement? Not that I knew how that could be done. Or *why*.

Who was James answering to? President Nguyen? Did it go up that high? Gray had led me to this spot and had visored into sensitive DataNet files. Known all the right passwords to get into the NIO basement.

As I stood there pondering all this, the visor powered off, obviously on some sort of strict timer. My efforts to power it back up were unsuccessful. I flung it away from me and did a quick search of the abandoned floor. No other clues. Gray had done his one good deed and left.

I moved to the elevator and palmed the CALL button. I watched the dim red circles above the door flash on and off, from floor one, and I counted up as the numbers did. For all I knew, the privacy visor had its own tracking system built into it, and agents were in that elevator, searching for me.

I readied my blaster. Finally, the thirteen lit up, and the elevator door opened.

Empty.

I sighed in relief, double-checked for peace of mind, then got in. It was my day off after all, so I didn't feel the least bit obliged to check in at the NIO. Agents were waiting to arrest me. I ordered the elevator to the first floor, and the doors closed.

I needed to let Alan know of my discovery, but I couldn't risk using my code card anywhere in Earth's solar system. Gray was right. The NIO couldn't monitor code card activity on other Union worlds because of the jump slots, which fried any cobweb hooked to a tracking system, even with a programmed worm forcing the issue. Alan would be safe messaging me with his code card once I got to Aryell. It dawned on me now why James had felt the need to question my decision to send Alan to Temonus, through Bardsley. For two reasons, actually. His monitoring cobweb wouldn't work there, and Alan might stumble into something on Temonus he wasn't supposed to stumble into.

Things had been so much easier in Seattle, running a private detective business that didn't do any interesting business. Sure, once in a while I got the privilege to get dirt on an unfaithful partner, or track an unregistered alien, or search for a missing person.

Contracting for the NIO had led me down a new path, and I was still learning the ins and outs of a more strenuous career. I hoped I learned fast enough.

The elevator doors opened up on the first floor and I half expected to see an armed security team waiting for me, but the floor was deserted. I walked out of the elevator, then out of Floor 13. I put as much distance between me and the building as fast as possible.

Fifteen minutes later, since the code card's messaging was being traced, I sent Alan the only possible communication I could risk: a lasergram sent from the New York Universal Telegram Station on Fourth to Midwest City on Temonus, Orion Hotel, strictly coded. Deciphering it would be Alan's problem. I hoped he remembered how to do a crossword puzzle.

I told him Plenko and Koch were the same Helk, we were being set up by the NIO, and that I would contact him once I arrived at our favorite backwater planet. I didn't specify, but he would know I meant Aryell.

Alan and I had stopped at Aryell for a few months during our year-long stint chasing Baren Rieser, a data forger from Seattle the police department had tried and failed to bring to justice for nearly a decade. We had chased him halfway around the Union before losing him, although we suspected he'd holed up somewhere on Helkunntanas.

That's how we met Cara Landry, a receptionist at the Flaming Sea Tavern, a local pub known for its high-priced sex workers. We didn't indulge in the ladies, but that's where Cara taught us the Flaming Limbo. That was three years earlier, before the NIO handed me my Movement commission.

Like a reccurring dream, Cara appeared and disappeared from my memory when I least expected it, and each time I awoke, I told myself I would go back to her.

Now was a good time.

I took five different auto-cabs and two shuttles to get to Minneapolis. I set my code card up with an alternate identity I'd uploaded years ago. Agents weren't supposed to do that without registering them, but we did it all the time. All I had to do was flash my card, say NIO and "Neil Ryan," pass the back of the card over their scanner, and I got a free ride. They'd bill the NIO later, of course, but the code card scans, while seemingly set to bring up Neil Ryan, would register a name I'd uploaded on the sly, that of Thomas Nelson, a journeyman agent I knew only by name, practically a kid, with less than a year's experience. I picked up a suitcase, clothes, and some necessities at a small shop in the spaceport, then purchased a ticket to Aryell. Thomas Nelson would have some explaining to do about his purchases and his flight plans today.

I waited impatiently for the drop shuttle to arrive. Had I managed to elude any NIO pursuit? If agents had been sent after me, and managed to keep up during my little jaunt, I'd give them all a bonus myself if I ever got back to New York.

The passenger lounge overlooked the launch pad, and as I gazed out the giant observation windows, the ground crew scurried about like tiny insects, insignificant. I saw my own reflection in the glass, as tenuous as the mirror images of the other passengers staring out the windows with me.

Out of work and on the run in a really big galaxy. Where was that Temonus whiskey when I needed it?

Six

itting in the restaurant at the Orion, eating breakfast and wondering about his next move, Brindos watched his waiter hustle over to his table, then drop a lasergram into his palm.

"Mr. Roberts," the waiter said. "Just came in, sir."

Brindos acknowledged him with a nod, and when the man hustled away, he thumbed the DNA lock on the top of the lasergram's thin resin and waited for the message to light up. Simple e-ink, flashpaper certainly too expensive for 'grams. It always annoyed him having to wait those seconds for the words to appear. He read it through, and it was not what he had hoped for. He needed solid information from Crowell to guide him through this mess, not chatty bullshit about how he and his roommate had stormed on the Temonus blue booze.

Then it hit him like a fistful of stupid. Dave Crowell didn't have a roommate, always the loner, never hitched, always making excuses, worrying about his mom, berating himself for not making things happen with Cara.

And the lasergram, while it came from New York, didn't have his name on it anywhere. It was in fact part of an emergency plan they'd concocted for troubled times should they ever come.

Brindos hit the encrypt node on his code card, flexed the membrane until the PROCEED prompt glimmered red above the node. He wrapped the code card around the lasergram resin and waited for the message to transfer. Crowell had designed a simple cipher with his code card, transferred it to the 'gram, and sent it to Brindos to decipher on his end. The idea being they couldn't carry around some obscure personal decoding program in their code cards for years without attracting suspicion. The design program itself was a crossword puzzle kit readily available in any software store, although Crowell had found a version of it on the DataNet, and stored it there in the ether where he could load in updates and tinker with its programming as needed. With a few simple modifications, he had himself a cipher builder. The sender wrote two messages, one for the across words, one for the down words, and the program designed a puzzle. Easy to code, but impossible to decode without the program on the other end.

Brindos set to work on it amid the impatient stares of his waiter. The message was long, so it took half an hour before he had it decoded.

Brindos read about Gray, the ultra thin level, the Plenko aliases, the Science Consortium, Temonus, and the NIO traces on them that screamed setup.

The last bit of the message read: *My code card is being monitored from home, but I'll be safe once on our favorite backwater planet. I'll contact you again with a Hancock when I've arrived. Find out everything you can about the Conduit and Plenko. Gray said you were in danger, so be careful. The assistant director knows you're there. Do not acknowledge this message.*

Hancock. Crowell would contact him with one of his alternate identities.

Brindos sighed, leaned back in his chair, and rubbed his eyes. Betrayed from above. This was not going to be pretty. He would have to keep his eyes open, try and sniff out NIO undercover agents, Terl Plenko and Movement sympathizers, and work even longer in the field. He'd never see his NIO desk again.

He supposed everything made a lot more sense, the Movement and the NIO, maybe even the Union, involved in something bigger than imagined. A carrier like the *Exeter* should have been more than adequate to clip the Conduit, but no one had anticipated the wire's durability. Those involved hadn't toured the destruction along the drag path like he had. Or maybe they didn't care if hundreds of innocents died. They didn't weep for Coral and Ribon either. His stomach churned, remembering the horrors visited upon Ribon. The very agency he'd spent three years working for might have had a hand in it all.

Crowell was going to Aryell. Brindos worried about his partner going to see Cara now, after three years. Three years of Crowell pining for her, never even telling her he was in love with her. If he'd thought either of them was the type of person to fly off the handle, Brindos would've alerted the vid networks and told them where they could find some juicy virtual programming.

Because he'd finagled his way onto the press shuttle the previous day, he'd been cleared to tap his code card into Temonus's newswire and pick up status reports. He logged in under his Dexter Roberts identity.

Released logs from the *Exeter* revealed coded changes in its navigational program. When the ship entered the planet's atmosphere it locked onto autopilot, running a curve that moved deceptively along routine reentry paths, but a last-minute course deviation sent it hurtling into the Conduit. He thought about the servo-robot flailing around in the wreckage of the *Exeter,* and wondered if someone had somehow programmed it to do the dirty work. The crew's only hope of overriding the program glitch, which was well-hidden and guarded by a triple fail-safe system DNA interlock, was to go back in time and get out of the transport industry. They had less than a minute to impact when the course deviation commenced.

Brindos wondered if Melok's article in *Cal Gaz* had appeared, if he made a case for sabotage. Most of the Temonus papers blamed the Movement. If the natives were getting restless, they didn't show it. Life moved along, and he continued to be treated as a welcome visitor, which of course made him nervous as hell.

His assignment had been to look for Plenko and Koch. That they were the same man made an impossible task only slightly more difficult. A real hole in his investigation had been a lack of a visual ID on Koch, but if he wanted a reminder, he only had to scan the local newspaper roll and read the *Stickman* comic, which seemed to be very popular here. The caricature of the superhero's nemesis bore a remarkable resemblance to the photos of Plenko in NIO files.

Crowell had suggested some new Plenko aliases. Tom Knox.

Tam Chinkno. Brindos figured, you want to catch a stray, stake out his watering hole and make some noise.

After breakfast, he told Joseph, the Orion's concierge, about his interest in sampling some Helk cuisine later in the day.

Joseph grinned. "Mr. Roberts, there's a restaurant in the city that does the real thing."

"Call me Dexter. Real thing?"

"Authentic."

Brindos said that if he took him there, he'd buy him dinner that night. He agreed.

Brindos met Joseph after his shift, about seven o'clock, outside on the hotel steps. He had exchanged his concierge uniform for an old gray wool suit, freshly pressed but looking its years. No doubt a remnant of Joseph's younger days on Earth. It hung loosely on his tall, age-thinned frame. His wispy silver hair, which Brindos had barely noticed before due to his cap, fluttered in the light breeze. He moved across the steps in a stiff, deliberate manner to greet Brindos. It occurred to him then that he'd encountered few other elderly colonists, if any.

The restaurant, he explained, was across town in a sector Brindos had not yet explored. "Can't quite recall the name," he said, thinking.

"I thought you knew everything there was to know about this town."

"I'm also damn old." He pointed to his head. "Brain cells going. Anyway, it's a place few tourists seek out, and I rarely go to that part of town myself."

They waited ten minutes for a ground bus. Few colonists owned personal transport vehicles, and auto-cabs were expensive here, a luxury used principally by tourists and the small upper class. Most rode public transit, or they walked. The bus took them across town, dropping them on the fringe of what appeared to be a ghetto district. The buildings were coarse but sturdy structures of stone and red brick. Many of the glass windows were broken or boarded over.

Brindos hadn't expected to visit a pre-human quarter. Helk settlements had been built decades before the establishment of the current colony but most tourists didn't realize that. It's how Earth had discovered the Helks, coming across the settlements when Temonus opened up as a colony possibility.

"The old district will be demolished and assimilated into the rest of the city plan before long," Joseph said.

"Do many live here now?" Brindos asked.

"A few. Not many. The restaurant, though. Whatever it's called, it's there because it always has been. The only restaurant in the district. Obviously, it has a good reputation, or it wouldn't be there."

The gray, cracked streets were empty but for them and an occasional soul who might appear a block off, then disappear, slinking down some side street. The streetlights, which came on in the early dusk, reminded Brindos of the old electric streetlights on Earth, complete with a flickering hum and harsh, unnatural light. The night's wary patrons dodged the sporadic spotlit circles like cockroaches.

A small wooden sign nailed above the front door of a dirty brick building had a single Helk word stamped on it, which Brindos couldn't read.

"Damn, that's it, of course!" Joseph exclaimed. "It's just called the Restaurant."

Joseph assured him it looked a lot better inside.

And indeed it did. The setting was formal and elegant. A plush, crimson carpet swept across the room, a vast red tide within a sea of lace white dining tables. The room floated in the aura of candlelight and boisterous dinnertime conversation.

Brindos turned to Joseph. "We should've made reservations."

"Who would've thought a Helk joint would be in such demand, eh?" he said, grinning.

All the employees Brindos saw were Helks. The large whitejacketed waiters danced around the tables, which looked like little doll settings. In fact, it struck him as odd that only a few Helk diners hunkered down to the small plates, tiny chairs creaking. Wouldn't they have Helk-sized chairs, plates, and silverware in a Helk restaurant? He started to ask Joseph, but the maître d' saw them then and, with a perfunctory smile, motioned for them to come with him.

They walked behind the Helk, smaller than most, probably Third Clan. Brindos caught glimpses of the other diners as he peered around his back. They were finally seated at a table near the back of the room, and within moments a waiter appeared, a Second Clan Helk.

"Good evening. My name's Jordan. Would you like to hear the specials?"

"Jordan, where are all the Helkunn diners?" Brindos asked, ignoring the specials.

"Sir?"

"Surely actual Helks would be a confirmation of the fare's authenticity. Joe here recommended the place. Frankly, I'm beginning to have my doubts."

From the corner of his eye, Brindos noticed Joseph, slack-jawed. The waiter took it all pretty well. He stared at Brindos for a long time.

"The truth is," the waiter said, "that the food you will receive, though excellent, has been altered slightly to fit the more delicate digestive systems of most of the restaurant's patrons. The real thing you would find painfully indigestible, and perhaps a trifle strong in flavor."

"What about the few Helks dining in here now?"

"They're entertaining non-Helk guests," he said, forcing a polite smile. "Many Helks frequent an adjacent room on the other side of the building that serves true Helk cuisine."

Satisfied for now, Brindos checked the menu and, on a recommendation from Joseph, placed his order for gabobilecks, a spicy meat sausage. Joseph ordered the same, plus a bottle of Helk white wine.

When the waiter had gone, Joseph leaned across the table and said, "I recommended the place, and you're complaining before even eating?"

"Sorry."

Luckily, the waiter came by a moment later, saving Brindos the trouble of trying to say something conciliatory. The waiter opened the wine and poured a small amount in his glass. He tasted it and nodded. An excellent bouquet of crushed apples and hazelnuts.

Okay, maybe he *had* been hasty.

The rest of the meal was, as Joseph had promised, excellent, a quality reflected in the final bill, which Brindos paid happily, with a hearty tip for the service. He excused himself, leaving Joseph to finish his wine.

An analog clock in the shape of a gabobileck said it was 11:00. Getting late.

The restrooms were in a dimly lit hallway. Thinking he might get a glimpse of the authentic portion of the restaurant, Brindos walked past the men's room door, down the hall, and around a corner. Ahead on his right, light spilled out of a bright room, along with the sounds of a kitchen. He walked quickly past, moving toward a large, crude wooden door he thought must be the entrance to the authentic portion of the Restaurant.

Curiosity got the best of him. He had his hand on the push-worn brass doorplate leading to the other half of the Restaurant, the door gently swinging inward, a warm draft of animal-scented air escaping past him, when the door slammed back into him, knocking him to the ground. He looked up to see Jordan, his waiter, in the doorway; Brindos apologized for getting in the way and started to get to his feet. Jordan must have been going off shift because he'd taken off his white jacket.

The big fellow leaned down to help, but he didn't look too pleased. He picked Brindos up with one hand around his throat, as if he were a sack of kitchen garbage, and carried him down the hallway.

"Fucking let go of me," Brindos wheezed, and he struggled, his hands over the waiter's. Brindos tried to pry them from around his neck, but no luck. Jordan's grip tightened, and he couldn't breathe.

They crashed through the exit door into the back alley. Jordan threw Brindos ten feet across the garbage-slick cobblestones and he crashed into the redbrick wall of the opposite building. He landed hard on the stone ground, consciousness dancing hazily in and out. His back throbbed. The alley looked pretty closed in, and the distance between him and the yellow exit door of the Restaurant kept him from even thinking about getting up.

"Jordan, what the hell?" Brindos said, massaging his throat.

"My name's not Jordan," the waiter said casually, as though he had just helped Brindos to his chair, "it's Tom Knox, and I'm glad to let you know it." He spoke with a calm Brindos found rather menacing.

"Tom Knox?" Brindos whispered. He arched his back, waves of pain running up and down his spine.

It wasn't possible.

He couldn't have planned the timing of this encounter better himself, at this restaurant, with this Helk conveniently placed in his path. How could this be Tom Knox? Or, more accurately, since Knox was an alias, how could this be Terl Plenko? Plenko was First Clan and this Helk didn't look anything like Terl Plenko.

Brindos couldn't maintain consciousness, and he succumbed to darkness.

Seven

After queuing through Heron Station in orbit around Aryell, I boarded the drop shuttle through the umbilical and eventually found myself at the planet's only spaceport. A light snow had fallen on abandoned ships, almost a cleansing, a futile effort to hide the dirt and gritty corrosion. I left the drop shuttle with fifty other passengers, towing my carry-on suitcase, a hard polymer plastic shell designed to withstand just about any attempt to open it. DNA lock, of course. Most of the passengers were tourists, I figured, here to check out the red-light district—the Flaming Sea Tavern in particular—or to ski and 'board some of the best snow in the Union worlds at any number of quaint, rustic resorts that boasted uncrowded slopes, but offered very few amenities. I'd skied as a kid in Montana, but that snow, even the famed deep powder, paled in comparison to the Aryellian slopes. That's why places like the capital city of Kimson did so well, and why tourist attractions like the Flaming Sea kept a steady business. It would be springtime on Aryell soon enough, and that meant the ski resorts would be closing down. Last chance for tourists to get to the slopes before the snow went away.

I shivered in my light cotton clothes; I hadn't had time to go on a major shopping spree during my run away from the NIO. Even though spring was just around the corner, I could've used a jacket. No ground car came to the pad and I swore at the inconvenience. We all walked to the terminal, a simple brown stucco building encircled by a gated fence. The Aryellan flag of blue and white vertical stripes fluttered alongside the green pennant for the Union of Worlds.

The man at immigration smiled when I approached, his pencil-thin moustache and slicked-back hair glistening in the lights that hung low from the ceiling. He took my code card, now set to passport mode, and glanced at it. I hoped he didn't pay too much attention to the size and shape, slightly different than the standard comm card civilians carried.

"Mr. Neil Ryan," he said, seeing only my alternate identity. "It says this is your first visit to Aryell?"

"That's right." It was my first visit as Neil Ryan, anyway.

He smiled again as he handed the code card back, then said, "All seems to be in order. I hope you enjoy your visit."

"Thank you. Can I get tranportation to Kimson City?"

"Oh, most certainly, sir. Ground buses come from the hotels to meet incoming flights. One should be here any minute to take you into Kimson. You can make connections from there to any of the ski resorts or local attractions. Do you have luggage to claim?"

"No," I said. I gripped my carry-on tighter.

"Very good," he said, logging me into his system. He smiled once more, then said to the man behind me, "Next?"

I found a seat in the corner of the waiting area. Actual smart posters, a rarity here, of the eight Union worlds adorned the stucco walls. They were always in motion, animated nature scenes or pictures of famous landmarks moving across the surface of each. The planet names were emblazoned permanently in ribbons of color diagonally across the left bottom corner of each poster. Along the top borders, bold black letters proclaimed TWT's universal slogan in alternating text blocks.

TRANSWORLD TRANSPORT, the posters announced. Then: WORLDS APART AND COMMITTED TO UNION. Just palm the posters and you'd get more information, or even book flights.

I stood up and found a drinking fountain. It actually had a handle—no sensors. I drank, then sighed. A backwater planet in many ways. Tourism kept it on the map, though. A brochure station next to the fountain had dozens of pamphlets advertising the various hot spots, including the Flaming Sea Tavern.

I returned to my seat and sent a message to Brindos from Neil Ryan. I was here. Be careful. Let me know what was going on. Were we fooling the NIO with all of this? Probably not. Messages from all over the Union poured in and out of Aryell every day. I hoped we could hide amid the chatter.

I hoped he'd seen my reports on the ultra thin files. Hoped he was okay and that my previous message had slipped past the NIO data hounds. From here on out, with the encryption program in place, we could use our code cards to communicate. We might be safe from NIO cobweb monitoring, hidden in the many jump slots between here, Temonus, and Earth, but NIO agents working locally, at least those with the expertise, could intercept messages.

No immediate response came from Brindos and I frowned. Too early to be worried, but nonetheless disconcerting.

I had plenty of credits data c locked in my code card from my Neil Ryan account, so I slipped over to the Monetary Services desk. An elderly woman helped me exchange credits for Aryellan paper currency, more than I'd possibly need, but I didn't want to do an exchange more than once because the NIO would trace it to me and know I was on Aryell now.

The ground bus arrived a few minutes later, and everyone crowded on. As the bus drove into Kimson, Cara's image dominated my thoughts. I thought about the first time we met at the Flaming Sea. Doing the Flaming Limbo on her breaks; after hours, traipsing off to the all-night diner on the corner opposite the tavern; sipping spiced coffee and nibbling homemade biscuits.

I stayed up late with Cara one night after Alan had left for the hotel. We talked, had wine, then watched the vid, me on the couch, Cara on the floor in front with her back to me. Her soft breath rose and fell like wind in the trees, and at some moment I touched her, not sure if she was asleep. Touched her neck. Traced a line down along her back. She turned around, a sudden request in her eyes, and that's how it all started.

I'd left Cara because the NIO had contacted me about working with them, and in my heart, I didn't believe I could really love her. That she could love me. It was all too fast. The thought of being paid more frequently contracting through the NIO, instead of waiting for cases to investigate on my own, had a lot of appeal. But now I was back, running from that job, from an agency I'd trusted, and in no position to see if loving Cara could ever happen.

Most of the passengers on the drop shuttle had boarded the ground bus. Most of them were human, but I didn't know which ones might be Aryellan colonists. Not many, I imagined. A few rows up from me I spotted the only Helk. Second Clan by the size of him. I didn't recall seeing any Helks on the drop shuttle. Had he boarded the bus at the terminal? I stared at the Helk's back; soon, he glanced back at me. It made me feel more than slightly uncomfortable. I smiled politely and turned to my window.

It was evening. Blocky stucco homes appeared along the road. The homes occasionally gave way to fields of stubby brown plants, the equivalent of Earth's native wheat. The earlier snow had dusted the broad limbs of the infrequent green trees. The famed Baral Mountains loomed in the distance. Some of the passengers around me chattered about the skiing, pointing out the mountains they thought might have the best terrain.

The bus rounded a bend, and Kimson rose up to meet us. A few pedestrians shuffled along the sidewalks. A handful of passengers got off on the second block, home to a number of hotels, and I kept track of who left, who stayed. Several folks got on. The Helk, his back still to me, remained in his seat.

The bus turned onto Amp Street and proceeded two blocks before grinding to a halt a block away from the Flaming Sea Tavern. I got out through the side door, hoisting my luggage to my shoulder. A dozen others left with me, but the Helk stayed aboard. A block down, the sign of the Flaming Sea beckoned to me, as if daring me to come closer. The bus powered up, rejoined the meager traffic, cruised past the tavern, then turned right, and disappeared around the corner.

I dropped my bag so I could rub my hands together. Again, I wished I'd had a jacket. Perhaps inside I could buy one with a Flaming Sea logo on it. The melting snow made the sidewalk a bit slippery. I heard the *buzz buzz* of the sign as it flicked back and forth from 3-D LED blue and white waves to red and orange flames rising out of a hint of green sea. The words FLAMING SEA glowed a steady yellow in an arc over the landscape. Quaint, as always. Sometimes backwater sensibilities were attractive.

A good number of the tavern's patrons milled about outside, their raucous laughter setting my teeth on edge. I picked up my bag again and walked toward the tavern. Within a half block the sidewalk cleared of snow.

Just as it had been on the bus, people loitering outside the tavern were mostly human; whether they were local or came from Earth directly or from colony worlds, I couldn't tell. I took a deep breath and made for the tavern's wooden door. The design mimicked that of a captain's door on an Aryellan keelhaul. I shouldered past the one Memor in the crowd, his long orange hair tied back in a ponytail. He frowned at me with his thick lips and pronounced cheekbones.

"Excuse me," I muttered.

"Glag-a-*doik*," the Memor spat. Emphasis on the doik. I knew enough Memor to recognize an insult, but I left him alone. Memors were lovers most of the time, not fighters, but I didn't want to test that right now. Memors had the toughest time communicating their needs, and often found themselves at odds with other governments. Governments of the human worlds such as Aryell, Barnard's, Ribon, Orgon, and Temonus, all colonized by the Union during its outreach from Earth, did their best to humor Memors and Helks when they felt the need to complain, even though humans would've remained in the dark if it hadn't been for the Memors and their jump-slot technology.

Most Memors preferred anonymity over ostentatious displays bragging about their jump-slot know-how. They tended to stay home, on Memory, and it was rare to see one of them elsewhere in the Union.

Which is why the article I'd given to Brindos about Lorway, the Memor scientist of the Science Consortium, had impressed me. She'd stepped into the spotlight with the Conduit project, but how much prompting had she needed? Only now, post-Coral and -Conduit disasters, she'd gone quiet with the rest of the Consortium.

The Flaming Sea opened up and I found myself pushed inside as four locals tried to get by. A hand gripped my shoulder.

"Pay," said a short bald man with gigantic shoulders. "Twenty squid."

I barely heard him over the noise in the tavern. A free-pop band played in a lighted cage suspended high over the dance floor, but one of the speakers sat right near the moneyman.

I handed him a couple of ten-squid notes. He produced a nanowand, pricked my hand with it, and said, "You're good until sunrise."

I didn't see a mark, but he had something behind his little stand that could read it, giving me in-and-out privileges. Of course, most of the patrons in here would pay a lot more for in-and-out privileges before the night was through.

He pointed to my carry-on bag. "Can't bring that in."

I smiled politely. "Yes, but I haven't checked into a hotel yet and—"

"We'll store it in the back. Squid and a half until sunrise. Squid per hour after."

Reluctantly I nodded, and the man took it, gave me a claim check, and motioned me out of the way so he could get to his next customer. I went up to the counter and got the attention of the bartender.

"Cara?" I yelled.

He pointed toward the end of the counter. An older woman sat in a sphere of glass. She spoke with clientele, a couple of humans, taking their money and motioning for them to head in different directions. As they left, others lined up to take their places.

Well, this was different. The management had done some remodeling during the past three years, added some new procedures. I got in line, suddenly feeling very nervous about seeing Cara again.

"I need to speak with Cara Landry," I said when it was my turn. A sensor picked up my voice and spit hers back at me.

"Cara's busy," she said in a flat voice.

"Who's she working for these days?"

"Kristen," the lady said.

"Don't know her."

"Only been with us a few months, but very popular." She glanced left, and a glow from the appointment board colored her face with a sickening green. "You want some action? You can have Kristen if you like. Or I've got Talmis in Six-F, or Sundy, ground-floor suite. Take your pick, sweetie."

"I just want to talk to Cara."

"Sure, hon." She leaned toward the glass. "You want to see Cara, you'll have to get on Kristen's list. If Cara has time to chat, then fine. You want on?"

"How long?"

"Three paying customers ahead of you. Hour and a half."

"Okay," I said.

"You're set, sweetie," she said, not looking at me, punching a holo-board with her long green fingernails. "I've left a note that you want to talk to Cara, not Kristen. No charge. Name?"

"No."

"Need to leave a name, in case we have to call for you."

I hesitated a moment, then said, "Aaron Lancaster." Cara wouldn't know it, of course, but I couldn't very well put Dave Crowell up on the list, and Neil Ryan needed to stay on the down low as well.

The next guy in line pushed me rudely out of line as I turned, and I swore under my breath. I noticed a seat at the counter just as one of the Sea's gals left it. She smiled as she passed, her face painted a light green, lips ruby red, tiny sequins on her forehead. A white flashstick, its holo-mist curling in multicolored patterns toward the ceiling, sat beside a glass half-full with a ruby-colored liquid. Lip-stick marked the rim of the glass. I didn't understand flashsticks, which were more for show than anything, the stimulants the man-ufacturers built into them relatively benign and hardly a reason to suck on them.

I sat down, ordered a beer, an Earth import, and the bartender plopped it down in front of me. I paid for it and waited for the time to pass.

The free-pop band, called Suzy and the Poppers, came back from a break and opened with a Zed Tomlin classic. The dance floor seethed with bodies swaying to the music like enchanted snakes. The tables were jammed. Seagals and Seaguys floated from one table to the next, taking orders, returning to the counter, piling drinks on their trays, and vanishing into the melee once again. I'd never seen the Flaming Sea so busy.

The band finished its set, and the glass cage lowered to the floor. The band piled out, and a man in black leather took a spot in the cage, prompting the crowd to applaud with wild abandon. I knew what was coming and smiled as the memories flooded back. The cage lifted above the heads of the crowd, and canned music started.

"Hehhhhhh-loooohhhh!" the man in black leather screamed.

The crowd yelled back in unison, "Hey-o . . . Daddio!"

"This is the place, this is the time, folks, and I am Daddio, your host for the Union-famous, Flaming Sea original!"

The noise in the place increased. A man next to me whooped right in my ear. I gave him a dirty look, but he ignored me, keeping his attention on Daddio in the cage.

"Ladies and gentlemen," Daddio chanted, "it's the Flaming Sea Limbo!"

Raucous music thundered in the room and about eighty people crammed onto the dance floor, squishing themselves into a knot of arms and legs right underneath the cage. Somehow, they managed to dance a little, if nothing more than hopping up and down, bending, twisting. The canned music intensified, and the cage cranked lower.

Slowly. Very slowly. People were ducking now, avoiding the bottom of the cage. Down came the cage another notch, and the dancers all bent at the waist. Feet on the floor, nothing else; that was the rule. People were forced out when they lost their balance and fell. Those still up made sure the guilty ones left the shadow of the cage.

"C'mon, you can do it!" Daddio screamed.

The music continued, the heavy bass booming like ground explosions. The cage lowered, and soon only ten people had managed the contortions necessary to remain on their feet. Then six remained. Then three. Then two.

One man in shorts and a Flaming Sea T-shirt stood an instant longer than a woman in a long white dress, and the crowd cheered and came over to acknowledge the man's dexterity, taking him out of the way as the cage lowered all the way to the floor. They took him to the bar for his free drink and coupon good for fifteen minutes free with the girl of his choice. The applause died down and Suzy brought her Poppers back in to do another set.

I shook my head. When Cara had taken Alan and me into the middle of that mass of people, I had tried to get out of it. I was one of the first ones out. They did the limbo three times a night at the Flaming Sea. On the third try of the night, I stayed up with the last group of fifteen people. Alan fell early and got his face stepped on.

I smiled to myself, remembering Cara's kiss after I'd managed to drag myself back to our table.

The Poppers kicked off the set with a Golden Oldie—a cut from Taz Monsoon's last disc. I pursed my lips and moved my shoulders to the drummer's pulsing back rhythms, tapping the bottom of my glass on the bar. I glanced casually down the bar and saw the Helk that had rode the ground bus with me. He wasn't paying any attention to me, just slowly sipping his drink through a straw. When had he got off the bus? I turned back to face my own drink and wondered if he was following me.

"Brings back memories, doesn't it?" a voice behind me said.

I turned, knowing it was her. My heart started beating faster than the Poppers' bass drum. She was dressed in a red blouse, a gray blazer, and a long black skirt. Her auburn hair hung loose and thick over her shoulders. I hugged her tight, her breasts pushing against my chest. "Cara. God, it's good to see you."

"Hello, Dave," she said, breaking our embrace and giving me a quick look with her hazel eyes. "I can't believe it."

"Me neither." A lump formed in my throat, and I wanted to explain right then and there why I'd stayed away, why I hadn't contacted her—why I hadn't told her I loved her—but the words stuck in my throat.

"You didn't write," she said.

Since arriving on Aryell, I'd thought about what I'd say to her. I said nothing to her now, not even "I'm sorry." I met her eyes, and I was sure she was just humoring me.

She glanced down the counter, avoiding my gaze. "Where's Alan? You bring him along?"

"No. He's slaving away as usual. You busy?"

"Always am."

"Don't doubt it. Business is booming, I see." Cara pulled down good money working for the Sea, checking clients in and out for her boss, taking their tips, scheduling off-duty appointments for twice the price. "The place has gone nuts since I was here last. Where did all these people come from?"

"Tell you later. Shall we go?"

"Kristen give you a break?"

"Yeah, well, sorta."

"You like her? She's new, right? What happened to Lexy?"

"Sexy Lexy left one night and never came back. Heard from her a month ago. Said she was settling down with a guy from Ribon, starting a family and all that."

"Oh, Jesus, Cara," I said, thinking about the disaster on Ribon. I wondered if Lexy had been one of the lucky ones to get off planet before Coral slammed into it.

"I started with Kristen soon after Lexy left. More beautiful than Lexy, a better, um, bedside manner, I guess you'd say. Better money for her, better money for me."

"And she's okay to work for?"

"Fine." She smiled and took my hand. "C'mon. I saw this name I didn't recognize go up on the board, someone who wanted to talk to me, and I soon spotted you in the monitors at my desk. Kristen owed me one, so I checked out for the rest of the night. Let's get out of here."

"My bag—"

"DNA-locked, right? Like always. We'll get it later."

The night had cooled further, and I wrapped my arms around my shoulders. We left the Flaming Sea behind, until we could no longer see the sign's flashing reflection in the snow on the sidewalk.

"Came to Aryell this time of year without a jacket?" Cara said.

"Yeah, I know. I was in a bit of a hurry."

I turned around to see if the Helk was following.

"What's wrong?" Cara asked.

I smiled calmly. "Nothing. Just thought someone might be following us." I glanced one more time over my shoulder, but I couldn't see anyone.

"You in trouble?"

"You see a Helk hanging around the tavern?" I asked.

"Tonight?"

I nodded. "This one's Second Clan. He was on the bus from the spaceport, and I saw him again inside the Flaming Sea."

"Don't see many Helks around here, so I guess I would've noticed him. What's going on?"

I couldn't tell her much. I had no idea what information might put her in danger. I also had to make sure whose side she was on. It'd been three years, after all. "A new case."

"Searching for Terl Plenko."

I stopped walking, surprised at her mention of the Movement leader. When we'd first met, I was a PI, I hadn't yet received my NIO contract to work on Movement operations.

"Hey, don't look so shocked," she said. "I know that much from watching the vids. Plenko and the Movement hog most of the U-ONE news broadcasts. Naturally the NIO would be after him with everything they've got."

I glared at her. "So?"

"Alan wrote me, a year or so ago. Said you were doing extra duty with the NIO. I figure you must be on NIO business, and most of the time these days, isn't it usually about the Movement?"

"He probably shouldn't have told you that."

"I will expose you both for the spies you are."

I laughed, relaxed a little.

"Plenko has a number of aliases," she said, "and I'm betting you've got him cornered somewhere. Alan's on his trail."

I said nothing.

"Where?"

I just shook my head.

"Right," she said. "Can't tell me. But you've found out something. You're on the run."

I looked at her. Smiled apologetically.

"Right, can't say," she said, smiling right back. "Alan know you're here?"

"I think so. Sent him a message before leaving. I'm waiting to hear from him before I decide what to do."

"You can stay with me."

I'd counted on it. "Thanks, but you don't have to. I can grab a room—"

"No, it's fine, although I've moved since you were here last. A bigger place."

Moved on. Making more money, doing well for herself. I wondered what else had changed in her life.

"That's great," I said. "I'm sorry about not writing."

She shrugged. "You're an interworld agent," she said. "Why would you have time for me?"

"I have no excuse. I'm a borrowed hound, after all."

"I really didn't expect to see you again. Honestly. I really didn't."

"Actually," I said, "I've not stopped thinking about you."

"Really?" she said, her voice quiet. "Did you come back for me, or did the job bring you here?"

"Both."

"Lucky for you," she said, reaching up and kissing me lightly on the cheek, "that I'm still here. Although during the past few months I've not been sleeping well."

"Thinking about me."

She made a dismissive sound. "Right. No, just some insomnia, at times, and then all of a sudden, I had this huge sleeping marathon, where I just could not wake up."

She put her arm around my waist and we started walking again. My feet crunched through the snow. "But you're feeling okay now?"

"Sure."

"So what's the big attraction at the Sea these days? Besides the obvious."

"Nothing the tavern's promoting," she said. "People want to be close to the world capital. There are rumors going around about Aryell breaking its ties with the Union of Worlds."

"Hearing the same kind of things on Temonus."

"Yes. But the rumors are true. Aryellian leaders have already started the process."

We kept walking. Cara knew a lot more about the Movement's involvement here than I did, because before leaving Earth, I'd heard nothing about Aryell moving forward with secession, even through the DataNet.

So how did Cara know?

Eight

Brindos awoke the next morning in his hotel room bed, feeling the relief one feels when awoken from a bad dream. In the nightmare he was on his back in a dark filthy alley, a bloodthirsty Helk leaning over him. He remembered thinking the Helk was going to tear him apart, then eat him. It wouldn't have been the first time, although nowadays they didn't generally consume other intelligent races, except as an act of war or terrorism. It was a fine point of etiquette with them. But as he tried to sit up, physical pain caused memories of the alley to surface.

It had been real.

Brindos propped himself against the headboard and soon realized it was not morning, but evening. How did he end up back in the hotel?

He reached for his code card on the nightstand, but it wasn't there. *Oh shit.* Without his code card—

He wouldn't get his message from Dave on Aryell. Couldn't contact him from his end. Not without compromising his whereabouts, unless he could get away with a lasergram. He wouldn't be able to encode it.

In a panic, he clambered out of bed and found his coat on a chair. No code card.

No blaster.

He checked his fingers. The capacitors, each with enough charge to knock a Helk cold, had been emptied. He wouldn't be able to recharge them until he could find a portable charger.

The room clock confirmed that it had indeed been eighteen hours since he'd gone out into the alley behind the Restaurant.

What the *hell*?

He attempted to piece together the previous evening: walking with Joseph through the old quarter, or what was left of it, he had said. A dead sector, but beneath the surface, a strange heart with a peculiar beat. And then they found the Restaurant. A sense of luxury laced with carnival atmosphere. The food remarkable, and their waiter, a Helk Jekyll and Hyde. Brindos had received friendly service, then the Helk had almost killed him. He could remember nothing beyond that.

The hotel room looked like his hotel room. Clothes scattered on the floor. These were *not* the same clothes he had worn to the Restaurant. They *were* his clothes, but he hadn't worn them yet. They were thrown there as he would have thrown them. Shoes under the table, but they were his smart shoes, not the loafers he had worn. Too bad. The smart shoes could've told him where they'd been if he'd been wearing them. As it was, the shoes had never left softmode, and the flash membrane under the shoe's insole reported no usage since he'd last worn them, two weeks earlier for a fundraiser event at the NIO building. Over a chair next to the clothes was a towel. He could tell it was damp, as though he had used it to dry off after a shower.

Brindos staggered over to the dresser mirror, spotting the loafers near the bathroom door. He examined his face; there were no marks. He felt for tender spots, but other than a little back pain from slamming against the brick wall, and a bruised throat from where the Helk had grabbed him, he seemed okay. The Helk *could* have taken his face off. Brindos was glad the Helk had been Second Clan instead of First. He felt a little dizzy, but that could have been a result of the Helk food.

If Brindos had indeed run into Knox last night, Crowell's alias hypothesis was off the mark. Knox, alias Koch, in no way resembled Plenko. Knox, as big as he was, was a good eight inches shorter than Plenko.

The newspaper roll on the table blinked red, announcing the latest update of the *Midwest City Tribune,* but he ignored it and looked things over once more: the clothes on the chair (the clothes he'd worn last night had seemingly vanished), the towel, his shoes, and the rumpled bed, which he couldn't remember crawling into.

He sat on a corner of the bed. Upon awakening he had considered the dilemma objectively, just a puzzle to be solved, but now reality caught up with him, and he felt a tug of fear. It wouldn't be wise to return to the Restaurant. He could obtain a better picture of what happened from Joseph, who must have whisked him back here. Risk and danger were not supposed to be a major part of his job now, and he didn't go looking for them. He'd been in military and government work for years before doing investigative work because the benefits were solid, and he had a little money tucked away for an early retirement. He never tried to think of it beyond those terms, but at the moment, he was having difficulty.

Brindos thought of the alley in the back of the Restaurant. *This Helk will kill me,* he remembered thinking, *and there's nothing I can do to stop him.* He felt his body ramming against the wall, over and over. He'd been afraid for his life, but he was more terrified of oblivion, of not knowing.

Now eighteen hours of his life were missing.

He went to find Joseph.

The concierge hadn't come on duty yet, so Brindos stepped out of the hotel, thinking he might find a street vendor selling bagels or pastries. It was evening, but his body asked for breakfast. The early evening weather was cool. Overcast skies threatened rain. He carried a black umbrella he'd purchased at the Tour Depot on his first day here. They could put a man on a ship to the stars but they still couldn't make an umbrella that would last. Already, two of the thin metal ribs had ripped free of the nylon, poking out like cat whiskers.

He walked a half block and came upon a street vendor on the edge of a small park. After buying a bagel and coffee, he sat in the nearby park to eat it. Before long, he looked up and found Joseph standing over him, looking old and inconsequential in his neat gray street clothes.

"Joseph, I—"

"Quiet now," he said. "You need to talk, and so do I, but this isn't the place."

Joseph led the way to a bar a few blocks from the hotel on Eagle Street, called the Blue Rocket. They ordered at the bar and took their glasses of Temonus whiskey to a booth at the rear. The light fixture above them was busted. Brindos could barely make Joseph out across the table from him.

Joe brought out a microfilament, which heated up almost immediately. He lit a candle that had nearly dripped its last drop, most of its wax stuck in a congealed pool on the tabletop.

He picked up his glass. The blue liquid moved through his parted lips like a frozen gas.

"Joe," Brindos found himself whispering, "what happened last night?"

He just shook his head and said, "I was hoping you could explain it to me."

Brindos just stared at him.

"You can't?" Joe's puzzled look of concern bore down on him.

"I woke up in bed not long ago," Brindos said. "But I have no idea how I got there."

The startled look on Joseph's face was genuine. He began to laugh, and Brindos chimed in with his own nervous hack. But this did not go on long.

"Look, Mr. Roberts," Joseph said with a smile that said he thought Brindos was the biggest screwup he had ever known, "I don't know what kind of game you think you're playing, but this isn't funny, not funny at all. Do you think I've gotten as old as I am by being an idiot? Maybe you think you're some big hotshot who can get away with murder, is that it? You best watch your back."

"Murder?" Brindos said, a little panicked. "I don't know what the fuck you're talking about. Joseph, this is *me* you're talking to—"

Joseph edged out of the booth and stood up, clearly upset. "And who are you? *Dexter.* What do I know about you? I can't talk to you about this if you refuse to cooperate. I must go."

As he moved away, Brindos's drinking hand rocketed from his

glass, hooking Joseph's coat. Joseph shot an angry glance, and Brindos chose his words quickly.

"Joe, I don't remember what happened last night. I must have blacked out. Something terrible happened, I can sense that, but I'm in the dark and you're the only one who can help me." He relaxed his grip, letting his coat fall free. "Please. Stay."

Joseph paused. "You blacked out?"

"Eighteen hours. Please," he repeated. "I don't blame you now for being angry at me, but the plain truth is I need your help."

Joseph reached into one of the deep pockets inside his overcoat. His hand came out with a flashroll of the *Tribune* that he thrust onto the table. Brindos cleared space and unrolled it. The same roll he had in his hotel room, which he had not taken the time to look at before leaving to find Joseph. His eyes went straight to the headline: "Waiter Slain Outside Old Town Restaurant."

Nine

ara lived in a two-story duplex at the end of a winding street, the pavement following the contours of a tiny hill bordering Kimson's residential park. The road ended at a series of narrow and steep steps that climbed to an upper hallway outside her building. She'd moved there, she said, about two months after Alan and I had left. Or, I should say, two months after I left; Alan had taken transport back to Earth a week earlier on assignment.

The new apartment lurked like a secret lover; I didn't know this place, didn't know the Cara who lived here. In the dim porch light, Cara fumbled with her keys, taking a few moments to insert the right one and unlock the door. No sensor.

We slipped inside the door, and without a word she turned and pulled me to her. Our lips met and I tasted lipstick as her mouth opened. Her rapid breaths warmed the back of my throat. My brain clung to the memory of our past together as she unbuttoned her blouse, then I reached behind her and unclasped her bra. As it fell to the floor, I spun us around and pushed her against the wall. Her breasts were small and pale, aureolas brown and nipples erect, and as I kissed them she unbuttoned my shirt and fumbled with my belt, sending shivers along my stomach. When I touched her she moaned so eagerly that it brought back the chills of our earlier times together. In an instant I was against the wall and she straddled me and rocked back and forth.

She pressed her face against my shoulder. She said my name in quiet, terse whispers, her shudders vibrating against my skin. I was still inside her as I lifted her and carried her to bed.

In the morning, sunlight streamed in through a crack in the window curtains, the passive heat bringing me out of contented sleep. Cara rested quietly beside me. I eased out of bed and padded across the path of sunlight on the hardwood floor. I peeked out through the curtain at the city center, and beyond the morning mist, Kimson's clock tower emerged behind the winding street that had brought me here. I hadn't realized we'd climbed so high. I threw back the curtains, and the sunlight invaded the bedroom. Cara stirred, and I returned to the bed and kissed her forehead.

She smiled with her eyes closed.

I snuggled next to her and we again became tangled with each other.

After a while, Cara spoke. "You didn't tell me what you thought."

"Fantastic," I said.

She laughed. "Not that."

"The new place is nice."

She slugged me in the shoulder. "I mean, about Aryell."

"Ah," I said. She stared at me, suddenly serious. I said, "Rumors about secession. We didn't talk about it last night for some strange reason."

She rubbed the shoulder she had punched. "Bad boy. But you've heard the same rumors about Temonus."

"Sure," I said. "And last night you said the rumors about Aryell were true."

"They are. Didn't you read the paper?"

"I just got here."

"You must be getting updates from the NIO if nothing else."

"Not really. And when have I had time to look? I came straight to the Flaming Sea to find you." I couldn't tell her about being on the run from the NIO. At least not yet. Not until I knew more about what she'd been up to.

"An article in yesterday's paper said the Union of Worlds is nearing a crisis point," she said. "You know what happened to Ribon. You probably heard about Temonus and the sabotage of their weather device too. The Movement, again, and Aryell is running scared. It's coming to a vote in a few days."

"Secession seem likely?"

"Very. President Nguyen's administration is faltering, he's losing control of the Union Senates, and we can thank Terl Plenko for that."

And maybe Tim James. Maybe President Nguyen himself. Thanks for nothing. "I've heard whispers of the same thing happening on Barnard's World."

"Barnard's too?"

"Plenko's got a hell of a reach, and he's not on Earth anymore. To tell the truth, I don't have a clue what's going on." So far, a true statement. I kissed her, featherlike. "I should get down to the Union Express office and see if I've got any new messages from Alan."

"Why Union Express? Can't you just use your code card to reach Alan?"

"It's damaged," I answered, which wasn't exactly a lie, since Gray had zapped the close-ops transmitter. It wasn't exactly the truth either. The code card was exactly what I'd use. I'd check it later for Brindos's message.

I just needed an excuse to get out of there, get my luggage from the Flaming Sea, poke around some more. What Cara had told me rang true, but I'd have to buy a newspaper roll and double-check her story. I pushed the sheets away and moved my feet to the floor.

Something bumped in the apartment below.

"Your neighbors?" I asked. "Downstairs?"

Cara's eyes widened. "That apartment's been vacant for five months."

"Are you certain?"

"I should know. I'm the resident manager here."

I froze, listening for more sounds from below.

"David?"

I motioned toward her closet. "Get dressed." I shot her a quick look, urging her to move quickly.

The clothes I'd worn the day before lay in a pile where I'd left them, sweet and musty with the smell of sweat. I propped myself against the wall and pulled on my pants and socks. Cara came out dressed in only a sweatshirt, and tiptoed across the floor. I squinted as I put on my shirt and listened by the door. I touched the doorknob.

The doorknob and the surrounding metal glowed red in an instant. My coat with my blaster hung on a hook next to the door. I looked back at Cara and pointed her back toward the closet, and as she moved, I reached for my weapon. The door burst open and slammed into me just as I put my hands around the gun butt. I'd pulled the blaster halfway out of the coat pocket, but the impact of the door knocked it from my hand and sent it skittering across the floor.

I stumbled back and fell. A Helk crashed through the doorway, saw me sprawled on the ground, and took that opportunity to perform a swan dive right on top of me. The air rushed from my lungs.

Oh, he was a big one. First Clan. The Helk smiled down at me and let me have it, throwing a punch that felt like a cement block smashing into the side of my face, even though I turned my head enough to cause a glancing blow. I heard and felt my jaw pop, the pain traveling from cheekbone to neck. He had my arms pinned beneath his massive legs, and I couldn't move. He hit me again.

"Give it to me or I'll hurt you," the Helk said.

A thought raced through my mind in a flash: No shit. For the first time, I managed to take a good look at him, even though my vision zoomed in and out of focus. It wasn't the Helk who'd followed me the night before. At that moment, I wished it had been. Last night's Helk had been Second Clan. This one was nearly twice the size in most aspects, the most noticeable being his goddamn fists. A sheen of sweat covered the dark skin of his head, and his white, razor-sharp teeth gleamed when he grinned at me.

"Give what to you?" I said, wheezing. I reached with both arms and got my hands on his legs. I let fly with my finger capacitors, sending the jolts full strength.

The Helk tensed a bit, looking down for a second. Then he realized what I'd done and laughed. "Finger caps? Please."

That was depressing. But a Helk as big as this? Yeah, not likely to be much affected.

"You know what I want," the Helk said. "The key. I want the key."

"Key? What key?"

"Oh, you prefer the pain? That's good enough for now. I won't kill you. Yet."

He raised both fists, clasped them over his head, and I closed my eyes. I didn't want to see that Helk sledgehammer come down on me. I expected pain, but never felt it. The air sizzled around me, and I snapped open my eyes. The Helk's face registered both pain and surprise, and after a glance at the bedroom door, he slid off me and fell, the impact causing the floor to groan and shudder.

I kicked his legs off me and scrambled up. Cara had my blaster, her hands holding it in the classic pose, her right hand around the grip, left palm under the butt, feet shoulder-width apart.

After a moment, Cara lowered the blaster, her hands shaking. "My god."

I went to her and took the blaster. "Thanks," I said, smiling weakly. "You saved me from a hell of a beating." And, I added to myself, you saved me from finding out anything about whatever key he thought I had.

The Helk lay on the floor, face up. I breathed with difficulty, my ribs aching, as I approached the downed Helk carefully. I trained the blaster on his head. I wasn't exactly sure where Cara had hit him. For all I knew she'd just wounded him and he was playing dead. When I reached his side I prodded him with my foot. A black hole marred the left side of his chest, just under the armpit, the fabric of his shirt still smoldering. Blood, almost black, seeped from the wound. My pulse lessened as I glanced at his face, the corners of his mouth still twisted in pain—

His eyes opened.

I jumped back. "Son of a bitch!" I aimed my blaster, ready to fire, but waited. He could barely move, and it was obvious from the wound and the large amounts of blood that he would die soon. There was little he could do, little I could do, except take this second chance to ask him about the item in question.

"What key?" I asked him, not sure if he could speak.

He coughed twice, and that almost did him in, but he did manage to say something. "Terl Plenko," he said quietly, turning his head slightly to see me better. He paused a moment, then said, "He'll find you."

My eyes narrowed. Did he mean Plenko was the key? I kept my weapon leveled at him. "Plenko's the key?"

"I don't know."

"Is he here on Aryell?"

"I don't know."

"Who the hell *are* you?"

He tried a smile, but that sent him into a fit of coughing. When he recovered, he paused for breath. "I'm Tony Koch."

Koch? The Helk I'd thought was actually Terl Plenko? This definitely wasn't Plenko. This Helk didn't look anything *like* Plenko. If this was Tony Koch, then who the hell did I have Alan searching for on Temonus?

"Do you work for Plenko or not? Another Helk was following me last night. Do you know him? Did you send him to spy on me?"

No answer.

"Where's Plenko?" But the Helk's eyes had closed, and the pain had vanished from his face. "Shit," I said as I felt under Koch's right arm. I failed to find a heartbeat. The Helk was dead.

Cara still stood in the bedroom doorway, but I couldn't talk to her yet. I searched the body for clues that might help me figure out what had just happened. Nothing.

Naturally.

"Recognize him?" I asked.

"Should I?"

"Just checking. It's Koch, Plenko's second-in-command."

She nodded. "I'd heard that on U-ONE. They didn't know what he looked like, though."

"Koch was an alias for Plenko. Or so I thought. Koch is dead in your apartment, and he's obviously not Plenko." I frowned, nagged by a growing sense of apprehension. "So if he *is* Koch, then this whole thing stinks."

"What do you mean?"

"Why send the Movement's point man to take me out instead of some expendable assassin?"

Cara shrugged. "He didn't want to take you out. He was after something."

"A key. Any idea what that might be?"

"He said something about Terl Plenko."

"Yeah, he changed the subject about the key. He wanted me to give him the key, but didn't even know himself what it was. He said Plenko would find me."

"Could it have been a warning to help you?"

I hadn't thought of that, but it didn't seem likely, not if this *was* the Koch we'd thought was on Plenko's side. "I don't think so."

I straightened and stared down at the body. Why had he confessed his identity to me? Could've been a lie to confuse me. And what about Cara? She'd taken out Koch with a blaster, *and* known where to shoot him. I sighed and finished dressing. I put on my coat and started for the door.

"Where are you going?" Cara asked.

"My carry-on. I left it at the Flaming Sea, remember?"

She came to me and put a hand on my shoulder. She lifted her face and said, "Don't leave."

"It's all right now," I said. "He's dead. We'll get rid of the body."

"I have a key to the apartment downstairs," she said.

I nodded. "Okay." I thought a moment. In all our years in Seattle, Alan and I had never had to deal with a dead body. At least not one shot by someone I knew and loved. "Okay. I'll drag the body down there for now. You have a sheet, or blanket?"

She went and got one.

"I'll drop him off if you could manage the cleanup here?"

Only after we safely stowed the body did I head down the hill toward the Flaming Sea. A check of my code card showed Brindos still hadn't messaged me back.

The Helk who had been following me—or had seemed to be following me—had dropped out of sight. Tony Koch, if he was Tony Koch, had found me somehow. Had he found me because I'd been recognized in the tavern? Because of Cara? Some of the tavern's

employees knew where she lived, including her boss Kristen. Anyone working in the tavern would've been hard-pressed to avoid
answering pointed questions. Especially when a Helk as big as
Koch was the one doing the asking.

Ten

As a minor player helping out the NIO, Brindos was just a micro switch in the circuitry of a massive complex machine that pretended to know all, and nearly did, aspired to be God, and nearly was. High-profile agents didn't go on suicide missions, unless they'd been tricked into doing so, but he'd been fair game. Sitting in a tavern staring at an article that connected him to a murder, he felt a little more than tricked. More like *betrayed*. An ink-black curtain of dread closed around him.

"My God," Joseph said. "Haven't you read this?"

Brindos shook his head.

Since violent crime here rarely happened, murder was front-page news. It was a large article, near the bottom of the page. The victim had already been identified as Jordan Dak, a Helk newcomer to Temonus about whom little was known—in other words, the typical colonist story. Jordan Dak. Not Tom Knox.

According to the article, Jordan had been waiting tables at the Helk establishment for less than a year. About midnight last night, some of Jordan's tables began complaining of neglect, the cook moaning because Jordan's orders had piled up. A waiter going out to the alley for a break discovered his body near the garbage Dumpster. While the cause of death had not been verified, the body had sustained multiple stab wounds, and the murder was under investigation.

"When I came looking for you, that was the last thing I expected to find," Joseph said, still standing. "You'd been in the restroom a long time, I'd had my fill of wine, and, well, my bladder isn't so steady these days. But you weren't in there. I looked for you in the hallway, you weren't there either. I had no idea where you were. Then I came to the hall that led to the door outside—"

Brindos cut him off. "You heard something? You saw something?"

"As I got closer to the door I heard voices. I got a bad feeling. I came up to the window and looked out."

"The last thing I remember," Brindos interrupted, "was that bastard leaning over me. He might have killed me. Joe, who was it? Who was it that zipped him?"

Joseph stared at Brindos's face as if it were a treasure map, looking for the X. "You bastard," he finally said, "it was you who did it, and you know it."

Brindos laughed, incredulous. "You could tell me I'd gone bowling last night, I'd probably believe you. Joe, I . . . can't . . . remember . . . *any*thing."

"You don't remember back at the hotel last night, later? You were shaky, but sober as a man on his wedding day. Baah!" He waved him off. "I must go." He started to roll up the newspaper.

Brindos grabbed his coat again, frustration fueling his anger. "Goddamn it, Joe," he said, "tell me a lie, tell me *some*thing, but don't leave me hanging here. For the hundredth time, I don't know what happened. This is no joke." Brindos stood up and forced him down into his seat, hard. "Now spill!"

The outburst didn't impress Joseph. He just sneered, pouring himself another drink. He downed it, placing the tumbler gently back onto the table.

The bartender hurried over, eyeing Brindos, sizing him up. "Joseph, you need anything?"

Joseph smiled, his voice oozing with sarcasm. "I'm good, Bill."

The bartender looked doubtful, but eventually he walked away.

"Joe," Brindos said. He had to get to the bottom of this, and he was starting to wonder what the concierge really knew about it all.

"Very well," Joseph said, to himself as much as to Brindos, "very well." He leaned forward, twisting the newspaper roll in his hand. "It was dark of course, but I could see the Helk facedown in the street, you on top of him. You had a knife to him, here." He thrust his hand under his armpit, a textbook Helk strike area, normally not too accessible. You usually couldn't just get one to lie down and play possum. "I could hardly believe it myself, but later you said it was the old electric handshake, or some such crap."

That could explain Brindos's advantage, but he hadn't heard a convincing explanation as to how he had regained consciousness to apply the megavolt jolt. Plenko's cronies knew Union agents had this capability, and that the capacitor design required feet planted on firm ground when actuating—Brindos's toes were a good six inches off when Knox carried him into the alley. He'd never had a chance.

"He was lying very still," Joseph continued. "I could hear talking, but who said what?" He shrugged. "You had one knee into his back, and then for whatever reason—because the Helk did not struggle—you stabbed the knife in hard and he fell limp. I heard footsteps in the hallway, so I ducked outside. That's when you looked up and saw me. I thought about running, but you stood up and called me. 'Joseph,' you said, 'he tried to kill me.' Well, something like that. You walked up to me covered in blood, dark Helk blood. You said he had tried to kill you, I guess in case I hadn't heard you the first time, that it was a dangerous Helk, one of Plenko's Movement, we couldn't spend time talking about it, we had to leave right away. Whatever had happened, I agreed this was wise." He paused a moment, staring at Brindos with eyes narrowed, as if trying to read his mind.

Joseph had, for all intents and purposes, confirmed that Brindos had killed the waiter. Murdered him? Or had it been self-defense? How much had Joseph really seen before coming out into the alley? At this point, Brindos wasn't sure he trusted the story. But Joseph had more to tell. "Go on."

"We split up and met back at the hotel. I disposed of the knife, then waited a long time for you. When you finally showed up you were in a state. It was a wonder you made it. You said you had twice woken up in the street, must have passed out, but you had taken side streets and were sure no one had seen you, it being so late and all. I went up to your room and got you clothes, using the service elevator. It was late, I'm sure no one saw me. As you changed, you told me the Helk must have thought you were out cold, that he went inside, brought back a knife. When he came back you played possum and zapped him. Anyway, you went up to your room, and I burned your clothes in the hotel incinerator. Your shoes weren't bad. I cleaned them up and threw them in your room while you took a shower." He leaned back in his seat and set the newspaper tube on the table. "That's it."

Joseph's story seemed to cover everything, except one thing he hadn't brought up. Brindos stared at him hard until he glanced away.

"You took something of mine," Brindos said.

The code card. It had been in Brindos's coat pocket at the Restaurant. If Knox hadn't taken it, Joseph had to have seen it. He could've taken it. Joseph had *helped,* had gone to the trouble of getting Brindos to hoof it back to the hotel, cleaned him up, but would he come clean about the code card?

"I found nothing unusual," Joseph said. "Took nothing."

If Joseph had found it, would he think it was a comm card and not the super tool NIO agents used?

"You're sure? Nothing in my coat?"

"Like what? A weapon?"

Brindos nodded.

"No, nothing."

Brindos looked down at the *Tribune* again, gathering his thoughts. "Joseph," he said, tapping the roll with his finger, "did you notice anything strange about the article?"

"Other than the obvious?"

"The time. They say the body was found around midnight. I remember the time clearly. It was eleven. I saw a clock on the Restaurant wall as I headed for the bathroom."

"It was eleven fifteen when I found you," Joseph said.

"Which means they didn't miss the body of a waiter in a busy restaurant for almost an hour."

Joseph nodded. "Seems odd, I agree. I didn't stick around to tell anyone. It seemed right to get you out of there."

Joseph's story stunk like week-old fish. Brindos wondered if the whole story was made up. Was Joseph an agent? Did he zap the Helk? Zap him, kill him, then drag Brindos to the hotel? Even though he couldn't get his head around it, Brindos said what he thought at this point Joseph would want to hear. "I guess a thank-you is in order."

He shrugged, letting that slide. "What are you going to do now?"

"I'm no cold-blooded killer," Brindos said. "You've got to believe that."

"All I know is what I saw and that it is likely I will be questioned. We were seen together. Look. I'm a pretty astute old bean. You obviously knew something about this Helk. You mentioned he might belong to Plenko's Movement. You've been snooping around the Conduit story, you went to East City about it. You seem to have lost a weapon. Maybe something else."

"What about it?"

He narrowed his eyes. "You're NIO."

Brindos stared at Joseph without saying a word, but his throat dried up.

"You are, aren't you?" Joseph asked.

Brindos stared at him some more.

"Come *on*, Dexter. I'm the concierge for the goddamn Orion Hotel. I poke around a little about you, I'll find out, won't I?"

No, he wouldn't. Unless he *was* an agent.

"Maybe you're here on low-level ops," Joseph said. "Dexter is an alias, didn't figure to come up with anything. Things heated up a little, and now you're vulnerable. Can your agency protect you here?"

Concierge or not, Joseph knew more than expected. Brindos picked his words carefully, holding back to see how Joseph would react. Technically, Brindos was *not* NIO. Not before as a contractor, and not now, on the run. "I know that the laws agreed upon by the Union of Worlds and your colonial government are strict concerning such secrecy as the NIO engages in," Brindos admitted. "If I *did* work for the NIO, I'd be an illegal monitor, and I imagine the NIO would disavow my activities."

Joseph leaned back and smiled. "Of course."

"Still," Brindos said, searching Joseph's face, "that Helk is dead, and I can't remember a thing about it."

"Well," he said, wrapping his hands around his drink. "Murder on Temonus is punishable by death. Even if it *is* a Helk."

"I'm well aware of that."

"If I can," Joseph said, "I will say nothing to incriminate you. You should consider checking out of Midwest City. At the very least, we should not be seen with each other. I am an old man, and living is enough of an adventure for me."

"You saved me the speech," Brindos muttered, but he now suspected Joseph had more than just living to keep him busy, that he had his fingers on the pulse of something big.

"Mr. *Roberts*," he said with a smile. And with that, he rose, and this time Brindos let him leave.

After downing one last drink, Brindos left the bar, stepping out into the cold night air. He felt pretty sober, considering the double punch of the blue devil liquid and the news Joseph had landed on him. Parked directly in front of the Blue Rocket was a land vehicle with police insignia. Two Helks unfolded themselves from the car and headed his way. One was female, and iron circlets adorned both arms, running up and down from wrists to elbows. A necklace, also of iron, was cinched so tight around her neck that she held her head at an odd angle, chin unnaturally forward. She had on a gold shift that didn't cover much, even if Brindos knew what it was supposed to cover. It didn't make her any less menacing. The male Helk wore traditional black leathers. Brindos couldn't imagine many Helks working for Midwest City Authority. They weren't in uniform, and that made him give them a wide berth as they continued on toward the tavern, talking their Helk gibberish.

Brindos stepped toward the curb, making as though he would open his umbrella. He heard the bar door swing open, the din of the bar becoming momentarily apparent, then quiet as the door sealed shut. A light rain had fallen, and there was a hiss of sparse traffic on Eagle Street, tires sliding over wet, mirror-black pavement. He glanced quickly over his shoulder, seeing a large figure coming at him.

They hadn't gone inside.

He drove the umbrella hard behind him, jabbing the point into the Helk's massive leg. He moaned loudly, the umbrella sticking out comically. Although he knew he couldn't outrun a Helk, Brindos shot for the street as the Helk limped along, only slowed slightly.

Then a deep painful heat ran through Brindos's body, every bone and muscle locking up. He tumbled to the ground, paralyzed but fully conscious. The injured Helk—the male—hobbled up, by now having removed the umbrella, and, picking Brindos up like an old suitcase, carried him swiftly to the police car while his partner holstered his weapon.

As he lay trundled up in the backseat, limbs shuddering involuntarily, Brindos found he couldn't move anything save his eyeballs in their sockets. He watched the shadows cast from the streetlights fade and jump on the back of the front seats. His blaster was gone. Code card gone.

The two Helks were silent as stones, obviously intent on their job, the one not complaining a bit about his wound. Not surprising. In any case, if Brindos could have talked, he might have asked where they were taking him, just to annoy them.

After a few minutes, movement in his neck allowed him to move his head a little to glance out a window. The lights and buildings of the city were gone. They had entered into the rural outlying areas, not on their way to the MWC police station. Brindos would've thought they were taking him out for his coup de grâce, sans trial, if it had made any sense. But they could have killed him right there on the street. Something else was going on. His pulse quickened, an odd feeling considering he could do nothing in response to it.

They'd been on the road about thirty minutes when he felt the car brake and turn off the smooth highway and onto an unpaved route. Trees cast their silhouettes against the moonlight. Some movement had returned to Brindos's fingers and toes, and he figured eventually he'd regain complete mobility. They must've known he didn't have a weapon. Or his code card. Or maybe they just weren't concerned about the possibility. They turned off the road onto rough ground, Brindos bumping around in the back, and then they came to a stop.

Their doors opened and shut, Brindos heard heavy footsteps,

then the door at his head opened. The female Helk reached in with one arm, pulled him out, carried him twenty feet, and dropped him in ankle-deep wet grass. Humbling. She mumbled to the other, laughing. Brindos felt movement returning, but not quickly enough. Maddeningly, Brindos tried crawling, willing his motor functions to return. He made growling noises in lieu of swearing, but intense pain turned him back, and he almost passed out.

The female Helk raised her weapon. Brindos was still sure they wouldn't kill him. Not yet. A beam burst past him, flaring into the ground, steam rising. The two Helks got a good laugh out of that. He didn't know if the event inspired him, or if he had finally just found his voice, but Brindos managed to say a choice Helk slur, which loosely translated had something to do with inadequacy of a sexual nature. The laughing stopped quickly, but they made no move toward their prisoner; they just glowered, checking their watches.

After three long minutes, the vehicle comm signaled, a soft spiraling tone. The one went back to respond while the other kept his weapon leveled. It was clear they all knew he could move now, but how well? The other returned and the two Helks spoke briefly. Then they waited in silence. At this point Brindos was beginning to feel that maybe they'd extended his lease on life.

Fifteen minutes later, a new car approached their spot. As it turned off the road onto ground, it rocked gently over the sinewy terrain, headlights sawing through the night. The beams swung sharply through the air, blinding them all as the car neared, then jabbing harmlessly into the earth as it came to a rest on the downward slant of a small depression. Two doors hissed open, then shut, followed by the crunch of heavy feet. A low fog hugged the ground, and in the spray of headlights everything was reduced to silhouettes. Brindos could make out the shadows of one Helk—First Clan, by the size of him—and a human.

Brindos found he could move enough to get to his knees, but it was an effort.

The two newcomers spoke briefly with Brindos's escorts, then the Helk shadow moved forward. He was impressive—all First Clan were—dressed in what appeared to be ebony black animal hide from toe to collar, including gloves that stretched over massive hands nearly big enough to encircle his waist.

Even as Brindos recognized him, he was caught off guard when the Helk spoke flawless English.

"Mr. Brindos," he said.

The hell of it all was that this Helk knew Brindos, had said his name without hesitation.

"Goddamn it," Brindos whispered. "Plenko."

Plenko crouched down. "As you see, Mr. Brindos, there has been a change of plans. You know me as Terl Plenko, but soon I will be more than a name to you, and you will be much more than a name to me. It won't mean anything to you right now, but on Helkunnta-nas, a name means nothing. What matters is ozsc."

Ozsc. Brindos knew that Helk word. It had no exact transla-tion, but roughly meant substance or soul.

Eleven

The sunshine had melted most of the snow and ice on Kimson's twisting streets and sidewalks, and tiny rivers cut across the top of the pavement. I stepped across them, trying to keep my shoes dry as I headed for the Flaming Sea. Sunny outside, but my mood was anything but sunny. The Helk who'd called himself Koch was dead, and I was as confused as ever about the whole mess.

The Flaming Sea's sign still flashed its wave and flame design as I approached, but because of the cloudless day, the LED colors looked washed out. No crowds loitered outside the keelhaul door, most of them, I'm sure, probably panicked at the thought of all the famous snow melting before they could get in their last ski runs down the slopes. The tavern was open though. The Flaming Sea never closed, just slowed down as the sun came up. I went in, and darkness swallowed me.

"I came for my luggage," I said to the man at the door before he could ask me to pay. "A carry-on bag." The small light of the podium revealed the same short bald man from last night. Didn't he ever sleep?

He held out his hand. "Claim check."

I fished in my coat pocket, came up with the tiny ticket stub, and handed it to him. He took it and looked it over carefully. After a moment he took the laserwand from his little podium and ran it over the surface of the ticket. An amber glow from a hidden inset monitor illuminated his face. He stared back at me, eyes narrowing.

"What?" I asked.

He shook his head. "Nothing. Your luggage is in the top-floor suite."

Where Cara's boss worked. I tensed, weighing the doorman's reaction to my ticket against the location of my luggage. "Kristen's room? What's it doing up there?"

He shrugged. "Cleaning the storage area. Had to move it. You can go on up. The girls don't work this time of day."

I wanted to say to this jerk that someone should bring down my luggage *for* me. Then I thought: at least this gave me freedom to snoop around. I didn't buy for a second that someone had hauled luggage out of the storage room and up to the top-floor suite just so some cleaning could get done.

"I'm not paying to get in again," I said to the man.

He waved me in politely. "Take your time. Have a drink if you want."

I mumbled my thanks and headed for the elevator. I noticed two stiffs in gray neck-to-toe jumpsuits hanging back to the left of the elevator, and two more near a curving stairwell to the right. Flaming Sea security, looking downright out of place on a slow morning. On the way there I felt the panic well up inside me, the Koch incident still under my skin. And Gray, the NIO, the setup. No electric handshake, with my finger capacitors drained, but the blaster in my pocket reassured me. I pulled it from my coat as the elevator took me to the top floor, then opened up to Kristen's waiting area.

The lights came up automatically, and I swore as the room came into focus. The place was a shambles. Someone had flipped over Cara's reception desk, and everything that had once sat on it lay strewn about on the carpet. The furniture had seen better days. Somebody had taken a knife to the cushions and pulled out the stuffing. Some of the stuffing dangled from the chairs and couches like icicles. A picture still hung, though crookedly, on the wall behind the desk, a photo of a breathtakingly beautiful woman with thick, shoulder-length black hair. A crack ran through the glass, cut through just underneath the woman's chin. This must be Kristen.

This would've been a better place for security to be hanging out. My luggage wasn't here.

The door to the next room—Kristen's room—stood open. The room lights were already on as I entered, blaster raised. The scene here mirrored the reception area, except instead of a desk there was a bed, and the bed had a body on it. I glanced quickly around the room before stepping to the bed to check who the body belonged to. Her face and hair matched the picture in the reception area. No blood, no marks at all. But she was most certainly dead, naked, her arms folded across her chest, feet together, hair combed neatly.

I shivered, realizing I could just as well have found Cara dead in the other room. If I hadn't shown up and asked for Cara, and if Kristen hadn't given Cara some time off . . .

"Kristen," I said aloud, as if trying to get the dead woman's attention.

"Katerina Parker, actually," a female voice said from behind me. "Earth girl, near the top of the Flaming Sea's list."

I spun and pointed my weapon. A young woman with long blond hair stood in the bathroom doorway, leaning against the jamb. She wasn't armed as far as I could see. She wore blue denims and a black-and-white checkered sweater.

She inched out into the room, favoring her left leg. "Looking for something?" she asked. Her voice was slow and deliberate.

"Every time I take a trip I lose my luggage," I said, trying to be funny. She didn't fall over laughing. I tried another approach. "Who the hell are you?"

"Don't get jumpy," she said, "but I'm going to pull out some identification."

I nodded for her to go ahead. She did, and pulled out a black code card from her pants pocket.

Huh. Just like mine.

"Jennifer Lisle," the woman said as she threw the ID to me. "Network Intelligence Office."

NIO. I tensed my grip on the blaster, thinking: they've found me. I palmed the card and a holo of Jennifer Lisle popped up on the black surface. Below the holo, data scrolled leisurely, in order of importance. Current assignment: CLASSIFIED. Common procedure, of course, nothing unusual about that. Last assignment: RIBON: U.U.

CORP INVESTIGATION/DORIE SENNALL. Now I recognized her. The undercover agent Dorie Senall had been with during the holo-vid recording.

I'd expected to see CLASSIFIED there, too but it wasn't. I figured she had *set* the code card so I could read it. Something she might do for another NIO agent.

"Okay," I said, looking up at her.

"Don't worry, I know who you are, if you're trying to pretend otherwise."

"And who am I?"

"A networker. A borrowed hound. David Crowell, private investigator from Seattle, on a four-year contract. Desk specialist." She smiled when she said that, eyes shining.

"You were on Ribon."

She nodded. "Took a sonic beam in the leg for my troubles there."

Yes, and she'd also been betrayed by an NIO insider, the recording of the incident with Dorie Senall having been fed into the dead woman's vid screen. Was she really still an agent with the NIO? If so, had they brought her into the fold about what was going on?

"They shipped me back home," she said, "and your partner dropped in on me at the hospital. Awfully nice of him. Still, I don't sleep much these days, remembering all that. One day I slept so long—" She waved a hand. "Never mind. I'm glad you showed up here."

"I was running out of places to look for my luggage."

She smiled and took back her code card. After stuffing it back in her pocket, she went over to the bed and sat on one corner, next to Katerina Parker's left foot. "Haven't been in the field much, I gather, since you tagged along with the NIO."

"Not much."

I managed a smile, but my gut told me to keep wary. She knew Alan and she recognized me at a glance. Jennifer Lisle was NIO, and the NIO had forced me to run. If she was here now, it was doubtful she'd learned about my security breach while in transit, but who knew what kind of information she'd received on her card since landing?

"You made a mistake," she said.

"Mistake?"

"Going over to Miss Kristen here without checking the bathroom first."

"Well, I just couldn't wait to see her."

Jennifer glanced at the body. "She's not your type."

"Her receptionist is a friend of mine. And I'm kind of *not* supposed to be here, so I wasn't planning on sticking around for a long, drawn-out crime scene investigation."

Jennifer shrugged. "Somebody was looking for something very important, seems to me. Kristen probably got in the way."

"Likely," I agreed. "You didn't come here to investigate this, though. You were already in transit before any of this happened."

"So?"

"*Why* are you here?"

"That's classified, Mr. Crowell. You saw my card."

"Just asking." I smiled innocently. "Doesn't hurt to ask."

"It's Movement."

Sure, big revelation. Everything was Movement these days. *I* was Movement. But was *she* still Movement, after all that had happened between her and Dorie Senall?

"Why are *you* here?" she asked.

"I told you. Her receptionist is a friend of mine. Visiting. I hadn't seen her in three years."

"Uh-huh."

"Union's honor. Can you tell me anything else?"

"I'm not allowed to divulge classified information to borrowed hounds." She narrowed her eyes at me, trying to look tough. And maybe she was, considering the hell she'd gone through on Ribon, with Dorie Senall trying to kill her. "Pardon me if I'm a little tight-lipped. Just following leads."

Following rumors, I bet. About Aryell's secession. And Temonus's. Barnard's. The Movement's hand in all of them. Searching for anyone with ties to Terl Plenko. Or to me. I shivered, wondering if the NIO had sent an agent to Aryell well in advance, knowing I might run here, even before I knew I was *going* to run here. If she was still an agent.

But the timing was off for that agent to be Jennifer Lisle. She probably did know about my disappearance by now. How could she not? Her code card, if nothing else, would've clued her in if there was an all-agent alert out on me. I wondered when would be the best time to bring up the subject. If I brought it up at all.

I'd been standing there with my blaster out since Jennifer came out of the bathroom, and now I put it back in my coat pocket. "So. Dorie Senall." I went over to a wingbacked chair and sat down amid a flurry of white stuffing. "Tell me about her. What was she like?"

"A loner," Jennifer said quickly. "Little respect for the law. Wild, and a bit crazy. Loved to take her RuBy and pop pills."

"But you slept with her." I recalled the marble camera recording from the apartment.

"It never got that far."

"Did you find her attractive?"

"Fuck yes." Jennifer shot a look at me that could have curdled molasses. "But I didn't love her. Her stint with the U.U. Corp was bogus; she was strictly Movement, slipping illegal recruits past customs. I was just doing my job, getting her to trust me, take me to Coral Moon."

"Lucky you weren't there when it took a nose-dive into Ribon."

"Lucky you weren't here in Miss Kristen's room when whoever it was decided to redecorate."

I looked over at Kristen's white face. "Whoever did this might also have been looking for me."

"Why would they be looking for you?"

"I don't know," I lied, thinking about the key that Koch had wanted. "Were *you* looking for me?"

"Of course not. Anonymous tip. We'd been keeping Katerina Parker under surveillance."

That surprised me. "What for?"

"Movement activities."

"But she was a Flaming Sea girl. You really think Movement?"

"Did you know her well?"

"Not at all."

"Well then."

I scratched at a hole in the arm of the chair, pulling out stuffing. "So does this look like Movement to you?" I asked, inclining my head toward Kristen.

She didn't say anything.

I got up and walked to the other side of the bed, searching the floor. I got on my hands and knees and looked under the bed.

"Looked around a little, before you got here," Jennifer said, "but I can't stick around."

I straightened and, on my knees, looked Kristen over, gazing up and down her body. "Why do you have to run off?"

"I'm out of my jurisdiction here."

"Bullshit. NIO trumps local authorities anytime Movement is involved."

"True, and I used that power to get up here. I gave the Flaming Sea's owner a cash incentive to hold off until I could get a closer look."

"Yeah, I saw their security people down there."

"But I really can't stay. When I give the word, they'll come back up, and the owner will call Authority."

Just when I decided to stand up, I spotted something tucked under Kristen's neck and caught in her hair. I made a show out of it, checking the neck for bruises, and when I pulled away, I grabbed the object, which I recognized immediately. A Helk rygsa, a small silver Second Clan earring that clasped to the inner part of a Helk's ear, which meant it wasn't visible to most.

I was surprised to find it, figuring Jennifer would've discovered it during her own search. Maybe because she was on a time schedule, she hadn't checked the body that closely.

Jennifer stood, wincing a little as she put weight on her bad leg. "Anything else you want to search for?"

"Do you know where my luggage is?"

"Yeah. Downstairs."

Now we were getting somewhere. "Nothing else up here, then," I said, palming the earring and slipping it into my pocket. "Let's go."

* * *

Downstairs, Jennifer gave a nearly imperceptible nod to one of the security members and he and the others headed toward the elevator.

Time to feel out the NIO smokescreen, see if Jennifer knew anything. I bought her a drink. Her NIO credentials would keep the locals off our backs for a while, but I wasn't sure how long I wanted to stick around.

"Have you been in contact with the NIO in the past few days?" I asked after we had sat down at a table near the limbo cage. Brilliant question.

"No."

"You going to tell me where my luggage is?"

"Your bag's still in storage," she said. "It was just one bag in there, no name on it, DNA-locked. Lucky for you I didn't have the equipment here to open up something like that, so I told the owner you were okay, and had the doorman tell whoever asked about it that it had been taken upstairs."

"Yeah, I heard his story. Not too convincing."

"Got you up there, didn't it?" She took a sip from her glass. "Where you staying?"

I held back a moment, staring at her eyes, getting a feel for her game. I waved at the bartender for a second drink. "With a friend."

"Ah. You mean Cara Landry."

I winced. "So you know who she is."

"Of course. And where she is. Keeping tabs on Kristen meant keeping tabs on Cara."

"Of course."

The bartender brought me the drink. "There you go, Mr. Norton."

Jennifer glanced at me, an eyebrow raised. "A borrowed hound with a borrowed collar, looks like."

"Woof." I guzzled half my drink.

"How many aliases have you used since arriving here?"

I clacked the ice in my glass and ignored her question. "Cara's a suspect?"

She downed her drink in a couple of gulps and stood. "Naturally. She worked for our stiff upstairs after all. Kristen saw no more clients after Cara checked out for the evening. I haven't mentioned Cara's movements last night to the locals, but they'll figure it out soon enough."

I couldn't disagree with her. If what Jennifer said was true, Cara could have been the last person to see Kristen alive.

I saw movement in the corner of the bar. At one of the back tables I spotted a Helk. Jesus. It was the one following me the night before. I gritted my teeth and fought the urge to jump up and go after him. He was someone I definitely had to talk to, and running at him like a crazy person wouldn't help matters.

"You'll be telling Cara about what happened," I said.

"Perhaps."

"You'll be gentle with her about all this."

"If I can be."

I nodded. "I suppose I'll see you later, like it or not." I realized we might be after the same person, but Jennifer's classified status left a lot to the imagination.

"You're part of my schedule now," she said.

"Am I a suspect?"

"You're not off the hook, that's for sure. And there's something on my code card about your disappearance from New York, and a pretty serious alert about you."

I swallowed, my mouth suddenly dry. So that was it. She knew. Although the NIO couldn't monitor code card activity outside of Earth and the jump slots, NIO updates and alerts still got through. Would she turn me in? Would I have to make a break for it? She didn't seem too concerned.

She narrowed her eyes again, that tough look coming back to her. "I didn't implicate you here. Not yet. I'll wait awhile. But I'll need to talk to you more later about everything."

"I figured as much."

"I'll be in touch. Don't leave town."

"And miss the skiing?"

She smiled, then left the Flaming Sea without another word.

Keeping my eyes on the Helk at the back table, I found a comm shield and called Cara. She was okay. Relieved that I'd called. I told her someone from the NIO was coming, but I didn't say who, and

I didn't say anything about Kristen. The dead Helk was in the vacant apartment below Cara, but I didn't really want her there when Jennifer and the locals started nosing around.

"Leave the apartment. Go somewhere for a while."

"Where?" she asked. I heard the confusion in her voice.

"Where's the nearest ski resort?"

"I don't ski. What's going on?"

"I don't know, but I don't really trust anyone right now, and I'd rather no one talked to you."

"You don't trust me either, do you?"

"No." I said it quickly, wanting her to understand how serious I was. I'd forgotten about the Helk for a second, and I glanced back over there. Still there, nursing his drink.

After a pause, Cara said, "I'll go to a resort, then, hang out in the lodge. Should I find a fake cast for my leg? Find myself a ski bum who—"

"Cara."

Another pause. "Fine. Do you want me to tell you where I'm going?"

"Not now. Call the WuWu Bar & Grille later in the day, leave a message for me. No, not me. Taylor Williams. I'll get there and ask for messages later."

Four aliases.

"All right."

"How will you get there?"

"Remember the vacant apartment below me? The couple left their flier. Entrusted me with it."

We said good-bye, and I felt a little better about Cara getting away from Kimson.

The next item of business would prove a bit trickier. How to approach a Second Clan Helk and accuse him of tailing me?

Easy. Oh, sure.

I was going to give him hell for tailing me, try to figure out what was going on with all that, but I noticed the obvious right away, and knew what to do.

Without regard for my safety, I strode quickly to his table.

The Helk growled and stood.

"Relax," I said. "Believe it or not, it's your lucky day. It looks like I found your earring."

The Helk stared at the earring in my hand as he poked inside his right ear.

"I think you'll find this is a perfect match to the one in your other ear."

He stared some more.

"This place is going to be crawling with local cops in a bit," I added. "I'm surprised you're actually sitting here, considering the circumstances, but we're moving this conversation elsewhere."

Twelve

Brindos's eyes burned—a side effect of his paralysis, he assumed. Blinking to clear his vision, tears coating his cheeks, he tried to look at Plenko's face. He heard the high-pitched hum of charged weapons; they would take no chances.

This was Plenko. *If I could kill him—*

All hypothetical, of course. If Brindos sneezed or sweated out the wrong pore, he would be a body in search of its limbs. Then, as if on cue, Plenko stepped to within inches of Brindos and reached down, holding a handkerchief.

"The condemned usually gets a cigarette with his blindfold," Brindos said. Not that they existed anymore.

Plenko smiled, and his voice boomed in the darkness. "No, it's all right, please take it, you look like you've been slicing Helk onions without a mask." And he continued holding it as Brindos sat, trying to assimilate everything, trying to look past the absurdity of it: Terl Plenko was offering him his hanky.

In the shadows behind Plenko, a tall, gaunt figure—human—walked forward, holding something gleaming in his hands. He moved slowly, in no hurry. He edged closer, and he was holding Brindos's umbrella. He turned the bloodied tip on its axis, testing it with a finger.

"Meet my One," Plenko said.

Brindos had trouble maintaining consciousness, felt his awareness of the situation slipping. He wanted to be back on a ship, shooting back to Earth, sleeping, oblivious. When the human came close enough, Brindos recognized him immediately and stopped breathing for a couple of seconds.

Joseph.

No. That couldn't be right. Not Joseph.

Joseph continued forward, stopping right in front of Brindos. He pressed the umbrella point into the flesh beneath Brindos's jaw and drew him to his feet like an accomplished puppeteer.

"Joe?" Brindos said, barely a whisper. "What the hell is going on? You're with *Plenko*?"

He didn't answer, just stared without a shred of emotion on his face. Plenko knew Brindos, called him by name, so Joseph knew him. He'd known all along. Looking into his eyes, Brindos saw a truly frightening deadness there. No, he thought, you're not with Plenko. Plenko is with *you*.

Meet my One.

"What is this?" Brindos asked. "Dinner at the restaurant. The story you told about what happened there. Goddamn it, I was out cold. What happened? What really happened, Joseph? What did you do to me? What did you do to Tom Knox?"

But Joseph didn't answer. A hint of a smile crossed his face just before he turned and walked away, using the umbrella as a cane. A minute later, a small craft hovered above them. It landed with a scream, its reverse thrusters whipping up dust. The side door opened and Plenko, Brindos, and Joseph were taken aboard. Plenko maneuvered Brindos to a seat at the rear and let him sit unrestrained. Plenko sat next to him. Joseph, whom Brindos was coming to see in a different light, sat in the rear-facing seat across from them, and at that moment Brindos found that he truly *did* fear him more than Plenko.

Joseph sat relaxed, his face impassive, his hands crossed loosely over the umbrella handle as though he were about to break into an old vaudeville dance number. Soft vibrations of the ship belied the fact that they were en route somewhere at a very quick pace. Brindos gripped the armrest tightly, his fingernails digging into the padding. He looked out the window, then back to Joseph.

"Where are we going?" Brindos asked.

Joseph gave an almost imperceptible sneer. Then, without a word, he calmly lifted one hand, like a magician. Nothing up my sleeve. He spread out his fingers like the leaves of a fan and his neatly trimmed fingernails began to glow very brightly, a white searing light.

Brindos awoke in what he presumed was the Helk historical quarter of the city—more precisely, in the ruins of an old gutted warehouse, ground level. The low walls and ceiling were blackened by soot. Canals of water several inches deep snaked around the rutted dirt floor. An odor of spoiled meat made his nose itch and his eyes water.

How long had he been out this time? He was getting awfully tired of this shit. Still dark, maybe middle of the night. He tried to view the surrounding streets through the hard light of the broken windows. He had a killer case of cottonmouth and a headache pounding at his skull. On top of all that, he had to pee so bad it felt like he'd wolfed down ten pots of coffee. What had Joseph done to him? Light had come from his fingertips, for Christ's sake, like Zeus bringing down lightning on mere mortals.

Standing up, trying to figure out where he might relieve himself, something definitely felt wrong. In his haste, he was hard-pressed to put his finger on it. The ground seemed oddly distant, as if he'd stepped onto a chair. He reached down to loosen his fly, but it wasn't there. He was covered by a rough one-piece suit. Only it wasn't a suit.

Brindos was naked.

The realization started slowly, built steam, then crashed through his mind. He cried out, his hands grasping at his body as if it were covered with deadly snakes. In all his worst nightmares, his subconscious would never have dredged up a dream as despicable as this.

He was a Helk. The clubbed feet, the thick legs and torso, the massive hands, the unmistakable brown fur. Brindos touched his head with swollen, grubby fingers, finding no hair, no fur, just a stiff, leathery skin. He dropped to his knees and buried his face in those gigantic hands, the world around him spinning, shifting, dizziness forcing him to shrink down until he had pulled himself into a ball on the floor. He shook head to foot, and heard himself whimpering, breathing in ragged gasps, until consciousness left him.

When Brindos came to again, he tried his best to settle the nausea, but was unsuccessful. Hurling as a Helk hurt much worse than he could've imagined, and the smell—he didn't even want to think about it. He crawled away from there as fast as he could, then crouched in a corner of the warehouse, his arms folded about him.

This was for real. Helk. Changed so much that he could barely comprehend the truth.

Maddeningly, on top of all that, Brindos still really had to relieve himself. He had a basic understanding of Helk anatomy, but hell if he could get a hold of his penis or whatever it was they used. Brindos willed himself to relax and think a moment. Okay. Their apparatus was hidden within the body cavity for protection. Still shivering, weak from whatever his body had gone through, Brindos fiddled around until he somehow found it about where a human stomach would be. Disgusted to the point of throwing up again, he released it and took care of business. Even that stung.

He sat down on a chunk of uprooted concrete, trying to settle his thoughts, get his bearings. As big as he was, Brindos felt inconsequential, somehow. Lightweight, as if he were a feather that might float away at any moment. A big, hulking beast, but fragile. He had a hard time trying to process this feeling.

Memories of himself—*Alan Brindos, I'm Alan Brindos*— seemed intact. How could they have done this? This was new tech, nothing he'd ever heard about before. Nothing in the known Union worlds. He didn't imagine an easy way of getting back to normal would pop up anytime soon.

Still, despite the extreme nature of his circumstances, despite his earlier despair, in his gut Brindos felt he was mentally in control. As he shook off the cobwebs, he realized he had never felt sharper.

His new body told him nothing about whether he had taken the place of an actual Helk individual or if he'd actually been *altered*. If he'd been altered, then to conserve mass, he had likely become less dense. Changed inside somehow.

Brindos didn't have any natural inclinations to speak a fluent Helk dialect, but he didn't speak the language in the first place. He didn't have a desire to beat, kill, and eat another species either. He felt no alien instinctual urges, though he was becoming aware of his heightened sensory perception and physical strength. Still, there had to be something else in this alien brain mass besides himself. But how would he know?

Questions were whirling. Brindos's size could only be that of First Clan. Why this body? Why here in the middle of nowhere? A partial answer came screaming up on the street just outside, sirens blaring. He suspected Joseph or Plenko had tipped the police, who were now out and about looking for some wayward Helk up to no good.

Car doors slammed, boots rushing over the pavement. Brindos quickly made his way through an interior door, marveling at the speed with which he moved, at the smooth gait that led him into a dark corridor. He reached another door. Locked. Forcing the door open with ease, he nearly wrenched it from its hinges. Even though he knew about it, the super strength surprised him, and he took a step back, blinking his eyes at the damaged door. He entered another large room, high walls, hospital green, covered with a coarse brown mold. Water an inch or two deep covered the worn, checkered tile floor, and wiring and plumbing gaped wildly from jagged openings in the floor and walls. Light leaked from a door on the far wall. He fled across the room and without thinking burst through the door, knocking it across a narrow alley.

A police prowler came screeching into view. Brindos fled across the alley and smashed through a door on the opposite side, scrambled up a short flight of stairs, bursting through another locked door. This led him into another corridor, which ended at a door covered by steel security bars. With a few hard tugs he pulled them free and tossed them clanging down the hallway. He almost missed the trapdoor in the ceiling above him, almost invisible but for the rusty padlock, and an easy reach for his newfound stature. He broke open the door in front of him, but instead of going through it, he ripped the lock from the trapdoor.

After batting the door open, Brindos pulled his weight up through the opening with some difficulty. It was a tight squeeze. Above the ceiling, a ladder led to a dingy skylight in the building's roof. He shut the trapdoor and prayed the ladder would hold him.

Now on the roof, he knew it was a matter of time before they discovered the trapdoor. He peered down onto the street; police ringed the area. He sat down for a moment, scanning the rooftop and the city beyond. It was a nice view of a place he was dying to leave. He had to get off this planet and find Dave.

Brindos walked quickly to the far end of the roof. The roof of another building waited ten feet across from him. He jumped and started running the moment he landed. He crossed the roofs of five buildings this way and came to the end of the block.

Directly below, the street was empty but for one police prowler on the far side next to a boarded-up building. Brindos watched it for a few minutes and decided he had to risk it.

A fire escape made the descent easy. He dropped onto the ground at the rear of the prowler, peered through the back window, and saw no one inside. He made another check up and down the street, then walked up to the car's passenger window, bent down, and took a look. A holo of the prowler's owner, a young Authority cop, looked out at Brindos with a stern look, and a tracer below the holo silently displayed his whereabouts, which, if Brindos was reading it correctly, put the cop about a block away.

A pretty good digital image of Terl Plenko glared from the computer monitor inset into the prowler's main console. There was a moment of reckoning as Brindos struggled with this information, then he looked into the side mirror. His nightmare got worse, and he pushed his back against the door of the prowler and slid to the ground, stunned. Now he knew why the prowlers had come looking for him.

Joseph, goddamn it. You played me, set me up, and threw me to the wolves.

Of course, it was perfect.

He was Plenko.

Thirteen

I walked the Helk outside, staying behind him after showing my blaster. "Next bar down," I said, and we entered Mack's Asylum, a glitzy bar a quarter of the size of the Flaming Sea. No sex workers here, just a circular bar in the middle of the room, a few gaming tables, and a small dance floor amid the regular tables. A Memor was playing a console game in the corner that screeched and whistled. His orange hair bobbed and weaved as he wrestled with the controls.

I motioned the Helk to a side table close to the door, told him to stay put, and went to the bar to order a few drinks, keeping him in my sights. Maybe I could loosen him up with a Helk ale. I ordered a glass of the blue poison for myself, left money, took both drinks, and sat down at the table, trying to look menacing.

"You going to talk?" I asked.

Probably not the best way to start a conversation with a Helk. Nearly an eighth of the Helk population is mute. Someone at the agency once tried to explain to me the nuances of defective genetic mapping, but he'd lost me at *defective*. So *fine,* I didn't wait for this Helk to initiate the contact. Didn't wait to see if he'd say hello or bring out a digipad. I had his earring, found at a crime scene—what would become an *official* crime scene as soon as the local police showed up—and I'd be damned if I was going to worry about Helk conversational protocol. He'd string some sentences together, I knew.

"Talking?" I asked as I dangled the earring in front of him again.

"Maybe," the Helk said, eyeing the earring.

Not a sentence, but at least he wouldn't be using a digipad. I hated those things. Turned a ten-minute conversation into thirty. The Helk reached for the earring, and I closed my hand over it and pulled back. "Not that I'm actually going to *give* it to you."

"What do you want?" he said.

I sipped at my drink. "Some answers."

The Helk snorted. "How original."

"You know where I found this?" I asked, tapping the earring with a finger.

"In the restroom?"

"Someone's dead in the room I found it in, if you need a hint."

He sat back in his chair and glared at me. So far he hadn't touched his ale.

"Don't waste that," I said, pointing at the ale. "Stuff's not cheap."

"I didn't kill the woman," he said.

So he knew. He'd most likely been in the room, guilty or not. "Kristen."

"Yes, Kristen."

He looked like a giant stuffed animal sitting there, until he suddenly leaned forward. I had my hand in my coat pocket, gripping my weapon, but even as I considered pulling it, he reached out and grabbed his drink. In one quick motion he downed half of it.

"When were you there?" I asked, making an assumption, relaxing again.

"She was already dead. On the bed. The place a mess."

"Things you might know if you'd killed her."

"It's not a Helk thing."

"Pardon me?"

"We wouldn't have positioned her that way. Remember how she was?"

"Remind me."

"Feet together, arms across her chest. That's a human ritual. Helks, we don't bury our dead or give them lavish funerals, we—"

I stopped him by waving a hand. "Yes, okay, I know what happens, I don't need the gory details." I leaned my elbows on the table and squinted at him. "So we didn't find Kristen in pieces in each corner of the room. Doesn't mean you didn't kill her. You know human rituals, you could have done it to lead the cops to the wrong conclusion."

The Helk finished his ale in a second gulp. He held out his palm. "I didn't kill her, Mr. Crowell. Can I please have my earring back?"

Someone else who knew my name. This was getting embarrassing. "I'm at a distinct disadvantage here. You seem to know me, but I haven't a clue who you are or what you're doing here."

The Helk nodded, his upper lip curling in amusement. "My name is Tem Forno." He smiled. "I'm here because of you."

"Me?"

"I was following you, waiting to see what you might find out. You left with Miss Landry. So I thought, maybe, just maybe, she had left something with Kristen. I went up there a few hours after you left with Miss Landry, but found the room just as you found it today." He shook his head. "Someone got there first."

What the hell was he talking about? "Wait, slow down, just slow down, for Christ's sake. So . . . what's your name again?"

"Tem Forno."

"You know Cara? You were following me because *I* knew Cara? How did you know who I was? And what could Cara possibly give Kristen that someone would kill for?" I imagined it was this fabled key Koch had been after, but I held that information back.

No answer. Instead, I got Forno's outstretched palm again. "The earring, please. If you want to know more. And there is much more to say, trust me."

I practically threw it at him. "There's your damn earring. Now talk."

"Hand out of your pocket."

If the Helk had wanted to kill me, he would already have tried. I removed my hand from my pocket without the blaster.

"Caps?" he asked.

"Spent."

Forno nodded, then stood up. "I can get them recharged for you on the way."

I froze, not liking how the conversation had turned. "On the way to where?"

He didn't answer, making a move to the exit.

I stood and tried to look menacing as I blocked his path to the door. "What were you looking for in Kristen's room?"

The deep lines in his massive forehead thickened when he frowned at me. "Something awfully damn important." He saw I wasn't going to move, so he sighed. "Mr. Crowell, if whoever killed Kristen didn't find what he was looking for, he will certainly go after it elsewhere."

"Maybe he already did," I said, thinking about Tony Koch at Cara's apartment.

As if reading my mind, he said, "And where is Miss Landry—Cara—now?"

"Honestly? I don't know."

"Then perhaps you don't need to know what's going on here on Aryell."

For the moment, Cara was safe, away from Jennifer Lisle. I didn't trust either of them. How could I? Cara was the last to see Katerina Parker, Miss Kristen, alive. Jennifer had been on Coral Moon. She was a Movement sniffer for James. How much did she know about the NIO's plan to make us scapegoats? Or Cara, for that matter? Scapegoats for something I didn't even know about yet.

"Cara's on vacation," I said. "That's all I'm going to tell you. And if I'm to go with you, you're going to at least tell me where we're going."

Forno loomed over me, looking hurt. "What, my offer to recharge your capacitors isn't enough?"

"Not in the slightest."

"Fair enough," he said. "We're going out to the Flatlands."

I frowned, remembering what Cara had told me about the heat-blasted Flatlands when I'd first met her. Even in winter, it never snowed, never got cold. At least I wouldn't need a jacket.

"There's nothing out there but miles and miles of dirt and rock," I said.

The Helk shook his head. "Not anymore."

*   *   *

I was surprised to find the sun directly overhead when we came out of Mack's, the temperature bearable. Midday already. I'd lost track of time. I made a quick check of my code card, but nothing new came up. Nothing from Alan, nothing from Jennifer.

No new NIO alerts. That surprised me. I mean, it was great not to see anything else about Alan and me splattered all over it, but shouldn't there be *some* alerts?

An automated street sweeper crawled by on Amp Street, and the first few police cruisers had pulled up to the Flaming Sea half a block down. The few tourists not skiing paraded up and down the sidewalks, enjoying Kimson's quaint ambiance, but they all stopped to gawk at the police activity. A half-dozen officers in green uniforms and several men and women in plainclothes got out and filed into the tavern.

Forno pointed down the street at a parked flier.

We boarded—it was a two-seater, probably imported from Earth, strictly an economy model from several years back—then headed for the Flatlands. Leaving Kimson and its gentle hills behind, the flier took us north, out past the spaceport where the terrain flattened out, trees giving way to scrub brush, scrub brush giving way to rock and sand.

"How long?" I asked.

"Half hour at the most." He pointed at my hands. "You want to recharge those capacitors? There's a unit in the back."

The flier reminded me of an antique sports car I'd had in New York: a sliver of space behind the seats for storage, the trunk practically useless with the spare tire taking up most of the room. The flier gave me the same sense of space as I twisted toward the back to scavenge behind the seat. I found the charger on the floor behind Forno, and I had to stretch awkwardly to reach it, jostling the Helk's right arm a few times in the process before grabbing it by its carrying strap. Charger in hand, I regained my balance and faced the front again.

Once I'd found the power cable and Forno had pointed out the correct socket, I plugged the charger into the flier's dash. I opened up the unit with a push of a button, snapped my capacitors over to recharge mode, then inserted the fingers of my left hand into the five matching slots. Suction pulled my fingers in, and the current surged, sending tickling vibrations up my arm.

"It's got an auto shutoff," Forno said, "just in case you want to rest your eyes for a while."

I was about ready to tell him I had no intention of sleeping, especially since I hadn't known him for more than a half hour, when the first waves of exhaustion passed over me, and I soon succumbed to sleep.

When I woke, the flier had landed, and darkness coated the windows like black paint. Forno was not on the flier, and that prompted me to reach for my blaster. It was gone. Cursing to myself, I checked my capacitors. Green power indicators glowed under my fingernails. Charged and ready. Strange. Why would Forno charge my caps, then take my gun? How long had I been out? Forno had said a half hour to the Flatlands, but the Flatlands stretched for forty miles in every direction. Still, it shouldn't be dark outside. Late afternoon, maybe, but not pitch-black.

Code card still in my pocket too. No alerts. No messages. I could crossword a message to Alan, see if I could find out what was going down on his end, but this whole silent code card thing had me spooked.

I tried the flier door, but it was locked. I couldn't blast my way out, not with caps. Only after I decided to sit back and wait, my side door thunked open. Sunlight slanted into the flier. Forno peered in, bent at the waist, one hand resting on the flier's rooftop.

"Shielding," he said to me when I squinted into the light. "This flier is in the Flatlands a lot, and it gets hot, even this time of year." He smiled benignly. "Come on," he said, taking a step back.

"Where's my blaster?" I asked, pointing my fingers at him.

"I've got it put away, safe." He slapped my hand away. "Don't point those things at me. I wanted to be sure about you."

I asked the obvious. "Where are we?"

He took another step back. "If you'll get out, I'll show you. You *did* want to know what's going on, right?"

I stepped out onto hard dirt and straightened. Though Forno had landed us in the Flatlands, he'd managed to find about the only bump in the landscape with enough elevation to give us a good view of what I'd come to see. Only I hadn't expected to see it.

It wasn't finished, I could tell that much. That's why I saw plenty of heavy machinery and dozens of workers scurrying around below.

"Know what that is?" Forno asked me, smiling. "Know what it *will* be?"

Slowly, as I inched forward, I nodded. "Yeah. They've got one just like it on Temonus." There was no wire, but I saw the first tower rising a half mile into the sky, and far down the hard plains of the Flatlands I could barely make out a second one. I said to Forno, "Another Transcontinental Conduit."

And all this time I'd thought Temonus, out of all the Union worlds, had the best way to tweak unfavorable climate, thanks to Lorway, the Memor, and the rest of the Science Consortium. But now I knew, deep in my gut, that whoever controlled the Conduits controlled something much more volatile than the weather. I just didn't know what.

Fourteen

Brindos thought: *I am Plenko.*

Sitting with his back against the prowler, eyes closed, he recalled Plenko's words when he had first seen him out in that deserted field: *Soon I will be more than a name to you, and you will be much more than a name to me.*

Ozsc.

Soul.

Had Brindos's soul somehow been lifted from his body and transplanted to Plenko's? Nothing he knew about could do that. Nothing. He shivered, knowing full well his human body might be walking around Temonus with Plenko's "ozsc" inside.

Nightmare upon nightmare.

He'd lost his identity, his blaster, his code card. His humanity. Stranded on Temonus, wanted for murder—hell, forget that. Plenko's list of crimes against the Union was as long as Brindos's new Helk arm, and murder didn't even top the list.

Take Ribon. What chance had it had against the Movement's planet killer? Coral Moon, a hammer coming down with little warning. Less than a week to kill a world. Some had escaped the slaughter, but too many had not. Not like the powers-that-be were going to let *that* one slide. Plenko was fair game, a "shoot-to-kill" target throughout the Union.

If Joseph had a hand in all this, if it had been his idea . . .

A hum startled him from his thoughts, and he opened his eyes. On the sidewalk, about twenty feet away, a Temonus cop stood poised, his weapon leveled. It was the prowler's owner, the young cop from the holo image. Young, probably fresh out of the academy; the gray and blue uniform looked brand-new. The blaster shook a little in his hands.

Brindos didn't blame him.

Funny. Brindos's first reaction *as* Alan Brindos would've been to put up his hands and shout "Whoa, whoa, whoa," adrenaline pumping through like RuBy shooting through an addict's veins. But while his consciousness had certainly taken root inside Plenko, some obvious instinctual behaviors of a First Clan Helk had not changed—well, as far as he knew, anyway, considering he'd been a Helk for less than a few hours. At least he had no desire to eat the poor guy.

Brindos felt calm. Confident. No anxiety. No concern for his safety. Right away he knew he didn't need to be afraid of this cop.

And yet: the Alan Brindos part of him had doubts. Hesitated.

"Midwest City Authority," the cop yelled out, a quaver in his voice. "Get up *now*. Hands high."

Could Brindos explain it to him? Did he tell this kid he wasn't Plenko, that he was human, an operative for the NIO? The cop would laugh himself silly—if he didn't drop dead from a heart attack first.

Brindos stood, letting the cop see what he was up against. Not once did Brindos take his eyes off him, and somehow, unbelievably, the young cop didn't flinch. He held his ground.

"Sideways," the cop said.

He knew the routine, that much was certain. Turn the Helk slightly to his right, expose the left side and, because of its location on that side of the body, the heart. Turning right would put the cop in a good position to fire at a point just under Brindos's armpit and blow him away if he did anything stupid.

Brindos decided to do something stupid. He turned left. Of course, the cop could've aimed for his head, but he was all textbook now.

"The other way, goddamn it!" he yelled. "To your right, to your right!"

Desperation had the cop a bit frazzled, and Brindos took that quick moment to move, zipping toward him faster than any human, feeling the near-thrill of moving that way. He reached the cop just as he fired his weapon.

This is what Helk quickness looks like, Brindos thought.

Accelerating and stopping. He knew about it now after running down alleys, through hallways, and across rooftops to escape pursuit. Acceleration got him to the cop in a flash.

Brindos had stopped suddenly right in front of him, and a split second later twisted out of the way, the projectile of the weapon missing.

This is what Helk power feels like.

Realizing its full potential in the blink of an eye, Brindos brought up his fist in an uppercut and connected with the cop's jaw. He grunted once as his feet left the ground, and he was out before he hit the sidewalk. The blaster clattered harmlessly beside him like a child's abandoned toy.

Brindos relaxed his hand and flexed the fingers as he took a single step to where the cop lay. Brindos might be an ugly son of a bitch, but he was starting to appreciate the super-strength thing.

More sirens warbled in the distance and he knew he'd have to get out of there fast. No use trying to steal the prowler—it would be keyed to the cop's DNA. He could probably start it up by getting the cop's thumb to the ignition, but he'd have to have the cop sitting in his lap to get anywhere. Brindos bent down and picked up the cop's blaster, but it also had a DNA trigger. Goddamn. He dropped it, straightened, and glanced at the cop's face.

His head rested against his right shoulder but his face looked away from Brindos, turned to the far left.

The cop was out cold and going nowhere soon. He'd have a hell of a headache, and would probably need jaw surgery.

He took a moment and peeked into the cop's prowler, rummaging around for anything that might clue him in on the ongoing search for him. As he studied the dash, he felt a moment of panic: he couldn't decipher half of what he was looking at. Finally, his brain zeroed in on a flash membrane inset on the steering pad that listed

Midwest City locations, most of them highlighted in a fluorescent green glow.

The third location down the list was the Restaurant.

He flicked the listing and the word SEARCHED popped up in red block letters. The cop hadn't taken the time to DNA-lock the screen. Brindos flicked again, this time on the red letters, and a city grid coalesced on the membrane. The Restaurant's blip snapped into place. Not far away, perhaps safe to return to if Authority had already given it a look.

The sirens suddenly got louder, as if someone had just cranked up the volume on some crappy U-ONE vid broadcast, and he left the prowler and took off at a run across the street in the direction the grid had given him for the Restaurant. He slipped into a narrow back alley, all thoughts about the cop on hold, his own survival now the only matter of importance.

The sun was coming up. Gray sky above, cracked pavement below feet that were not his feet. Tired. When had he last had a regular night's sleep? Quite a while, if he didn't count the numerous times he'd been out cold. He slipped through the alley, barely taking notice of the buildings themselves, which looked to be in much the same shape as the rest of the district: rundown, neglected, mostly deserted. Only a little bit of garbage, wrappers and containers for foods and drinks he couldn't identify, some boxes, cardboard, and plastic, and not a lot else.

Brindos kept moving, sticking to alleys and side streets, and the sirens faded. Finally, some distance. Of course, he had no idea where the hell he was, or how he was going to get out of his genetic Helk suit.

He was hungry. How much did a Helk have to eat to quell his hunger? At least Brindos could go into the Helk section of the Restaurant to eat, but would he actually enjoy the food? What Joseph called the "real thing"?

Goddamn you, Joseph. He slammed his fist into a brick wall as he passed by, knocking a hole in it. He didn't even slow down. He wasn't surprised in the least that he could do it. Was it because he was losing his humanity, losing his connection to who Brindos was and truly becoming a Helk? He still didn't know yet whether all his thoughts were his own, and he was pretty sure a Helk psychiatrist would just end up declaring he should be hauled away to the nearest Helk looney bin.

Brindos moved into another alley, barely aware of his surroundings, but hoping his sense of direction was taking him in the right direction, toward the Restaurant. Thoughts circled like buzzards waiting to claim his soul.

His ozsc.

And then he was at the end of the alley. A dead end. Surrounded by brick on all sides, Brindos knew he had stumbled into a blind alley. A glance to the right revealed it wasn't exactly a dead end, though. A slim passageway, dark and ominous, looking like the entrance to some forbidden tunnel, was tucked tight against the right angle of the brick walls coming together. He wasn't sure he could even squeeze into that space. Not sure it was smart to even try, but at the very least, it could turn out to be a decent hiding place if the cops suddenly showed up.

He slipped into the darkness, discovered he had plenty of room to walk, and inched farther into the passageway.

Pitch-black.

Walking with his hands out in front of him, Brindos managed to shuffle along without tripping over anything or bumping into any walls. Soon enough, a glimmer of light appeared in front of him. Emboldened by this, he moved faster, until he nearly fell out of the passageway.

Along a redbrick wall, Brindos saw a few waste containers tucked in tight against a wooden platform. Next to the platform was a door. A yellow door.

Yes. He was outside the Restaurant, near the spot where Tom-Knox-who-was-supposedly-Jordan-Dak-the-waiter slammed him against the wall.

The place where he'd blanked out and lost eighteen hours of his life. Hours Joseph had filled in, insinuating Brindos had killed the waiter. Saying he'd helped get Brindos to his hotel, keeping the incriminating evidence to himself. Then Brindos had met Terl Plenko. Then Joseph turned out to be more than he had let on. Brindos's last image of Joseph had been his haunting smile and his fingertips glowing white.

Two Second Class Helks came through the yellow door. Brindos waited a moment, then moved forward into the dim light. They saw him and raised their stunners.

He needed to remember he was a Helk. Shit, not just a Helk. *I am Plenko.* He had startled these two Helks, that was all. They had raised their weapons because he'd appeared so suddenly. If he just played a Helk, he'd be fine. If he just played *Plenko,* he would be even better.

Brindos looked the part, but could he bring off the rest of it? Would the first words he uttered give him away?

The Helk to Brindos's left was the first to ease his guard. He had on a blue jumpsuit that covered everything but head, hands, and feet. "Terl?" he said, giving Brindos something to work with. "That you? What are you doing *here*?"

The other Helk's jumpsuit was red. He lowered his weapon in relief. "Scared us."

"Sorry," Brindos said, keeping his voice low. He pointed back toward the dark passageway. "I decided—I mean, I just thought—"

Blue Jumpsuit took a small step forward. "You okay?"

"Sure," Brindos said. "Just . . . you know. A walk."

Blue and Red looked at each other. Then Red said, "Without any clothes?"

Brindos looked down, remembering he was naked. Naked as a Helk could be, considering its leathery skin and massive furry body. A slight flaw in his plan to blend in.

There was distrust in the Helks' faces when Brindos glanced back at them. "Yeah. About that . . ."

Blue's stunner inched upward. "We haven't seen you for a week. We were told you were in East City."

"East City," Brindos said.

"You know. Tower One?" Red said.

"Tower One," Brindos repeated.

Did he mean the carrier disaster? The *Exeter* running into the Conduit, ripping out the tower, dragging it, the wire down, a section of East City destroyed.

"Destroyed," Brindos added, trying to sound authoritative.

"Well, yeah, we knew that. You were going to assess the damage, see how bad everything was. See if the patterns are compromised, if you could get near enough to check."

Brindos nodded. "Of course."

Now Red's stunner leveled. "Of course? You got in? Patterns lost? Destroyed?"

This was getting tricky. "Destroyed." Brindos pointed back behind him, realizing he'd made a big mistake coming here. "You know, I'm just going to go back and look for my clothes."

"Maybe you should come on inside for now," Red said, waving his stunner a little.

Brindos turned, prepared to run at full Helk speed, fear motivating him to get far away from the place. Red and Blue had him pegged before he'd taken a few steps. The tingling started at his leathery head and permeated his entire body, and as he lost control of his limbs, his fading thought was:

Not again.

================ Fifteen ================

Another Transcontinental Conduit.

The one on Temonus had been mysterious enough, as Brindos had figured out. But here on Aryell?

Soon there would be a new Conduit, and maybe the old one would still be usable if repaired—whatever that meant—and two planets had already progressed to the point that they were ready to leave the galactic club, thanks to Plenko's Movement.

I knew without a doubt that Forno had orchestrated the twists and turns needed to get me to this place now, standing a short distance from a technological marvel and a conspiracy bigger than Terl Plenko's Movement.

"Forno," I said, "just what the hell is going on?"

Forno took several Helk-sized steps away from his flier and looked out over the Flatlands at the tower that would soon host the thin filament of a Conduit said to control the weather. He stood tall, his Helk frame massive in front of me, and he didn't seem to be at all concerned about being visible here on this small hill overlooking the expanse of the Flatland, with the afternoon wearing on.

When he didn't answer, I said, "Honestly. Is there really that big a need to control the weather here?"

He shook his head. "Not really."

I eyed the workers down there at the near tower. "And who are they?"

"You ever wonder why they built the first Conduit on Temonus where they did?" he asked. "In the cities? East, Midwest, West?"

"I've got nothing. Answer my question."

He nodded at the workers. He hadn't looked at me since he'd stepped away from the flier. "They're just Aryellians doing their jobs. Someone tells them to build this engineering behemoth, and off they go."

"Out here in the Flatlands."

"Back on Temonus, they built the Conduit right in the middle of everything," Forno said.

"They?" I said.

"Before the Movement started gaining notoriety."

"You mean the Science Consortium."

Tem Forno finally looked back at me. "Yes."

"Are you saying the Consortium has enough pull to organize a second one of these, so soon? I hadn't heard or seen anything in NIO circles about this second one."

Forno laughed. Or burped. I wasn't sure which, but the volume and grating intensity of it said the same thing. He was amused. "Of course you didn't," he said. He pointed at the tower. "You think Plenko has the resources to do that? He's been on the run for years, ducking in here, sliding in there, little hit-and-runs, coaxing out Union planes and Arks to chase him as if it were a game—"

"What about Coral? The Movement base there, and Coral's destruction. Planet Ribon."

"It's not Movement."

"Dorie Senall. Jennifer Lisle."

"Not Movement."

"Then it's the NIO, like you warned me about."

"They did set you up."

I thought about my silent code card, no agency activity popping up on it at all, and wondered. "Who are you, really?"

"Told you. Tem Forno."

"Are you Movement?"

"No."

"Consortium?"

"No."

I took a step back. The Flatlands seemed a little hotter. I could've used some of that shielding Forno had on his flier. I wondered how those workers down there at the tower could stand it.

Forno looked straight into my eyes. Actually he had to look down quite a bit, but the effect was the same. He held my gaze for several seconds. "I'm Gray."

Gray. I took another step back. "Who?"

I flashed back to my run-in with "Gray" at Floor 13. The person in the shadows who told me about the ultra thin level. The setup. Tony Koch and Terl Plenko being the same person. Aliases. But not aliases. The Science Consortium, Tim James, NIO involvement . . .

"It was you?" Keep stepping back, Dave, I told myself. I stepped. "You're Gray? You left the privacy visor? You *shot* me."

"Stunned you," Forno said.

"You son of a bitch!"

"I got you out of there. That's all that mattered. I took a flight ahead of you since I didn't have to work as hard to lose anyone."

"What the hell? Why Gray? Why not tell me you were Forno?"

"Trust issues." Forno stood like a colossus, barely moving. Intimidating. Then he shook his head. "Gray is an accurate name, however."

"How so?"

"I worked for the Kenn. Helk intelligence."

"You're an agent?"

"Was."

It came to me as I remembered the indoctrination the NIO had given me about the other intelligence groups. "Kenn. It means Gray. In Helk."

Forno nodded. "The Kenn are famous for doing whatever needs to be done to insure the safety of the Helks. So we straddle the line sometimes. I mostly did undercover work, infiltrating the larger, more troublesome districts on Helkunntanas, working the underground. RuBy sniffers, data forgers, you name it."

"Why are you here? Why me? If the Kenn knows something—"

Forno shook his head. "They're compromised just like the NIO. I can't trust the Kenn, and you can't trust the NIO."

"Why can I trust you then, if you're Kenn?"

"I helped you. I'm not your enemy."

"Who is, then? The Consortium?"

He shrugged. "Sort of."

"What do you mean—"

"Director James."

"He's the enemy?"

"Sort of."

"For god's sake—"

"James and the Consortium."

Sounded like some free-pop band. "You mentioned the NIO funding the Consortium. Something about the Plenko commission order coming from Timothy James. And by the way, just how in the hell did you get a hold of a privacy visor and get into the NIO basement?"

"NIO has secrets, the Kenn has secrets. And I had reason to use our secrets to access yours, trust me. Uh, sorry about the visor not giving you anything else. That's as far as I've been able to dig into the NIO basement. The rest of what I know has come from . . . direct involvement."

"James didn't make the order to fund them?"

"The NIO could get the cash, but someone else made the order. I think the Consortium did."

"Through James."

"Through James who's not James."

My thoughts whirled. I walked past Forno, toward the tower, hand to my head, then spun around, walked back, toward the flier, and regained my original spot.

Forno said, "Is that helping?"

"Shut up."

"Fine."

"No, don't shut up," I said. "Listen and see if this is right. Tony Koch isn't Plenko's right-hand man, he *is* Plenko. But no, it's an alias. But no, he didn't look anything like him. My partner Brindos said something about crap going on where he was. Tom Knox not being Tom Knox—"

"I was going to get to both you and your partner, get all this explained earlier. But then you sent Brindos to Temonus."

"Sure. Following leads—"

"Brindos is in a lot of trouble," Forno said. "You've got to get to him, because I think he knows something the Consortium doesn't want him to know. They may be making an example of him."

I stared at him.

"I understand this is confusing, Crowell. And there's more to tell. But we need to get back to the flier and get out of here. I have another place I have to take you. Another puzzle piece. Then you'll know as much as I do. The rest of the mystery? That I can't figure out. I'm going to need your help."

"My help? Forno, I don't know anything about this mess. Or you."

"You were inside the NIO. You were a part of it, a contractor. When the NIO set you up, they did it because you knew something, or they did it because of someone you know. Something you saw. Everything's been thrown in your path. It's true you may not have known anything then—or you don't *know* you know something—but you may know something *now*."

I found myself nodding, but not because I understood him. Or believed him. I just wanted him to make me understand what the fuck was going on.

"I can't trust anyone else in the Kenn or the NIO, not even the provincial and Union governments. It became clear to me that I needed to bring you in on this, if you weren't already compromised."

"You've decided I'm not."

"Yes. I wouldn't take you to this next place only to show you the sights."

I followed him back to the flier. As we clambered inside, he handed me my blaster. Having it back did not get rid of my uneasiness. My brain tried to wrap itself around all that Forno had said so far.

Then I remembered Cara. "Cara's involved," I said, as if it had already been proven true.

"You suspected so, didn't you?"

"Yes, but I have no idea how."

Forno lowered the shielding and hit the ignition. The flier's engines fired up almost immediately. "I only know that she's associated with Kristen, the woman she worked for at the Flaming Sea. I think she might have something Kristen gave to her. A key. That's what I was looking for at the Flaming Sea."

My eyebrows went up. "Tony Koch said something about a key before he died."

The flier had taken off now, and Forno shot a quick glance my way. "Koch? Dead?"

"Cara and I had a run-in with him. He kept saying we had the key, that Plenko would find me. But I don't know what the damn key is. Do you?"

"No clue. Cara didn't have any idea?"

"Didn't seem to."

He pursed his lips. The fleshy parts of them were bigger than my hand.

"This key," I said. "It opens something? But they don't know what it is or what it does?"

"That about covers it."

"And *you* don't know what it is."

"No clue."

"Nothing?"

He shook his head. "You've been thrown into this mess, Plenko is looking for you, so you've got to help me figure it out."

"Yeah, everything's so clear now."

"So what do you think?" Forno asked.

"No clue."

Sixteen

Awake again, greeted by a soft, reddish light. Brindos was sprawled on a hard floor, inside somewhere. A strong odor actually made him wince.

Four or five times coming up out of unconsciousness in the past day and a half. Another few times and he'd be a pro at this.

Plenko. *Me*. Still getting used to it. Where was he? *Who* was he? Brindos the Helk. Shit, was he now thinking like a Helk?

No. Under the surface, he was Alan Brindos. He remembered the last words out in the alley, about the Conduit being attacked again, the main tower "compromised." He knew who he worked for, he knew his partner's name, and he knew what had happened to his own body.

His body of fur, still without clothes. It wasn't that unusual for Helks to walk around without them, particularly since the "objectionable" parts of Helk anatomy were out of sight.

The Helk stunner had done quite the number on him. Evidently humans and Helks suffered some of the same effects. Dizzy, Brindos tried to sit up three times without success. He decided just to stand, so he rolled over, pushed himself to his knees, and managed to haul himself off the floor. He half expected to see Red and Blue in a corner keeping watch, stunners leveled. The other half expected to see Joseph and his glowing fingers. He shuddered.

No one else was in the room. The red light came from a single bare bulb in its socket that dangled from the middle of the room on a rope, the wires snaking up to the ceiling and disappearing there.

The walls were made of the same redbrick of the alley, the floor made of concrete. A wooden door, old and warped, tempted him from the far side of the room. It was tall enough for a First Clan Helk to walk through without stooping.

Big enough for me *to walk through without stooping.*

White light seeped in around the edges. He had the feeling that if he tried, he could easily break the door down. Stacked against the wall on both sides of the door were plastic see-through canisters filled with something, but in the low light he couldn't tell what.

Brindos moved toward the door, and the strong odor he'd smelled when he woke up grew stronger. It was coming from the canisters, and he nervously approached one. As soon as he did, he knew he wouldn't find something horrible inside, even though for a moment he considered he had become part of some horrible genetic experiment to create Helk replacement body parts. He identified the smell right then.

Spices. The effect of the pungent, biting aroma on his eyes and nose told him they were Helk spices.

Brindos had seen the yellow door of the Restaurant just before Blue and Red knocked him out with their stunners, so he wondered if this was a storeroom in the back.

Looking behind him, he spotted more containers along the back wall. Then he eyed the door again. Familiar.

And then he knew. He was on the other side of it now, but it was the same door he'd come to before Tom Knox had grabbed him by the throat. The door he'd thought led to the authentic portion of the Restaurant. He wondered if the place had an authentic portion at all.

Perhaps the place was a front after all. Not for body parts, but something Joseph and Plenko had involved themselves in. Something Movement.

Brindos eyed the door, but without warning, his stomach did a few flips. Thinking the spices were affecting his part Helk, part human body, he closed his eyes and held his nose.

No use. The pain that came suddenly shot through his midsection like a hot knife slicing through skin and muscle. He screamed a guttural, nonhuman yell and fell to his knees, arms clutching his stomach. He forgot about the fur, and it surprised him not to touch bare skin; a moment later it didn't matter as the pain doubled and he fell and curled into a half moon on the floor.

This was not human.

Brindos had never considered pain in that way before. Pain built for a Helk, and yet he felt he couldn't endure it another second. A wave of stabbing sensations traveled up and down his body and he cried out again, unable to control anything.

Soon every inch of him throbbed with red-hot agony, and there didn't seem to be an end to it. He would just suffer until whatever was affecting his body passed. If it passed at all.

The door opened.

He didn't see it open, but the quality of light changed, the red washing out. The door squeaked a little on its hinges.

"Hold him down," a deep voice commanded.

Brindos wheezed, now cradling his head. The knife stabs had moved there, ripping at his brain.

Large hands grabbed at his arms, and more hands snagged his legs and feet. He thrashed, screaming louder, but his captors held him down. Two of them, probably. Red and Blue? He thought they must be Helks for them to manhandle him so easily. *Helk*handle him.

"Got him," said a voice near his head. "Stick him."

Panicking, Brindos doubled his efforts, hoping to escape them and the cutting pain at the same time. A viselike grip clamped on his arm at the elbow and a second later something sharp punctured his shoulder. It might have hurt if the other pain hadn't so consumed him.

Brindos opened his eyes and found himself staring straight above at the red lightbulb. He still couldn't see who was holding him down, their grips tight on his limbs.

"Relax," the voice said. "We've got you. It'll be another moment. Just *relax*. Do you understand?"

Brindos managed a deep breath and squeezed out a raspy reply. "Who are you?"

The voice that had spoken first said something next; he was holding Brindos's feet. "You'll be okay in a little bit."

A wave of nausea slid through him, but the pain was lessening with each passing second. "Who are you?" Brindos repeated, then he felt warm all over, and his vision started to blur.

"Who we are doesn't matter," said the voice at his feet. "Who *you* are does, and we'll find that out soon enough."

Head spinning, eyes closed, and, unbelievably, the pain subsiding. "You know me. I'm Terl Plenko, and I demand you let me go, or so help me—"

"Or what? Even if that were true, you'd be in no shape to do anything."

"You—" Brindos struggled to get out the words. He took a deep breath and opened his eyes. The red lightbulb blurred in and out. "You tell Joseph. Tell him I want to see him. Now. *Now*, do you hear?"

A face appeared over him, a Helk face. He caught a flash of blue around its neck.

"Joseph," the Helk said. He moved his head to look toward Brindos's feet, and the underside of his jaw was clothed in blue. "We know any Joseph?"

"That's enough," the other said. "There's certainly no Joseph here. No more questions."

And with that they let go, quickly exited the room, slammed the door shut, and left Brindos on the floor. The pain that had so incapacitated him subsided to a dull ache, but now he had another problem.

He couldn't move.

At least he didn't pass out.

For nearly an hour he lay there unable to move. Unable to sleep. Unable, even, to think about his horrific transformation, capture, or what he could do about it. Nothing. He just stared at the red bulb in a fog. A fog that enveloped and fed him with a sense of euphoric abandon, but also debilitating dread. He remembered turning his head slightly at one point, seeing the door to possible freedom a few body lengths away, then giving in to the fog of apathy and bliss. He turned his head away and closed his eyes.

Who cares about revolution?

Who cares about Union?

Who cares about goddamn Alan What's-His-Name?

About humans, Memors, even the human race. Fuck Helkunntanas.

He smiled, and the sensation of leathery skin around his face
wrinkling felt oddly satisfying. Then the light washed out again,
the wooden door opening. He didn't bother to turn his head, preferring to luxuriate in the miasmic fog. Footsteps on the concrete.
Two Helks looking down. Maybe he'd seen them before. So what?
They were blocking his light.

"Sit up," one of them said.

Didn't they know he couldn't move?

"You could've got up a half hour ago."

"I like it down here," he said, barely remembering why he was
there in the first place.

"Get up," another of them said, his voice rattling like a garbled
transmission. First Clan. He leaned over with a snarl.

"Who's going to make me? You and whose army?" he said,
remembering some witty saying from his distant past. He thought
it clever and laughed heartily.

Immediately they set upon him, grabbing and lifting him to his
feet. It did take both of them, though, because at that moment he
found he could indeed move, and fought against them the whole
time they grasped and pulled him over to sit on the containers full
of Helk spices. He took a deep breath and took in the smell, suddenly very hungry. The spice wasn't bothering him now at all. He
recognized kelska, a subtle spice that Helks used like salt and that
most humans couldn't stomach even in small amounts.

"You've got a visitor, Terl," the Helk said. He didn't see which
one said it, because his eyes were closed, enjoying the aromas. "If
that's who you are."

"Who else would I be?" he said.

"She'll know better than anyone," the rattling voice said, "considering you're married to her."

He sobered up. He opened his eyes and followed the entrance
of a young human woman into the storeroom. She was tall and

slender, and a trace of amusement flashed in her brown eyes as she stopped in front of him, her hands on her hips. Mixed marriages between Helks and humans were rare, but not unheard of. Still, he could hardly believe that this wisp of a human woman could love, let alone *love*, a First Clan Helk.

Love *me*, he thought.

She looked like she could float away at any moment. She wore a black jumpsuit that clung to her curves and accentuated her wide hips.

Even though he was sitting, she still had to look up at him. She pulled her long black hair back behind her ears. "Poor thing," she whispered.

She reached up and touched his face, and it made him wince. Not due to any pain. Not revulsion. But because of the tenderness in the touch, as if she were afraid he might vanish from her sight in an instant.

"Terl, what have you been up to?" she asked. Looking him over head to toe, she shook her head. "Where *are* your clothes?"

"So it's him," one of the Helks said. Red jumpsuit. "You're sure."

The woman turned to him with a frown on her face. "Well, of course it's him, Chinkno. Are you blind as well as stupid?"

Chinkno held up his hands. "Hey, listen. Knox and I found him like this, and I've never seen him act this way—"

"He's been through a lot over the past few weeks, and you know it."

Yes, I have been through a lot, he thought. But he couldn't remember anything.

"It's just that he didn't talk right," Chinkno said. "He seemed . . . off. He didn't seem to follow what I was saying about where he'd been."

"You gave him that sedative, so how could he have said anything that made any sense?" the woman said.

"But what about before then? He didn't seem to know about the sabotage at Tower One. He tried to run away from us out back. Then all that yelling and screaming."

"Look, I'm his mate. I know my husband when I see him. I'll find out what the screaming was about," she said. "Leave us."

The other Helk spoke up then. "I'm not sure it's safe."

She gazed into his eyes, squinting a little. "He's fine," she said, the whisper coming back to her voice. "I'm safe. I've got something else to calm him if he needs it. Now *go*."

Chinkno shrugged, then headed out the door. The other followed. Once the door shut, the woman took a step back and reached inside a pocket of her black jumpsuit. She pulled out a couple of red, coarse papers and held them to her nose. She took a deep breath, then smiled.

"You don't know who I am, do you?" she asked.

His fog had completely disappeared now, but he didn't understand any of this any better than before. "You don't know who I am either," he guessed.

"You're not my husband," she said.

"I'm Plenko."

She tilted her head and frowned. "You're not Plenko."

"I'm a Helk."

"That much seems true. But who else are you?"

"Who else?" He lowered his gaze to his clubbed feet. *Who else?* "I don't know. I don't remember."

She touched his shoulder, the one someone had stuck with a needle, or whatever it was, to administer the sedative. "Don't worry. I'll help you remember."

When he looked up she was stepping back again, and now she had her hands around those red papers, slowly rolling them. She licked them both, and red dye stained her tongue. She popped one in her mouth and handed the other one to him.

"It's RuBy," she said. "It's going to help a lot. Take it."

The red paper nearly disappeared in his hand.

She went over to the wall, pulled a container out, and positioned it in front of him. She sat down and craned her neck up to look at him. "We better find out who you are."

"What about the others?"

"I lied to them. I have a secret." She winked, then closed her eyes as the RuBy hit her. When she opened them, they were glazed over, looking gray and dead, as if she were blind. "Now to get better acquainted, dear husband of mine."

She stuck out her hand.

He popped the RuBy, catching a slight odor of cinnamon, then carefully held her hand. "Okay."

"I'm Dorie," she said. "Dorie Senall."

Seventeen

Heading south, we left the Flatlands behind, Forno's flier cruising low over rocky, sandy terrain that soon gave way to the evergreen forest surrounding Kimson on all sides. Patches of white where the snow had not yet melted mixed in with the green, creating a nice little patchwork quilt.

Forno stayed to the west of Kimson's hills, continuing southwest toward the Baral Mountains and its ski resorts. I didn't actually know any of the names of the resorts, or even the names of the specific mountains.

"We going skiing?" I asked. "Here I am without a warm jacket, and I hear the rental equipment isn't cheap."

Forno gave me a look that told me I should shut up, so I did. For now.

He looked out his window as he banked the flier to the left, a little east. He aimed for a natural pass between two mountain ranges, gaining altitude. My command of Aryellian geography included Kimson's hills and the nearby spaceport. And of course, now, the Flatlands. I had no idea what awaited beyond the mountains.

I kept thinking about the key. The key Forno knew about. The Helk didn't know what it was, but he knew someone had been looking for it. Someone had thought Kristen had it. Forno had gone looking. Jennifer Lisle had gone looking. Had she gone looking for the key, or for Kristen and Cara, two suspects high on her list? Someone else had arrived before all of them, killed Kristen, and left the room in a shambles. Koch, maybe. If Koch, he hadn't found the key. If someone else, the key—whatever it was—could have been found.

Nothing new on the code card. It might as well have been some antique music player for all the good it was doing me now. I didn't think telling Forno about the NIO's silent treatment was a good idea. Not yet. But I was oddly comforted knowing that no other NIO alerts had appeared on the code card since before Forno took me out to the Flatlands.

Forno also knew about things that cluttered my brain so much that I couldn't even begin to put two and two together. One and one, for that matter. The Science Consortium. Director James. Plenko.

The flier shot through the pass. Seemingly, no one in Aryellian government minded air traffic buzzing around wherever it pleased. I grabbed a quick peek at Forno and he looked tense, his knuckles white as he gripped the controls. A few beads of sweat trickled down his leathery face.

"You okay?" I asked.

Forno nodded, but kept his eyes front and center.

"Expecting anything"—I searched for the right words, but couldn't find them—"interesting?"

"*Look,*" he said, the loudness of the single word in the cabin of the flier making me jump slightly. Now he looked at me, held my gaze for a couple of seconds before turning away. "I've only been out here once before. Things can get a bit . . . touchy."

"Touchy? What does that mean? And where's here?" With the mountains behind us, the land had flattened out again. We hadn't passed any foothills. The mountains had just stopped, and a grassy plain stretched as far as the eye could see. "And why are you taking me out here? I believe all you told me in the Flatlands—at least everything I can comprehend—so come clean and tell me."

Forno's massive arm nearly hit me as he pointed out the right side of the front window.

"See it?" he asked.

"What?"

"Over there. Look."

I *was* looking, but hadn't figured out what I was looking at. In the distance, I saw a field of patchy brown that seemed to waver and undulate, as if alive.

The flier closed in on those brown spots, the movement almost hypnotic, and I started to tell him he'd stumped me when Forno's little ship bumped hard, as if we'd hit something, and a bright light shone through the window.

Startled, I pulled back from the window. "What the—"

"Hang on," Forno said. "This'll get a little rough."

Bright white light, followed by blues and oranges, flashed through the flier, forcing me to look away from the front window. The cabin lurched sideways toward my side, then up, like a scream elevator at a virtual fun park. I grunted and nearly flipped over the back of my chair. Nowhere to go, however, with that small utility space back there, but the sudden movement made my stomach queasy and my head spin. The flier dropped suddenly and I exhaled as if I'd been hit in the stomach. The light outside turned a nearly translucent gray, with flecks of white shooting through it like lightning.

The flier bumped along, slew to the right, and Forno struggled to keep us steady. Bronze lines like old-fashioned telephone wires appeared in front of us, and I ducked instinctively. We passed through as if nothing had been there.

"Forno!" I yelled. "What *is* this?" Another thing he forgot to mention to me, of course.

The Helk concentrated on the window in front of him and kept quiet. If he'd been expecting this, I could understand his earlier tension. The buffeting from side to side, as well as up and down, became unbearable, and I held my head in my hands. The next wild swing, to the left this time, threw me against the door about the same time a high-pitched whine assailed us. I wondered if the flier had malfunctioned and the engine had gone out, but just as quickly as the noise had sounded, it stopped.

Movement calmed slightly, and I relaxed somewhat. I'd yelled out at Forno due to my confusion, but as I settled down, I felt that I should know what this was. I squinted at the swirling colors, the plasma-like fluctuations.

"Datascreen," Forno said, almost at the same time I realized we were caught in some kind of defense mechanism.

"What the hell's a datascreen?"

"It's virtual," he said. "Like camouflage. And a deterrent. I found something out about this place when I accessed the files in the NIO basement."

Like a hot zone. But I'd never seen tech like it. Unless the Memors had hidden it until now. "This place? What's this datascreen keeping us from getting to?"

"Oh, we'll get there. The datascreen is automatic. The fields and data coils react to our flight path, but we'll pass through it. No one actually starts and stops it, and very few even hang around to maintain it."

"But someone wants to keep ships away."

He almost smiled. "Most definitely."

More science from the Consortium? Another gift from the Memors, from Lorway? "The datascreen's weakening," I said, the colors and grays dwindling to a swirling muddiness, becoming more transparent.

"Check out below."

I followed his arm, lifting myself off the seat a little so I could look down through the front window. We were almost through the datascreen now, the virtual shield giving way to the natural colors of the Aryellian sky and earth. Those patches of brown I'd seen earlier stood out in stark contrast to the disappearing gray and white, the last remnants of the datascreen, and now I understood why they had seemed to waver.

They *were* wavering.

Or, more accurately, fluttering.

"Tents?" I said in a whisper. I whispered it, because the tents extended along the flat plain for miles in all directions and I could hardly believe it possible.

Forno nodded out the window. "Welcome to New Venasaille."

"New—" I narrowed my eyes and took in a breath. "*What?*"

"I've got to land this thing."

"Did you say New Venasaille?"

"The datascreen's automatic, but that doesn't mean they don't have people out here keeping watch from time to time."

"New Venasaille? Like Venasaille on Ribon?"

"There's a spot I used the first time I was here. Well out of the way, hidden for the most part."

"Ribon? The planet my partner barely escaped from?"

"I can land this thing there, keep out of sight."

"Forno!"

Forno stopped and finally looked my way. "You haven't figured it out?"

I had, in that instant, realized what I was seeing. I nodded, but didn't say anything right away. In my mind, I saw the copy of the police surveillance holo Alan Brindos had made for me, the one the Venasaille Police Lieutenant Branson had played for him. I watched it, knowing what followed on Ribon after the incident. Wincing during the recording, when Dorie Senall pitched over the edge of the apartment in the Tempest Tower, her freefall down one hundred floors captured by the marble cam; I couldn't help thinking she might have been one of the lucky ones.

Luckier than the ones who didn't make it off the planet and had to watch Coral Moon fragment above them.

Possibly luckier than these people here, in New Venasaille, depending on the conditions.

A tent city. A *massive* tent city.

"This is the classified spot the Ribon refugees ended up," Forno said. He put the flier into a steep descent, and soon I couldn't make out the tents anymore, a copse of wispy trees rising to meet us.

As he set us down in a small clearing in the trees, I found my voice. "Are they all here? I heard they managed to evacuate nearly five hundred thousand people before the disaster."

"Five hundred fifty thousand," Forno said. "Humans mostly, but some Memors and Helks. All that's left of Ribon's population."

I looked at him, my question still unanswered.

"They're all here," he said.

We left the flier behind and Forno led the way out of the clearing and through the evergreen trees. Here, away from the Flatlands, the temperature had dropped considerably, and patches of snow and ice slowed our steps. It was also getting on toward evening. I shivered.

A warm Flaming Sea jacket would've been nice right about now. My blaster felt awkward tucked into my pants, but I didn't want to be carrying it. Not with the footing a little tricky.

Eventually we came to a small rise pocked with shrubs and dwarf evergreens, and the ground cover became less dense. Forno crouched low as he neared the top and motioned for me to get down. On our elbows and knees, we scrunched upward until the tent city came into view.

I could now make out individual tents, door flaps, rainflys. Once in a while, I spotted movement and realized these were refugees of New Venasaille walking around with no apparent destination in mind.

"But," I said, searching for understanding, "what do they *do* here? Five hundred thousand people. They're just hanging out in tents? Isn't someone trying to relocate them? Are they looking for jobs somewhere? Are there first aid centers, food cantinas, water wells? I mean, what the hell, Forno?"

The Helk nodded knowingly, looking across the tent city. "Hard to fathom, isn't it?"

"Can you do some fathoming for me, then?"

He glanced my way and he narrowed his eyes. He jerked his head at the tents. "You up for a sprint?"

"Sprint?"

"To the nearest tent. Take a peek. Have to be careful, though. Don't want to be discovered."

I frowned, not sure I was up for the challenge. "I'm not going to win a footrace with a Helk." Particularly since I hadn't had a chance to get to the gym for a while.

"I'll hold back a little."

"A lot."

He stood and brushed off his trousers. "Ready?"

I nodded as I rose. "When—"

"Go!" Forno yelled, and he was off.

It wasn't quite a race after all. I followed him, and we just picked our way down the backside of the rise, sidestepping snow and brush, keeping as low as we could. No one seemed to take any interest in us, although I had to believe some of the tent people noticed our scramble toward them. I trailed Forno most of the way, but we weren't going to get separated or lost.

As he ran, Forno pointed to the tent we'd reach first, then made a circling motion with his finger, indicating we should sneak around to its backside. Forno wanted to make sure we were as close to the tent as possible and found a spot out of sight from whatever and whoever would see us. Did he worry about the tent people, or just the brass who put them here?

We made it to the first tent and crept around it a bit, until Forno was sure all was okay. Due to his size, he had to crouch closer to the ground than me to keep his head lower than the top of the tent.

"Let me take a quick peek inside," he whispered. He held a Helk stunner now. I hadn't seen him grab one in the flier. "See if anyone's in there."

"If there is, then what? We keep looking until we find a tent that's empty, right?"

Forno gave me a funny look. If Helks actually had eyebrows, one of Forno's might have risen.

"No?" I said, nervously scanning the next nearest tent.

Forno shook his head. "We *want* someone to be home."

"Some *tent* person to be home," I added.

"Yes."

"And why's that?"

His mouth became a thin line. "You'll see. I found this place, got out of here quick, and now you need to see. Maybe you can help shed some light on this."

He motioned me to hold my spot, then inched around to the front. Once he'd slipped out of sight, I crouched even lower, making myself as small as possible. I pulled the blaster out and held it tight in both hands. Not long after, Forno's shadow appeared, moving around inside. This tent must have had what Forno wanted to show me.

His shadow came close to the side where I crouched. "Come on in," he said, his voice muffled.

Still in a crouch, blaster raised slightly, I worked my way to the front tent flap. I took a moment to glance down the aisle of tents, and six or seven tents away, a man and a woman stood watching me. Somehow, I avoided aiming my blaster at them. I froze, certain they would raise an alarm of some sort. Yell. Scream. Point. Jump up and down.

They just stared at me.

They didn't move a muscle.

"Okay, that's creepy," I muttered aloud. Another few seconds passed and neither of them budged, so I slipped into the tent, happy to get away from them.

I stopped just inside, a chill prickling my skin. Even in the dim light, I could make out a male stretched out on a cot. Human, yes. Alive, yes. Moving, no. His eyes were open and he stared intently at Forno, who was on his knees next to the cot. Forno's head still grazed the top of the tent.

A strange odor permeated the tent, and I couldn't quite place what it was. Strong, though, as if someone had spilled something.

It looked as though the tent person wanted to say something, because his lips moved ever so slightly. No sound came from him, though, and I shot Forno a look, waiting for an explanation. I held my blaster loosely at my side.

"He knows we're here," Forno said in a half whisper. "He's aware, but feeling very little. Can't talk or do much of anything because his whole body has shut down." He shook his head. "I hadn't realized it had gone this far. Not already."

"Jesus, he's in La-La Land," I said. "What's wrong with him?" Scanning the tent, I spotted an open trunk with clothes jammed inside, a small folding table, a small unlit oil lantern, and a cardboard box that I couldn't see into.

"Drugged," Forno said. "Pretty much gone over the edge too. I was afraid of this."

Forno back at it, dredging up more mystery. I was ready to ask more questions, but then my eyes caught a glimpse of something on the dirt.

Blood.

A ragged red square of blood.

As my eyes adjusted to the dim light, I noticed more of it, the blood spattered haphazardly along the floor, each square almost uniform. On the table too. Only . . . the red squares on the table were three-dimensional. They were in stacks. *Piles.*

This wasn't blood.

Forno inclined his head toward the table. "You know what it is?"

I nodded, now connecting the strong odor to the drug. "RuBy."

"RuBy," he repeated. "What do you know about it?"

"Not enough," I said quickly, although I knew it had been developed on Helkunntanas. In my mind, I recalled the holo-recording again, the image of Dorie Senall taking the drug before sliding over to Jennifer Lisle, before asking her about adventure. About the Movement.

"It's nasty stuff," Forno said. "Particularly for humans."

I craned my head around and stared at the tent entrance. "They're all drugged? Five hundred thousand of them?"

Forno got up off his knees and walked in a crouch to me. "In various stages, I imagine," he said. "Men, women, Helk, Memor, and children."

Children?

"No one's looking for them?" I asked.

"No one's looking for them. Family, loved ones, friends—they were all told they didn't make it off Ribon."

"But everyone knew there were refugees. The Union government had to—"

Forno shook his head sadly. "The ships were commandeered on the way through the slot with a recalibration of the tracking signals via cobweb. Brought here to Aryell, hushed up, the datascreen put in place. All very quiet."

Picking one of the red squares off the ground, I felt a surge of panic. That stale cinnamon smell made me wrinkle my nose. All that Forno had shown me, all he'd told me, had brought me to this moment: here I was, on a world far from home, in a tent city of massive size, a wild conspiracy ongoing, holding up a square of red paper. So flimsy. I could crush it, roll it in my hands until it crumbled into dust, harmless. I stole a glance at the man on the cot.

I figured Forno would tell me everything now.

But no.

He didn't know everything. After he showed me this place, he'd said. After he told me about what he knew. The rest of the mystery? Even he didn't know it.

But I knew things he didn't. I hadn't heard from Alan in a while, my code card as silent as the RuBy addict in the tent, but I suspected Alan knew things *I* didn't. If, as Forno had told me at the Flatlands, Alan was in trouble with the bad guys on Temonus, he might know *too* much.

"This is fucked," I said, blinking away the tears brought on by the ever-present smell of too much RuBy.

"Now," Forno said, sitting on the ground, "I'll tell you the rest of what I know about the plan to tear apart the Union of Worlds."

Eighteen

The RuBy hit him quickly, hazing his vision and numbing his head. Arms and legs rubbery. Sitting on the container in front of him, Dorie Senall scanned his face, trying, no doubt, to see how he would handle the stuff. The stuff he didn't think he'd ever taken before.

I am Plenko.

Surely, at some point in his life, he should've popped a RuBy before this. It *was* a Helk drug.

But he was *not* Plenko. Not exactly. This woman who claimed to be his mate had said as much. Needed to find out who he was. Had the person he was before this taken RuBy? Some goddamn wimp, he suspected, since the drug wasn't playing very nice; he was definitely having trouble with it.

He shook his head, groaning as an echo of the knife-pain from earlier washed through him.

"Breathe slow," Dorie Senall said. "Deep. You'll be totally Rubed out in a moment. It hits fast, holds on to you hard, doesn't last too long."

He forced himself to relax, breathing in and out as slowly as possible. It was almost automatic once he'd been reminded about the breathing, as if someone had wired the rest of the procedure directly into his brain. Count backward from ten. Tongue way back in the mouth, teeth apart, breaths full, clench the muscles in legs, arms, stomach. Then relax, head back, and close the eyes.

He closed his eyes and watched the pretty lights.

* * *

"Are you awake? Are you with me?"

The soft voice brought him out of the light show, and he became more aware of the high. A new fog. This fog felt different from that which had rolled in on him when Chinkno and his buddy had stuck him with the needle. Earlier he'd felt euphoria, true enough. But he'd also felt a palpable fear, even though he didn't know what he was afraid of.

This time, the fog gave an understanding. The electricity punched all his pleasure buttons, but the dread had vanished. A shift took place inside his consciousness, one that allowed him to perceive his environment, his world. He felt Helkunntanas, most definitely, but he recognized another imprint. The world of Dorie Senall. The world belonging to the person he had been.

Earth.

"Earth," he whispered, opening his eyes.

Dorie stood on the container, level with his face now, intent on his eyes, which felt heavy with fatigue.

"Yes?" she asked.

"You're from there?"

She shook her head. "No." She laid a hand on his forehead. "Well, I was born there. But I lived most of my life on Ribon."

Sadness washed over him. Her world gone. "I'm sorry."

She shook her head, as if shaking it free of the memories. "No, that's okay. I belong to Union, you see. I just find myself temporarily homeless."

Me too, he thought. Both Earth and Helkunntanas, they didn't exist for him at this moment. He couldn't figure out where he belonged, and the images he had of both flickered in and out like ghosts, not real people, not real places, and the uncertainty weighed on him like stone. Only the RuBy kept the ghost-worlds from crushing him.

"But I found you, Terl," she said. "I found *you.*"

"You said—"

"I know. You're not him. Not exactly. But a part of him is in there with you, whoever you are."

"Will telling me about him help you figure out who I am?"

She shut her eyes a moment, probably working her way through another wave of the RuBy. She whispered something to herself before opening her eyes again, and jumped off the container. She laid down on it, turned onto her side and faced him, then rested her head in the crook of her elbow. He could still see her eyes, and they had softened from the earlier RuBy-induced high. She was coming down from it.

"I met him on Ribon," she said. "Terl Plenko was a First Clan Helk like any other. He didn't advocate violence. 'Union bright,' he used to say to me. 'Union bright.' He said it was a rally cry. Said there used to be an old saying, 'Honor bright.' It was a promise. He *cared* about Union.

"He was smart. He spent most of his career developing many of the DNA locking mechanisms we take for granted these days. He was creating new strategies for the next generation of DNA-locks, contracting with provincial governments, even local Authority and intelligence circles. But also, because of his interest in local politics, he decided to run for provincial mayor of Venasaille. That's when he recruited me. I was a graduate student at the university, and he met with a bunch of us at a rally."

"And you fell in love."

She raised her eyebrows. "Love? No. We married for convenience. We hoped to help knit the rift between Helkunntanas and Earth with a show of commitment. Our secret. We married, but we never consummated it." She smiled. "I've heard stories about that sort of thing between Helks and humans, but still . . . I wasn't too thrilled about finding out."

He looked past her, staring at the hanging red bulb as the RuBy did another tour through his system. He experienced another ghostly image: an apartment, lavishly furnished, high up on a black tower overlooking a city. He saw his ghost-hands, immersed in some kind of activity, a knife of some sort in his hand. Cutting. Carving.

"He was an artist?" he asked.

Dorie smiled. "Indeed. Sculpture, and very good at it. This is helping. Are you seeing things?"

"Some."

She nodded, then rolled onto her back. She seemed to have fought through the effects of the RuBy. "We lived there in Venasaille. I grew to love him in my own way. I know he loved me. He didn't win the election, but he didn't mind. He'd proved his point, made his policies known. He sculpted."

"What were you doing during this?"

"I continued at the university. I did enough rabble-rousing on my own without him. Terl had introduced me to RuBy, but had warned me about long-term use. I didn't start abusing the drug until later. Until after . . ."

She trailed off, and his body reminded him that the RuBy still had its claws in him. The fog had dissipated a little, but the drug's strength still summoned enough ghosts to help him follow Dorie's story. His eyes closed again.

Evening. On the roof of the tower, lying on a cot, her presence at his side. Looking up at the reddish moon that dominated the sky. Coral.

"We took a vacation trip to Coral," she said.

He nodded as the image haunted him. "You lost him."

"He excused himself at the rock quarry where we were taking a tour of the mining facility there. The Rock Dome had been mined out for several years, but there always seemed to be people there. Anyway, he said he wouldn't be long. 'Union bright,' he said, and slipped away to use the bathroom. Security reported later that his ident card had been used to leave the Rock Dome. But he never used it again after that. He vanished."

And then reappeared, he thought.

The Movement of Worlds leader. The more Dorie talked about it, the more he understood he was not really Terl Plenko. Not on the inside, anyway.

What had happened to Plenko?

The ghosts were leaving him as he came down from the RuBy, the room around him assuming its former shape and colors. He tried not to give in to it, hoping to keep it with him, or to at least integrate the fading experience with the newly discovered images of his consciousness. Would those stay with him when the effects wore off completely? Would he understand then who he was?

Perhaps as he reentered normality, he would let go of the Plenko patterns and change his personality. Alter his defenses. Pliable, bendable, like iron in the fire.

Before Dorie, before the RuBy, he had believed he was a Helk. He believed he didn't care about anything or about anyone. Something else had a hold of him now, and he didn't like it. Also, the fire seemed to be winning, and a few of the pains he'd felt upon first waking here started making themselves known again.

"I hit the RuBy hard," Dorie said after the long silence. "I did everything Terl had told me not to do with it." A tear rolled down the side of her face even as she tried to turn away to keep it hidden. "There were days I didn't get out of bed, almost comatose. There were days I went out into Venasaille and partied until the wee hours, having almost no recollection of what happened. Not so bright, my Union."

She wiped the tear with her hand, rubbing it out like an erasure, from her chin to the corner of her eye. Then she sat up and stared at him, her brown eyes moist. He waited for her to collect herself.

"During one of the days inside, zonked on RuBy, I lost myself. I have a vague recollection of all these hands grabbing me, holding me." She shook her head slowly, an almost imperceptible motion. "I woke up here, on Temonus."

"In this place?" A sharp pain tore up his side and he grimaced, placing a hand near his hip.

"Nearby. In a house where I live now in the Helk district. Are you feeling sharp pains?"

He nodded. "A little."

"RuBy's worn off."

"I figured."

"I don't know if I should give you any more right now. Not before . . . well, later on . . ."

Another stab pierced his stomach and he exhaled noisily. "I can manage for a while. Go on."

"Not much more to tell," she said. "Terl started popping up

around the Union, making his Movement known, started doing his thing. I couldn't believe it. It didn't sound like him at all."

"And he showed up here?"

"He showed up here," she echoed. "I was waiting tables. Turns out he now owns the place. He clocked me out, took me to my house, and told me I was done working. Limited my freedom, assigned some of his cronies to me. You met a few earlier."

"Chinkno?"

"Tam Chinkno, his top guy. And others you need to remember. Tony Koch. Tom Knox."

A pain hit below his shoulder, in his chest, right as a tendril of the non-RuBy fog swept through him. Koch, Knox. The names seemed familiar. Why?

"I can't know for sure," she went on, "but I've been here on Temonus almost a year, with very little access to anyone. From time to time, Terl has come and talked to me. One minute he seems to long for the old days, but the next minute I don't believe a word of it. He doesn't come on any regular schedule, and every time I see him he looks more haggard, more irritable. Even Chinkno is nervous around him."

"You used that to your advantage when I showed up."

Dorie nodded. "I knew you were not my Plenko. I knew it for the same reason I knew the Plenko who owns this restaurant is not my Plenko. My Plenko was killed. Murdered. Do you follow me?"

"A little," he said, wincing at a number of pains that hit him all over, one after another. "The Plenko who came to you here is not the Plenko you fell in love with. He's no more the real Plenko than I am."

And so why the hell were there so many of them? Of him?

"It's my secret," she said. "The one I told you about. For a little while, I wasn't sure about you."

He looked toward the wooden door, looking weak and not-so-well insulated. "Should you be talking to me in here?"

"No one but Plenko gives a shit about me. And he does because he thinks I know something—" She stopped and shook her head. "Well. I've got them fooled. They think Plenko has a hold on me. I did my Dorie-strung-out-on-RuBy tough-girl act to win over

Chinkno once I realized the truth about you. It didn't take long after looking at you. Listening to you. I know who my Plenko was, and there's no doubt about who *I* am."

"But you know more than just whether Plenko is Plenko or not. You know something bigger."

She nodded, and her eyes glinted with excitement. "Plenko's revolution isn't his own." She stood suddenly, came close. Her voice lowered to a whisper. "He's being used. It's not just a revolution, it's an invasion."

"What?" he whispered back.

"It's a thousand monkey wrenches thrown into the inner workings of the Union. And you, my unknown friend, are right in the middle of it."

Who cares about revolution?

Thoughts he'd had earlier when waking up in this room returned. He'd thought he was a Helk. When he'd decided nothing mattered. When he was ready to give up.

Who cares about Union?

Something had a hold of him. A fire inside. A fire that was growing, changing him. A fire RuBy kept at bay.

Who cares about humans, Memors, even Helks? Fuck Helkunntanas.

Yes, he had thought that earlier, in this very room. Indeed, RuBy kept the fire under control, but RuBy had started it all.

Who cares about goddamn Alan Brindos?

He stood up so quickly, Dorie fell backward onto the container she'd sat on earlier.

"Alan Brindos."

"What?" she said, getting up.

"That's who I was. The name just came to me." But who exactly *was* Alan Brindos?

She walked back to him, motioning him to sit down again so she could look into his face. "This is good. It's coming back to you, as I hoped. I was afraid the RuBy wouldn't work this way."

"What way? What's it doing?"

"It's counteracting the stuff they injectioned you with."

He swallowed hard, not liking where this was going. The fire overtaking him chose that moment to scrunch his gut like a fist squeezing an inflated balloon. He cried out as the pain punched him there, then pounded him seemingly everywhere else inside.

Dorie put a finger to her lips. "I know, I know, it hurts, but you don't want them coming back in here now."

"Maybe that *is* what I want. That injection stopped the pain the first time."

"No, you don't."

"I don't?"

"You're this Alan Brindos, whoever he was. Do you want to be a Helk?"

"I don't know. I doubt it."

"Do you like being used? Do you want to be a part of chaos? Or do you want to be free?"

"I don't even know what that *means*."

She reached up and held his hairless leathery head in both hands, her eyes radiating kindness. "It means, Alan Brindos, that you have a chance, and the Union has a chance. Union bright." She gave him a sad smile. "But if I don't free you, if you don't figure this out, you will die."

He stared at her hard, and his own eyes watered as the floodgates of memory let loose.

Alan Brindos.

The pain doubled, everywhere, as if dozens of red-hot brands burned through his skin, torching his inner organs, but he clenched his teeth, somehow managing to keep screams from escaping.

With the pain came understanding. With the pain came everything.

His partner, Dave Crowell. The National Intelligence Organization. Everything flooded back. The Conduit. Plenko. Joseph. *Meet my One.* And—

Dorie Senall.

"Dorie," Brindos whispered. "Oh, Dorie."

She frowned, pulling back a little. "Listen, I know it's hard to understand. I've got to give you this now." She pulled out another square of RuBy, rolled it for him, and coaxed it into his mouth between his teeth. "I know you don't want to die, so if we figure it out—"

"No," he said as the RuBy dissolved on his tongue. "It's you. Your apartment at Tempest Tower. I saw you fall off the balcony."

"What?" Her eyes went wide as Brindos leaned back against the redbrick wall.

"Dorie, I saw you die."

Nineteen

How I'll tell you about the plan to tear apart the Union of Worlds. That sentence from Forno should've sent an electric current through my body, shaking me from top to bottom, but when he said it, I didn't feel a thing.

Of *course* that was the plan. It had been Plenko's goal long before I'd signed on with the NIO. But that wasn't everything. Without a doubt, Alan and I had become involved in something much larger than Plenko's Movement. We were part of a large-scale Union-shattering plot, one that Forno had also stumbled onto.

"Is it safe to talk here?" I glanced at the RuBy addict on the cot, who lay still, staring wide-eyed at the top of the tent.

Forno said, "Not even remotely safe."

"Oh," I said. "That's . . . encouraging."

He nodded at the cot. "He's not going to tell anyone a thing. Poor fellow will be dead before too long."

I gulped, and I imagined I could actually taste the RuBy at the back of my throat. I'd never tried the drug, and although the cinnamon odor was strong, I didn't know how it really tasted. Another five minutes in this place and I believed I'd be addicted to the stuff myself.

"All right, tell me," I said. If we truly were not safe, even hidden in here, then I wanted him to get on with it. I squeezed purposely on the blaster I still held at my side. "Start with the Conduit. It's supposed to be a weather control device. I read the specs."

Forno drew his knees to his chest and wrapped his massive arms around them. "That was the story the Science Consortium told. Hell, they even *showed* it. In theory, it could work that way. But it was designed, ultimately, to do something else."

"To do what?"

"To replicate people," he said, his eyes distant. Then he shook his head. "Well, no, that's not the right word. They're altering them."

That part seemed only too true, considering what I'd experienced so far, and what Alan had told me from his end, before he went silent.

"Helks?" I asked. "Humans?"

"Anyone changed into anyone," Forno said, his voice hushed. "The tech I came across in the NIO basement is way beyond me. I did my best to understand and internalize it, because I had no way to transfer the information. The Science Consortium's using ultrafast x-ray technology, something light-years ahead of anything I've heard about. Something about acceleration and diffraction. Heating matter, shocking it. Signals shooting through a superaccelerator."

"Jesus. The Conduit's an accelerator?"

Forno nodded. "In part, due to its ultra thin wire. The Conduit's used to change these pulsed, ultrafast x-rays, and the particle acceleration creates—" He paused, looking me straight in the eye. "Dave, they've discovered how to change the very structure of matter."

Ultra thin wire. I thought back to my encounter with Forno at Floor 13, the warnings, the information about the ultra thin level. He'd hinted then at the Science Consortium's involvement with the NIO, hinted at topics such as Temonus, Ribon, Coral, and the Conduit.

"They've come up with a way to change the physical structure of life forms," I said, trying to follow him. I didn't think he was following himself very well either.

"It's no wonder my brain hurts when I think about this stuff," Forno said.

"Yeah, tell me about it."

I wondered how much of Lorway's Memor know-how figured into this. Did the Memors really have this kind of advanced technology at hand? I didn't think so.

"They've developed nanoscale machines," Forno said. "They can even mutate and engineer chemical reactions in the body, at a molecular level, probably even smaller. They not only change living beings physically, they alter their brain chemistry, essentially allowing them to match anything, or any*one* they have on file."

Making nearly perfect copies.

Forno went on. "They can even give the subjects a type of computer memory, using the ultrafast light pulses in lieu of binary switching. With ease, they could control how much old memory a copy has or doesn't have, depending on its uses. Some of this tech has been around a long time. Nanomachines, in particular. But no one's been able to figure out how nanomaterials *transform*. But this ultrafast acceleration idea? Seems to have done the trick."

"How fast is ultrafast? How thin is ultra thin?"

Forno shrugged. "Approaching the speed of light. And that Conduit wire is minuscule."

Something really bothered me about this. Besides the obvious, of course. I didn't doubt Forno's explanation about the Conduit, but even the idea of superaccelerating via the agency of a thin wire seemed ludicrous. What kind of material could allow that sort of thing? Even I had heard a little about some of this tech, but how could it have made such a giant leap forward in such a short time? The Memors were quiet, often stingy with their technology, but this didn't sound right.

"We're dealing with unknowns here," Forno said, "so if you're thinking about temperatures, superconductivity—I've reached the end of my knowledge base."

"Helk snot," I mumbled, realizing the truth. I glanced quickly at Forno. "Um, sorry."

Forno shrugged. "My snot is not offended."

I walked over to the man on the cot and stared at his red-rimmed eyes. The tent became very still. Sweat cooled my forehead and my own words rumbled in my head.

A flicker in the RuBy addict's eyes. A slight tic along one bottom lid.

Even sitting, Forno's gigantic, silent presence became almost unbearable. I stood there a long time, several minutes passing as I stared into the addict's eyes, Forno waiting me out. Suddenly, I didn't like it. The silence was oppressive. Someone in this tent needed to talk to me.

As if he heard my thoughts, Forno said, "They've subdued these people with RuBy. Why?"

But I had it now. I had it, and I didn't want to have it. As if someone had slapped me on the back of the neck, forcing the words from my throat—words I didn't want to say—I said, "They're making an army."

"An army?"

Now I was ahead of Forno. "New Venasaille—it's a soldier factory. Not an army as we would think of it. It's for a quiet, hidden war, and the soldiers are pawns in the reshaping, with the goal of infiltrating every possible known position of power and prestige. You and I both have already seen it with the NIO and the Kenn."

The evidence in front of me, I still could not come to terms with this new horror. But nothing fit. I couldn't even begin to jam these puzzle pieces together.

"Forno, it makes no sense that the Science Consortium would do this. What could possibly cause five scientists to want to reshape the Union? To want it so bad that they'd do"—I swept my free arm around in a large circle to indicate the tent city—"*this*? These atrocities?"

He shook his head.

Another terrifying realization came to me and I suddenly felt helpless. "Ribon," I said.

"What?" Forno said.

"It was done on purpose."

"Sure. Part of the Movement. An act of terror—"

"*No.* Coral Moon was deliberately thrown into Ribon's path, not to destroy it, not to demonstrate a show of force, but to displace some of the world's population. To give them these refugees to turn into soldiers."

I heard Forno's voice catch in his throat. "How many people *didn't* make it off Ribon alive? They sacrificed a world, decimated its population, all for . . . I lost family there. Friends."

He couldn't finish.

I nodded in sympathy.

And still . . . nothing could make me believe the Science Consortium would stoop to something this evil. I didn't believe Plenko's Movement could have done it. Helkunntanas itself? A world against the Union? Maybe. But why would they want to?

"Something else is going on here," I said. "It's not adding up."

"I agree," Forno said. "Everything that's happened has been done to lead away from the real truth. Plenko's implicated. The Consortium is implicated. The NIO is implicated, the Kenn, maybe even the Memors, the MSA—"

I looked up at Forno. "We can't trust anyone in the NIO. Any one of them could be . . . altered. Like Tim Jim."

"It's the same reason I can't trust anyone on my end, in the Kenn. Crowell, they could be anywhere. Anyone."

"Could they have President Nguyen?"

Forno shrugged. "Maybe. Can't know for sure. What about Plenko? You were on the Movement commission."

"He was a law-abiding citizen, and even ran for office on Ribon. Intelligent. DNA-lock expert. Contracting with big business and big government. His whole Movement is probably a by-product of this larger conspiracy."

Whatever was going on, it had reached a crisis point. New Venasaille's "soldiers" might enter the fray soon.

I looked again at the cot. The man still had not moved. "What happens if these victims don't get the procedure?"

Forno shook his head. "If we managed to free some of these people? The extreme RuBy addiction, the sudden loss of the drug—it would kill anyone human or Memor. Helks might survive."

So who was really behind everything? Who had the power, who had the desire, to do something on such a large, destructive scale? I still couldn't buy the Consortium. I stared hard at the man on the cot, wondering about his fate.

Forno got up from his sitting position and crouched. "What do you think?"

"The Consortium is the logical choice if we're talking about new science, but I don't believe they have the motive."

"That's what I've been thinking."

"Then all we have to do is figure out who does. Who would create this in order to do serious harm on a galactic scale?"

I waited for Forno to say "no clue," but he just stared at the cot.

The real Plenko could be alive, but deep down I thought it unlikely. Which other "originals" besides Plenko were out there? "Plenko had nothing to do with the Conduit disaster?"

Forno looked a bit surprised. "No, of course not. Why would he sabotage the very thing that made him? Experts who've looked at the crash vid now say it was a servo-robot that reprogrammed the ship midflight. The damage to the robot was extensive, but they might still find evidence of who tampered with it. But it'll be covered up by the NIO, or Temonus Authority if they're compromised as well."

"So someone else knows about the Conduit's true purpose? Tried to destroy it?" At a high cost, I thought, thinking of the civilians killed, the damage done to East City.

"No clue."

"And after all that, the Conduit's still working, isn't it?"

"Don't know that either. It doesn't seem possible, with the current state of the tower, but I've not been able to get close. It could be working well enough, which is why you need to find and warn your partner."

"Unless it's too late."

Forno paused a moment. "Yes. It would be better to completely take out that tower."

"If I could trust the NIO, trust *any*one, it would be as simple as calling and getting an Ark to Temonus to finish the job."

I heard the unmistakable whine, barely audible, of a reverse thruster. Some kind of ship was making its way toward us. The wind had picked up a little too, the tent ruffling a bit. The flapping of the tent canvas reminded me of sailboats in the breeze during lazy days as a teenager at the Hammond Marina on Flathead Lake. But here, in this tent city of pain and death, the snaps and pops sounded like distant gunshots.

"We'd better go," Forno said.

I stood. Took one last look at the man on the cot. "There's nothing we can do for him? For any of them?"

Forno shrugged. "Some of them, maybe, if they're not too far along."

"All right," I said, taking one last look around the tent. I picked up a handful of red squares and slipped the RuBy into my pants pocket. "Let's get out of here."

Forno poked his head out the tent door for a moment, then said, "C'mon" as he disappeared outside. I followed right behind him, keeping close. It was late afternoon. The man and woman who'd been standing in the aisle of tents had gone. We backtracked around the tent and headed up the small hill. A cold wind now blew steadily, spring's foothold in the last gasps of winter weakening. I couldn't wait to get back to the shelter of the ship.

Shouts from below interrupted my thoughts. Forno looked back an instant before I did, then said, "Trouble."

About two dozen people, presumably all refugees who weren't totally flipped out on RuBy, had left the perimeter of New Venasaille, in pursuit, flanked by two armed and uniformed Helk guards. They were too far away to tell what clan they were.

"Just when I thought things couldn't get any worse," Forno called over his shoulder.

"We've got enough distance on them!" I yelled, and we ran faster, scrambling up the icy slope, no longer worried about stealth. I had my blaster, and Forno had his stunner, but there wasn't any reason to open fire yet. I had my finger caps, fully charged, thanks to Forno, but those only worked in close proximity. Once we made it over the top of the rise, we no longer saw them, but I didn't believe for a second that they'd stopped following.

We entered the trees, heading for the clearing where we'd left Forno's flier. I glanced back again before the trees enveloped us, and they still hadn't crested the little hill. At least the flier had a quick start-up sequence; I felt confident we could at least get off the ground before the pursuit reached us. After that, I had no idea. Did they have any anti-aircraft weapons? Something other than the datascreen to warn off uninvited guests? None had been in evidence on our arrival.

As we neared the clearing, The trees thinned.

"We'll make it!" Forno yelled.

I took a deep breath as I pushed myself, inching closer to Forno. Even without my workouts lately, I was in good shape, and the run felt almost exhilarating. We burst out into the clearing. Once we got out of there, we just had to figure out who we were really dealing with, find them, and head off their invasion somehow. Easy.

Forno had stopped dead in his tracks. I nearly ran into him.

"We did in fact park here, right?" he said.

"What?" I looked around his body, which had been blocking my view.

The flier was gone.

"That," Forno said, his voice distant, "is bad."

"You've got to be joking," I said, my eyes automatically scanning the clearing for a sign of the missing flier. My own voice cracked a little. Heart pounding, I felt the blood drain from my head as I stared in disbelief at the empty clearing. No way out of here.

The mob from the tent city came into the clearing behind us, and we turned and froze. They stopped at the tree line, and the Helks, unflinching, looking quite huge next to the refugees, aimed their stunners at us. I guessed they were Second Clan. No time to make a run for it, no chance to get to the far side and try and lose them somewhere in the trees.

"Now it's my turn to say it," Forno said, looking at me. I raised my eyebrows, then he shook his head and said, "Helk snot."

I didn't even smile. "What was it you said earlier about things not getting any worse?"

"I don't know what I was thinking," he confessed.

Someone grunted behind us, then began to laugh. A woman's laugh, mocking and caustic. "It just got worse," she said, and the air went out of me. I felt like a total fool, because I knew right away who it was.

I turned around slowly, as did Forno, and I stared hard into the smug, self-assured face of Jennifer Lisle. She had come out of the trees on the other side and now stood there, her defensive posture absolutely textbook perfect.

Her NIO-issue blaster aimed at my head.

Twenty

Dorie Senall seemed on the verge of bursting into tears. Could he blame her? Brindos would have found his own death pretty hard to take. He felt guilty thinking it, but he was glad someone else had to process this heavy shit for a change.

Then again, maybe he *had* died, thinking again about his Helk suit.

Still leaning against the brick wall, he relaxed in the warmth of the second dose of RuBy starting to take hold, even as Dorie struggled with the news about her fall from her balcony in Vena-saille. She closed her eyes, fighting the emotions, then he closed his, welcoming the RuBy relief. Neither of them spoke for a while, and during the silence Brindos's memories solidified. Mentally, he felt like himself again. When he opened his eyes and looked back at Dorie, her eyes were already open, and a new hardness had set in them, as if she had passed off her death as a momentary loss, something she'd practiced plenty of times. Now that she'd dealt with it, she was ready to move on.

But he doubted it would be that easy.

"It happened to me and I didn't even know it," she said, almost whispering.

And yet Brindos was sure she must have wondered. Her Plenko had vanished, she had lost time, woke up here in Midwest City, and now the Terl Plenko who was not her Plenko had appeared to her. . . .

Then Brindos showed up: Brindos/Plenko.

He couldn't imagine how anyone could have accomplished such a thing, but the Dorie who fell to her death on Ribon had been a double.

"That time before I woke up here," she said. "That's when it happened."

"You were . . . copied."

"And *you* are a copy, Mr. Brindos," she said.

"But not a copy. I'm still Brindos inside, thanks to you." Should he tell her he was NIO? She had a link to Plenko and the Movement. One Dorie was dead, but this one still dealt regularly with Plenko and the other Helks.

"Don't thank me yet. They're still planning on using you somehow." Dorie lowered her eyes. "As I'm still being used."

"This invasion you talked about."

She nodded. "A lot of people are being changed. Altered. Even the Plenko who hangs around here is being used."

"Used by whom?"

Dorie shook her head. "I don't know."

She didn't know, he didn't know, and he wondered where Crowell was, and if he knew. If this was the kind of trouble Brindos had managed to get himself into, what sort of craziness had Crowell found on his end? Probably dealing with his own doubles. Brindos had no way of knowing, because his code card had disappeared after the run-in with Tom Knox, before meeting Plenko and Joseph. *Joseph.* When Joseph had done his thing—

Fingers glowing white.

Joseph was not human. How could he be? It couldn't have been some parlor trick. He wasn't a Helk. He wasn't Memor. So who was he? *What* was he?

Brindos leaned forward, away from the wall and closer to Dorie's penetrating dark eyes. He decided he'd tell her about the NIO and let whatever happened happen. The NIO he once knew didn't matter much right now anyway. They were part of the problem. "Dorie, I was contracting for the NIO before all this happened."

She nodded. "I figured it had to be something like that."

He relaxed a little, knowing she had intuited some of it already. "Will you help me? I've got no other way to go here."

"Yes, of course. I was willing to help you even before I knew who you were."

Right to the point, then. "Do you know how the copying is being done?"

"Something to do with the Conduit."

"What, exactly?"

"I don't quite know. From what I've gleaned, they have a scan or a pattern of Plenko, and they use it to create copies of him out of other people—like you."

"And they have a scan of you, and they made a copy of you."

"I guess so."

"Do you know anyone or have you seen anyone around here who calls himself Joseph? Or Joe? I was *here* with him. We ate, and Tom Knox was our waiter." He winced at the memory. "Or so I think. Knox attacked me outside in the back alley. Did a hell of a number on me."

Dorie was silent for a time. Then she shook her head. "I don't recognize the name."

He closed his eyes again. Thoughts were still catching up to his Brindos self. The RuBy kept the pain manageable, but didn't do him much good when trying to think cogently.

Okay, so after his run-in with Tom Knox, aka Jordan Dak the waiter, he woke up at the Orion Hotel with eighteen hours of his life missing, perhaps in the same way Dorie had lost time and ended up in Midwest City.

So had he been scanned then? Prepared for the process somehow? Maybe. But now he was a copy of Plenko, and that had happened after Joseph knocked him out. *After* the Conduit disaster. That meant the device still worked, even with the tower down. He didn't even want to think about how that was possible, considering the differences in their sizes. Crowell had the better head for science, but he doubted even he could figure this one out.

Most likely Tom Knox was a copy of Jordan Dak. Somehow. It was *Dak* who took their orders that night. Tom Knox happened to be at the Restaurant, in the so-called authentic Helk area, or this very storeroom, and had listened in somehow and heard his name. Or, more likely, considering what happened to Brindos later, he had been waiting for him. Knocked him unconscious in the alley, and Jordan Dak kept waiting his tables, oblivious. Dak came out to the alley ten minutes after Knox and found Brindos unconscious. Concern for his own safety could have made Dak pull a knife. Brindos must have woken and seen Dak/Knox with the knife and panicked, thinking Knox was going to finish the job. Used his finger caps in order to get the jump on him, then used Dak's own knife to kill him. Joseph said he'd seen Brindos attack and kill the waiter. That was possible, but he didn't remember any of it, including their escape from the alley and the subsequent hours at the hotel.

But the timing: the body wasn't discovered until midnight.

Tom Knox must have gone back to wait on Dak's tables for an hour. Long enough to allow Joseph to do what he needed to do to get them back to the hotel. He'd concocted a whale of a story when Brindos asked what happened.

He rubbed his temples, opened his eyes.

Dorie stared, lines creasing her forehead. "You doing okay, Mr. Brindos?"

Managing a smile, he nodded, then sat down again. "So you don't recognize the name Joseph."

"No. Is he someone the NIO wants?"

"The NIO may want him, or they may already know about him."

"What does he look like?"

"Tall, skinny man. Older, maybe in his sixties, early seventies. I don't know his last name, but he put me out cold somehow. Plenko was there, and he called Joseph his One. Then Joseph did something with his fingers. Something . . . alien."

"Alien?" she repeated, her voice taking on a tone of disbelief. Then her face brightened. "Wait. I don't know if it's him or not, but on several occasions I've seen an older gentleman with silver hair talking to Terl here, in the authentic portion. A tall man, quite thin, shabby clothes."

Brindos perked up a little, suddenly hopeful. He had a lead on Joseph. "That sounds like him."

"I don't know anything about him. Just thought maybe he was a restaurant supplier or something."

"When I met him, he was a concierge at the Orion Hotel."

"That's a nice place," she said.

"I have to go back there."

"You can't."

"If he's still there, if I figure out who he really is—"

"He could be a copy."

He blinked at her.

"Or," she said, "the person who put you out could be a copy, and the Orion concierge could be the original."

Had Brindos in fact been dealing with two different Josephs all this time? If, as Dorie had suggested, there was an original and a copy, he could've talked open-air baseball with Joseph one day, and found himself knocked senseless by a different Joseph another day.

"But," he said, "if he's alien . . ."

"He *looked* human, right? He could have copied himself to blend in." She shook her head. "What are we talking about here? Am I actually believing you when you say new, unknown aliens are trying to take over the Union? I'm not even high on RuBy anymore." She managed a small smile.

"You're the one who mentioned invasion."

"I just didn't think it would be . . . aliens."

"I have to find out," Brindos insisted. "The Orion is the only place I know where to look."

"You can't."

"I *must*."

"Look who you are! You're not Alan Brindos on the outside. Terl Plenko can't just waltz into a posh hotel in the middle of Midwest City! There's a price on your head."

He stood quickly, startling Dorie. She leaned back, even though he circled right, hand on his forehead, thinking. Difficult, though, with the RuBy haze muddling his brain.

She was right, of course. He wouldn't have a chance getting to the Orion Hotel. He couldn't walk up to the main lobby and ask for Joseph.

But Dorie could.

He paced a complete circle and stared down at her, the idea already buzzing.

It must have showed in his eyes, because Dorie shook her head emphatically. "No, no, I can't. They watch me like— There's no way Terl's men will let me out of the Helk district."

"There must be a way."

"They escort me from the Restaurant to the house two blocks away, and back again for my work shifts."

"I'll help you get past them."

Dorie smirked. "How are you going to do that?"

"By doing a little of what you do. Play-act. If you can convince them that I'm your husband, I can convince them, as their boss, to do something that will keep them out of the way."

"Such as?"

"The Helks who brought me in here said I'd been gone a week?"

"Yeah, around there."

"Well, then. They can't begrudge a husband and wife their time alone."

"Mate," Dorie said. "We don't use that term. So we'll finally consummate the marriage after how many years?"

"Do they know we haven't?"

Dorie raised her eyebrows. "I guess not."

He smiled. "I'll give Chinkno and whoever else—"

"Knox."

"Knox. I'll give them the night off."

The look on Dorie's face told him she was warming up to the idea. The corners of her mouth twitched upward, her nose flaring just slightly.

"I think it'll work," he said.

"What I think is that you're totally Rubed out."

A little pinch in his side made him wince. "And thank Union for that. I'd rather not feel that other pain ever again."

Dorie reached up on her tiptoes and touched his cheek, her face darkening. "Oh, Mr. Brindos," she said, "I'm afraid you're not going to have any say in that."

Dorie left Brindos in the room for about fifteen minutes while he nervously thought about her statement. He didn't like the sound of it at all. Earlier, she had told him that he would die if she couldn't "free" him. The little twinges had come back, and he worried he might not get more RuBy before the twinges became excruciating pain.

She returned with some clothes: a gray one-piece tunic similar to what Red and Blue had worn out in the alley. She left again while he put them on, the tunic a little loose, but serviceable. When she came through the door again, she had a simmering plate of gabobilecks and Helk red rice. He hadn't eaten since his earlier trip here with Joseph. This time, the food was authentic, and he devoured it with no ill effects, ignoring the utensils, spicy juice dripping down his chin. He wanted seconds, but didn't send her back for more. Even playing the part of Plenko, he couldn't just wander around the Restaurant looking for more food, since its patrons weren't all Helks. Someone—the wrong someone—could recognize him and alert the authorities.

Dorie left again with the dirty plate, then came back to the storeroom, ready to move them out of there, ready to blend in. As she put it, she hadn't seen face or fur of Plenko's Helk entourage: Chinkno and Knox, both of whom had been around the Restaurant when Brindos got pulled in.

"I'd rather you not run into them considering the state you were in when you got here," she said. "You're well within your rights as Plenko to walk me out of here to my place, but it would be better if we went unnoticed."

A pain similar to a punch to the stomach made him suddenly double over. He forced back a groan.

"This is all for now," she said, and gave him half a square of RuBy. "It'll ease the pain, and it's not enough to make you stagger through the hallway like a drunk."

He nodded, letting the RuBy dissolve on his tongue. He motioned for her to go ahead. Once she deemed it safe, Dorie led him out into the hallway and they turned right toward the back door. The hallway was as he remembered it, the lighting yellowish and dim, the space wide enough to accommodate several Helk waiters side by side. A tinge of Helk spices and an almost overpowering smell of boiled meat bombarded him. A constant clatter of dishes came from the kitchen area behind them, and just before they reached the entrance to the authentic portion of the restaurant, a loud crash from within, followed by some choice Helk curses, made Dorie jerk back in surprise.

She recovered quickly, walked a little faster, and motioned him farther down the hallway. "Hurry," she whispered as they approached the exit to the back alley.

Brindos had no idea what he might say if one of the Helks was out back. Luckily, no one lay in wait in the alley. Dusk was coming on. He'd been in that little storeroom almost a whole day. He glanced to his right at the narrow passageway he'd squeezed through last night, then they headed in the opposite direction, their footsteps on the cobblestones echoing off the brick walls.

"It's not far," Dorie said over her shoulder once they came out into a main street. The stone buildings here seemed to be mostly homes and apartments, some of them deserted, and they crowded the street, making him feel a bit claustrophobic.

Joseph had known about the original Helk settlement in this district. He'd seemed knowledgeable about a lot of things regarding Midwest City, but what had he really admitted that night? That the city planners would demolish the old buildings, modernize the district, and squeeze out whatever Helk heritage remained here. Joseph hadn't really given it much weight, a typical reaction of Temonus colonists who didn't exactly care about Helks and their claims to the planet. That, more than anything, convinced Brindos that the Joseph from the Orion Hotel was different than the Joseph with the glowing fingers.

The question was: did Joseph know he'd been copied? Their conversation at the Blue Rocket bar, where he'd learned about the murder of Jordan Dak, suggested he might.

"Have I lost you again?" Dorie asked.

Brindos blinked away the thoughts. "Sorry. Found me." His little twinges had gone away, thanks to the RuBy, and he took a moment to focus on their surroundings.

They rounded a small bend and came upon a one-story home that seemed almost out of place compared to the buildings around it. It was a wooden building instead of stone or brick, painted red, four tall windows on the side facing the street, all intact. Set back a little farther from the street than the other structures, the home had an actual sidewalk to the front door. Although the day had not completely given way to darkness, a solitary lamppost behind them had flickered on.

"Home sweet home," Dorie said. It was an Earth saying, so the sarcasm in her voice had extra punch. She'd been born on Earth, but she hadn't told him how long she'd lived there before moving to Ribon. Temonus was not her home; this little *house* was not her home, and she was not happy about it.

The door was wooden too, painted yellow like the back door of the Restaurant. As Dorie walked up to it, Brindos wondered if it would be locked. Would Plenko let her have a key if they were watching her, escorting her from place to place?

But she did have one. After fumbling around in her pockets, she produced a single silver object. "They let me unlock, open, and close the door," Dorie explained. "To make the place feel more like my own, I guess."

She pushed the door open, letting a little light into the dark room.

They saw the person sitting calmly in the large upholstered chair in front of them, feet flat on the floor, arms behind the head, eyes reflecting the light of the lamppost out on the street. They froze, and Brindos made ready to do something desperate if needed, but the person made no move toward them, no threatening gestures. Brindos's eyes hadn't adjusted to the lighting, but he had no doubts about what he was looking at, and it wasn't really a person.

It was a Helk.

The Helk fidgeted a little, as if trying to get more comfortable in the chair. Brindos rolled over in his mind what he was going to say, unprepared for this moment, even though he'd been the one to suggest giving Dorie's watch-Helks the night off. A wrong gesture, an incorrect turn of phrase, or a failure to recognize which Helk sat here in the near darkness—well, he'd be found out and turned over to the Midwest authorities. *Look who we found!* they'd say. *The evil terrorist Terl Plenko!*

No more Union bright. Good-bye, Union. Good-bye, Alan.

He didn't have a clue, of course. Chinkno? Knox? Koch? Dorie hadn't moved a muscle, and wasn't giving any hints. Brindos glanced quickly in her direction; her eyes were wide, mouth open.

Say something, Dorie. Help me out here.

She remained silent, so Brindos took a chance and stepped forward onto a hardwood floor, raising a hand in a nonthreatening greeting. "It's okay," he said, his voice low and guttural. "I've got her."

"Oh, do you, now?" the Helk said.

Brindos nodded, putting a hand on Dorie's shoulder. "Going to spend some time . . . with my mate."

The Helk laughed. "That's funny, coming from you." He reached over and turned on the lamp on the side table. "It's actually something I would've said."

Terl Plenko stood up and grinned, and Brindos felt a pang in his heart, which was not at all a pleasant sensation considering its new position in his body. Plenko walked over slowly, eyes glittering with amusement.

Goddamn it, Brindos thought to himself, looking at Plenko. *At me.*

Plenko had come close, his face inches away. He looked into Brindos's eyes. "Well now, this is quite impressive," he said, and he seemed genuinely surprised. "They certainly did a nice job on you."

Twenty-one

Jennifer Lisle stared at us over the barrel of her blaster, and by the look on her face I could tell she was more than pleased to have us in this position. She wore jeans and a dark blue sweater. At least I thought it was dark blue. The sun had dipped behind the mountains, and the sky had darkened quickly.

The uniformed Helks had separated themselves from the mob, coming up on either side of us, their own weapons raised.

Jennifer nodded at one of the Helks and they both moved toward us, one coming right up to me. He made a "give it to me" motion with his stunner, and I reluctantly gave him my blaster. Forno was relieved of his weapon too.

"Code card," Jennifer said.

I pulled it out of my pants pocket and threw it at her.

"Your flier is impounded and will be thoroughly checked," she said. "New transport will arrive soon, and we'll return to New Venasaille." Now that the Helks had their weapons trained on us, she put her own blaster away. "I've got better things to do than chase you two around."

I wondered what things. "Kidnapping," I said. "Sedition. Enslavement. That sort of thing."

Jennifer smirked. "Funny man, Mr. Crowell."

Next to me, Forno cleared his throat. He fidgeted, then bumped me a little with his arm. He was trying to tell me something, and I knew what it was.

Everything she had told me at the Flaming Sea had been on the level. No way would she have said those things if she was going to put a gun to my head later and take me prisoner. This wasn't the Jennifer Lisle I'd talked to earlier in the day. She wasn't dressed the same. Her demeanor had changed. If Forno hadn't told me his story, if I hadn't figured out who this was, I might have given away something about Katerina Parker. Or Cara Landry.

"You're a copy," I said.

Jennifer shrugged. "I'm real enough, Mr. Crowell. Oh, and we know all about your visit to the Flaming Sea. I guess Mr. Forno here told you what he knows about us?" She reached out and ran her finger along my jawline, the trace of wind catching her blond hair and blowing it across her face.

I narrowed my eyes at her, holding back my anger. I wanted to reach out and smack her. Lean into her and zip her with my finger caps. Wouldn't come to anything, of course. Probably get me knocked in the head, but I wanted to do it more than anything.

"Who's done this to you?" I said to her dark eyes.

She backed away from me, glancing at Forno. "Who they are does not matter. I don't matter, you don't matter." She looked at me again. "Names mean nothing. What matters is ozsc."

Substance. Soul.

"That's a Helk concept," I said. "You're not a Helk."

"The concept is appropriate. We are One. That is all."

I heard a rustling behind me, and after a moment, the Helk closest to Forno walked away toward the sound. When I braved a look over my shoulder, I saw that the tent mob had turned away and were headed back to New Venasaille, escorted by the armed Helk. They disappeared into the trees.

Almost immediately, I heard the whine of an approaching craft; from the sound of it, this flier was larger than Forno's flier, probably a Helk transport ship, the thrumming engines ominous in the near dark of the clearing. I looked up and caught sight of the craft as it flew in over the tops of the trees from the direction the mob had gone. It hovered over us for a bit, its landing lights blinking; then, after a shriek of its thrusters, it settled down in the very spot where Forno's flier had landed earlier.

The engine noise lessened and a moment later a side door

opened up in the craft. It was so dark now I could barely discern the outline of the hull. Someone ducked through the door and jumped the short distance to the ground.

The figure came up behind Jennifer Lisle, walking so slowly that I thought maybe some sort of handicap was holding it back. But no, not an "it." She was a human female. I saw the shadow of long, flowing hair, a thin frame, a careful, purposeful walk.

"Meet my One," Jennifer Lisle said.

I shivered at those words, at the slow reveal of this person. She slipped in next to Jennifer and I saw her face, saw who she was, and I sucked in my breath. Next to me, Forno swore.

Cara.

Oh, please, not Cara. *Not Cara.*

She took another step toward me.

"Cara?" I whispered.

Forno jumped in quickly. "I swear I didn't know."

But it didn't matter. I knew it wasn't really her. A copy, of course. She didn't say anything to me, just scanned my face without emotion. Without . . . *anything.* Her eyes were glassy, the pupils dilated, and they barely moved in their sockets. I just stared into those dead eyes, ignoring the others in the clearing, and a feeling of helplessness overcame me; my earlier shiver returned, my whole body quivering. I felt absolutely afraid of her.

This wasn't just another copy.

I could read the *otherness* of her from her demeanor. This wasn't simply a matter of the Science Consortium altering her molecular structure and manipulating or mutating her DNA or brain chemistry. It wasn't that she was just a pattern, a perfect copy. It wasn't just binary switching. It wasn't just nanomaterials transforming.

She was something else.

A barely perceptible smile crossed her face, as if she realized that I understood at that moment what she was. I *didn't* know what she was—not at all. I needed to know, though. I needed to know for the sake of the entire Union.

Cara's smile—or what passed for a smile—was fleeting, and disappeared just before she turned on her heel and walked calmly toward the transport.

Jennifer Lisle motioned us after her. "Watch out for his finger caps," she said to the Helk. "We'll discharge them inside."

I groaned to myself as the remaining Helk moved in and nudged me with his stunner.

"Move," he growled.

He herded us into the transport. A row of seats with armrests in the back faced another row. The Helk pushed us into the back row, then sat in one of the rear-facing seats, on the end farthest from the door. Jennifer Lisle and Cara sat next to him.

Before I could even attempt anything, Jennifer reached over and covered my hands with a neuralizer designed for the purpose of discharging finger caps quickly. Its soft material automatically formed to my hands and I soon felt the tingle that meant I had lost the charge in my caps.

I stared at Cara. She had yet to say a word. She looked as though she might melt into the seat, she was so calm. Hands folded in her lap, she didn't even flinch when the transport rumbled with sound, shook madly, then took off.

I held on to the armrest, my head against the back cushion, but I never looked away from Cara. The corners of her mouth lifted ever so slightly. It wasn't so much a smile as it was a gesture of contempt, and coming from someone like Cara, whom I had loved and cherished, it made me cold inside.

Still silent, she lifted her right hand, spreading her fingers as if she hoped to teach me what the number five was.

Then, slowly, her fingernails, followed by her fingers, began to glow. The glow intensified, enveloping her hand in a blinding, white light.

I didn't remember passing out. I awoke thinking: *what the hell was that?* Cara putting me under with a glowing hand? Cara the copy. Cara the *alien*. I had decided that much just before getting into the transport. She was not just a copy of the original Cara, but a transformed version of an entity here to invade the Union.

Mouth dry, head throbbing, I needed only a moment to figure out where I was. They'd taken me back to New Venasaille and dumped me on a cot in one of the tents. It was dark. I wondered what time it was, whether just past sundown or almost sunrise. I had no way of knowing at this point, my code card gone. Cut off from the real world, from the agency I worked for. The agency now compromised by an enemy disguised.

"Forno?" I whispered, hoping they'd put him in the tent with me.

"Don't you wish," came the voice of Jennifer Lisle.

I sat up on the cot and spotted her in a chair in front of the tent opening. A faint light outside made her an indistinct shadow. "What've you done with him?"

"We're very glad he saved us the trouble and came to New Venasaille. The Kenn told us they had lost him."

"You killed him."

"Well, not yet."

My eyes adjusting to the dark, I scanned the tent, looking for an advantage.

"Several guards are posted outside and around the back," she said. "Trying to escape would be foolish, since they've been ordered to kill you if they see you alone outside this tent."

Throat scratchy, I swallowed, still trying to recover from the effects of Cara's light show.

"Mr. Crowell," she said, "you know about something important we need." She took a moment and inched the chair closer to me. "Where is the key?"

"Tell me how the Conduit works."

"When you tell me about the key."

"When you tell me about the Conduit."

"I'm not privy to nor do I understand the technical stuff, and can't give you specifics."

"Do your best."

She sighed. "It won't do you any good knowing about the procedure. So you might as well tell—"

"This procedure you talk about. It makes a copy of an individual, right?"

She shrugged, giving in. "Two different procedures. The first makes a copy from the original. Or, more accurately, makes a pattern based on the original that is then stored. The process doesn't kill the original, but we could easily make the original go away. The second procedure transforms bodies—such as these tent dwellers—into any of the stored patterns on record. Now, the key—"

I held up a hand to stop her. "So let me see if I have this straight," I said. "You took Plenko on Coral Moon. Plenko Prime is copied into storage. Then you grab someone, like one of these RuBy guys, and use the Plenko pattern to turn this guy into a Plenko clone? But he's not even half Plenko's size. There *has* to be conservation of mass. You can't make someone into an alien three times his size and break that law."

"The density decreases," she said. "Mass stays the same, but there are internal changes to make the body bigger."

"I'm guessing that doesn't end well for anyone that happens to."

"No. We decided initially we would gather up the biggest Helks we could find and replicate them. Plenko was quite the find. Put a copy of him in charge of a terrorist group. Dial up a few extra Plenkos. Confuse the authorities trying to find him. An alias here, an alias there, but nothing matching up, the visuals never quite right."

"No one knows who to trust."

She smiled. "As you're finding out."

"You're a copy of yourself, so there's no mass degradation, I'm guessing. And your memories?"

"My One decided how many to keep. As it turns out, I have most of them."

I stared at her, her outline fleshed out now, physical details coming into focus. "Your guy Koch first mentioned this key to me. But I have nothing. You took the only thing I had on me of worth when you took my code card."

Jennifer Lisle stood, and anger radiated from her. "You're lying."

"Maybe. You're not going to find out for sure, though, if you kill me."

"We'll see." She turned toward the tent opening, yelling out something in Helk. The same two Helks from the clearing came into view. She said something else to them, then looked back at me. "You're not long for this world, Mr. Crowell, just like Mr. Forno. Your meddling in our affairs has proven most troublesome."

She left the tent abruptly, and the Helks made their presence known by standing where I could see them through the flap, one with his back turned to me, the other facing the opening.

Forno had showed me the unfinished Conduit in the Flatlands. The towers were complete, and evidently the way and means to capture the patterns lay inside the towers. But making the physical copies, according to Forno, required the thin wire of the Conduit itself. They couldn't do anything like that here on Aryell with the wire missing, and I wasn't going to get to Temonus now to warn Alan. And what about the rest of the refugees here? They couldn't just shuttle five hundred thousand bodies to Temonus. No, the aliens needed the Conduit on Aryell working.

Did the Conduit on Temonus still work, even after the carrier pulled over the tower? It seemed possible. If it could be destroyed completely, the bad guys—aliens controlling the Science Consortium, NIO, Kenn—had no way to move forward with their plan to invade the Union on a large scale.

I wondered about their reasons for invading, or why they'd chosen to come at us in this way instead of with guns blazing. Their weapon technology might not be as advanced as their body-morphing technology, but I honestly didn't know enough about them even to make guesses.

This tent had been cleared of RuBy. I certainly didn't see any stacks of the red paper anywhere, and I didn't notice any of the telltale cinnamon odor. Stuffing my hand into my pocket, I pulled out one of the RuBy squares I'd put in there earlier, fingering it thoughtfully. If they were going to kill me anyway, perhaps I should spend my last moments conked out on the drug.

I brought the paper to my nose and sniffed. Only now did it actually smell enticing; before, in the tent of the addict, the odor had overwhelmed me.

Maybe just a taste. Just a brief flick of the tongue on the red dye of the paper.

Eyes closed, I put out my tongue.

"Don't do that," came the voice of Jennifer Lisle.

I was ready to ignore her, resigned to my fate, willing now to pop the whole thing in my mouth. But something stopped me. Something other than her order to do so.

I opened my eyes, and Jennifer stood inside the tent, right in front of me. Blinking to regain my focus, I stared at her eyes, and even in the dark of the tent I could make out the blue color. Her words still rolled around in my head. Without thinking, I looked down and took in the rest of her.

She had changed her clothes. She wore the same blue denim pants, and still wore a sweater, but now it looked thicker and warmer, and it was checkered in a black-and-white pattern. Something clicked inside my head as stark realization came to me.

These were the clothes I'd seen her in at the Flaming Sea.

I looked up and her eyes and the set of her face told me, *Don't say a word.*

"You're coming with me now," she said.

She had a Helk stunner at her side, which she raised now. I stared at it. Then, with her back to the tent opening, blocking the view of the guards, she flipped the stunner in her hand and gave it to me, handle first.

"It's me," she whispered, so faint that I almost didn't hear.

The real Jennifer Lisle.

Twenty-two

Brindos could have struck Terl Plenko hard in the face the instant the Helk came close to admire the view. The RuBy was partially to blame, because it seemed to slow everything down, and he found it hard to see through the fog.

He missed his chance. Plenko pulled back quickly and raised his stunner. Brindos hadn't noticed it earlier in his left hand.

"There," Plenko said, pointing to the chair he'd been sitting in earlier. "Now." Without taking his eyes off Brindos, he said, "Dorie, more light."

Plenko kept backing up, moving to Brindos's left as he did so. Brindos walked to the chair and slumped into it just as Dorie turned on the room lights overhead.

He hadn't called Brindos by name, so did Plenko know who he was? Maybe not. Brindos kept quiet, just in case. Unless all the other Plenkos wore the same thing, this was the Plenko he'd seen the night with Joseph. The black pants and high-collared shirt of animal hide seemed to suck up the light. He flexed his fingers inside the same black gloves Brindos remembered him wearing. Helks often wore the same outfit for days at a time. Other than the clothes, he looked too much like Brindos.

I look too much like him.

Goddamn, Brindos had seen way too much of Plenko in the last few days, and his chances for getting a break from him didn't look good.

Plenko sidestepped back in front of Brindos, but kept his distance, out of reach of any sudden lunge. Nothing Brindos could do now. The idea of finding Joseph at the Orion Hotel—or Dorie seeing him and arranging a meeting—seemed more and more unlikely.

Plenko called over his shoulder, his voice gruff, the anger obvious. "Dorie, what the hell?"

Brindos figured Dorie would wilt under the pressure of Terl Plenko questioning her. But she surprised him.

She put on her little show. Her RuBy act.

Since she hadn't said anything since entering the house, she had the advantage of altering her speech now. She slurred her words a little as she practically tiptoed toward him. "I didn't know." She seemed to disappear as she neared him and gave him a tentative hug. "It's you? Really you?"

"Please desist," Plenko said, looking at Brindos instead of her as she tried to reach around his torso. When she didn't, he forcefully pushed her away, still looking at Brindos. "You're not helping, Dorie."

She stumbled, and the momentum from Plenko's push caused her to fall and sit hard on the floor.

Plenko stared at Brindos. "Nice outfit," he said, smirking. "Dorie, you couldn't find him something better to wear of mine than this?"

From the floor, holding her head in her hands, Dorie said, "I thought something had happened. You weren't due back from your tour of the tower, and he"—she looked up and waved a hand in Brindos's direction—"showed up, distraught, screaming, looking hurt, no clothes. I don't know, I was confused. I thought . . ."

She broke off and lowered her head.

Brindos *had* been distraught. He still was. Especially now, considering she had told him he would die if he didn't get free of whatever it was that had changed him. This Terl Plenko had played a part in that change.

Brindos wondered if Plenko would see through Dorie's charade. Keeping quiet, Brindos looked on as Dorie continued her game, standing slowly, working her way back to Plenko, her eyes twinkling with a mixture of seduction and submission.

"Don't be mad," she said, her hand reaching for his shoulder.

Plenko grabbed her by the wrist and pushed her away a second time. She stumbled back and Brindos tensed, wanting to jump out of the chair and help. Although matched for size in every detail, Plenko still held the stunner, and Brindos didn't dare try anything. Brindos had other disadvantages, including trying to wrap himself completely around this body; he doubted he could control it well enough in a fight. And then there was the RuBy, although he had started to ease out of its grip.

"I'm stupid, I guess," she said.

"You're more than stupid," Plenko said, a growl in his voice. "You're *nothing*. If you didn't know it was me at first, you should have figured it out. You go through your RuBy like candy, and your judgment is so impaired that I wonder sometimes whether you'd be better off in an asylum somewhere. I don't trust you, Dorie. Is it any wonder we watch you day and night?"

Dorie shook her head. "Don't say that. Don't. I told you I would help you."

"Which is the only reason we've kept you alive," he said. He folded his arms across his mammoth chest, the stunner tucked for a moment under his right elbow. "Maybe that's not enough of a reason anymore. The last help you gave us didn't turn out so well, did it? There are at least two deaths on your head from that little incident."

"Well, then," Dorie said, disgusted, "I'm sorry I don't know about your precious key."

Brindos frowned, having no idea what Plenko's "precious key" was. If Dorie had knowledge of it, if they'd kept her alive for that reason, she was walking a thin line. Brindos wondered if she could bring off her act, keep Plenko guessing about what she knew, and convince him to keep her around.

Then again, if this key was something Plenko and his cohorts desperately needed for their cause, would it be better if they had no chance of getting it?

Brindos looked at Dorie now, uncertain. If Plenko didn't trust her, should Brindos trust her?

Plenko's eyes became slits. "Do not discuss that here. That slim chance you might still lead me to it keeps your life hanging on a thread. You should not have brought him here, to your house."

"It's not my house."

"You know what I mean, Dorie."

She shrugged. "He didn't know anything. I thought bringing him here—because I thought he was you—might dislodge something. Make him remember."

Now Plenko made a deliberate turn toward Brindos, studying him as he kept still in the chair. "He doesn't remember?" he said.

"He remembers waking up without any clothes. For a while he thought he might be someone else, but all he thinks now is that he's you."

"Terl Plenko," Plenko said.

Was he saying it directly to him? Brindos lifted his head slightly, trying to show recognition of the name in his eyes and face. Since opening the door to the house, no one had said Plenko's name aloud. Who wouldn't be confused, seeing another Helk identical to himself? So if he responded to Plenko's name, perhaps he could work his way out of this.

"Why do you look like me?" Brindos muttered. He didn't need help looking confused. He was. And some of the earlier pain had seeped back into his stomach as the RuBy wore off. "What's going on? I've been held against my will, stuck with needles, drugged—"

In an instant, before Brindos could react, Plenko covered the distance between them and hit Brindos across the face with his open palm. The strength of the blow knocked Brindos out of the chair, and he fell hard to the floor. Pain spread across his face. For a moment he lay on the hardwood floor, stunned, his eyes trying to focus on the tiny grooves between the wooden slats.

Roughly, Plenko turned Brindos over, and his leathery head bowed down, his face lined with fury. "Who are you?"

Brindos rubbed his jaw. "I don't know," he lied. Did Plenko not know Brindos was Brindos, or was Plenko just trying to find out if Brindos's memories had atrophied completely? Was Brindos the Helk he'd turned Alan Brindos into, or did he believe Brindos was some other Plenko duplicate?

He brought his forearm down hard and slammed it into Brindos's jaw, and he cried out and turned his head. Plenko kneeled on
Brindos's chest, grabbed his head with one hand, and forced him to
look at him. He took his forearm and wedged it under Brindos's
chin, choking him.

"You were once human," Plenko said. "Do you know that?"

Brindos tried to speak but could get out nothing but a wheeze.
Plenko let up a little, less pressure on the throat, and Brindos struggled to get out his next words. "I have a feeling that I was, but I
don't know who."

Plenko spoke to Dorie, who had come up beside him, barely
moving his head in her direction. "Where were Chinkno and Knox
when this happened?"

"Outside," she said. "They brought him in unconscious. Later
they gave him the treatment."

"Treatment? Why?"

"You weren't acting like yourself, and they figured you'd missed
one. They were confused too, and brought me in. I was sure it was
you."

"Where are they now?"

"I don't know. They left me alone with him. I thought they
might have come here."

Plenko studied Brindos again. He removed his arm from Brindos's throat and put his hand firmly on his chest, holding him
down. "Are you feeling pain now?" he asked, smirking. "Besides
your face."

Brindos nodded. The fire in his gut had returned, and tendrils of
pain crept through his torso, burning, aching, threatening to consume him.

"You don't know who you are?" Plenko said. "Really?"

"I don't."

Plenko sighed, as if he'd decided to give in. Indeed, the pressure
on Brindos's chest lessened, and Plenko raised his head, staring off
into one corner of the room.

"I believe," Plenko said, his tone even more severe, "that you
are lying to me."

Brindos thought he was going to convince him otherwise. His

body wanted to sink into the floor, but the pain wouldn't let go, acting like a buoy.

Plenko looked Dorie's way. "You're lying to me too, Dorie."

"Terl, I—"

"You've given him your RuBy, haven't you?"

No answer.

"You might as well tell me the truth," he said to Brindos. He cocked his head. "No? Then I will tell you. You are Alan Brindos, part-time agent for the Network Intelligence Organization. You and your partner David Crowell were pulled into the game at the suggestion of Director Timothy James. You figured it out—a little, anyway—and went on the run. How am I doing so far?"

Goddamn, he did know. Would anything Brindos said to the contrary make any difference? "I'm not following you in the slightest," Brindos said.

Plenko then went on explaining a little about the Conduit. What it was for, how it worked—Brindos didn't understand much of the techncial side of things, but at the very least he understood that the Conduit's ultra thin wire had done its number on him.

"We took the initiative," Plenko continued, "when you came into our sights here on Temonus. You'd either become one of us, get caught by the authorities, or die most uncomfortably."

At that moment, Brindos knew nothing he said or did would change the fact that Plenko had found him out. "Seems like none of those happened," Brindos said.

"Not yet." Plenko sent a hard look to Dorie. "Thanks to Dorie."

Dorie hung her head.

"But she's a RuBy addict, and doesn't know better," he added.

"So I'm guessing the RuBy counteracted the treatment," Brindos said. Plenko still didn't know that although Dorie took RuBy, she wasn't the addict he thought she was. She still had Plenko fooled with her act.

"A little." Plenko stood, backed away, and pulled Dorie with him. He slumped into the chair Brindos had been assigned to earlier and left Dorie standing next to it. Brindos sat up and Plenko pointed a beefy finger. "Stay there."

Brindos stayed, feeling more and more like a puppet in Plenko's control. Not caring whether Plenko saw him or not, Brindos glanced at the door, which stood open. No one else had been out there when they had come in, and no one else was out there now. If he made a break for it, he thought maybe he'd get away before Plenko could do anything. The pain was bad enough now that it almost begged him to go through the door.

"Or *don't* stay there," Plenko said, amusement in his voice. "Door's open. You want to leave, go right ahead. I won't stop you."

Brindos gazed longingly at the door again. "Why would you let me go?"

"Your treatment."

"My treatment?"

"I'm the only one who can give it to you."

"The stuff that Red and Blue gave me."

"Who?"

Dorie interrupted. "Chinkno and Knox. The jumpsuits they were wearing."

"Ah. Yes, they can give it to you too, if they have it around them."

"Why did you make me into you?" Brindos asked. "You're fighting against the Union, but it's something bigger."

"It's a long story, Mr. Brindos."

"I've got time."

"No, you don't."

Brindos squinted at him, remembering Dorie's warning about the treatment. His gut twisted as the hot needles there poked and prodded.

"The copy process isn't foolproof," Plenko continued. "The 'stuff' you were given keeps you well enough to interact with society. Did Dorie tell you I'm a copy of her own beloved Terl Plenko? It's true."

"So if I don't get the treatment?"

"A few missed treatments," he said, leaning forward in the chair, "and you will die."

The door didn't seem so inviting anymore, even with the escalating pain.

Plenko leaned back and smiled. "The problem of pattern rejection is considered an acceptable risk, considering the instances of it happening are rare."

Brindos gulped. "It didn't happen to you?"

"No. It happens only to those individuals whose size changes. It's a problem with internal density. I went from Plenko to Plenko. You went from human to Helk."

"So I have to keep taking the treatment to survive."

"The degradation of the pattern is continual, even with the treatments. Eventually, even the treatments will not save you."

"Terl," Dorie whispered.

"Mr. Brindos, you have no hope beyond what little I give you. You will die within the week, one way or another."

Brindos swallowed, fighting back his anger. His despair. He lay back on the floor and Terl Plenko kneeled and brought his face close. He whispered in Brindos's ear, and Brindos should have heard him clearly, but didn't. Or maybe he did, but decided it was nonsense. Brindos lay back, giving in.

Brindos stayed on the floor and forgot about the door.

A loving fog shrouded him from all manner of evil. Oh, yes. Good-bye to the concerns of the Union. For now, anyway, the pain was gone, and he could relax.

Plenko left the chair and walked to the back of the house. Brindos turned his head to watch Plenko enter a room and flick on a light, revealing the kitchen. A moment later Plenko brought out a travel bag. It only took a few moments more for him to open the bag, pull out a syringe, and prep it.

"You'll retain all your memories," Plenko explained. "Alas, the RuBy has seen to that, but no matter. We still need you."

"Why?"

Plenko ignored him.

Brindos needed his treatments to stay alive, and Plenko knew Brindos wouldn't leave. At this point, Brindos couldn't figure out why he'd want to, but his head still struggled to catch up with all the drugs he'd been subjected to. He didn't struggle when Plenko injected Brindos's upper arm. The needle pinched and stung, but he didn't mind.

"You *will* keep a close eye on him, Dorie," Plenko said.

Brindos had no intention of moving a single inch from his spot on the floor. The hardwood felt good, actually, and he traced the little grooves around him with his fingers, preferring to lie flat on his back.

"You're leaving?" Dorie asked.

"I'll be back to give him another dose in an hour. We'll double up on the serum, see if Brindos's system can handle it. I'll send Knox or Chinkno back later."

Then he left.

Good riddance, Brindos thought. *Good-bye, Plenko.*

Dorie said something about there being a couch in the room he could rest on, but Brindos ignored her; almost immediately he fell asleep.

Light.

The fog thinned and Brindos had a brief glimpse of someone's face above him.

Noise hurt his ears. An argument. Garbled words, spoken rather heatedly.

Brindos thought he might be dreaming, because the face staring down at him looked like his own.

No, not me. Plenko.

Another pinch in his left arm. A second dose.

Brindos smiled and succumbed to sleep once again.

Light.

The haze still surrounded him, and this time the noises were random, little pops and deep rumbles that seemed to be far away, sometimes very close. A strong acrid smell made his nose itch. The light dimmed and blurred, brightened and faded as the pops and rumbles echoed around him.

Brindos wondered if Dorie had slipped him some more RuBy.

And yes, there was a voice. A voice he thought he recognized.

His eyes seemed to clear, but the haze didn't go away. The smell bothered him.

It wasn't anything from Plenko's treatment. Brindos recognized it now for what it was.

Smoke.

That urgent voice called to him, and he jerked fully awake.

"Brindos! Please!"

Dorie.

Outside, thunder boomed close by, and the house shook.

"Brindos, wake up. Over here. *Here!*"

Brindos stood quickly, almost toppling back over, and located Dorie. She was pinned under a wooden beam. The beam had once held up part of the roof of her house.

"Fucking hell," Brindos whispered, staring at the night sky above her living room. Something had torn it apart. He stumbled to Dorie's side and kneeled next to her. "Dorie, are you all right?" No, of course she wasn't all right. "What happened?"

"I think I'm okay. I just can't get out of here."

It didn't take but a few seconds with his Helk strength to move the beam aside and free her. She got to her feet and she winced a little when she put weight on her right leg.

"You okay?" Brindos asked.

"Twisted the ankle a little, and I think the leg's bruised pretty bad. But I can walk."

"What *happened*?" he said again.

Dorie glanced at the hole in her roof, then around the room, at the mess. Windows had shattered, much of the furniture was overturned, and the door had popped off its hinges and fallen inward.

"They're attacking the Helk district," she said.

"The whole *district*?"

"Looks like they're willing to accept the collateral damage. We're definitely not where we want to be."

"Union. It has to be Union, not the NIO." The NIO was compromised. He guessed President Nguyen had decided to take a proactive approach to getting rid of Terl Plenko.

"We've got to get out of here," Dorie said. "You've been out of it most of a day."

"A whole day?"

"It's the next evening." She rushed to a nearby closet and scrounged around inside until she found a large, heavy gray coat and a matching wide-brimmed hat. "Put these on."

"I'm not cold—"

"It's to hide you."

"What?"

"They're after *you*, Brindos. They're after Plenko."

His blood froze. Join them or get caught by the authorities, Plenko had said. Joseph and Plenko had originally set him loose in the Helk district near where the Midwest City Authority had set up patrols, hoping he'd get caught. A scapegoat for the real Plenko. Or, Plenko had hoped Brindos would lose his memory and be primed to do their dirty work, whatever that was.

Dorie helped him put on the coat, covering him the best she could. She grabbed a jacket of her own, a black rain slicker, one with a hood. She pulled up the hood as he plopped the hat on his head. "Come on," she said, urging him toward the kitchen. "There's a back door."

Goddamn.

Brindos hadn't been set up to take a fall for the NIO. He'd been set up to help Plenko. Help Joseph, whoever he was.

If NIO operatives and agents had been replaced with copies— and he had to assume now Timothy James was one of them—then he and Crowell might be the only ones from the organization who knew the whole truth about the Conduit and the fake explanation the rest of the Union had been told. The compromised NIO would tell President Nguyen anything to confirm and perpetuate the lie.

Brindos wished to God he knew what was going on with Crowell. If Brindos had fallen prey to this invading force—whatever it was—here on Temonus, was Dave Crowell okay on the backwater planet of Aryell?

An explosion on the street lit up the house and the concussion shattered a window near the door. Brindos pulled Dorie out of the way just as the overhead light fixture crashed down within inches of them. Dorie pointed him to the kitchen and he rushed in there with her, giving support by holding her under her arm as she limped.

Brindos stopped suddenly. "Dorie," he said, looking around at the counters, at the wooden table in the corner.

She knew what he'd stopped to look for. "He has it with him," she said. "There's no time now, we have to go."

Terl Plenko had his bag. The treatments that would extend his life. Plenko might already be dead somewhere, caught in the brunt of the attack.

They crashed through the back door and slipped down a red-brick alley, Dorie pointing out the way she said would get them out of the Helk district.

Brindos had nothing to lose.

You will die within the week, one way or another.

And, finally, Plenko's whispered words, the ones Brindos thought he had misunderstood, came to him loud and clear.

You are a Thin Man now, Mr. Brindos.

Twenty-three

The real Jennifer—I hoped she was the real one—said, "Follow me" as I tucked the stunner into my pants and draped my shirt-tail over it. Turning, she led the way, and I followed, my eyes sullenly downcast.

The Helks stared at us as we walked into the night air, passing between them. One practically growled as I neared him. Nice of him to care so much. I hadn't wanted to be that close, but the Helks' own proximity to one another didn't give me much room. Deciding to help me, he put his mighty hand on my shoulder and shoved me forward. I was so tense that I was able to shuffle ahead without losing my balance.

Jennifer slowed down and followed suit, pushing me ahead of her, saying, for the benefit of the guards, "Move. Haven't got all day."

We kept walking, down the aisle, and I couldn't figure out which way we were headed. Behind me, Jennifer whispered, "Eyes forward. Straight ahead."

"Wait," rasped one of the guards.

Jennifer said over her shoulder, "If I don't get him to Cara immediately—"

"Stop," the guard continued, "or I *will* shoot."

"Stop," Jennifer said, and I did. "Face forward." I heard her turn around, her voice subdued when she spoke to the guards. "What's the problem?"

"What happened to your leg?" the voice asked.

"My leg?"

"You're limping."

Damn. The sonic blast she took from Dorie on Ribon. I hadn't seen her limp in the tent when I first woke up, and walking out of there in front of her hadn't noticed it until the Helk said something. I inched backward, not wanting to draw attention to myself, getting as close to her as I dared. Cover of darkness helped.

"I twisted my ankle a little on the way back here," she said.

"Is that so?" came the gruff voice. "And that's not what you were wearing."

"You're mistaken," she said.

"Who do you think you're talking to?" the Helk asked.

He was right. Some Helks could be downright stupid, but they had a better memory than even the brightest of humans, and even some Memors. They never forgot a face. Or a sweater.

Jennifer must have realized this could be a problem, giving me a stunner earlier. I hoped she had her own. Carefully, I pulled the stunner free from my pants waistband and held it in front of my thigh.

Then I heard the unmistakable sound of the Helk's own stunners powering up.

I made a decision. "Now or never," I whispered. "Go left!"

She slid left, I edged right, and we both fired. Unfortunately, the Helks fired almost simultaneously.

A sharp pain erupted in my side as the sonic blast clipped me; the muscles there screamed. I fell to my knees, but the guards went down and stayed down, motionless. I'd caught my Helk right in the head; Jennifer had hit hers on its left side, dead-on perfect for a Helk.

"You okay?" she asked as she bent down, concern on her face.

I extended an arm. "I hope."

She hoisted me up and glanced at my side. I pulled up my shirt a little and checked out the skin, but of course a stunner left no mark.

"Grazed you," she said.

"Lucky." A full hit would've scrambled my insides and boiled the muscles. Goddamn Helk stunners. I looked at her. "So they made a copy of you."

"Funny, huh?"

"Not so much."

"I told you about my sleep issues when we were at the Flaming Sea. I slept a day and a half in the hospital. That's when they must have done it."

"You don't know how it happened?"

She shook her head. "After everything that went down on Ribon, and Dorie Senall, and someone betraying me with that vid feed into her apartment, then losing those hours . . . Well, by the time I saw you at the Sea, I realized I was in trouble with the NIO. That's why I didn't turn you in. I'm no longer an agent, Crowell. I'm on the run, just like you."

"How the hell did you find me here?"

She smiled. "Forno told me."

"Forno?" I felt a surge of relief. "You found him? He's alive?"

"He's alive."

"In one piece?"

"Whole as a Helk. I ran into him on the far side, in a tent near a small landing field. Took care of the few guards there. We'll use my ship, because Forno's was nowhere to be found."

"You just pulled into a parking spot in their own shipyard?"

"My ship's official, NIO clearance. They didn't challenge me."

I had plenty of questions for her: about how she found us here, about the NIO and what she knew about the invasion, about Cara—my Cara—but now was not the time.

"That hot zone wasn't much fun," she said.

I nodded. "You noticed. Datascreen, is what Forno called it. I'm guessing it's alien technology."

"Memor?"

"Something else."

The air, crisp and cold, smelled slightly of ozone due to the sonic discharges. I tried to use my keen sense of direction to figure out where I was, but it failed me. "We should move," I said. "The other Jennifer—"

"Is dead," she said.

I stared at Jennifer in confusion. "What? How?"

"Forno got her as she came to his tent. I'd already freed him. Unfortunately, we didn't get—" She paused, glancing my way. "Cara. The copy escaped. She made it to another shuttle ahead of us, and before we could get to her she blasted out of here."

I nodded, my earlier optimism drying up. I imagined it had been a bit strange for Jennifer to see herself killed.

"This way." She pointed behind me. "You going to live?"

"I'm fine." As we jogged between the tents, my side ached, but it was nothing serious.

Jennifer never paused as we moved down the aisles, her path among the tents deliberate. Ten minutes later we came to the landing field, barely noticeable in the darkness, a small bit of flat land crudely fenced in with some sort of black plastic material about six feet high. Only two ships rested there, a one-seater flier, and a larger shuttle that rumbled quietly during its start-up sequence, the running lights turned off.

"That's mine," Jennifer said, pointing at the shuttle. I nearly tripped over the bodies of two Helks sprawled on the ground near the shipyard's entrance, which basically consisted of a gap in the plastic fencing. Just as we reached the shuttle, its side door flipped upward and Tem Forno stood there, silhouetted in the light from its cabin.

"Need a lift?" he asked.

"It's *my* ship," Jennifer said.

"I doubt that," Forno said. "In fact, I'm not sure how much I trust this NIO-issue shuttle, considering I don't trust the NIO. Or you, for that matter."

"Then hop off and you can walk home," she said.

Forno grinned, his leathery face wrinkling with the effort. "Glad to have you aboard," he said, reaching down to help us up to the deck.

Forno steadied me as I scrambled up. The darkness was thick, the night sky punctuated by stars that looked cold and very distant. "Didn't find the key, I presume," I said.

"Nope. Or your code card." He reached for the shuttle door above him and pulled it down. It thunked into place. "Cara's gone."

I nodded. "The *copied* Cara's gone," I said. "Jennifer's copy called Cara her 'One.' Definitely not like the other copies. I felt the difference."

"Agreed," he said. "Now we need to figure out what she is, and from where, if possible." He locked the shuttle door, slipping the bolts into place. "Can we get out of here now?" he asked Jennifer. "Preferably be*fore* the tent people and any remaining guards get here?"

Jennifer was already on her way to the controls. "Strap in."

That reminded me about something I'd wanted to ask earlier. As we sat down and buckled up, I asked, "How'd you find us? What made you think to come out this way? Why didn't the datascreen discourage you from looking here, specifically?"

Jennifer pointed at Forno.

Suddenly a bit nervous, I retreated a step.

Forno said, "Relax, Dave." He pulled off his rygsa, the earring I'd found on Katerina Parker's body and given back to him. "It was the earring."

"Earring?"

"I found it before you did in her room," Jennifer said. "I rigged it with a nanotracker and put it where I was sure you or Forno would find it. I didn't know for sure about either of you. I didn't know who killed Kristen—Katerina Parker—and I was awfully nervous about the NIO finding me."

"Thanks for the confidence in my abilities to find it," I said.

"It worked, didn't it? It led me right to Forno."

"Yeah, you found us," Forno said, "so can we now get out of here?"

Jennifer turned and palmed some sensors on the control panel. The ship shuddered a bit as it took to the air, banking right, putting it on a path over New Venasaille.

The datascreen was nowhere to be seen.

Forno smiled. "Did I forget to mention I'd solved that little datascreen problem? I disabled it. Made quite a mess of it, actually." He pointed to a pulse rifle near him. "Comandeered it from one of the dead guards. It's amazing how much damage one of those can do."

"They'll have it back up and running in a few days," Jennifer said. "But we'd better hurry, because it's a good bet whoever put the screen up knows it's down."

"Sure," he said. "Probably. But at least we can get out of here without going through that thing. And just *where* are we going?"

Now that I knew what was going on, I had no doubt about where to go.

"The WuWu Bar and Grille," I said.

Forno narrowed his eyes. "Helk's breath! After all this, you want to go have a drink?" He blinked a moment, then said, "Well, yeah, maybe that'd be a good plan."

"I need to get back to the Flaming Sea," Jennifer said, working her hands over the controls, the sensors responding to her touch with short pulses of light. "Why the WuWu Bar and Grille for you?"

The shuttle had banked again and now accelerated toward the mountain range Forno and I had passed through on our way to New Venasaille.

"A message from Cara."

Jennifer and Forno glanced at each other, then at me.

"Cara?" they both said.

"Yes, Cara. She's been . . . hiding. But now that I know she's been copied, and copied somehow to disguise one of these aliens working with the Science Consortium—well, it's obvious there are a few things she's not telling me."

"I knew it," Jennifer said.

"I think she may know something about this key of yours, Forno."

"You told me she had no idea what the key was," he said.

"I said she didn't seem to."

Forno leaned back in his seat.

I sighed. "Look. You have somewhere else you want to go right now?"

"Yeah, but my boyhood home on Helkunntanas is a long way away."

Jennifer smiled thinly, then turned back to her console. "To

Kimson, then," she said. "I'll get us close by, and then you're on your own."

"To Kimson," I said, staring out the front window at the approaching mountains.

To find Cara.

Twenty-four

You are a Thin Man now.

Plenko's words confused Brindos, but so had everything else about this ordeal.

When he'd asked Dorie about the Thin Man, she said it had to do with the Conduit and the copy process. She'd heard Plenko say it a few times about people who'd been copied.

The first rain he'd seen on Temonus began falling as Brindos and Dorie wended their way through the streets, away from the chaos of the raid on the Helk district. Clouds and smoke from the attack obscured the night's stars, and the sporadic streetlights made it easier to hide and disappear when needed.

Dorie had given him a half square of RuBy, carefully doling it out now, trying to ease his pain, but not wanting him to get hooked on the stuff. It was hard having it shown to you that you're not immune to addictions; RuBy had an insidious way of catching your brain on fire.

Not that it mattered. If Brindos had a limited amount of time, if he had to die anyway, he might as well have no pain. It wouldn't matter if he became addicted to RuBy or not.

Dorie moved well enough, even with the discomfort from her sprained foot and bruised leg. They slipped through the district by means of so many alleys and passageways that Brindos was soon completely lost. He'd been pretty oblivious to his surroundings to start with. Dorie insisted she knew where she was going, however, and promised they'd get to the Orion Hotel before too long. The discomfort in his gut and the haze in his brain kept him from worrying about it much, and besides, he had no one else to trust but Dorie.

That was saying something, considering Brindos had seen the police holo-recording on Ribon that had presented her as a drugged-out fanatic.

When several Midwest City Authority police vehicles sped past, they slunk into the shadows of a tall brick building on the edge of the district, a ragged awning providing cover. Dorie grabbed his shoulder and leaned out to check the street, then pulled him across it and down another alley.

They continued this way for a half hour until, well clear of the Helk district, the sounds of destruction had disappeared underneath the steady thrum of the larger, more populated areas of Midwest City. The Orion, he remembered, sat on the opposite end of town from the Restaurant, so they still had a sizable journey ahead. Now, too they would be more conspicuous, since few Helks strayed from their district, particularly these days.

Brindos huddled as best he could in the overcoat Dorie had given him, trying to diminish his presence. He ducked his head and the raindrops dripped from the wide-brimmed hat. If he'd a flash-stick and its curling holo-mist, the scene would have been nearly cliché, but he sure as hell didn't feel like the private detective he used to be. He was First Clan Helk, and nothing, not even a hunched posture and a baggy overcoat, would hide that fact. His hope was to at least keep Terl Plenko's face hidden long enough to get to the bottom of this mystery.

They spent a good half hour passing through residential areas made up of the mostly human residents, the prefab homes of the various housing projects looking shiny and new compared to what Brindos had seen in the Helk district. Traffic increased along the now rain-soaked streets, the few privately owned cars mingling with the city's ground buses and taxis. Once in a while, a Temonus Authority cruiser rushed past in the direction they'd come, or a small air vehicle whooshed by overhead.

Residential gave way to blocks with a mixture of more elaborate homes and actual stores and shops. More colonists, mostly human, braved the sidewalks, dashing in and out of storefronts, avoiding the rain.

The sharp pains started pinging inside him again, seemingly coming back faster than before. He endured them without saying anything to Dorie. He suddenly felt the need to breathe free, to exist without RuBy in his system, and he gritted his teeth, wondering how long that desire would win out over the agony of his reality.

Brindos fought to bear the pain as they drew nearer to the business district. Even here, the buildings never became extreme or elaborate. As he'd noticed when first landing on Temonus, most colonists had taken a chance on this planet, starting over, in many cases, and the small minority of well-to-dos kept their posh homes along the outer edge of the cities. But even those residences paled in comparison to the excesses on Earth. Excesses that had crippled her, and sent her inhabitants scrambling for the other planets of the Union to begin again.

So much for that.

A glass window of a tiny shop shattered next to him, the crash startling him from his reverie. He turned to watch the shards spatter against the sidewalk. The shop sold clothing—a few mannequins with heavy coats and scarves stood in the display window. Dorie pulled him down, but something still hit him in the shoulder. Looking back out across the street, he fixed upon the dark shapes of three older kids, drenched in the rain because they had no coats or umbrellas. Two girls stood on either side of a boy a good three or four inches taller. The boy casually tossed a rock in the air.

The pain in Brindos's shoulder went away quickly. Nothing compared to that inner burning agony he was fighting off now, and he nearly growled at them, making a slight move in their direction. Dorie did her best to keep him down.

"You can't," she said.

"Helk, go home!" the boy yelled across the street, his voice booming.

Laughter from the two girls. One of them threw a rock, and this time, Brindos instinctively gathered Dorie within his large frame to protect her. The rock sailed over their heads and hit the door of the clothes shop with a loud thunk.

"Stickman, Stickman!" the boy yelled. "Save us from that louse!"

The others joined in. "The Movement's here and Plenko's near—"

Goddamn them to hell. Forgetting secrecy, Brindos succumbed to the pressure and stood up, removing his hat and coat. He let them have a good look. They shut up so quickly that for a moment they seemed frozen in place. For effect, Brindos made an audible growl.

"O you better be afraid," he said, finishing the street rhyme. He took two steps toward them and they came unstuck from the pavement and dashed off to the end of the block. They disappeared around the corner.

Dorie sighed. "Okay, now we *do* have to move. That wasn't the smartest thing to do right now."

"I didn't want you hurt," he said, putting the coat and hat back on.

She looked a little surprised at his protectiveness, but she managed a smile. "Thank you, but if those kids say something to anyone—"

"We'll be far away from here."

And they headed off toward the Orion, which Dorie said was still a good half mile away.

"How are we going to do this?" he asked as they continued to keep to the shadows, inching forward as breaks in street and foot traffic allowed.

"Anywhere along here, now. We need a place for you to hide. I need to find this Joseph."

They had hit the full business district, but the cover of night, and the later hour, was making it easier to make progress toward the hotel.

"What if he's not there?" she asked.

Brindos didn't know Joseph's hours or what days he worked or didn't work. During the handful of days he had stayed at the Orion, there hadn't seemed to be much of a pattern in his work schedule, other than the fact that he seemed to be there nearly all the time.

"He'll be there," Brindos said.

"Here," she said, pointing to an alley between two of the tallest buildings—as tall as they got here in Midwest City, anyway. "There should be very little foot traffic coming through here. Pull some of those refuse containers closer and sit between them."

The black containers, although large and bulky, didn't pose a problem for his Helkness. He quickly arranged them into a small cave and sat down on the rough, wet pavement.

"I'll be back as soon as I can," Dorie said.

"He knew me in my human form as Dexter Roberts. Dexter Roberts. Remember. And if you can't find him, don't stick around. You come back here and we'll figure something out."

She smiled. "I'll find him. How're you feeling?"

"Like a two-ton dead weight is sitting in my stomach," he said, "and all the nerves, all the blood vessels, are pinched shut."

She fumbled around in the pocket of her black rain slicker and found another square of RuBy. She tore it in half. "I don't know how much more of this I can give you. The effects start diminishing with time, and as usually happens, the body craves it more and more."

"I'm dying anyway, right?"

She held out the red paper, he stuck out his tongue, and she put it there, watching it dissolve, watching him—his life—dissolve with it. "Not so fast, Brindos. We'll figure something out."

"You were married to him."

"What?"

"To Plenko. Married to him."

"Yes—"

"What does it mean to you, to see me here now? To be doing all this, with so much at stake? You loved him."

"That was—"

"I know." He put his large hand on her shoulder, gently. "This is difficult for you. You didn't have to do this. I'm not him. I'm not the man you married."

She nodded, warmth in her eyes, a sad smile on her lips. "How can I not help? I look at you and I see the love and joy I felt for Plenko in those days before—"

"Shhh."

She stopped and gazed into his face that had once belonged to her husband, the Helk she had lost and would no doubt lose again.

"You should get going," he said.

"Yeah." She stuck the other half of the RuBy square in his coat pocket. "Keep it dry. And don't take it unless you absolutely have to. Okay?"

"Okay. Be careful."

"Of course."

"You come back for me."

She smiled. "Union bright."

She rested the palm of her hand on his leathery cheek for a moment, then she straightened, turned, and ran off quickly to the street.

The rain stopped a few minutes later. That was something, anyway. Drifting into himself, waves of euphoria crashed down. He closed his eyes to the alley and the world.

Awake.

The monotony of this crap really pissed him off. Awake, passed out, awake, knocked out, awake, passed out, awake, drugged out, awake . . .

Still dark. How long had it been this time? Previously, in Dorie's house, a whole day had slipped by. Brindos took stock of his surroundings. Still in the same place. Trash bins shielding him. Stars out. Sky clear now, the pavement still wet.

Then came the slow realization that he no longer felt the raging pain inside him. Why? Because very little time had actually passed? Or had his system somehow figured out a way to undo the damage? Maybe he had become immune. Something in his biochemistry had counteracted the drugs, the unknown, alien process roiling his insides.

Perhaps Dorie had come back, unsuccessful, popped another square of RuBy in his mouth, and ran off to try again? Or had she given up and left him there to fend for himself? He didn't think she would do that. Not *this* Dorie.

Still. She knew something that Plenko and the others wanted.

"They" were keeping her alive because of it. A key. She would have to answer about that soon enough; he just didn't have time to worry about what side she was on any longer. If it was important to one side or the other, she would have to tell him.

A dull ache forced him to think a bit more clearly.

The essence of something that wanted to be pain still tugged at him, so the whole "beating out the process and becoming immune" idea seemed unlikely.

For the first time, Brindos wished Dave Crowell was there with him. He missed him. Missed the days in Seattle, the two of them taking on those few cases that would pay the rent and put food in their mouths. Jobs had been few and far between, considering most of the people had headed off-planet, or at least to the largest cities like L.A., New York, or Chicago, where the skeleton of society still included a backbone.

Some of Earth's population had come here, to Temonus. Some, like Cara Landry, to Aryell. Some, like Dorie Senall, had found Ribon, the largest and most industrialized of the colonies. Some had braved Memory, living among that race of beings. Some to Orgon. Or to Barnard's.

Even some on Helkunntanas. Enigmatic, mysterious Helkunntanas. Here he was, one of the most well-known Helks of them all. But not. How much did the Helks really have to do with all this? Or was it all instigated by the likes of Joseph, whoever he was?

Having Dave Crowell here would have put his mind at ease. He had a way of defusing even the heaviest of situations. Brindos liked the way Crowell's brain worked its way around problems, although he doubted Crowell had had much luck figuring this shit out.

Brindos felt a punch in the gut, and cramps wrenched around his middle. He growled as he scrunched into a tight ball and waited for this new pain to pass.

So much for his earlier theories. If Plenko was right, if *Dorie* was right, the pain would get worse, his body would rebel, the treatments would not be forthcoming, and he would likely not see Dave Crowell again.

The pain got worse.

Brindos fumbled inside his coat pocket, fingering the half square of RuBy. Not unless you absolutely have to, Dorie had said. How much more pain should he endure? If he took it now, and she came back shortly after, would it make any difference? She could just as well come back and give him another dose anyway.

Or she could get herself captured, or worse, killed, and never come back. Then what would he do?

He would have to make a run for the Orion Hotel himself. He had no other sane option, seemingly, than trying to talk to Joseph, and if that meant walking through the hotel's front door, grabbing him by the neck and demanding answers, then so be it. He might get answers. He might get blasted. Captured, detained. Executed.

Well.

He figured he'd find something out one way or another. Get a chance to talk to someone before the inevitable happened.

Plenko's words still haunted him. *You will die within the week, one way or another.*

He fought back another wave of pain, this time spreading from belly to chest and arms, as if jabs of hot needles were perforating his skin. Outside and inside now.

A sensation akin to a needle poking his left eye made him cry out, and he covered it with his hand. The pain didn't let up, not one bit, his whole body now crawling with fire, and he figured this might be his "absolutely have to" RuBy moment.

The half square was already in the palm of his hand. He'd gone from fingering it to grasping it, probably when the pain had ripped through him. Although crumpled, the RuBy looked more beautiful than anything he'd ever seen. The low light turned its red color almost black, and because of the dampness, some of the dye coated his hand, but that was about the extent of his thinking before placing the paper on his tongue.

The RuBy flashed through quicker than ever, relief coming almost instantly. If Dorie was right, the drug would wear off faster, and he'd ache for more and more of it.

If he was going to do something on his own, he needed to consider starting now. He struggled to his feet, crouching a little to keep low in case anyone chose that moment to walk by the alley opening.

No one walked by. He straightened and walked out from his cave of refuse containers, sliding close to the wall of the nearest building, back pressed hard against it. His head cleared somewhat, even as the RuBy haze filmed his eyes. The alley was quiet, and no noises came from the main street either.

What time was it? He'd become so unstuck from the normal passage of day and night. Daybreak could be an hour away, for all he knew.

Brindos inched toward the street, pulling his coat tighter around him, pulling the hat down over his eyes. On the street he'd just be a stupid Helk out of his district, subject to the ridicule of street urchins and bigots.

At the same time, the attack on the Helk district had likely changed things. Since it had happened under the cover of night, the general public, particularly here, across town, might not have heard about it. If they had, it was possible any Helk found outside the district would become a target, not just Terl Plenko.

Conceivably, however, Brindos could work his way to the Orion Hotel without too much trouble. The trouble would arrive when he got there.

Out he went to the street. Not a soul there. The lights up and down it seemed brighter than they should be, but toward the heart of the business district, they were even more numerous, glittering in the windows of the tallest buildings. In a flash of recognition, he saw the tallest building rising from behind the others, a single word near the top glowing in bright white LEDs: ORION.

Here we go, he thought, walking forward, his right shoulder brushing against the building.

The timing was anything but propitious.

A vehicle turned onto the street off the side arterial before him and came his way. He didn't look too closely at it, but it was black, and quite small. Definitely not a ground bus or other public transit vehicle. Brindos took its appearance as a sign to hurry forward, thinking he might be able to blend into the night or that they would not see him close to the building. Then he could turn up the arterial the vehicle had just left.

A good plan in theory, but the moment the vehicle passed, the tires screeched on the wet pavement as someone inside applied the brakes.

Goddamn it. Brindos ran for the corner. He heard the engine gun, then whine as the vehicle reversed. Could he lose them once he made it to the side street? Duck into another alley? Just before he reached the corner, the tires screeched again and the vehicle ground to a halt. A door opened.

"Alan!"

Brindos paused halfway around the corner of the building, recognizing the voice. He turned and eased back to the main street. "Dorie?"

"Get in!" She stood next to the back door of a small passenger car, her thin frame, black hair, and rain slicker all recognizable in the streetlights.

Brindos ran toward the open door and hunched to squeeze inside. Dorie bent down and disappeared inside just as he started to wonder how he would fit in there. It didn't matter, because nothing was going to keep him from folding himself into this car.

He threw himself in headfirst, crawling over the seat as Dorie, coaxed him toward her on the far side. His head in her lap, he pulled his legs in, jamming his knees into his chest.

The car took off abruptly, the door pulling shut with the sudden speed.

"Got you," Dorie said in a whisper, one hand stroking the top of his bald head. The car turned left, then accelerated again.

"Thanks," Brindos said. He had a narrow view of the space between the front seats, the driver hidden except for the back of his head.

The gray wispy hair a dead giveaway.

The car slowed considerably, and then the driver turned toward him.

"Hello, Mr. Roberts," Joseph said.

Brindos grimaced as a sliver of pain sliced into him.

Joseph smiled. "I was right about you," he said. "NIO through and through."

"Joe," Brindos said, "I'm definitely through with the NIO."

Joseph twisted his head back to the front while the car made another turn, this time to the right. Dorie held Brindos around the middle, doing her best to keep him from sliding around.

"You think so, Mr. Roberts?" Joseph said loudly over his shoulder.

"Alan Brindos."

"Brindos. Yes, Miss Senall told me as much." He turned toward the back again. "But honestly," he continued, "do you really think you're through with the NIO?"

No, he thought. *Not at all.*

Twenty-five

Jennifer landed her shuttle on the outskirts of Kimson, close to the main road into town. Night had given way to the light of day, although it was still quite early. That didn't stop a good tourist town from rolling out its sidewalks and attractions early, getting a jump on the day.

Forno and I hopped out and Jennifer told us to be careful, that it was possible word of what had happened at the tent city of New Venasaille had reached Kimson. We needed to lay low the best we could.

Of course, finding out Jennifer Lisle had a copy out there made things even more interesting. Although Forno had killed the copy, someone here in Kimson could be waiting for her to make an appearance. She didn't want to go barging into the Kimson police station, or connecting with any NIO office, if one even existed here. So we told her to mind her own advice and be careful.

She knew that, and said she'd land the shuttle on the opposite end of town. She could track Forno's earring if she needed to find us again. She fired up the shuttle and left us there.

"The main road from the spaceport goes straight into Kimson," Forno said. "A few more blocks and it'll run into Amp Street."

"Yeah, I know," I said. "I was here years ago too."

"That's right. When you met Cara."

I nodded. "Things were a lot different then, obviously."

"Obviously. You know where the WuWu Bar and Grille is, then?"

"Haven't been there since that first visit, but yeah. I know where it is. Straight down on Amp Street from the Flaming Sea, a couple of blocks."

Forno nodded. "Should I go in with you?"

"Be my bodyguard?"

"I'm only Second Clan, but I'm bound to be bigger than anyone else in the WuWu."

"Comforting."

"Of course, I'm on the hit list too, if we run into any Thin Men."

I twisted his way. "Pardon? Thin Men?"

Forno shrugged. "It's the code word I found on the ultra thin level in the NIO basement. Those who've been copied are called Thin Men. Because of the Conduit."

The thin wire. "So Jennifer—the deceased one—she was a Thin Woman?"

"They don't make that distinction."

I took stock of our surroundings. Not a lot of places to hide here. The trees were sparse coming into town, mostly to allow tourists good views of the mountains, but they grew taller and more numerous closer to town.

"We can't just walk in on the main road," I said. "We'll have to take whatever cover the trees give us."

We took to walking, skirting the main road, and worked our way through the trees. Our progress was slow due to a low, dense brush, but it gave us time to pick the path that offered the most cover. Once in a while we came upon some of those blocky stucco homes stuck back in the trees. No roads or sidewalks led to them, and I wondered how the homeowners managed the walk into town. We gave the homes a wide berth, and sometimes makeshift paths did indeed show up. We declined to use them.

After a half hour we started angling toward Kimson's main road. Eventually we came upon a good dozen houses, and the first real streets. Now we hurried, slipping in behind the few trees that lined the streets, bolting out toward other trees, or a house or two, until we felt comfortable trudging along the side of the streets themselves. Tourists and locals around now. We could blend in a little, since Kimson's tourist crowd included Memors and Helks as well as humans.

Main Street appeared before us suddenly, wider and better maintained than any of the other streets. The bustle increased dramatically, the tourists more numerous, many ground buses and private transports passing by. As the day wore on, the buzz of excitement, the foot traffic, the lines of ground buses—all reached a sort of mad frenzy.

Forno pointed us toward Amp Street, and we took off at a jog. Nothing that would make us stand out, since many of the tourists hustled from place to place, from gift shop to restaurant, from open doors to buses.

We passed the Flaming Sea Tavern and its flickering neon sign, then slowed down again after a few blocks. The WuWu Bar and Grille sat on the same side of the street as the Sea. It was much smaller, and it didn't have the panache of its bigger sister. The food wasn't as good, the bartenders not as friendly. No cover charge. They had a license for prostitution, but the girls did their own advertising and found their own customers from the main floor.

And they sure as hell didn't have the limbo.

All in all, of the bars and brothels in town, the WuWu was the most laid-back. The most quiet. It was exactly what I needed right now.

A simple brown wooden sign hung over the entrance on a couple of chains, and simply said WUWU in huge red letters.

We passed through a painted red door that swung freely on its hinges, and were just about to walk over to the bar when a man at the door stopped us.

"Five squid, sirs."

I stared at him. "Since when?"

"Last year. Still fifteen squid cheaper than that overpriced place down the street, let me tell you!"

Forno said, "What? You didn't know?"

I gave him my "Shut up, Forno" look and dug in my pocket for the cover charge. Forno kept looking down at me, expectantly. "You don't have any money?"

Forno shrugged. "The Sea tapped me out."

"*I* paid for your Helk Ale."

"Yeah, nice of you. Thanks."

I sighed, then passed the man ten squid.

"Appreciate it, gentlemen," he said. "Enjoy yourselves. Any questions, see Talia at the bar."

We moved into the WuWu. It was still early, but a few patrons already nursed drinks at the bar, and a few more talked with some of the hired help at the various scarred wooden tables scattered haphazardly on the main floor. I pointed Forno toward the tables while I checked in at the bar.

Behind the lacquered bar, an older woman, maybe late fifties, early sixties, glanced at me as I stood near one corner. Her black hair, cut shoulder-length, had streaks of gray so evenly distributed that I wondered if she had colored it that way on purpose. She had on a long dress that seemed to be made out of light. The black material shimmered in the lights hanging low from the ceiling over her service area, and as she came toward me I saw that the dress was covered in tiny mirror beads.

"I'm Talia," she said, smiling as she wiped down the bar in front of me with a rag. "You have the look of someone who needs to know something."

I smiled back. "I'm wondering if you might have a message for me. Taylor Williams." It was the name I'd told Cara to use when she called in. "Might even be from yesterday."

"Sure," Talia said. "I remember. Hold on."

She walked to the far side of the bar, to the register and waiter station, and hunched over a stack of papers. A moment later she straightened and returned to me, a note in hand.

"Taylor Williams," she said, passing the safe-note to me, still sealed.

The paper, folded several times, had my alias scribbled across the top.

"Can I get you a drink?" she asked. She smiled broadly, and her teeth also gleamed in the light. Her front teeth had been fitted with mirror caps.

"Blue poison," I said. "And a Helk Ale."

She looked at me, then nodded behind me. "Ah, for your friend at the back."

I turned and saw Forno trying to get comfortable at a small table near the rear of the WuWu. "That's him."

"I'll bring them to you," she said.

"Thanks."

I paid her enough for both drinks, added a healthy tip, then joined Forno at the table.

"Find your message?" Forno asked.

Nodding, I unsealed the note. It had just two words. "Snowy Mountain."

"Nice," Forno said.

"Nice?"

"One of the better ski resorts, but a little less known because it's not as close to Kimson. Silly name, though, don't you think?"

"Could be worse. How's the snow?"

Forno snorted. "How would I know? Helks don't ski. No snow on Helkunntanas, and we hate the cold."

That was true. Helkunntanas bottomed out at about eighty degrees in the habitable areas.

"And we don't exactly fit in the lifts," he added.

"So she's at Snowy Mountain," I said. "How do we get there?"

"I used to have this nice flier," Forno mused.

"Jennifer's parking her shuttle on the other end of town. If the NIO doesn't track it down and take it back, maybe she'll give us another ride."

"Her schedule's not going to match ours, and she's already in trouble with the NIO. I'm sure the word's out about her. Another scapegoat added to the list."

"Then throw me another idea."

"About?"

"Getting to Snowy Mountain."

Forno shrugged just as Talia arrived with our drinks. She put down two coasters, both embedded with flash membranes alternating between the WuWu logo and advertisments for other Kimson attractions.

"Here you are," she said, placing the drinks on the coasters. She winked and headed back to the main bar.

A moment later, Forno said, "It's a free ride."

"What is?"

He took a sip of his ale and picked up the flash coaster. A flick of his finger at the top of the image, and the membrane froze with an advertisement for Snowy Mountain. He held it up for me to see.

It took a moment, but eventually I made out the smaller print near the bottom. "Resort bus to Snowy Mountain leaves every thirty minutes from the front of the Flaming Sea."

"There you go," Forno said. "A free lift to Cara. Say, how did Cara get there?"

"A flier. From the apartments she managed. I just told her to get out of town. At that point, I didn't trust Jennifer."

"Or Cara."

I shot him a glance, but he was right. I took a sip of my drink. "And I guess I still don't, considering the circumstances."

"Well, then," Forno said, downing the rest of his drink, "I guess it's time for us to smack the hills."

"That's 'hit the slopes,' " I said.

Forno laughed. "Just messing with you."

I shook my head, but managed a smile. Forno was more human than just about any Helk I'd ever met. Of course, I really hadn't met that many. I found that I truly did trust Forno now. I liked him, even though I hadn't known him long, and didn't know a thing about his past, other than what he'd said about being in the Kenn, and going undercover in the Helk underground. He could be abrasive and annoying, but what he lacked in tact, he made up for most noticeably with ... well ... *size*.

I was glad he was on my team.

Fifteen minutes later, after I bought some WuWu Wear—a warm coat and some rubber overshoes—we walked down to the Flaming Sea and did our best to look inconspicuous waiting along the sidewalk in front. When the resort bus arrived, we waited while other passengers loaded some of their equipment underneath in the storage compartments and placed their skis in the racks all around the sides of the bus. Then we entered the bus, having decided to sit apart from each other on opposite sides and opposite ends. The wide, somewhat rickety bus, nearly full, soon made its way down Amp Street.

I'd been on any number of transport vehicles over the past week, but this one trumped them all. I felt every bump and pothole in the road out of Kimson, the vibrations making my teeth rattle. It was a resort bus, so it serviced resorts other than Snowy Mountain. The bus stopped at three other ski areas before ours, and it didn't get to that first one until after an hour's drive. We endured a tedious drive up the first narrow, twisting mountain road to let off one batch of skiers, then waited for the skiers from the previous day to load on before continuing back down to the main road and the next resort.

By the time we reached Snowy Mountain, a good three hours had passed. Now I knew why diehard skiers started out so early in the day.

The spring morning, now inching toward midday, continued to do its damage to the resort, the snow nearly all melted in the parking lot, little rivulets working their way down the road. The sound of dripping water was everywhere.

The sun reflected off the snow on the slopes and hurt my eyes a little as I scanned the parking lot, easily locating the modest ski lodge and the surrounding buildings: store, pub, snack shop, and ticket booth. Near the buildings I spotted three chairlifts that whisked skiers to the tops of the various runs. No fancy mag-lifts here on Aryell. Not yet.

"It's the smallest of the resorts," Forno said, "but it's still a big place. Where are we going to find her?"

"The lodge. Like you, she doesn't ski."

"Yeah, well, I'm going to look way out of place here."

"You think you'd blend in better in the pub?"

"It's a thought."

"Check it out. If she's not there, then just stay there."

Forno held out his hand. "Expense money?"

Again, I couldn't help sighing. "You're paying me back," I said as I scrounged around for more money.

"Of course."

He took off for the pub, and a short jog brought me to the lodge, its entryway broad and spacious, two large wooden doors protecting the main foyer from the weather. On my right, a gigantic stone fireplace crackled with a roaring fire, and a dozen overstuffed, high-backed chairs and couches ringed the hearth. I saw only a few people in them because of the way the furniture was situated around the fireplace. To my left was the registration desk, which took up most of the space behind the couches and chairs. In front, down the aisle between, was the entrance to the restaurant, and a wide staircase led up to the balconied second level.

I stepped toward the fireplace so I could get a look at the folks lounging on the furniture, but none of them turned out to be Cara. There *was* one guy sitting there with a cast on his leg. Probably not fake.

I continued on to the restaurant, which had no host. A sign said SEAT YOURSELF, so I walked in, taking the long way around, checking the tables and booths. No Cara.

I passed somebody intently studying the menu, and I was just about ready to leave and start checking guest room floors when a voice from behind me said, "About time you figured things out and got here, Dave."

I recognized the voice and stopped midstep. I could hardly believe it. I turned and saw he had put down the menu and twisted his legs out from under the booth.

"Alan?" I said, my voice weak. I put a hand on the back of the booth to steady myself.

Alan Brindos stood and smiled. "Shall we find Cara and get the hell off this backwater planet?"

Twenty-six

Joseph the concierge—the *real* man, Brindos hoped—did have a last name: Sando. He drove the tiny black car through the streets of Midwest City in no apparent pattern, with no apparent destination in mind. Probably he was making sure they weren't being followed, while giving them all a little time to sort things out.

Dorie put another square of RuBy on Brindos's tongue, then explained that she had found Joseph at the hotel right at his concierge stand, giving him Brindos's alias, Dexter Roberts, urging him to help. He had done so readily, she said, because of all that had happened between them. Luckily, it was slow at the hotel, and the second concierge had come in early, so Joesph checked out.

When Joseph finally pulled the car over to the curb, it was in a residential neighborhood so devoid of traffic and pedestrians that Brindos thought they had entered the area from the Conduit disaster, everyone evacuated. But that was East City. Joseph ran his hands over the console in front of him, the car coughed a few times, then fell silent.

Now he was able to fully turn around and face them. His eyes narrowed and the wrinkles in his face deepened as he studied Brindos. "So they got to you," he said. "These aliens Dorie told me about. The real threat. Unbelievable."

Brindos looked up at Joseph, still terribly uncomfortable in the cramped quarters of the car. "They got to *you*," Brindos said.

"Apparently."

"You going to tell me what happened with all that? The Restaurant, the night at the hotel? The minor details like the goddamn reason why you didn't tell me about being copied?"

"Calm down, Mr. Roberts—" He shook his head. "I mean, Mr. Brindos."

"You see the shit I'm in. Don't tell me to calm down."

"How do I know you are who *you* say you are?"

"Come on, Joe, why would we be in this predicament right now? Dorie coming to get you? Didn't I just mention the Restaurant? The night at the hotel? How about the Blue Rocket, when you told me everything you saw in that alley."

He shrugged. "Things the copy could know."

"You told me you were the reason I didn't get hauled into jail by the Midwest City Authority. I killed a man, and you witnessed it."

"Then there you were, biting out cold in the alley next to the body."

"Yes."

"Or a copy of you."

"Jesus, Joe!"

Joseph turned away from them. Dorie continued to keep a comforting hand on the top of Brindos's head, but Brindos knew she was looking at him differently, not having heard about this. He was surprised she wasn't in pain from most of his weight pressing down on her.

"Joe," Brindos said. He didn't need to argue with him, he needed answers. "We talked baseball. When Cecil wouldn't help me get to the disaster site."

Joseph didn't move, just gripped the wheel of the car. "What team?"

"Tigers. Detroit Tigers. We complained about the open space laws shutting down the game."

Joseph visibly relaxed, loosening his grip on the wheel. "Look, I don't know anything about what happened."

"Nothing about what happened to you? To me?"

"I only know that one evening several weeks ago, I missed an entire shift at work."

"You lost time."

"Fifteen hours. I just thought it was some sort of exhaustion that put me out for so long. I'd been working long hours. Only . . . something didn't seem quite right about it all. There was all the craziness around the Conduit disaster, but I somehow put it out of my mind."

"But why you? Why copy a hotel concierge? And a copy that an *alien* is using?"

"I don't know for sure, but probably because they could watch you through me. How would you know if it was me or my double talking to you or doing concierge duties in your presence?"

"It was obviously you who talked baseball to me and got me the cab to the airport."

"Yes. But there could have been other times the copy of me was there, when I was off shift."

"True." He remembered wondering—even asking—if Joe ever slept. He seemed to always be at the hotel.

"And it was you who took me to the Restaurant?"

Joseph nodded. "What I saw there I truly did see. It happened the way I told it to you at the Blue Rocket. Hearing you talk about your perceptions of what happened, about waking up with all those hours missing? Well, I didn't want to believe it might be connected to what happened to me. Then you walked out of the Blue Rocket, and that was the last I saw of you." He turned fully back to them again, his discomfort gone now. "But I didn't know about"—he pointed at Brindos, his eyes looking him over, up and down—"your change. I didn't know about . . . what Dorie said . . . about another *me*."

Brindos stared out the window, at the prefab houses across the way taking shape in the morning light. He raised his arms and looked at his furry hands, the size of them still unbelievable. "I wasn't even Alan Brindos for a long while," he whispered. "I'm not me at all on the outside. But Dorie saved me on the inside."

Dorie's other arm, the one not cradling and stroking his head, tightened around his torso. He understood her need to help him. To be close. He was her husband. *Had* been her husband. If the situation had been different, would he have even taken notice of someone like Dorie?

Dorie saved him.

But it wasn't enough, he knew. She saved him from being Plenko, but she wouldn't be able to save him from the aftereffects of the change. Already, the last RuBy he'd taken had begun to wear off, the ache inside starting to build again.

"What happened?" Joseph asked.

Brindos told him about walking out of the Blue Rocket, the Helks grabbing him, taking him out to meet Plenko.

To meet his One.

Joseph closed his eyes when Brindos told him about what the Joseph copy had done to Brindos.

"I don't have much time," Brindos said. "According to Plenko, the process that turned me into this is not without complications. I have a day or two at best."

"I'm sorry," he said.

"Don't be. None of it is your fault. As you said, you were helping me out."

"If I hadn't, you'd have been saved this agony."

"A death sentence for murder, you said. End result the same."

"But you've found out a lot," Dorie said. "You've helped me too."

True. There was a sense of urgency now. Whatever was happening could take over the Union as quickly as any cataclysmic event. Brindos's severely shortened life span should only keep him more focused and determined. He tensed as pain rippled up both arms, both legs.

"Then help me understand, Dorie," Brindos said. "Plenko said you were alive now only because of something about a key. Something you said you could help him find."

Dorie grimaced, then looked away, obviously nervous about something.

"What is it?" Brindos said.

She pursed her lips, her eyes darting back and forth. Not looking at Brindos directly. She shook her head, as if deciding she couldn't come up with a reason to tell him.

"Tell me, Dorie."

"I can't."

"Why not?"

"I don't know what it is."

Joseph piped up now. He'd been listening intently. "You don't trust me. It's only logical. Maybe you don't even trust Mr. Brindos, here."

Dorie shook her head. "No, it's not that. I just don't *know*. Plenko seemed to think I should know. But maybe my copy knew. Before she killed herself."

Joseph frowned. "You're copied too?"

She nodded. "While I've been on Temonus, Plenko has kept asking for the key. He didn't even know what it was."

"He kept you alive," Brindos said, "based on what you knew, which was nothing?"

She nodded. "But he thought I might understand at some point."

"So you honestly don't know what it is or what happened to it?" Brindos asked.

Dorie shook her head, and she drooped her shoulders, her eyes downcast. "But I told them *some*thing without thinking about it. They set off on a little side mission, and it did buy me some time, but I got a couple of people killed because of it."

"Where?"

"On Aryell."

Brindos raised an eyebrow. "My partner ended up there. It wasn't him—"

"No, no. One was a woman. Katerina Parker. She was a friend of mine. Well, then she became a friend of my copy."

"Katerina."

"She went by Kristen. She replaced a girl at the Flaming Sea Tavern named Lexianna. Lexy for short."

Brindos's pulse pounded in his throat.

Sexy Lexy.

Cara Landry had worked for her. If what Dorie said was true, Cara might have worked for this Katerina Parker. Katerina Parker who was now dead.

Crowell could be right in the middle of it.

If Dorie wanted to talk about trust, then turnabout was fair play. Brindos said nothing about Cara. He shook off a strident buzzing echoing in his head, then endured a gut twist. For the love of Union, the pain never went away now, only added sharp barbs in spite, each one harder to bear. He looked at Joseph, who ignored him and stared at Dorie.

"Who was the other person killed?" Brindos asked Dorie.

"Some Helk of Plenko's," she said. "That's what Plenko said. Could have been anyone. One of the Chinknos, a Knox, or Koch."

Brindos sighed and tensed the muscles in his arm against the jangling of his nerves and the snaps of pain running from his fingers to his shoulder.

"I've got nowhere else to go," he said. "I'm the most wanted Helk, Terl Plenko. I've got to get off Temonus and find my partner Dave."

Joseph leaned back as far as he could between the seats. "But if it's all happening here—"

"The Conduit's down," Dorie said.

"I was copied after that happened," Brindos said, "so it must still be working in at least some limited capacity."

"All the more reason to stay here and fight this thing," Joseph said.

"They're gunning for me," Brindos said. "The Union government is looking for Plenko. *Me.* If I can get off-planet, find Dave, find out the bigger picture? I don't know. So much has already happened, and I feel like I'm no closer to the truth of it all. Maybe Dave knows more."

A new twinge of pain ran through him then, and he grunted.

Joe said, "You need help."

"Joe, you were the only person I thought might be able to help."

"If I turned out to be who you hoped I would be, that is."

"Yeah."

Joseph turned completely around to the front again and restarted the car. "Then we best get moving."

"Moving?" Brindos said. "Where to?"

"I'm the goddamn concierge for the Orion Hotel," he said back to them, pulling onto the street. "I've got connections."

* * *

Dorie switched to the front as Joseph drove them to the Orion. He entered the hotel to make calls to some of those connections only a concierge seemed able to make. When he climbed back into the car, Brindos saw he had also grabbed a hotel comm-phone so they could make some calls on the way. It looked like a simple block of black plastic, almost antique. He assured them the phone was not trackable.

"I'll have proper clearance," Joe said as they drove to the airport. "The lockouts have no effect on my car, and I can bypass any travel routine the suits try to program into the grid."

"Who did you call?" Brindos asked, fondly remembering this Joseph as the friendly, knowledgeable man who had helped him during his first days in Midwest City.

"A gal I know who works for the Authority, and an old friend at M.W.C. Airport who can get my car past the security checkpoints going in, since nonessential traffic is still limited."

"Then what?" The view between the front seats revealed the wet streets flashing by a little too quickly for his comfort. Brindos gripped Joseph's headrest.

"I'm working on it," he said, waving the comm-phone in his free hand.

Twenty minutes after that, they reached the entrance to the huge facility, Joseph's car passing the initial checkpoints without incident. Dorie kissed Brindos's forehead and gave him some more RuBy as they arrived in the public parking area skirting the TWT terminal and the dozen or so launch circles. During the drive from hotel to airport, Joseph stayed on his phone, making half a dozen different calls. The names he used had no significance to Brindos, but each call ended the same, with Joseph hanging up, shaking his head, and mumbling curses.

Temonus's spaceport bustled with activity, with drop shuttles landing on the launch circles and shuttles taking off from other circles, bound for Solan Station in orbit or to West City. Once in a while, the occasional press shuttle cleared for East City headed off to cover the Conduit disaster, or the attack on the Helk district. According to Joseph, the scene at the Conduit still had everyone over there scrambling.

They sat in the airport parking lot, gazing out at the arriving and departing flights. Joseph and Dorie sat in the front seats of the black car, and Brindos remained low in the back, spread out the best he could, enduring his escalating pain.

Now, sitting in the parking area, they all reached the same conclusion. They hadn't a chance in Helkunntanas of getting on a drop shuttle.

"I'm sorry," Joseph said. "I thought I could get us on a ride out of here."

Dorie looked back at Brindos. "You feeling okay?"

At the moment, because of the RuBy, he wasn't feeling much pain. He nodded. "But it wears off faster now."

"I know." She searched his eyes as if trying to gauge how much time he had left. "This is getting awfully difficult, Alan. I'm about out of my RuBy, and I don't know how we're going to get any other treatment to you."

Brindos shook his head. "I can last awhile longer."

"That's just it," she said. "I don't know how much longer you have."

His gut churned, and he closed his eyes. Not much longer. Not much. Soon he would be dead, if what Plenko and Dorie said had any validity.

"Then we have to figure something out, and fast," Brindos said. He shook his head and stared at the nearest shuttle, which happened to be loading up with reporters.

An idea started to take shape.

"Joe, those press shuttles. Can they make the trip to Solan Station?"

Joseph shifted in his seat, looking out at the same shuttle. "Sure."

Brindos felt the first trickle of hope run through him, the first in a long time. Dorie still scanned his face, her eyes narrowed.

"What for?" she said.

"Joe," Brindos said, ignoring her, "you know anyone at *Cal Gaz*?"

"Cal who?"

"It's a Helk newspaper."

"Oh, you mean *The Monitor*."

"Yes, that's the translation. The English version."

"They're all Helks there, but yeah, I know one. Reporter. But you're not going to get him anywhere close to this airport."

"I met a *Cal Gaz* reporter at the airport in East City named Melok."

"Melok." He pondered a moment before shaking his head. "No, I don't know him."

"He's human. The only one working there."

Joseph lifted his eyebrows. "Human? Unusual. I still don't know him."

"Doesn't matter. Whoever you know over there, see if you can get him to get Melok to contact us."

"Why would he help?"

"Don't know if he will. But he was sympathetic to the idea that the Conduit had been sabotaged. He gave me his card, but I kind of blew him off."

"You have his card?" Joseph offered his phone. "Why don't you call—"

"I don't have it anymore. It was in my pants pocket, but of course that disappeared along with my clothes when I was altered."

Joseph pulled back the phone.

"Alan," Dorie said, "just because he seemed sympathetic—"

"He's a go-getter," Brindos said. "I think I can entice him by promising the story of a lifetime."

"An awfully big risk," Joseph said.

"You don't know; he might be one of them," Dorie said.

"He wasn't."

"He could be now," Dorie said. "You changed. Same could've happened to him."

Joseph nodded. "Like I said, an awful risk."

Brindos said, "What other choice do I have?"

Not long ago he'd thought about risk and its implications. Brindos, a little wheel hidden somewhere on a big machine that kept plodding along no matter what direction he tried to turn. All he had was his little map and a general direction.

"I may not get out of this alive," Brindos said, the seeping pain reminding him of just that, "but I can do some real damage before all is said and done. More than that, I owe it to my partner. Make the call, Joe."

After one final sharp look, Joseph sighed and turned his attention to the phone.

A moment later, he put it to his ear and they waited out the silence in the car. Outside, the nearby shuttle roared as it rocketed from its landing circle and climbed out of sight.

"Bertram?" Joe said into the phone. "Joseph from the Orion. I need a little help locating a reporter of yours. Human named Melok."

Dorie and Brindos stared at each other as Joseph listened to the voice on the other end. Brindos couldn't decipher any of the low scratchy words seeping out of Joseph's receiver.

"Yes," Joseph said. Another pause. "No, I don't know him personally."

Brindos edged closer to Joseph's ear, watching his other hand tighten on the steering wheel. He still couldn't make out anything from the other end.

Joseph said, "Really? You're certain? How come?" His voice sounded disappointed.

"What?" Brindos whispered, getting impatient.

Joseph waved him off. "Bertram, can you tell me where I could find him? No? Bertram, this is extremely important." He waited, listening. "Privacy? What does he need with privacy? Maybe I want to offer something he needs . . . No, no. I was just following up on something a client told me . . . Some-time soon. Of course. When my schedule quiets down a bit."

Brindos heard the voice on the other end say a few words, then Joseph clicked off and frowned.

"What's wrong, Joe?" Brindos asked.

Joseph puffed out his cheeks, then shook his head. "Apparently, Mr. Melok no longer works for *Cal Gaz*."

Brindos blinked. "What?"

"They fired him yesterday."

"You're kidding."

"Something about some stories he wrote. He wasn't being a good team player."

"Wasn't a good *Helk*," Brindos said. "He wrote that sabotage article about the Conduit, I bet."

"Bertram said it was more than that, something a lot more serious. Something about putting Helks in a bad light. I asked where I could find him, but he wouldn't give me anything. I figured it was better not to push it, not knowing who's really who over there at the paper anymore."

"Your friend Bertram included," Dorie said.

Brindos had hoped Melok could get them onto a press shuttle somehow. He'd felt so hopeful, and now the shuttle idea was out of the question.

Brindos pondered Melok's name, turning it over and over in his brain like an old-fashioned washing machine. Why did it seem so familiar? He had thought much the same upon first meeting him in the airport cafe.

The three of them sat in the car, lost as to what to do. Pretty soon, some official at the airport would get suspicious about the little black car in the parking lot and they'd be on the run again.

If Brindos had not been a Helk, he'd have had no trouble boarding a shuttle. How the hell had Plenko managed to get around from planet to planet without capture? Transworld Transport's best customer indeed. The truth was, he really hadn't done a lot of planet-hopping. His aliases had done the work for him. The Kochs and Knoxes, all different faces.

If he could change his face. If he could change his race.

But he couldn't, even if he knew how to do it, even if he braved the consequences. The Conduit might have put this face on him, and it might still be working, but trying to get to it somehow was out of the question. He didn't have the kind of time he'd need to work that out. His gut squirmed as if acknowledging his thoughts, and he grimaced and closed his eyes.

Anyway, to do the process again would probably kill him outright.

You are a Thin Man now.

Plenko's name had an ominous, surreal quality to it, and the idea that Brindos had become one of his ilk made him sick to his stomach. Plenko had said Brindos would be dead before too long due to errors in the copy process, so was Brindos really one of them? *Am I anyone?* An orphan, left on his own most of his life. This is what it came to, just going out of the world the way he'd left it. A stranger to himself and everyone around him, except maybe Dorie.

Dorie, who loved him without knowing *him*.

Pain rippled from the top of his head to his neck, a particularly sharp stab attacking his left cheek. The painful sensations didn't seem to target any one area of his body, always moving, always unique. He tried to do his suffering in the backseat without alarming Dorie.

Finally, Joseph said, "What now?"

"Let's get out of here," Brindos wheezed. "Anywhere. We'd need an army to get to any of those shuttles."

Dorie looked back. "Maybe we can find one."

"Sure," Brindos said with a snort. "Joe, have any standing army contacts?"

Joseph said nothing, but pulled out of the parking spot. Soon, he had them on a path back toward the business district.

He hadn't gone more than three blocks when Brindos yelled for him to stop. Brakes screeched, the car fishtailed, then came to a halt in the middle of the street.

"Hold on," Brindos whispered, fighting nausea, which gave way to a crunching pain through hips and legs. He closed his eyes, waiting a moment.

When he opened them, Dorie and Joseph were looking back at him, surprise on their faces.

"Across the street," Brindos said.

They stared out Joseph's window and Brindos wriggled around so he could get a better look out the passenger window. A tiny shop sat in the middle of the block, a somewhat rundown building with a modest sign over its door that seemed out of place compared to the glitz and flash of the surrounding stores.

"Temonus Tales?" Joseph said.

"Yeah," Brindos answered. "Media store, right?"

He nodded. "Flashbooks, download hubs, DataNet visors and immersion specs, fiction rings, implant journals. Even some rare paper books and some old used electronic books. What are you thinking?"

Brindos smiled, but even that hurt now. "Comics."

Brindos stared hard at the front door. He'd barely had a moment for the thought to gel in the intervals between pain and disappointment, but then it was there, triggered by the sight of the bookshop.

"Comics," Dorie said. "You . . . want to buy comics?"

"One particular comic. In whatever media I can find it." He looked at her, excitement overcoming some of the pain now, knowing he was on to something. "*Stickman.*"

Dorie shook her head. "Excuse me?"

"I just remembered how I know Melok's name," Brindos said. "It's *Paul* Melok."

"And you remembered his name how?" Joseph asked.

"He's the writer." They both gawked at Brindos as if he'd told them he was pregnant. "Paul Melok writes the comic *Stickman.*"

Twenty-seven

Alan Brindos stood in the lodge's restaurant, waiting me out, an amused smile on his face. He had taken me completely by surprise.

"Alan, what are you doing here?"

He raised his eyebrows. "Doing fine, Dave, thanks for asking. And how are you?" He waited a couple of beats before continuing. "Goddamn, Dave, relax." He slapped me on the shoulder. "It's good to see you. I'm relieved that you're okay. I expected the worst."

I wasn't relaxed because of all I'd seen since coming to Aryell. Meeting Cara. Jennifer Lisle. Forno. And then: Jennifer and Cara again, only they were not Jennifer and Cara. One of them now dead. And now here was Alan, on this planet, showing his happy face, which he rarely brought out for anyone.

Alan? Really?

No.

Did this copy really think he could fool me? Would *I* be able to fool *him*?

"The worst *has* happened," I said, working in a response as quickly as I could. My brain whirred crazily, trying to come up with what to say next while continuing with small talk. "But I'm fine."

"Really?" he said. "You'll have to tell me, but it's pretty urgent we get out of here. I've lots to tell *you,* and I'm still recovering from that little trip you made me take to Temonus."

I nodded and forced a little smile. "How'd that work out for you?"

"Work out?"

"I lost contact. Your code card. What happened to it? What happened to you?"

He came up to me, hooked his arm in mine, and pulled me away from the booth toward the hotel's main lobby. "Plenko."

I walked with him. "You found him."

"He found *me*."

"And you lived to tell the tale."

"I got away from him, but he had already taken my code card."

I nodded as we passed by the front desk, Alan gently leading me toward the large front doors.

"So what about Cara?" he asked. "How is she?"

Once again, he took me by surprise. I could tell he had no idea she was here at the resort. He'd wonder why I'd stopped, though, so I said, "Wait a minute. How'd you find me? Here, at Snowy Mountain?" It's a question I would've asked the real Alan if he had made such an unannounced appearance.

He made a gesture with his arms, hands palm out, shrugging a little. "Hey, it's me. Aren't I the sleuthy one?"

I waited.

He sighed. "The Flaming Sea. Your alias."

"My alias."

"Yeah, only you didn't use your normal one. Neil Ryan. Good thinking, of course. The folks at the Sea, as usual, were very accommodating. Naturally, I know a number of your other names. Lancaster. Norton. Bouncer at the front door said you'd left, come back, talked to some folks, left again. I thought maybe you'd been under duress, because he mentioned seeing you with a Helk. I did a couple of quick searches around town, threw in some official posturing, and turned up your Taylor Williams alias at the WuWu Bar and Grille."

"That's why we pay you the big bucks," I said, doing my best to act casual.

"Gal there—Talia, I think her name was—said she heard you talk about skiing."

I'd thought Talia hadn't been near enough to hear all that. She certainly hadn't read the sealed safe-note.

He smiled, motioning me toward the front door. "I know, I know. Bad stuff going on. Come on, let's get out of here."

Outside, the sidewalks and service road that wound through the resort buildings were nearly deserted, since by this time most of the skiers were on the slopes, or taking lunch up at the cafeteria at the top of the mountain or in the pub. A tractor of some sort rumbled, coming up the service road, its rear grooming attachment lifted so it wouldn't scratch the bare and wet pavement.

Almost deserted.

Three Helks formed a triangle, one of them directly in front of me on the other side of the road, the other two on either side of me just inside my peripheral vision. I kept walking down the steps, Alan at my side, staring at the Helk in front of me. It was Tony Koch.

A different Tony Koch, of course.

I stopped and turned toward Brindos, but he had already looked away, toward the Helk on our right.

Another copy of one of the supposed Plenko aliases. *Knox.*

I looked left quickly. The Helk there stood about fifteen feet away. *Chinkno.*

Back to the Brindos copy. I hadn't done much fighting in a long time, but if I didn't want to be taken, I'd have to try, and the timing would have to be dead-on perfect.

"I know you," I said to Alan's back when the tractor had come close to the Helk on the left. The muscles in the Brindos's neck tensed. "And you know I know."

The Brindos turned back to me, smiling, holding up a hand in a calming manner. "Dave, relax," he started to say.

I narrowed my eyes and took a single step toward him.

"Honestly, Dave, I don't know these three—"

"Bullshit."

Suddenly he lunged, and I took back my earlier step, retreating and leaning away from him as he swung at me hard with his fist. I stuck out my own arm and blocked most of the blow's power. As I reeled backward, the Koch and Knox Helks slipped their stunners from their tunics and started to fire, the pulse beams slicing into the lodge behind me, the entryway, and the stairs. Warning shots, I supposed, due to the Brindos's close proximity. The Knox copy, across the street, ran forward. Chinkno, behind me, had to be coming up too, and I wouldn't have much time with the Helks's lightning-fast speed.

I leaned forward and twisted around, putting the Brindos in front of me. As he drew his own weapon, I smacked his face with my open palm. He staggered back and I grabbed at him to keep him from falling, latched on to his arm with the blaster, found the trigger finger, aimed, and shot Knox in his left side. He fell, and I had just enough time to round about with my leg and thunk it into the groin area of the charging Chinkno behind me, also catching the hand carrying the stunner. Pain raced through my leg, but Chinkno grunted and stopped a moment. Before the Brindos could recover, I elbowed him in the nose, and took that moment as he brought his hands to his face to wrench his blaster free. I spun and blasted Chinkno in the head.

The driver of the ski tractor stopped the vehicle when he realized what was going on, and slipped off the far side and ran. The tractor was directly between me and Koch. He'd been waiting across the road, obviously not expecting me to have made it this far, waiting for some cue from the Brindos.

I let the Brindos go in favor of racing toward Koch, the more formidable enemy. With almost careless abandon, I charged the ski tractor, which now completely obscured the Helk. With the blaster stiff-armed in front of me, I clambered onto the tractor and came up firing, surprising Koch, who'd been quickly sidestepping to the front of the tractor. I hadn't had a chance to aim, and a few shots went wild, but two blasts caught his torso, and he went down.

I leaped off the tractor, the pavement sending a jolting pain through my lower legs. I winced, but recovered and looked up quickly, trying to track the Brindos. He was running up the road to my right, toward the far ski lifts and the pub, and he had quite a jump on me. Taking a deep breath, I sprinted after him, the blaster held high in front of me. Screams sounded around me as the few tourists nearby ran for cover. Could I shoot a man I'd known so well for so long, if I had to? I aimed the blaster in his general direction and fired, but my intent was not to hit him. Chances would've been slim to hit him at this distance, with both of us on the run.

Instead, I had aimed at the pub in front of him, mindful of the by-standers scrambling out of the way.

At this point, I just wanted to hit the pub. I kept firing, the sonic beams lashing across the service road and ricocheting off the pub's front facade.

"C'mon, Forno," I muttered as I ran. "A little help."

The Brindos glanced over his shoulder at me as he drew near the pub. If I wanted to now, I could hit him. Not kill him. I wanted him alive, see what I could get out of him. My blaster's sonic beam could cut him down, trip him up. Making up my mind, I readied myself to aim, but just then, the Brindos copy stopped and spun, and in his hand was a Helk stunner. While I was vaulting over the tractor to get to Koch, he must've picked up the weapon from the dead Knox before racing toward the pub.

He raised it.

I dove to the road, rolling left just as he fired. The stunner's beam struck next to me on the pavement. I rolled some more, try-ing to find cover. Another beam just missed my head, and my hair stood on end. I would've thought my rolling helped, but I realized he'd missed on purpose. He didn't want me *dead*. Yet.

I kept my sights on the Brindos, who had stopped firing and turned to the pub again.

Then Cara ran out the pub's front door, Forno right behind her. She slipped on a patch of ice, lost her balance, and pitched forward—

"Cara!" I hollered.

—right into the Brindos copy's grasp.

She cried out a sound of fright and surprise as he kept her from falling, throwing his left arm around her neck, pulling backward and twisting her a little to put her in between us. At the same time, his right arm whipped up and he fired the stunner at Forno.

I didn't see where it hit him, but Forno stumbled backward, then fell in front of the pub's doorway. He lay facedown, and didn't move.

I scrambled to my feet and put myself in position, blaster up, pointed toward the Brindos. Cara struggled, but he had a good grip around her throat. She couldn't even speak.

"Dave!" he yelled, swinging around with his weapon. "Not a good idea, Dave."

"Let her go!" I yelled back.

He shook his head, stepped back, and put his stunner to Cara's head. "I'll kill her, Dave."

I blinked hard, realizing as I stood there that I could now feel the ache in my leg from kicking Chinkno, the pain in my feet from jumping down so hard from the tractor, and the hurt in my shoulder from hitting the pavement and rolling. I fought to keep my blaster steady. I was sure resort security was on its way, but I didn't imagine they'd be prepared for this kind of standoff at a ski resort.

I took four determined steps forward, blaster level.

"Don't," the Brindos said.

"What do you want?" I said. "Let her go."

"She's not going anywhere. Not until she—or you, if you're privy to the information—tells me what I need to know."

"I don't know where your goddamn key is," I told him.

The Brindos laughed an eerie, not-Brindos laugh. "I think you do."

Somewhere above, close by, I heard the whine of a transport in the Aryellan sky, but I tried to stay intent on the Brindos.

"The key, Dave," he said.

"Don't know. Don't have it."

He jammed the stunner under Cara's chin. "I suppose you don't have it either?" he said to her. She shook her head, but her eyes stayed on me. Eyes wide with fear.

I stared at this counterfeit Brindos, anger rising in my throat. Behind him, in the pub doorway, I saw Forno stir. He was alive, but I didn't know how badly he was hurt. Didn't know how much the stunner might have damaged muscles and tissue.

"You don't have any way out of this," I said.

He laughed again. "I don't need a way out of this."

I narrowed my eyes. "Let her go. You kill her, you're a dead man. You know that."

"Dave, why should I care—or anyone else care—what happens to me? What do you think? I'm just a copy. A copy, Dave. I came from a Brindos pattern in the buffer. They got your partner, scanned his pattern, and turned him loose. If he's lucky, that's all they did to him. They could change him from a dozen captured patterns if they wanted to. His pattern is *there*. It'll be there long after I'm dead. After your partner Alan Brindos—wherever he is—is dead. The aliens gave me his memories, or some of them. As many as I needed to do this job."

"Who *are* you?"

"I don't even know anymore. They used Brindos's pattern to burn me out. Decided to fill me with his memories, and lock my own away from me by injecting me with some shit."

In the pub doorway, Forno made an effort to turn over. He seemed to be looking for something. His own weapon?

"I want the key, Dave," the Brindos said. "And if you don't give it to me, then I'm done."

Done? My heart thumped as I realized what he might do. *Cara*.

The whine I'd heard earlier came from a shuttle, and it was now somewhere over the resort, perhaps the parking lot behind us.

"Terl Plenko," the Brindos said. "He will find you."

The shuttle flew in, its thrusters screaming overhead. I didn't dare look up as it hovered above the road, flurries of snow whipping around us.

"The key, Dave!" the Brindos yelled.

Someone shouted from the shuttle, but I couldn't hear what.

Brindos brought his weapon up and fired a few quick pulses at the shuttle, and my eyes flicked upward. He hit the fuselage, scoring it from door to turbines. It wavered a little as it tried to stay in place, correcting as it slew to the left. No one up there returned fire, and I didn't have a clear shot at him myself.

Tucked in tight behind Cara, he said something to her I couldn't quite hear. My eyes darted from her face to his, and I stepped forward.

"See you around, Dave," he said, then straightened, giving me the clear shot. But as I aimed the blaster, the Brindos pulled the trigger of the stunner underneath Cara's chin.

I screamed, running now as I fired at the Brindos, catching him on his right shoulder. I saw another beam strike him from behind. Forno had found his own stunner.

Cara fell. The Brindos fell too, the smile on his face cemented there, and he was dead before he hit the ground.

I rushed to Cara as the shuttle's high-pitched whine modulated, the thrusters backing off. I knew the shuttle was lowering, settling onto the service road. I reached Cara's body, falling to my knees.

Time slowed.

Forno coughed next to me.

I breathed, and tears came to my eyes. I turned my head as the door of the shuttle opened. It clacked into place and Jennifer Lisle stood perfectly still in the opening.

Twenty-eight

orie came out of Temonus Tales and jogged back across the street with a bag in her hand. Before going in, she'd given Brindos some RuBy, a whole paper. At best it had numbed the pain, which never let up now. He wasn't sure how much more of the ups and downs he could handle. He'd missed the timing for at least one treatment, maybe two, and he wouldn't last long after missing two, according to Plenko.

Dorie opened the passenger's side front door and ducked inside, offering the bag. Inside the bag was a flashbook of the latest issue of *Stickman*.

Letters and numbers glowed red on the outer skin of the rolled-up flash membrane: *Stickman 38.*

"Number thirty-eight," Brindos said, flicking his fingers over the green-tinged membrane, unlocking the roll.

"There've been that many?" Joseph asked.

"*Stickman* debuted long before Plenko started up. It's only in the last few years that the story line's moved toward the whole Plenko archenemy thing."

The membrane, flexible and stretchable, powered up, opaquing enough to keep bleed-through away. The front cover snapped into place, filling the membrane completely with the image. It showed Stickman, a normal-looking human by most accounts, except for his extreme thinness and, of course, his special power of elasticity. He held a pose that suggested he was about to have his head handed to him on a platter, for he was stiff and rigid, not engaged in his well-known Stretch-O mode he'd acquired after some type of scientific experiment went haywire. His gray head-to-toe uniform (specially designed to morph with his elastic body) glistened with some yellow ooze. Near the edge of the cover, standing bigger than life, was the massive bulk of Terl Plenko, his mouth set with an evil laugh, his unnaturally clawed hand holding the weapon that spewed the yellow ooze.

Brindos hadn't read a lot of comics as a kid, and when he did, it was usually via immersion specs at a few of the foster homes he'd stayed at, none of them very up-to-date, and he certainly could never have afforded implants, or even the earliest flashbook models. But this cover was like those his great-grandfather had told him about, explaining how the images themselves gave a hint of the story to come inside.

He thumbed the lower right corner for acknowledgments, and words snapped into place at the bottom of the cover, announcing "Pictures by Tad Anthony, Story by Paul Melok."

"So," Dorie said, "Melok was with *Cal Gaz*, but he was probably also researching a future issue of the comic."

"But what can this tell us?" Joe asked. "It's just stories."

"Stories based on reality," Brindos said.

Joseph pointed at the comic. "Mr. Brindos, the likelihood of this story line in this particular issue being of any use to us—"

"I know," Brindos said, nodding, but he concentrated on the issue, flicking the control nodes embedded in the flashpaper to navigate the comic. The art was damn good, the inside art matching the feel of the cover, the colors bright, the likeness of Plenko nearly flawless. Stickman, in Stretch-O mode, twisted all over the page, allowing for writer and artist to work together to create an almost sinuous look.

Brindos might not get any hints from the story, but it might help them find Melok.

He found the search node, brought up the contents list, and ran his finger down until he found the staff box. He flexed the membrane there and pulled, the text zooming out large and bold until he found the publisher's name: Skinny Press. Underneath was a logo of the letters *S* and *P* looking like sticks branching off each other. The publisher had included a holo-animation within, the logo morphing slightly, the colors of the letters switching between red and blue, a halo of white light appearing every few seconds to orbit around them.

Below was the address.

"Skinny Press," Brindos said. "Twelve-A, New York Avenue. Please tell me, Mr. Concierge, you know where that is."

Joseph gave a hurt look, then accessed his memory a second before answering. "That's residential, not too far away."

"Do you think Melok publishes the comic himself?" Dorie asked.

"He might. He might do the work from home and send it out from there. Only one way to find out. It'll save a lot of time if it's Melok's house."

"Then hang on," Joseph said. He pulled his black car out into the street, then turned left at the first corner he came to. "Have you there in five minutes."

During the ride to New York Avenue, Brindos skimmed *Stickman 38*. Dorie and Joseph were right. Just stories. Based on fact, but nothing in the story line gave any real hints about what was happening to the Union. Only Plenko and—by default, it seemed—the Helks seemed to be implicated and based on some measure of reality. Brindos wasn't that impressed with Melok's storytelling abilities, but the juxtaposition of the words with Tad Anthony's art, along with the odd, somewhat flawed character of Stickman himself, pulled him through.

Flawed. *Sounds like me,* he thought.

A stampede of various aches and pains rushed through him all at once on its way over a goddamn buffalo jump. He didn't want the crash at the bottom. Closing his eyes, taking deep breaths, he let the dust clear before returning to the comic.

In *Stickman 38,* Terl Plenko had taken innocent humans hostage, ready to sell them off one by one to the various crime lords of Temonus as slave labor to help solidify the alliances the Helks had with each of them. Plenko's internal monologues, however, spoke of betrayal, and how his Movement would eventually make the crime lords bow at his feet. At the same time, having perfected his Slime Stunner, Plenko had baited Stickman with the human hostages and trapped him with the slime that neutralized the Stretch-O ability.

And there it ended. Despite himself, Brindos smiled. He enjoyed a good cliffhanger.

"Just ahead," Joseph said.

Brindos caught a look at the neighborhood as the car slowed down. The prefabs were older here, or at least less cared for. Otherwise, they looked similar to most homes outside the Helk district.

"That's the one," Joseph said, and pulled over across the street from a white two-story that looked in better condition than most.

Brindos was sure the money was good for Melok, since *Stickman* had quite the following. If this was indeed Melok's place. There was only one way to find out.

"All of us out," Brindos said. "Strength in numbers."

Joseph laughed. "You've got my strength somewhere in your little finger, I think."

Brindos rolled and popped another square of RuBy, then they exited the car and crossed the street, which luckily was as quiet as the rest of Midwest City this morning. The rain from earlier had come back in a thin drizzle. Brindos kept to the side of the door, out of sight, and Dorie and Joseph positioned themselves in front. Brindos nodded to Dorie, and she reached up, her rain slicker swishing a bit with the motion, and rang the doorbell. All the quaint customs of an earlier era. No fancy sensors, recognition programs, or greeting routines. Just a button that when pushed made a bell inside say *ding dong*.

A few moments later, someone answered the door. Brindos kept his eyes on Dorie and Joseph.

"Yes?"

Joseph smiled. "Mr. Melok, by any chance?"

A pause.

"Who wants to know?" came the voice.

Brindos tried to remember Melok's voice from the airport, but that had been awhile ago, and frankly everyone sounded a little different to his Helk ears.

"I'm with the Orion Hotel," Joseph said. "The head concierge."

"What does the Orion want with me?" he asked. Then he snorted. "Wait, don't tell me. They want to carry *Stickman* in their gift shop, is that it?"

Stickman. That was enough for Brindos. He left his spot and came up behind Dorie and Joseph, towering over them.

"Hello, Melok," Brindos said, keeping his voice low and menacing.

Melok's eyes went wide as he looked up, his face blanching at the sight of the Helk Movement leader. He was as skinny as Brindos remembered, and of course it all made sense now: the writer of *Stickman,* not much more than a stick himself, writing himself into his comic. Now, on his doorstep, right in front of him, was Stickman's archenemy, Terl Plenko, and he was about ready to pee his pants.

It was delicious. Brindos wanted to play the part, grab him by the collar and shake him, ask where the Stick was, threaten him with some horrific method of punishment if he didn't talk.

"Plenko, I—" He glanced down at Joseph, then at Dorie, shaking his head.

Brindos wedged between Joseph and Dorie a little so that he had an unobstructed path to the writer. He was so hazy now from the constant RuBy-induced high that he could barely hold on to any cogent thought. Haze and pain were constant companions now, and he couldn't escape either of them.

Brindos flexed his arms and leaned forward.

Melok flinched, his face growing paler by the second. He was not happy to have the leader of the Movement on his front doorstep. "What do you want?" he croaked.

"Why did *Cal Gaz* fire you?" Brindos asked.

He frowned. "What?"

"Because of your article on the Conduit disaster?"

"You know about that?"

"I know *you,* Melok. At the airport. You talked to me over lunch. You had a patty melt and I had the California burger."

He kept staring, unnaturally long, until finally light dawned in his eyes. "Dex?"

"Dexter Morrison was the name I gave you," Brindos said.

"What the hell?" he said, looking Brindos over head to toe. "You're not Plenko? How is this possible?"

Several cars passed by on the road behind them, and Brindos cringed. "Inside," he said. "We need privacy. I'm not exactly supposed to be running around Midwest City."

"That's a fact," Melok said. He might not have wanted to invite them in, but he didn't have much choice, considering Brindos's size.

They entered a small entry room with dark hardwood floors and white walls filled with framed paper covers of *Stickman.* Several stills of the covers hung there, too, and a few of them even had holo-animations, superhero and foe grappling with each other, looping in five-second intervals. Melok moved into the main living room, where the hardwood gave way to stone tiles that nearly matched the color of the earlier wood floor. A number of leather couches and chairs made a circle around a lush, circular woven rug. Melok sank nervously into a chair, and didn't look the least bit comfortable sitting there.

"You can sit if you'd like," he said, his voice weak. Where was the earlier bravado he'd shown at the airport, challenging Brindos about locals being ignorant of their world's importance?

"I'll stand," Brindos said. So did Dorie and Joseph.

"Okay," he said.

Brindos got right to the point. "Dexter is an alias. I was undercover, working for the NIO."

"Tell us about *Stickman*," Dorie said. She'd been quiet since Melok first opened his door.

"It's my own side business," Melok said. "I've put my own time and money into it. *Cal Gaz* never paid me much, but I had enough to get started on *Stickman,* and then it became very popular. I was lucky, even if a bit brave for doing it under *Cal Gaz*'s nose. They found out about it, mulled over the fact that I had made a Helk a bad guy—"

"Plenko the terrorist *is* a bad guy," Dorie said.

"And just who are *you?*" Melok asked.

"I'm Dorie . . . I'm Plenko's mate," she said, and Melok's eyebrows raised. Dorie shook her head. "His wife. The Plenko I was married to was copied and taken away from me. He's dead now."

She gazed at Brindos, seeing him, he knew, as the Helk she had loved. She felt closer to him as she tried to get farther away from Plenko the bad guy.

Melok looked at Brindos. "If you're Dexter—"

"Alan Brindos."

"Yes. So . . . you're a copy?"

"Copies everywhere," Brindos muttered. "Created by the Transcontinental Conduit. You were right about it. It was sabotaged, but we don't know who was responsible. We're trying to stop the Science Consortium, and stop Plenko's revolution, but we really need to thwart the real villains behind it. An alien race we know nothing about."

Melok leaned back slowly in the chair, his eyes wide. "An alien threat. Not Helks?"

"No."

"What can I do about it? Look, I'm a writer. I just wanted my work out there. I love adventure stories, and hell, what could be better than Plenko and a superhero trying to stop him?"

"You're more than a writer, you're a journalist with a keen knowledge of getting yourself from place to place at a moment's notice. I know you have knowledge of the press shuttle."

Melok shrugged. "I guess I do."

"You can help us stop Plenko for real," Brindos went on. "We need to stop the aliens making copies. They're infiltrating every corner of the Union, little by little."

Melok shook his head. "The Conduit is down. Inoperative, from what I can tell."

"We don't think so."

"You realize, don't you, that the Union government okayed the construction of another Transcontinental Conduit a few months ago? I did some digging. I *am* a good reporter, Dex. I mean, Alan."

"Another Conduit?" Joseph murmured. "I'd heard rumors. Where?"

"Aryell."

Brindos's heart twisted a bit, and not because of the tearing-down process going on inside. "Crowell," he whispered.

Melok shook his head. "Who?"

"My partner. He's there. We've been out of touch since just before this all happened to me."

"Well, that Conduit?" Melok said. "It's barely started. Just towers. They still need the wire."

Wire. Thoughts bombarded him, some of them jumbled due to his less-than-perfect state of being, but many of them began to make sense. The wire of the Temonus Conduit that came crashing down during the disaster, but sliced a cruiser in half, the ship pulling and uprooting a massive tower and dragging it for many city blocks.

A very thin wire that had not broken.

"What's the wire made of?" Brindos asked.

Melok smiled. "You know, if you'd asked me this question at the Temonus Trolley, I wouldn't have known, but shortly after speaking with you, I found out from a reporter who'd been on assignment here. Sadly, a reporter who no longer has a paper to work for."

"He was from Ribon," Brindos said.

"The *Venasaille Observer*. Anyway, it's not even a guarded secret, but the wire is made of a metal found only on Coral Moon."

Brindos had the name on his tongue in an instant, and the gears of his mind clicked into overdrive. "Mortaline."

Melok leaned forward again. "But good news. No more Coral. No more mortaline."

He shivered. "Not true."

There *was* more mortaline. Coral had been mined out years back, but there was definitely more, and the aliens were out to get it. Brindos hadn't paid much attention to the fact that many NIO operatives had made noise about the stockpile. And now he knew why. The NIO had been infiltrated with copies of this alien species, including Timothy James.

Yes, more mortaline. The problem was getting to it.

"Not true?" Dorie asked, staring.

Brindos came out of his reverie. "I'm not sure if I even have enough life in me left to do this, but we definitely need a ship now. I know where there's a stockpile of mortaline. On Ribon."

"Ribon," Melok said. "You're kidding, right? The planet destroyed by its moon?"

"Not destroyed, of course, but mostly uninhabitable." The constant pain ratcheted up a notch and made Brindos second-guess his own knowledge. "There's a DNA-secured vault in Venasaille, near Ribon Provincial, and currently it holds the last mortaline mined from Coral. It's valuable, like gold."

"Wait," Joseph said. "Then why haven't the aliens, bad guys, Plenkos—whoever—taken this metal from the vault already? I mean, if it's there—"

"I doubt they know where it is," Brindos said. "It's underground. Impenetrable, made of steel-flex several feet thick. The Big Bang wouldn't open it. A fail-safe lock was installed within the last year." "DNA coding, of course, and a special locking mechanism workable only workable under the right conditions, and with the right hardware to boot it."

"Who did the coding?" Joseph asked.

"Someone on Ribon. Someone contracted with the NIO to do the work."

Brindos heard Dorie's indrawn breath of surprise. "Dear god. The key."

"They want the key to the vault," Brindos said, nodding. He was immediately sorry, because all the loose things in his brain spun around and seemed to impale every square inch of his head.

Knees weakened, he put his hands on his thighs to keep from falling to the floor.

"Alan," Dorie whispered.

He waved a hand at her. "I'll be okay."

"Alan, I'm out of RuBy."

As a person fighting an alien-induced pain, Brindos did not like this news one bit.

Still, he imagined his Helk physiology was helping out a little. He couldn't imagine trying to combat all this in his human body.

"Melok," he said, "we need to get on a press shuttle, and you need to help us."

Melok shook his head. "You can understand why I don't like that idea much."

Brindos said, "Think about *Stickman*." Brindos paused for effect and grinned, making Melok sit up slightly in his chair. "Think of the story you could tell. You'd have a hell of an ending, and we could give you some first-hand information."

Melok put his elbows on his knees, then rubbed his face with his hands.

"What do you say?" Brindos asked. "Is it possible? Can you get us on a press shuttle?"

"I don't know. I was fired—"

"Do you have your credentials?"

"Sort of."

"Sort of meaning you have them, or sort of meaning you could wing it?"

"Wing it with what I've got. *Cal Gaz* didn't get everything back yet." He stood slowly, keeping a hand on the arm of the chair, as if to steady himself from his uncertainty. "I don't see how you're going to do any good, even if you can get to Ribon. Even as a Helk. Even as *Plenko*, how can you save the Union?"

"We can work that out if we get that far. But we don't get that far if we don't get on that shuttle, and as a Helk, I'm not getting on it without some help."

Melok shook his head. "You have to have more of a plan than that."

"The press shuttle to Solan Station."

"And from Solan?"

"I was thinking about taking the press shuttle through the slot."

Melok blanched, eyes widening.

Brindos noticed Melok's fear. "It's been done, and you know it. Most off-world reporters have to have some jump-slot training."

"It's not that I don't know how. But the shuttle isn't equipped with all the fail-safes. It would be like taking a fishing boat across the ocean."

"No choice," he said, "unless you know someone with a cruiser we could borrow that's docked at Solan."

Melok was quiet a moment. "Then what?"

"Destroy the mortaline," Brindos said quickly, with no doubt in his mind now. Without the mortaline, the Conduits could not be built or rebuilt. No more copies. They could gain control of their worlds, root out the copies and alien intelligences.

"What else can we do?" Joseph said, breaking his silence. A wisp of his gray hair fell across his forehead and he flipped it back with a veined hand.

"We have to do whatever we can to take the mortaline out of the equation," Brindos said.

"Maybe you can get to that vault, somehow," Melok said, "but how will you open it? You don't have this key everyone's looking for, do you?"

Brindos stared at Melok a moment before answering, the edge of pain insinuating itself into the silence. "No," he said. "But we know who installed the DNA lock. Dorie's mate, the real Teil Plenko."

Dorie was frozen in place, disbelief on her face.

"You know it's true, Dorie," Brindos said. "You told me he was an expert. You two were on Coral. He disappeared. The hunt for the key began."

"My god," she whispered.

"I'll pass for Plenko," Brindos said, feeling the skin of his face ruck and wrinkle as he pushed back the anguish coursing through him. "With the key, I can open it, and I have to do it before the Plenko copy does."

"Why open the vault?" Melok said. "Maybe that's what the aliens are hoping you'll do."

"That crossed my mind," Brindos said. "But to make sure the metal is not used we have to open the vault. I have to try, because that metal has to be eliminated. Completely."

"So what the hell is the key?" Melok asked.

Brindos looked at Dorie.

She shrugged. "Like I told you, Plenko never said. He thought I knew something, but I didn't. He wouldn't give me any specifics."

"Whatever it is, how'd it get lost?" Melok asked. "How'd it get away from the NIO? I mean from the bad guys?"

"I don't know," Brindos said. "Dorie's Plenko did something

with it. Probably realized what was going on with the mortaline, and hid the key."

"Plenko asked for it and obsessed over it," Dorie said. "Even he didn't know what it was. He doesn't have all of my mate's memories."

Brindos caught his breath, realizing something important. He fought off nausea and a millon pinpricks inside him to put words to his thoughts. What an idiot he'd been. *Plenko. Goddamn Plenko!*

Brindos said, "He was a DNA lock expert."

"Yes," she said.

"And an artist."

She frowned.

Shit. Brindos had held the key in his very own hands. A key that even warned about the alien threat.

"Joe, if there's any way I could get a coded message off-planet through the slot, I'll buy the hot dogs and Cracker Jacks at that baseball game."

Joseph raised an eyebrow. "I don't know about strictly encoded, but—"

Brindos turned to Melok. "We have to get on a shuttle *now*."

Melok stayed where he was, unmoving. "Because?"

"Because I know what the key is, and I know *where* it is."

Twenty-nine

Although it was the last thing I wanted to do, we left Cara's body with the resort's ski patrol. Jennifer Lisle might have had enough pull to work out the details with them, but who could we trust?

We loaded into the shuttle after Forno brushed off the ski patrol doctor's attempts to get him to a hospital. If he'd been human, he would've been seriously hurt, the injury severe enough to threaten his life, but his Helk physiology had saved him.

"I'm taking you to Heron Station," Jennifer said once we had left Snowy Mountain behind, "and I've got to do it now before I lose my clearance completely. It's not usual for an NIO shuttle to make a trip directly to orbit. And there's no telling what the alien copies have access to."

I nodded, distracted for the moment from thoughts of Cara. "You've arranged passage for all of us?"

"A special Union Pass. An open ticket, good to anywhere the jump slots will take you."

We had reached the upper atmosphere, the sky darkening as the shuttle slowly transitioned to space.

"I looked into our deceased, Kristen," Jennifer said. "Katerina Parker."

"Yeah," I said. "What did you find out?"

"She was a friend of Dorie Senall."

I shot a look at her. "Dorie?"

"Katerina replaced Lexianna Shumann at the Flaming Sea."

I nodded. "Sexy Lexy, they called her."

"Right. We were watching Katerina Parker because she was Movement, as far as we knew."

"Do we know who killed her yet?"

Jennifer sighed, glancing at me for a moment before returning her attention to the front screen. "Cara."

"You're sure?"

"Flaming Sea surveillance caught it. You know we're talking the bad Cara here. Right?"

"Yes," I whispered. "Just—" I paused a moment, flustered at the thought of the alien imposter. "Call her Landry."

Calling her by her last name seemed right. I needed to distance myself from the cold reality of Cara's death.

Jennifer nodded. "Landry must have thought Katerina had the key," she said.

"Which means Landry thought Katerina had obtained it from Dorie before she died," Forno said.

"Yeah, but Dorie died on Ribon," Jennifer said.

"Just before the Coral Moon disaster," I added.

"The key could have been there, then."

"Possibly. But where?"

"Her apartment? The Towers? A place to start, anyway."

Forno cleared his throat. "May I remind you both that Ribon had Coral pieces slam into it? It's probably off-limits. Not to mention uninhabitable."

"That's going to stop us?" I said.

He shrugged. "It'd stop a lot of folks from trying. Maybe even our bad guys."

"Do you still want to find your partner on Temonus?" Jennifer asked me.

I thought a moment, weighing the decision amid the recent turmoil. If Alan was still alive, if he'd learned the truth about what was going on, if he wasn't just another copy looking to kill me, then maybe he'd come up with the same conclusion.

A lot of ifs.

"I can trust the real Brindos," I finally said. "If I can find him."

Jennifer nodded, and Forno grasped my shoulder sympatheti-
cally.

"I don't suppose that open ticket is good for Ribon," Forno
said.

"Why not? You'll just have to talk the folks at Heron Station
into it." She jerked her head behind her. "I found some items to
help you do that."

Forno scrounged through the storage locker behind Jennifer
and pulled out a few blasters and a pulse rifle, cradling them in his
arms. He raised his eyebrows. "Will this be enough of an incentive
to get the station to accept our Union Pass?"

"Jesus, Forno," I said. "These weapons *are* your Union Pass."

He looked down at me and stared a moment before he got it.

"This might help too," Jennifer said. She reached in her pocket
and pulled out her code card. "We can't use it to communicate with
anyone on our own, but it's good identification."

"As long as the Heron Station staff isn't compromised," Forno
said.

I stared at her code card, wishing I still had mine.

The shuttle hit space and we were silent for nearly five minutes.
And then Jennifer's code card chortled, a wavering sound of short
pulses and whistles.

"What's that?" Forno asked.

"Incoming message," Jennifer said.

My mind started ticking off the code card's communication capabilities. Anyone with a code card on Aryell or in Aryell's space
could track an agent on the other end, but messages sent through
the jump slots, although rare, could not contain tracking cobwebs.
There wasn't any way to tell where the message was coming from
until the agent toggled the DNA-locked activation node.

"Hit it," I said.

Jennifer looked long and hard at me, then palmed the node. She
stared at it for a moment before holding it out for me. "Does this
mean anything to you?"

It was a crossword puzzle. It meant a lot.

"It's from Alan," I said, my hand shaking a little at the realization. The real Brindos. I had no doubt. "He's alive."

"How do you know?" Forno asked.

"You've a DataNet connection here, yes?" I asked Jennifer, ignoring Forno.

"Sure."

"I need you to download a little crossword program."

"Crosswords? Now?" Forno laughed. "Is there a comics flash too? *Stickman* back issues?"

Jennifer hesitated a moment, then said, "A cipher."

I nodded. "And as soon as I have the puzzle kit, I can decode it. It's a message. Sent to you, the only NIO agent Alan spoke to before going to Temonus."

"He visited me in the hospital on Ribon," she said to Forno in answer to his puzzled look.

Jennifer went to work with her code card and a few minutes later had the crossword kit I needed downloaded to memory. "Ten minutes to Heron Station," she said as she passed the code card to me.

The message was short, I could tell, so it wouldn't take that long to decode. I expected to have the message before we made it to the station. As it turned out, I had only minutes to spare. "Ribon," I said, reading the result. "Venasaille police. Mortaline."

Jennifer frowned. "What does *that* mean?"

"Mortaline," Forno said. "That's what the Conduit wire is made of."

I smiled. "The key is too." The five spokes of Heron Station had appeared in the viewscreen. "Get ready, everyone," I said, snagging the pulse rifle from Forno's armload of weapons. "Brindos knows what the key is, and *where* it is. We're taking a trip to Ribon after all."

"Do *you* know?" Forno asked.

"Yeah. It's a goddamn sculpture." I turned to Jennifer. "Can you send a message back?"

She nodded. "You have time to crossword a message?"

"No. Send this," I said, pronouncing very carefully. "'We have the crossword. Understand the key.' But spell it this way."

I spelled it out.

Jennifer looked up at me, her brow furrowed. "What the hell is that?"

"Now who's laughing about all those antique Earth books I love?" I said.

She shrugged, clueless.

"It's Pig Latin," I said. "There's nary a Helk or alien alive in the Union who will know what Pig Latin is."

Thirty

Brindos had seen the key. He'd held it.

The planet-shaped sculpture with the thousand tormented faces screaming on its surface. He was sure of it. Created by one Terl Plenko. He'd watched the holo-vid of Dorie and Jennifer recorded at the Tempest Tower, then left with Branson of the Venasaille police department to the crime scene. Found the sculpture in a cubby under the vid, Plenko's DNA all over it. Plenko the artist. Plenko the DNA lock expert.

No one else besides the deceased Dorie had known where the key was before the Tempest Tower incident. The real Dorie had never seen it, but she had known Plenko was capable of sculpting something like it. She knew his work.

Jennifer Lisle's cover had been blown when the image of Dorie's apartment appeared on the vid screen, transmitted by the marble camera Jennifer had placed there. Brindos still didn't know who'd betrayed her, and maybe he'd never know—some NIO agent, he was sure—but the important thing was that Plenko's key, the mortaline sculpture, was in Venasaille, most likely in some evidence locker at the police station.

Other than Captain Rand at the Venasaille station, Branson had said no one else had seen the recording. Maybe the brass had transferred the sculpture somewhere, but he truly doubted it.

One city. One specific place to look on an entire world shredded by its moon. Brindos liked the odds, but it depended on the extent of the damage to Venasaille. He took time to tell Dorie where to find the police station, how to find Ribon Provincial, and how to locate the vault. Just in case.

It depended on if he had time. He fought back nausea. He fought back pain.

Every bone ached, every muscle seemed on fire with debilitating agony, but he mentally threw it away, holding on to the task ahead of them. He explained everything to Dorie and Joseph while Melok, who had finally made the decision to help them, went looking for the press credentials he hoped could get them on that press shuttle.

Flying that shuttle to Solan, prepping the ship for the slot to Ribon—it remained to be seen whether they could pull that off.

It turned out Joseph had something valuable to offer as well. Valuable beyond what he'd already done to help the cause, of course. His comm-phone from the Orion had the ability to send messages through the jump slots to any of the other worlds, a perk given to many major hotels and businesses throughout the Union so they could stay in contact with clients and partners. Apparently, use of the comm-phone by concierge staff was strictly prohibited. By allowing Brindos to use the comm-phone to send a message to Crowell, Joseph had, for all intents and purposes, given the hotel evidence to terminate his employment, since every call or message sent out, although untrackable, would register on the hotel's records. Joseph had checked the phone out. The time stamp would incriminate him for sure. Joseph didn't care, and offered it without hesitation; he wanted to help.

He told them, however, that he wouldn't go with them to Solan Station. "I'm an old man," he said, and not for the first time. "Living is enough of an adventure for me."

Brindos went with tried-and-true, putting together a cipher in the guise of crossword clues, descriptions for down and across. Keeping the message short to keep the decode time down to a minimum, he keyed it into the comm-phone and sent it on its way.

He didn't know if Crowell would be able to read it. If his partner didn't have his code card, the message would just get lost in the ether.

So he took a chance and sent it to Jennifer Lisle. The last he'd seen her, she'd been in the hospital on Ribon. Whether she'd been copied or not, he didn't know, but he had to risk the communication. Only one of her would have a code card, and he hoped the original would be the one holding it. Crowell being with her and the message getting read at all was a long shot at best; it was unlikely anyone could decode the message without his input. Crowell would have to procure the crossword kit from the DataNet, because Jennifer Lisle certainly wouldn't have it.

Melok had access to M.W.C. Airport with his *Cal Gaz* credentials, and, more important, access to the press sector. Most press shuttles were operated by TWT pilots, who contracted with the various news organizaions and pulled in extra freelance duty from DataNet files.

Joseph still had his contact to get him clearance past the lockouts and to bypass grid routines. They entered the airport without mishap and entered the public parking area next to the TWT terminal. They pinpointed the press sector, and the private press-only access point. Brindos made himself as small as he could in the backseat. Melok leaned across Joseph and revealed his credentials to the gate attendant, who peered in through Joseph's window. The flash photo and holo-ident expanded to viewing size as the attendant reached across and swiped the surface of the membrane.

The attendant let the car through without a glance at the backseat. Airport security didn't seem too concerned about mayhem happening in the press sector. There was no way a blaster or a Helk stunner would've made it past the perimeter, even with lockouts disabled, so Brindos hoped they'd get aboard the shuttle without the weapons. He also hoped his size would dissuade the heroics of any zealous Authority cop.

"There it is," Melok said, pointing to the launch circle hosting the press shuttle. They parked as close as they could to the shuttle without raising any suspicion from the two Authority cops standing nearby.

Brindos hoped TWT hadn't heated up the landing circle perimeter with electronic hot zones and virtual deterrents. Holo-signs hovered around the circle every few feet warning about trespassing, listing the consequences in pulsing letters.

This is where Joseph would leave them.

"I still mean what I said about that baseball game," Brindos told Joseph as they readied to leave the concierge's car. "Next time you're on Earth."

"It'll be a pleasure," he said.

"Good-bye, Joe."

Joseph shook his hand. Brindos, breathing hard, focused on ignoring his hurt and climbed out of the car, Dorie and Melok close behind. As soon as they were out, Joseph sped away and was gone in an instant.

"Here we go," Brindos said. "Be ready."

Melok slipped to the front, and Brindos fell back, once more wrapped in the big gray coat and wide-brimmed hat Dorie had given him. The pain ratcheted up, and it made Brindos double over. He stayed bent down to minimize his size, breathing through his nose, every step an effort.

By the time Melok stopped at the front of the shuttle, Brindos could barely stay on his clubbed feet. He concentrated on the surface of the landing circle and watched the embedded warning lights of the outer ring pulse and zip along like a marquee.

"Hey, folks," one of the Authority cops said, his body padded with blaster protection gear, "you shouldn't be here. Shuttle's not due to go out for a few more hours and this is only for the press." He kept a hand poised over his blaster.

"*Cal Gaz,*" Melok said, holding his credentials high. "We have a pressing need to board. No pun intended." He smiled good-naturedly, but Brindos imagined the man was more than a little nervous.

"A Helk newspaper? You expect me to buy that?"

"Does this look like a human or a Memor behind me?" Melok said, pointing back at Brindos, who hunkered down some more and tried not to growl as he clamped down on the pain that had turned his legs to jelly and his head to mush.

The cop acknowledged Melok with a nervous nod, and Melok began a spiel about Crasp, a Helk sickness that, as Melok described it, could turn a Helk's insides out. Bullshit, of course. Crasp was real, but it was hardly a killer, more like a heavy-duty flu, and humans were immune to it.

"And her?" the cop asked, pointing at Dorie. The other cop,

younger, the protection gear hardly fitting him, situated himself to the right of Brindos and Dorie, inching slowly behind them.

"She's his handler," Melok said.

The cop nodded, glaring at Brindos's hat, then reaching out with his arm toward Melok for a better look at his credentials.

Melok started to give the card to him, then dropped it inches from the cop's hand. At that moment, Brindos tested his super Helk powers, hoping his constant pain wouldn't limit their effectiveness. He slammed his elbow into the face of the younger Authority cop, who'd come up closer to check them out. The cop fell backward even as Brindos yelled out, the blow heightening the waves of nausea crashing through him, heavy, throbbing pain traveling down his arm into his chest.

Heart pumping too fast. But Brindos didn't hesitate. He *moved*.

The older cop, who had started to bend slightly to retrieve Melok's card, had no chance, even though he straightened and went for his blaster.

Brindos got there first and simultaneously wrenched the weapon from the cop's grip and pushed him back into the door of the shuttle. The cop grunted when his head hit the hatch, the air wheezing out of him, then he fell sideways to the landing circle and didn't move.

"Take this," Brindos said, and gave the blaster to Dorie. "I can't even grip it." He grimaced, his hand and fingers cramping up. He could hardly use the thing anyway, not being able to get his large hands around the firing mechanism. To Melok he said, "The other weapons."

Melok retrieved blasters from the two cops as the hatch opened, the pilot emerging to investigate the disturbance.

Dorie waved the blaster at him. "Stop there."

The pilot, a skinny wisp of a man, immaculately dressed in his dark blue TWT uniform, saw the blaster, saw Brindos towering over him, and stopped abruptly, his hands high.

"Name," Brindos ordered. "Now."

After a beat, the pilot replied, "Thomas."

"Inside, Thomas."

The pilot nodded, backed up into the shuttle, and Dorie followed. Brindos entered the hatch door next, and nearly had to fold himself in half to get through the opening. Melok came in last with the two extra blasters. He took a moment to get his bearings, and while Dorie kept her blaster trained on the pilot, he set the weapons on an acceleration couch near the back.

"What's the deal here?" Thomas said. "This is a press shuttle. There's nothing here you want."

"Relax," Dorie said. "We're not here to steal shit."

Melok needlessly flashed his credentials at Thomas as he came back up front. "I *am* with the press. *Cal Gaz* will add to your contract for this," he lied to the pilot. "No questions. No alarms. You don't have to believe me when I tell you this is a Union matter of utmost importance, but this is what it is. You can cooperate, or I'll turn my Helk friend loose here."

Thomas flicked a nervous look at Brindos, who didn't even have to act upset with the constant agony shooting through him. Brindos knew the pilot couldn't see his Helk face too well, perhaps only seeing it black and twisted by the pain, maybe deciding it was a look of contempt. The pilot showed no sign of recognizing Plenko.

"You'll disable all the shuttle's countermeasures and trackers," Melok said, "as well as the outgoing comm and DataNet link. I know these shuttles well; more than a few pilots have helped me get to where the news is. I've had many lovely tours of shuttles and cruisers. I'm an off-world journalist so you know I've had schooling in the jump slots. So you will not mess with me by trying anything funny. Understood?"

Thomas nodded quickly.

Melok said, "Good. You'll see that we get safely to Solan Station."

"Solan? But—"

"And from there through the slot to Ribon."

"You're joking!"

"Off-planet mode. You know the settings. The press shuttles pop up to Solan all the time, it's not unheard of."

"But through the slot. And Ribon is off-limits—"

"*Cal Gaz* will pay for any damages," Melok lied again. "Cover funeral expenses and provide for your family if need be. Everything else doesn't matter. You have no choice."

Thomas visibly gulped, but he nodded.

Dorie gestured with the blaster. "Fire it up."

Brindos inched up behind Thomas, who coughed nervously. Thomas quickly moved to the front and sat in the pilot's seat, Brindos staying close, trying to stay upright.

Thomas ran a hand through full, curly black hair, pulled at the collar of his TWT uniform, then reached out and accessed the bubble controls. The engines cranked.

Melok kept a steady eye on him. After a moment, he said, "And the slot tracker." He pointed at a node pulsing blue along the upper arc of the bubble.

Thomas touched it and it stopped pulsing. "Without the slot tracker we could—"

"I know what it means," Melok said. "You can worry about getting lost if you *get* lost. You know all the insertion codes?"

He nodded.

"Morph the code to Ribon. Now."

Brindos looked on in fascination as Thomas's fingers whispered along the bubble until a portion of it pushed out like a glop of black gel and formed into a clear plastic rectangle the size of his hand. Traces of light whirled around its edge as the insertion equations morphed into the plastic, and nodes emerged along the surface. Thomas touched the nodes, almost randomly, but the rectangle soon darkened and the holo-image of Ribon appeared, embedded into the plastic.

He leaned to the right of the bubble and with his thumb, pushed a cheap-looking resin panel that protruded from the control board. DNA-locked. But now the panel snapped into place and a flash membrane not much bigger than a square of RuBy emerged from a slot below the panel. Melok released it, the membrane flashing and scrolling with data, and handed it to Dorie.

"That's the lockout. Once he's engaged, none of the nonflight settings can be changed, including lockouts and countermeasures, except by someone outside the bubble." He pointed to the steady-blue node. "The shuttle's proximity to the jump mechanism, plus the preprogrammed insertion code Thomas configured to Ribon, means we'll be automatically slotted. Once we're in the jump slot, we reinject the slot tracker back below the panel and we'll be fine for any return trip."

Dorie nodded, then glanced at Brindos, who was breathing down Thomas's neck.

Brindos understood the look. She knew as well as he that they couldn't afford to take Melok with them. "Melok," he said with as much force as he could, "you're not going."

Melok ignored him and said to Thomas, "Engage the bubble and take off."

"The takeoff protocols—"

"Forget them."

"They'll query my status."

"Ignore them. You can't respond anyway. The comm is set one way. Now, *engage.*"

The pilot rubbed the controls in front of him and the bubble fully engaged, engulfing the pilot in a transparent film. Brindos backed away from the pilot's chair just in time.

"Melok," Dorie said.

"After all the trouble you took to get me here, you want to leave me behind?" Melok asked. "Too dangerous for me, huh? No big ending for Stickman?"

Brindos smiled. "You'll have it. We'll bring it back to you. You can do more for us by keeping up appearances here. If we don't succeed, you'll need to—" He faltered. "Well. I don't know what you'll be able to do."

They remained silent a moment as the press shuttle whined, preparing for launch. Dorie waved Brindos's weapon at Melok. Brindos didn't think it was a threatening gesture. Melok wouldn't resist. It was time for the reporter to clear out.

"Good luck," Melok finally said.

"Thanks for this," Brindos said. "You're a regular Stickman."

Melok frowned. "Please. I don't even have Strech-O mode." They said good-bye, and Melok left the shuttle.

They strapped in to acceleration couches near the front so they could keep track of Thomas. Only one Helk-sized couch was positioned in the front row, so Dorie took a human couch right next to it. Brindos scrambled into his, groaning as the sides of the couch dug into his torso, aggravating his hurt. His legs hung slightly over the end. Probably designed for Second Clan. His head spun with vertigo, the needles of pain contantly poking at him.

The pain had often come upon him randomly, had often been inconsistent in strength and intensity, and attacked his body at will. He assumed something about the copy process, something about the rejection of his Helk self, had caused the abnormal pain.

But that had changed, and it plagued him constantly now.

Dorie had run out of RuBy, and he had nothing to counteract the missed treatments. Very little of his body, inside or out, escaped the raging pain. Every little movement he made triggered an avalanche of agonizing side effects.

Thomas went through preflight procedures quickly, totally at the whim of the bubble, the lockout now seeing to his cooperation.

Thanks to Brindos's groans, the never-ending grimaces that twisted his facial features, and his bulky coat that covered a lot of him, he was pretty sure Thomas still didn't know he was Terl Plenko, the pilot not having had a chance to get a good look at him, but he sensed the pilot wanted the Helk off his ship as quickly as possible. He wondered what the pilot was hearing from the port, those flight directions ignored because Thomas couldn't confirm them.

The pain in Brindos's gut twisted so violently that he barely held back a scream. A moment later, Dorie reached over from her couch and wiped blood from his nose.

"It's starting," she said over the shuttle's engines.

Brindos waited for the pain to subside a little, then wheezed out, "How long now?"

She shook her head slightly, put a hand to his forehead, which was sweaty. Her small hand felt good on his leathery skin. "I don't really know, not having seen something like this actually happen to anyone." She glanced away for a moment before continuing, her eyes finding his face once again. "But it can't be long before—"

Brindos stopped her by placing a finger on her cheek, the motion causing his insides to twist and his head to pound even harder.

"I'll have long enough. And if not, you'll have to do your best to finish for me."

"I don't know if I can—"

"Promise me."

She hesitated, then gave a slight nod. "Union bright, Alan."

He didn't know how to say what he really felt. All his Brindos thoughts about her converged into the center of his brain, and he wanted to coax them to his mouth. To tell her that above everything else that had happened, meeting her seemed more than an accident. He wanted to make her understand what he felt as *Brindos*, not as Plenko. But even that contained deeper, unintentional regret.

He wanted to say he cared for her.

But he didn't. It was a complication she didn't deserve.

"Just channel the bad Doric and you'll do fine," he said instead, pushing back the other thoughts.

Just then the pain caused him to turn away and cough violently.

The shuttle took off with a roar, and the pressure caused Brindos's skin to prickle as if from hundreds of needles. This time, he wiped away the blood from his nose and mouth himself.

Thirty-one

A sculpture.

That's what all the fuss had been about. The only thing standing in the way of a cache of metal needed to complete a device capable of creating thousands of doubles to penetrate the Union's positions of power.

I had seen it, Brindos had held it.

Now I had to go get it.

Docking at Heron Station was easy because of the NIO clearance Jennifer Lisle's shuttle gave us. Getting to a jump vessel? That was not going to be easy. We hoped that it would be minimally guarded. The fact was, not a lot of jump-slot travel passed through Heron Station on any given day, unless it was the middle of the ski season when the snow was at its best. But even then, the station had nothing on the Egret Station at Earth, or, until the Coral disaster, Swan Station above Ribon. The number of TWT officials needed to run Heron Station varied with the known flight schedules, but it was conceivable that a handful of armed men and women could overrun the place. If they knew the layout, and if they had a plan.

We had neither, and there were just three of us. Two of us, once Jennifer hightailed it back to her shuttle, which wouldn't happen until she knew we had found a jump vessel and a pilot.

Things would've been a hell of a lot easier if Jennifer's shuttle had had jump capabilities.

"Three TWT guards at our door," Forno said when the shuttle had latched to the umbilical.

"Ready to sweep the way and marshal us to knavery," I muttered. Through pursed lips, I added, "Let it work."

Forno stared at me, the question in his eyes.

"Hamlet," I said.

"To be or not to be," Forno said. He shrugged when I looked at him. "That's all I know."

I checked the pulse rifle and nodded to Jennifer and Forno to do the same with their blasters. Earlier, we'd loaded up the weapons and stuffed extra ammunition packs wherever we could stuff them.

Whoever stood in our way would be fair game. We couldn't afford to miss this opportunity. If the TWT had been compromised as well, then we would do what we could to counteract their plans.

"Blow them at the moon," I whispered, false bravado keeping me from panicking.

"Let's go, sweet prince," Jennifer said, and she slid the shuttle door open.

The fingers of my right hand curled around the pulse rifle's trigger, and my eyes moved, locating the three guards as we stepped out of the shuttle. They were waiting at the end of the umbilical, weapons holstered.

They didn't know who we were, seemingly, but I noticed them tense a little when Forno appeared.

We walked out in a line, Forno in front, shielding us from view. A blaster in a Helk's hand probably looked like a toy, so I hoped that would buy us a little time to edge closer to the TWT boys.

"Idents, please," a guard barely in his twenties said nervously. Not that he was expecting anything; I'm sure it was just the presence of Forno.

We were close enough now to fan out and surprise them.

"Right here," I said, going left of Forno. Jennifer peeled off to the right.

The TWT guards moved simultaneously, reaching for their weapons as if on the same remote control, but Forno shouted "Don't!" in his loudest, most menacing voice. They froze, and we got to them an instant later, Forno knocking two of them down with one powerful arm while Jennifer and I covered the third.

"Drop it and be smart," I said to the third man. He did.

Forno pulled the blasters from the downed guards, then picked up the third weapon.

"Up," I said to the two on the floor, and when they were vertical I motioned all of them into the corridor that was the outer hub of Heron Station. "No noises now," I said. "Walk ahead of us."

"Who are you—?"

"No questions," I said. "Just walk. You know this station. We want the nearest jump vessel, but it needs to be one you know will be slotted soon and has a pilot. Understood?"

The guard who'd asked for our identification nodded, then we told them to turn around and walk in front.

"Be happy tourists now," Forno said, and he took the rear.

We had our weapons ready but held low. I wasn't sure how many others we'd come across on the outer hub, but it was likely there would be more than these three. Likely, too, that shooting would commence.

The next umbilical came up, but no ship was docked there. One guard stood at the entrance, and he waved at his fellow guards, then frowned when he saw us trailing them.

"Where—?"

Forno didn't hesitate. He fired his weapon and the guard dropped. The other guards spun around, but Dorie and I showed them our weapons and told them to forget it. I read a little more fear in their eyes now. This definitely was not anything they'd signed up for when joining TWT.

"We have no qualms about shooting anyone," I told their backs. "Now can we get to a ship with as little bloodshed as possible?"

"Next umbilical," the young one said. "Ship's scheduled to go in ten minutes."

"Perfect," I said.

"But," he said, a nervous flutter in his voice, "as a matter of protocol, all TWT officials are outfitted with a sensor system that automatically sends a panic signal when we use our weapons—"

"Which didn't happen," Forno reminded them.

"—or we leave our assigned area without a call-in."

I closed my eyes and thought a moment, but one of the other guards chimed in then.

"Hidden cameras too. You were spotted the moment you came out of your shuttle."

We rounded the bend and saw the jump vessel docked at the next umbilical. A medium-sized cruiser, glistening white and yellow in the station's lights, looked ready to be slotted for jump at any moment. Heavy, flowing script across the ship's bow read TWT VOLANTIS. I saw passengers through most of the cruiser's tiny windows. Perhaps twenty, maybe thirty. This was our ride, but these passengers certainly were not expecting to go to Ribon. We'd have to get them off the cruiser.

At the junction of hub and umbilical were four Helks with stunners, two First Clan in front, and two Second Clan in the back.

Between the First Clan Helks stood the alien, Landry. I could tell immediately by the firmness of her face, the coldness in her eyes, and the fact that she just stared, no emotion, saying nothing.

The Helk on her right was one of the Tony Kochs. I also recognized a Chinkno to her left. Somehow, they had tracked us after all that had happened on Aryell.

Landry didn't say anything, but now it seemed like she wanted to. Was trying to. Her mouth moved a little, an eerie gesture that only made her alien nature more threatening.

What did she want to say to me?

I'd seen Cara murdered in front of me. Thoughts flashed through my mind now that I was seeing this alien version again. How could I forget what I'd witnessed at Snowy Mountain? How could I forget that Landry was an abomination? Could I act without hesitation?

Hell yes, I could.

The Koch looked at Landry before he said in a gravelly voice, "This is where it ends."

"For her, maybe," I said, and in an instant, I stepped to the side of one of the TWT guards, brought the pulse rifle up, and shot her, left side and high.

Doing it without warning, I hadn't given Jennifer and Forno much of a chance to react, and although Landry fell unceremoniously to the floor, four armed Helks still stood facing us.

The Helks immediately raised their stunners, but Jennifer and Forno brought up their own weapons. I got off another shot just before I slipped back behind the surprised guard and grabbed him by the neck. I hit the Koch with another pulse, but he fired right afterward, stunning the guard I was holding before falling to the deck. The guard became dead meat and I couldn't hold on to him.

Unprotected like that, I should've slipped in quickly behind Forno, but I saw Landry on the floor, her body motionless, her eyes open and staring at the bulkhead.

I blinked back the frozen moment just as Jennifer edged out from behind the second guard and aimed, fired, and hit the Helk closest to her. Chinkno. Forno simply picked up the third guard by the neck and rushed the other two Helks, screaming as he did so, his own blaster raised. The guard took the damage from the nearest Helk's stunner just before Forno threw the body forward. It landed on the Helk's head and shoulders, and Forno took advantage of the confusion to zip the Helk three times in the torso with his weapon.

All this happened in slow motion, and I looked up in time to see the fourth Helk fire before anyone could train a weapon on him. I heard Jennifer grunt, then saw her fall.

Forno and I fired at the same time, marking the last Helk in the heart on his left side. Forno sidestepped to the bodies and shot two Helks who were still moving. Just like that, nine bodies littered the deck.

One of them belonged to Jennifer Lisle.

Thirty-two

Nothing could be done about the blood.

The light-brown fur of Brindos's forearms and wrists were now stained red with the constant wiping of his face. He didn't know if Helks had allergic reactions, but the blood on his fur made his arms look as if they'd broken out with splotchy rashes.

When he wasn't wiping at his nose or mouth, Dorie reached across from her couch and held his hand.

At some point, the pain reached a crescendo and he couldn't even begin to handle it.

He passed out.

He saw light, Dorie's voice urging him awake. Saw black space. He was weightless, held down by something, and the hurt did not diminish.

Dorie said something, but it trailed off into the fog as he lost consciousness again.

Awake, with lights, and movement. Dorie above, jostling him.

"Stay awake now," she said. "Can you hear me?"

He did, and nodded.

He was flat on his back on the couch, the blood tracking his face making him more hideous than ever, he was certain. He tasted blood on his tongue and it pooled in the back of his throat. The pain was less, but maybe that was because his body had become numb with it.

"Thomas?" he whispered.

"He's nearing the jump slot," Dorie said. "Remember? He has

the insertion code, and we'll take our chances through the slot. No one's trying to stop us." Her voice sounded distant, barely there. "He's taking us to Ribon."

Going to Ribon? Brindos remembered something about that. Something important. The planet not quite right. He centered on an image, a metal planet, a thousand faces screaming and writhing, trying to tear themselves out of there.

"Are you with me?" Dorie said.

"I am a Thin Man now," he wheezed.

"You're Alan Brindos," she said. "You're human, you hear me?"

Do you love me, Dorie?

"You need to stay conscious," her voice said from somewhere. "Keep awake."

He fell asleep.

Thirty-three

I had never completely understood how Helk stunners worked, but then again, I'd never come across that many until thrown into the contract work investigating the Movement of Worlds. What I knew was that stunners were all about paralytic disruption and turning muscles to oatmeal. An energy pulse that hit a critical area could, in an extended burst, cause organs to burst. Invisible death.

Rushing to Jennifer's side, I feared the worst. She grimaced, but was not screaming in pain, which is what I'd expected her to be doing.

She'd taken the pulse in the left leg. Serious, of course, but treatable. The leg bent at an odd angle, some of the muscles damaged, possibly paralyzed.

Jennifer tapped her leg. "Same leg Dorie got with her blaster. Nerves are all shot, so I'm not feeling much pain."

"Can you walk?"

"Not a chance."

She couldn't get back to her shuttle and fly out of here, so we had to take her with us. Maybe there would be medical help on the *Volantis*.

"You have to go," she said.

I nodded. "But not without you."

"You have to—"

"Be quiet." I positioned myself to lift her.

"You can't," she whispered. "You've got to get those passengers off and beat it. You don't have time for me, and—"

"No."

"—I can get help here. Someone will come."

"You don't know who is going to—"

"Doesn't matter," she said.

Forno came up to us, fresh worry in his eyes. "Something's going on with Cara." He looked at me. "With the alien."

The air whistled with a sound I only then realized had been building slowly. "What is it?"

"There's this glow around her," Forno said.

Glow. Like the glow around her fingers when she'd knocked us out back at New Venasaille. Looking in her direction, I saw Forno was right. A soft whiteness surrounded her like an aura.

Jennifer held out one arm.

I pulled her to a sitting position, and she checked her code card. She made a few swipes across the surface and pulled up an alert. She stared at it a moment. "Shit."

"What is it?"

"Something's setting off the radiological alarm."

"Radiation?" Forno said. He crouched low, but I still had to crane my neck to look up at him.

"Actually, no," Jennifer said. "Something else. Something I'm not sure I understand."

"Is it that glow?" Forno asked.

Jennifer took a moment before answering. "Yeah. An energy spike. Negative particles. A trace of—"

An audible, strident pulsing issued from her code card, and I recognized the sound.

It meant get the hell out of there now.

"Gamma rays," Jennifer said, putting out her arms so Forno could pick her up. She stood on her good leg. Her ruined leg I tried not to look at.

"Like Ribon," I said, realizing what the presence of gamma rays meant. "The detonation on Coral."

Jennifer looked at me, face grim. "Antimatter, Dave. She's got some kind of antimatter core."

I jerked my head to Landry's prone body, the glow around her almost too bright to look at. "We've got to go *now*!"

I ran to the umbilical, and Forno followed, carrying Jennifer.

"What about the passengers!" Forno yelled, having a difficult time navigating the cramped umbilical.

Risking a glance back at the hub, I saw only a bright, pulsing glow where Landry lay.

"We can't leave passengers here," I said. "The place is going to go to shit any moment."

"What about the key?" Forno said. "The mortaline. Finding your partner?"

The *Volantis*'s main door was open.

"We'll do all that," I said. "But it looks like the passengers are coming with us to Ribon."

Panicked passengers streamed out the ship's main door, running the best they could through the umbilical, but my blaster, my assurances the place was going to blow, and Forno's size—as always, a good deterrent—pushed them back.

The scene at the door was chaos, but somehow we managed to talk them—or in Forno's case, *scare* them—back inside.

The TWT pilot needed no urging to disengage from the berth and prepare the *Volantis* for the jump. His own radiological alarm had gone off and he understood what was happening.

"C'mon!" I yelled as the pilot engaged his navigation bubble. I held the blaster outside the bubble so he could see it, and forced him to reprogram the insertion point from Barnard's World to Ribon. The pilot's hands flew over the controls, gel forming, equations morphing, nodes activating. Soon, a holo of the planet Ribon appeared, slightly hazy and unfocused as I saw it from outside the bubble.

We were a dozen cruiser-lengths away when the antimatter blew. Bright white mushroomed and overtook the berth where the *Volantis* had been minutes before.

I couldn't tell how much damage Landry's death dealt to Heron Station, but the destruction didn't follow us out toward the jump slot. A few minutes after the glow died down, as we scrambled into our acceleration couches, the ship reached the insertion point and slotted, taking us, and more than twenty passengers, to the ruined world of Ribon.

Thirty-four

When Brindos next awoke, Dorie sat on her couch beside him.

After all the urging from Dorie to stay awake, he was surprised to be alive. Surprised that he was even *able* to waken. Surprised that the process that had made him Helk had not run its course and put an end to him.

"How?" he said, his mouth barely working, body fighting the pain that burned like hot irons branding every inch of his skin. He stayed as motionless as he could on the floor.

"Thomas," she said. "Our pilot. He had RuBy, and I talked him out of the few squares he had on him. They were enough to revive you, but the time you have—"

Brindos made a slight motion with his head, signifying, he hoped, a nod. The movement set off ice picks in his head. He could still taste blood.

"We're on Ribon," she said. "We punched through the jump slot a little while ago, and I ordered Thomas to take us all the way down, bypassing Swan Station."

"Where is he?"

"He's here. He's okay, don't worry about him. I told him what was going on. I had to, in order to get his cooperation. He doesn't have much choice, stuck here with us on a nearly dead planet."

"Okay," Brindos said. "Venasaille?"

"Venasaille. It's mostly intact. Not a lot of structure damage, since the big pieces of Coral came down halfway around the planet, but it's hard to tell, as it's nighttime here."

"We close to the police station?"

"Big park one block away."

"Can we breathe down here?"

Dorie shook her head. "We'll need breather masks. Only one problem, though—"

"No Helk-sized ones."

Dorie set her mouth in a grim line.

"Probably no suit either," he added.

"No."

"Then you have to go on your own."

She looked panicked at that. "I don't know if I can find it."

"I told you what it looks like, Dorie, and you know your husband's work better than anyone."

"I know."

The fuzz of the RuBy eased up, and more of his Helk pains took advantage. He fought through it. "Go to the police station. You can find it."

"Yes, but where?"

"Go through everything in there. Storerooms. Evidence lockers. Filing cabinets."

"Then we'll go to the vault?"

"Then the vault."

"Across town from the police station, you said."

"There's a fortified entrance we'll have to get through."

"The vault's DNA-locked. We'll need you to open it." Dorie frowned, her face going pale. "You can't make it to the vault without some kind of mask."

"Nope."

"Then how—"

"My DNA is good whether dead or alive. Cut off my finger."

"No!"

"Dorie, I'm one dead Helk, any way you look at it."

She was silent as Brindos grimaced, pain distracting him, the RuBy wearing off.

Thomas stood nearby. He looked frail, his blue TWT uniform loose on his thin frame. "It's quiet and dark out there," he said. "If you're going to go, you better go now. Don't want to stay down here much longer."

Brindos reached up, carefully, slowly, and held Dorie's arm. The pain had numbed his body. It was almost bearable. He thought, but did not say, *Union bright*.

There were two extra blasters that Melok had retrieved from the downed guards, but could he trust Thomas with them?

Something was wrong. Thomas and Dorie were frowning, looking off in different directions.

"What?" he asked, slowly, painfully, working his way into a sitting position. Dorie steadied him the best she could.

At that moment, he heard what they were hearing. The unmistakable whine of reverse thrusters.

Thomas went to his console. After a moment he said, "Another shuttle."

"Whose?" Brindos asked.

"I don't know. It didn't show up on my tracker, so it must've come down directly from the jump slot, like we did."

Brindos still held on to Dorie's arm. He shot her an urgent look, his body protesting. He wasn't sure he could give her cogent directions at this point. He pushed with all his might, coaxing his brain to work. "Okay, you guys go now. Thomas, take a blaster."

Dorie said, "I have the lockout membrane, Thomas. You'd have to kill me to get it and fly out of here, and I'm not letting that happen."

"I understand," he said.

Dorie let go of Brindos's hand, headed to the back, and took an extra blaster. She threw it at Thomas.

Brindos said, "Okay. Go to the police station before that other shuttle lands and realizes we're here."

Thirty-five

Aryell to Ribon was the shortest of all jump-slot trips between colony worlds, and we hit Ribon space after about six Earth hours.

Forno warned our pilot about any undue alarms, and after getting clearance, the *Volantis* docked unceremoniously at Swan Station, which was nearly deserted. Only two vessels circled the hub of the station, one jump vessel and one shuttle, and they both looked like they'd been docked there awhile.

Swan Station had a skeleton crew, according to the pilot, and indeed, no one came to meet us at our umbilical when we debarked. Apparently, Union officials weren't too worried about traffic coming and going, and TWT didn't care either.

"What're we doing about the crew and passengers?" Forno asked on *Volantis*'s bridge. "We'll need a ride out of here."

"The shuttle has slot capability," the pilot said. "I've piloted it before. An old cargo shuttle for supplies from Ribon to the station, but fitted with insertion gear for smaller export runs to the other Union worlds."

Forno left with the pilot to find the shuttle, and I went to check on Jennifer in the ship's medical area. She lay on her back on one of the diagnostic beds, her legs covered with a blanket, her blond hair tied back in a ponytail. I told her the situation.

"I can pilot the shuttle through the jump slot," she said.

"You can? Since when does the NIO give its hounds that kind of training?"

"Before the NIO." She managed a weak smile, no doubt feeling the damage to her leg, despite her telling us otherwise. "I worked awhile for TWT. Might be a little rusty, but I could get us home."

I didn't say anything, just checked her out, trying to confirm whether she would be up to the task or not.

"I don't need my leg to pilot," she said.

"And the *Volantis*?"

"You should let them go."

"To Barnard's, where they were originally going."

She shrugged, moved her right leg beneath the blanket. "By the time they get there, this'll all be over one way or another, won't it?"

"One way or another."

"I'm not going down to Ribon with you, so this is something I can do when you get back."

"If we get back."

"You will."

Later, after Forno and the pilot had returned to confirm the shuttle's jump-slot worthiness, we found a spot in a deserted waiting area down from the ship's berth, and Forno carried Jennifer there. We made her as comfortable as possible, and I gave her my WuWu coat. She tried to give me her code card.

"It's no good to either of us right now," I said, "but you should hang on to it. In case—" I stopped, not wanting to verbalize the possibility of not returning.

The *Volantis* left for Barnard's fifteen minutes later. Forno and I situated ourselves in the cargo shuttle.

"You *can* pilot this down, can't you?" I asked Forno.

"Not my usual, Crowell, but I can do it."

He found the drop coordinates for Venasaille while I made sure we had breather masks for both of us. At the last minute, I stopped at a crew lounge and lifted someone's leather flight jacket. At least it didn't have the TWT logo on it.

Forno grinned. "Finally, a decent jacket."

"You're jealous it won't fit you. Let's go."

Then we debarked and made our descent to Ribon.

*   *   *

I'd never been to the Venasaille police station myself but knew the general area downtown, and we buzzed over the area a number of times, the shuttle's floodlight shining down on the dark buildings, before coming across it. On one of the rooftops downtown, I recognized the Ribon Authority logo depicting Ribon and a circling Coral Moon on a blue shield with an old-fashioned sword raised along the left side.

We found a clearing nearby to land the shuttle. As we descended, Forno said, "Shit, there's another shuttle here."

I leaned closer to the front window and saw a shuttle almost identical to ours parked in the clearing, its engines off, the area around it quiet.

"No way to tell whose it is," I said, grabbing the pulse rifle. "We have to consider the possibility that one of the aliens, or some of their Thin Men, are watching the police station."

Forno finished the landing sequence, and once the shuttle hit ground, he powered down, grabbed his weapon, and turned to me. "You'd think they'd have a whole army here."

"No, we know where the army is. They're sitting in the tent city on Aryell. Whoever these aliens are, they're not many, and they probably haven't had a lot of time to make many copies, these Thin Men. At least not enough to do much more than they've already done infiltrating the NIO and sending authorities on wild-goose chases after Plenko and the Movement."

Forno scratched his leathery head with his blaster, looking at the shuttle across the clearing from us. "Well, at this point, it would only take a few of them to make it difficult for us down here. If we fail and they get the key, they'll be able to finish their Conduit and take their own sweet time building their army at New Venasaille."

"We can't fail."

Forno pointed out the window with his blaster. "That could be your partner, for all we know."

I grabbed one of my breather masks and slipped it on. "Only one way to find out."

"What if it's not him?" Forno asked. "What if it's Plenko?"

"Then we kill him," I said without a thought.

Thirty-six

Thomas and Dorie secured their breather masks and went out through the airlock. They were well out of sight, disappearing into the darkness, by the time the other shuttle settled nearby.

Brindos couldn't keep watch over the other shuttle. He fought his demons in a haze of pain and frantically struggled to stay awake.

No more RuBy.

If he fell asleep now, he was certain he would stay asleep.

No more Brindos.

Thin Man, Thin Man, coming to our house.
Save the day! Save the day!
O save us from that louse!

Brindos didn't know for sure because he was lying down, but he didn't think his legs would work if he tried to walk.

He had heart palpitations, he was sweating, and his arms were shaking against the floor of the shuttle. The pain was a tidal wave, gaining strength for one last devastating blow.

He was lightheaded. Thomas's RuBy was wearing off. He heard a soft clanking sound outside the shuttle.

The Movement's here and Plenko's near
His revolution made.

Brindos wasn't going to make it.

Never fear, the Thin Man's here,
O don't you be afraid.

There was nothing he could do. Blackness seeped around his eyes, and the wave crested and crashed, twisting him around, battering him against the rocks.
Union dark.
Drowning him.

Once again, Brindos was surprised to wake up.

His eyes regained focus, and a blurred shadow turned solid. Brindos stared at himself. At the Plenko copy, leaning over him.

"Plenko's near," Plenko said.

"Son of a bitch," Brindos murmured.

"You missed me, I see," he growled.

Brindos wanted to get up and strike at him, pummel him with his fists, never let up until the Helk was on the floor here instead. His pain seemed in abeyance, and he wondered how that could be. He blinked away tears and fuzziness and took a better look at Plenko. Plenko straightened, shook his head, and raised one hand, which held a syringe.

"A treatment?" Brindos whispered.

"Do you realize," Plenko said, "that you were rambling on with that despicable nursery rhyme?"

"Why did you give me a treatment?" Brindos asked, confused. He lifted his head off the deck for the first time in a while. "Why save me?"

Plenko leaned down again, closer, and anger sparked in his eyes. "Goodness, this will not save you. It just allows me to talk to you. Do you think you're my Stickman, Mr. Brindos? Is that what you think? That you're going to take me out?"

Brindos closed his eyes and put his head down again. "I don't think anything."

Plenko patted him on the top of the head. All it did was set his head on fire.

"You should be thinking about your mission, shouldn't you?" Plenko swept his hand around the shuttle. "You didn't come down here alone, and you came looking for the key. You were hoping to find it before I did."

"I'm not telling you anything about it. You should have let me die."

"Not so easy." Plenko extended his hand, the one not holding the syringe, and motioned for him to grab it. "Come on, off the floor."

"I'll kill you."

Plenko laughed. "You're back among the living, but you're still not yourself. You're in terrible pain. You're weak. You've missed too many treatments. Get up." He waved his arm a little. "Or I just kill Dorie and take the key from her dead fingers."

Dorie? He had Dorie? He did his best to move his head and glance around Plenko.

Dorie sat in the pilot's chair, eyes wide, mouth a thin line that quivered a little.

His thoughts flew back. Plenko had known where they were going and waited for them to make the first move; Brindos led him right to the key. Plenko had Dorie, and now he had the key. Brindos didn't think Plenko would kill her, not after all this time with her, but he didn't want to chance it. He put out his arm, Plenko wrapped his hand around it, and pulled Brindos up, causing a landslide of pain to roll over him.

Dorie held the not-quite-spherical sculpture made of mortaline that Brindos had seen once in the Venasaille apartment. At the moment, he couldn't see the fine details of the people writhing beneath and atop its surface, because Dorie's two-handed grip covered it.

"Sorry about your pilot, by the way," Plenko said. "He tried to keep me from getting to Dorie and things got a little messy." He grinned, showing sharp teeth.

Brindos made eye contact with Dorie, trying to give her a calming look. She didn't relax at all.

"Are you hurt?" Brindos asked.

She shook her head.

"She's fine," Plenko said, "except for the fact that she's a RuBy freak. Nice of her to share with you, though. I can't imagine you'd have made it this far without some."

"What do you want from me?" Brindos asked, voice shaking.

"Such a simple thing," Plenko said, staring at the planet sculpture cupped in Dorie's hands. He got to her seat in one step and wrenched the sculpture from her. He held it up to his face. "I would've never guessed it would be something so simple. It truly is a piece of art."

"You really didn't know what it was?" Dorie whispered.

Plenko looked back at her. "No. Just that it was something your husband gave to your copy. He created it for the vault on request of the NIO. Unfortunately, he found out about the Ultras and he took it."

"Ultras?" I asked.

"That's the name we've given them."

The aliens.

"Why are you doing this for them?"

Plenko cradled the sculpture in one hand, studying it. "A deal was made years ago with a number of special envoys from the eight worlds of the Union. Human, Helk, Memor. The five members of the Science Consortium brought in."

"What deal?"

"When the Ultras discovered mortaline here, they enlisted help to create the Transcontinental Conduit. They enlisted help to cause unrest throughout the Union—that's where I came in, of course. To cause unrest, to destroy faith in the Union. But ultimately the Movement set out to devastate this world to have access to thousands of refugees the Ultras could use to make copies and build their secret army.

"When the key went missing and evidence piled up about Kristen's connection to the real Dorie, after you became involved in the death of the Dorie copy, the NIO set you up. The Ultras already had control of the NIO through copies of Timothy James and others, so it was easy enough. They didn't expect Crowell to send you to Temonus. Didn't expect him to run, didn't figure the two of you would make so much trouble along the way." He patted Brindos on the head again. "Worked out in your case, didn't it?"

Brindos brushed angrily at Plenko's arm, but he didn't even have the strength to do that, and didn't come close to it.

"One of our own Tony Kochs tried to get the key from Crowell's girlfriend, Cara. She was chosen, you see. To be One with the Ultras."

"You made a copy of Cara?"

"Yes. Well . . . sort of." He waved it off. "The point is, *that* Tony Koch disappeared. I assume your partner managed to kill him. We sent our own Cara to kill Katerina Parker, whom I thought might have the key."

"We."

He spread out his arms. "The Thin Men."

Brindos stared him down, waiting for him to continue.

"The Ultras are determined. The Thin Men will finish the other Conduit for them, continue building the army to infiltrate the Union. No one in the NIO will question the purpose of the Conduit because most of the NIO belongs to the Ultras. Most of the Kenn too. Eventually, we will copy all members of the organization, or dispose of them. We'll infiltrate all the provincial governments and envoys, and all the intelligence organizations."

"And President Nguyen?"

"Did the Ultras copy him, do you mean? Kill the original?" He bared sharp teeth when he grinned. "No. Not yet. But the inhabitants of the Union trust who they trust. They trust Nguyen, and they'll trust the copy when the real one has been eliminated."

"We'll stop you."

Plenko laughed. "*You're* Plenko now. Plenko's Movement will die with you. Your knowledge of the Ultras will die with you. The Union will see the horrible terrorist Terl Plenko dead and praise Nguyen and the NIO for all their efforts. It'll be too late for those who know the truth because no one will believe them."

"You said it was a deal. It sounds like the Ultras get everything. What's in it for you?"

Plenko laughed again, enjoying the moment, but he didn't say anything else.

Time seemed to slow. Brindos wrestled with Plenko's revelations, but he also fought to stay cogent through the fog of pain. He glanced at Dorie, who gave him a panicked look, her face pale.

A shrieking whine erupted from outside the shuttle. Surprised, Plenko practically growled.

Another shuttle was landing nearby.

Brindos wondered if it might be Crowell. Dear God, he *hoped* it might be. "Give up," he said to Plenko, standing taller, hoping to exude confidence. "That's my partner now."

"I hope so," Plenko said, holding out two breather masks he'd brought with him from his own shuttle. "Time to get ready."

Thirty-seven

We didn't debate for long how we would handle the other shuttle. Time was not on our side. Forno fitted us with breather masks and we exited the shuttle, weapons ready and aimed at the other shuttle. A good hundred yards separated us. The sky looked to be turning a little lighter, night giving way to early dawn.

A blanket of hardened ash covered the ground. I didn't see any vegetation. Most likely the rains had also poisoned the plants, if they'd not been suffocated by the ash. Some of the nearest buildings, damaged by numerous earthquakes, looked like they could fall at any second. Others were burnt out. I smelled smoke from somewhere. A few towers were missing windows, the glass blown out.

But I had to focus on the shuttle in front of us. Plenko could be in there. Brindos could be in there.

We had no cover. We crouched low but stayed put near our shuttle. If someone decided to open fire, we still had a chance to scramble to safety. We were making ourselves known to the occupants of the other shuttle, if they were even looking.

No one fired on us, so after a few minutes, we edged forward, taking a more defensive tack to show them we were not planning any overt assault. Of course, I didn't know if that was entirely the case. We drew within twenty yards of the other ship, my stomach churning.

Then the door of the other shuttle opened, and out stepped a ghost.

Dorie Senall.

Even though she wore the breather mask, I could tell she was the woman from the holo-recording. The woman I'd seen plummet to her death on Ribon.

As Forno and I raised our weapons, she held her hands high, the rain jacket she wore rising up past her hips; she was unarmed.

Following her was Terl Plenko, also unarmed, dressed in a loose-fitting gray overcoat; he stepped in behind Doric. Right behind him came—

Another Terl Plenko.

He was armed with a Helk stunner. I gripped the pulse rifle tighter and trained it on the Plenkos.

A black animal-hide tunic covered the second Plenko neck to foot. He slipped in behind the first Plenko.

Forno whispered, "What the hell, Crowell."

Both Plenkos glanced at Forno. Dorie Senall kept her head down.

"Well now, I don't know you," the second Plenko said through his breather mask.

Forno glared at him.

"But I know you, Dave Crowell," Plenko said. The voice, even muffled, boomed in the quiet of the clearing.

"I guess I thought I knew you," I said.

"You *know* who I am."

"Well," I said, inching a little closer to them, "since there are two of you, I'm not quite sure I *do* know you. You seem to be holding the other at gunpoint, so that tells me a little."

Plenko nudged the first one with his weapon. "Tell him."

The Plenko in gray looked back for a moment, then down at the ground. He didn't look well; his hands shook.

"It's me, Dave," he said. "Brindos." He looked up at me. "Alan."

I stared at him so hard my eyes watered. "Bullshit."

"I sent you the crossword. Told you about the key."

I waited for him to say something more, something more telling.

"You sent me to Temonus to find Tony Koch," he added. "You told me before I left that the inflatable Plenko Halloween costumes were quite lifelike, and you had one just my size." He managed a weak laugh, throwing out his arms to announce his Helk presence. "Well, here I am. Didn't think it would happen so literally."

"Alan," I whispered.

"Son of a—" muttered Forno next to me.

"It is indeed Brindos," the armed Plenko said. "The process to create a Plenko from a much smaller human is not without its side effects, and it is slowly killing him, although I could keep him alive for a little while longer with the proper treatments. Certainly not forever." He moved directly behind Brindos, his stunner buried in his neck. I thought of Cara at Snowy Mountain, of the not-Brindos there who had murdered her. He had stood behind her in much the same way Plenko now stood behind my partner.

"It's true," Brindos said. He narrowed his eyes at me, tilting his head ever so slightly. "I'm a dead man no matter what. Plenko and some others made a deal, helping the Ultras get the mortaline, make the Conduits—"

"Ultras?" I asked. "That's what you call them? Who are they? Where are they from?"

Plenko smiled. The look on his face was almost reverent. "You'll never know. You cannot know. They're beyond scrutiny. Can you believe that just a handful of them have put the Union on the brink of revolution?"

"But why?" I asked. "Why are they doing this?"

"They want to learn from us."

"Learn? Are you kidding me?"

"They are One with us. They can mimic our thought patterns, understand our physical superiority, and weed out our mental deficiencies. They can rebuild themselves by tearing us down and re-creating us."

Brindos was faltering. Swaying a little, his face contorted, he cast a desperate look toward me, then to Dorie Senall. I seethed, wanting to get to Plenko right then. Brindos said nothing.

"You'll never know them, never find them," Plenko said. "Never understand them."

Riddles. Still riddles, even at this point in time, with everything on the line.

Brindos grunted, folding his arms around his stomach and bending over slightly. He mumbled something, words that I understood, but in an order that made no sense.

Sweet mother of Memory, but he was dealing with excruciating pain. It seemed to emanate off him in waves. He was dying. . . .

"No one will trust anyone," Plenko said, "and so we will continue to create the Thin Men, and the Ultras will come to our worlds in greater numbers, and soon we'll be free, and soon we'll have peace."

"We had peace!" I yelled. "Before this all started. You turned everything upside down, and for what?"

Plenko put more pressure on Brindos's neck. "I will live, you will not. It's simple. Your weapons. Throw them far away from you."

I looked over at Forno. His hand clenched his weapon so firmly I thought he might crush it. For a moment, I wondered if he might be able to use his super speed and surprise Plenko.

Plenko expected to win. He could have stayed in the shuttle, but he was brimming with confidence, firm in the belief that things would go his way. Because he thought he was immortal?

Because he knew he had the upper hand. He was a Helk. Ruthless. Quick. He could shoot Forno before I even took a step in the Helk's direction, and he'd have that stunner locked back on me in a split second.

I frowned as I realized what had to happen here. I caught Brindos's eyes—his Helk eyes—and stared long and hard. It didn't matter that he didn't look human. I could tell that was my partner in there. My *friend* in there.

When Forno looked my way, I gave him a nod. He frowned and shook his head.

"It's okay," I told him. Plenko needed to know we were complying.

"Over the shuttle," Plenko said.

Forno took his time, but he finally threw his weapon in a high arc that took it up and over the shuttle to the other side and out of sight.

"Now you, Crowell."

"Let my friend go," I said, "and I'll surrender mine."

Plenko looked at me with pity. "You don't really expect me to be that stupid, do you? I certainly don't expect *you* to be that stupid. Do you think I'm alone? That I came here without other Thin Men? You don't have a choice."

My heart raced faster, as if someone had simply turned up a control knob. Other Thin Men *where*? In his shuttle? I didn't think so. He would've come out with them.

At the vault, maybe.

Or he was bluffing. A party of Ultras. Maybe a good number of copies made, but where were they all? Scattered around the Union? Could the Ultras, through Plenko, possibly get a large number of the Thin Men together in one spot—on a ravaged planet hard to reach by normal means—to help secure the metal they needed for their takeover plans?

Brindos and I, we'd just been a couple of borrowed hounds on the run, even included in their plans to discredit the Movement and heap praise on the NIO and draw attention from what was really happening there and around the Union. Why would the Ultras think they needed to worry about us?

Then Dorie surprised me as she turned and stepped away from Brindos. "Terl, you can kill these guys if you want, whenever you want, but how about doing something for me first?" She smiled up at him.

Plenko seemed startled. "Dorie—"

"You have some, don't you?" She patted the pockets of the rain jacket. "Just a square is all I need. My head really hurts. I won't give any of it to Brindos."

Plenko pushed her away. "I have none."

I thought then I understood what Dorie was doing. She had taken herself out of the line of fire. I remembered the squares of RuBy I had taken from the tent in New Venasaille.

"I've got plenty in my pocket, Dorie," I said.

She looked at me with glassy eyes, that haunted look of a RuBy addict, but I realized it wasn't the drug making her eyes glaze over. She had tears in her eyes.

"Crowell!" Plenko yelled. He aimed his stunner at Brindos's head. "Your weapon."

There was an interminably long pause while we stared each

other down. I shifted to Brindos, and in his eyes shined the torment of the moment, like the eyes of the thousands of churning, tormented bodies aching to be free from the mortaline sculpture.

Brindos smiled the briefest of smiles, made a barely perceptible nod.

I knew what he wanted. I steeled my resolve, knowing I couldn't think too much about it, or the moment would be lost. I lifted my chin and gave Terl Plenko an icy stare.

Plenko clicked something on his stunner, the buzz of a power-up, a killing pulse to come.

"I'm not giving in to you," I said, hoping to keep my voice from cracking. "Not to you. Not to the Ultras. There's only one Thin Man I'm giving in to."

A second passed, Plenko and I frozen like chess pieces, waiting. But it was just a second.

I whipped up the pulse rifle and shot Brindos in the chest. Alan Brindos, my friend and partner, fell to the ground like a lead weight.

Terl Plenko did what I expected. He watched Brindos fall, stunned by what I had just done, his weapon tilting toward the ground. By the time he realized what had happened and came back to the reality of it, I had the split second I needed to fire again.

The blast threw Plenko backward into the shuttle behind him. I fired three more times before he slipped down in a heap and lay still.

Thirty-eight

And now the pain changed.

Crowell's pulse rifle had ripped that other pain from him. Brindos was a Helk, physically, and his heart wasn't where the sonic beam ripped into his chest.

But it was close enough. Enough for Crowell to get the jump on Plenko. Enough for Brindos to get the hell out of there and leave all the pain and suffering behind.

"Goddamn Plenko," he said as Crowell scrambled to his side.

"He's dead," Crowell said.

"I meant me. Look at me. Shit of a way to go out."

"I'm sorry."

"No, no." Brindos caught Crowell's shoulder with his hand. The movement brought a new dimension to his pain and he waited for the chaos inside to die down a little. "We have the key. Dorie found it, Plenko found us—"

"We've got it now," Crowell said.

Dorie came up beside Crowell, pulled RuBy squares out of his pocket. She rolled several squares quickly, then placed them on Brindos's tongue. "This will ease your way," she whispered into his ear.

"Dorie," Brindos said. He swallowed, the cinnamon of the RuBy coating his throat, the fog enveloping him once more.

"We'll finish this for you, Alan."

"Union bright?" he asked, fighting back tears.

She smiled as she leaned over, her teeth like pearls, shining as if streaks of sunlight illuminated them. And indeed, at that moment, rays of Ribon's sun bathed the clearing in light.

"Union bright," she said, and kissed him.

Crowell held onto Brindos's shoulder for another few minutes. All the while, Brindos watched Dorie's face. Soon, he turned his head and saw Crowell. One corner of his mouth lifted in a half smile.

"This borrowed hound hopes you kick Tim Jim's ass," Brindos said.

Crowell smiled back and said, "You can count on it. Rest, my friend."

And then Brindos was gone.

Thirty-nine

We put his body on the shuttle we'd take to the vault. He'd had no family, but we couldn't just leave him on Ribon. Also, Dorie took us to the police station where we found Thomas's body. He deserved a ride home too. Plenko had shot him point-blank multiple times with his stunner. I looked away from the misshapen corpse while Dorie and Forno found some body bags inside the station. We wrapped Thomas in one of them and Forno carried his body back to the shuttle without too much trouble. Dorie carried the extra Helk-sized body bag for Brindos. Eventually we had both of them in the back of the shuttle.

It was Dorie who said Brindos hadn't expected to live long enough to get to the vault and that she should cut off his finger for the DNA lock, so Forno found a laser knife and took one of Terl Plenko's fingers. I didn't give a shit about this Plenko. The rest of him could rot down here for all I cared.

After rounding up the weapons—Plenko's stunner and the blaster given to Thomas—we lifted off in the shuttle Forno and I had come down in. Day had come to Venasaille, a ghost city, largely intact, although some buildings had been damaged or had collapsed, probably from earthquakes, heat, and fire. Dorie held on to Terl Plenko's sculpture the whole way, and at that point it seemed that an army of Helks couldn't have wrenched it away from her.

She explained to us who she was. The mate of Terl Plenko. How she met Brindos on Temonus, about the run-in with Plenko in the

Helk district, meeting Joseph, Melok the writer, and how they'd worked together to get to Ribon.

"Your friend was a good Helk," she said with a smile.

I smiled back. "He was a good human."

She nodded. "Physically he was Terl, of course, and for a while he was on his way to becoming a true copy of the Ultras, but I helped him find himself. In the end, he was Alan Brindos." She paused for a second, thinking. Remembering. "He was a lot like the Terl I married. I felt something for him, and I think he felt something for me."

"I'm guessing so."

"It was hard to tell because of his pain."

We left the conversation hanging there as the shuttle cruised low. I could only imagine the emotions streaming through Dorie Senall upon seeing two Plenkos, so like her husband, killed in front of her. I kept quiet, and left her alone.

We were looking for the large triangle-shaped building of Ribon Provincial. The vault was several miles away in an underground building. The only way to get in was via a kiosk that marked the vault. No one had access to the kiosk except the top brass on Ribon, and I wasn't sure we'd have any luck with this strategy either.

The shuttle flew over Ribon Provincial about ten minutes later. I pointed Forno toward the kiosk visible behind the building's south triangle point.

"It's damaged," I said, seeing jagged shards of metal jutting from the sidewalk.

"Someone's been here," Dorie said.

"There's a Memor transport a half mile down," Forno said, pointing it out. It was spherical, five landing struts extending outward from the sleek surface, making the ship look like a beetle. It was colored a deep orange.

"Plenko said they knew where the vault was," I said, "so we might indeed have company. I would expect, even if their numbers were few, they wouldn't leave it all to Plenko."

"They're waiting for the key," Forno said, "and we're taking it right to them."

I knew that. It was a risk I was willing to take. We could take what we knew back to Earth, but who could we trust? Certainly not the NIO.

I said, "We can't just take the key and leave that metal there."

"Any plan yet as to how we're going to get rid of it?" Forno asked. "If we can even get close to it? You didn't think there'd be much of an army down here—"

"And you said it would only take a few of them to take us out. I know."

"Seriously, though, how *are* we going to destroy that mortaline?"

I peered straight ahead at the kiosk.

Forno sighed. "I'll land us right in the street. Might blow out a few windows, though."

"No one to care," I said, and gathered the weapons and breather masks.

We were up for a fight, but we didn't find one outside the kiosk.

After landing, the three of us secured our breathing masks and checked our weapons. I left the pulse rifle in favor of a blaster. Not as much firepower, but more accurate in close quarters, and easier to carry. And easier to hide, if need be, in my newly acquired flight jacket.

Forno had Plenko's finger, wrapped in plastic and secure in the gray coat Brindos had worn. Forno had asked Dorie if it was all right to wear it. Dorie carried the mortaline sculpture in one hand, blaster in the other.

The building containing the vault was quiet and completely empty when we climbed down the ladder ourselves. I took this as a good sign.

Three access doors that would've required force to open had been blown apart. This I took as a bad sign.

We continued down the last passage, weapons drawn, until we came near the end, and a sharp corner to the right. I motioned Dorie and Forno back a few steps as I glanced quickly around it.

Twenty paces away, a heavy glass wall and door blocked the passage, and visible on the other side of it was the vault. As far as I could tell it was locked tight, the huge steel door glinting in the spotlights overhead.

That was the good news. The bad news was the presence of three First Clan Helks on the left-hand side of the vault door, and two Memors and two humans standing on the right-hand side. They wore breather masks, and all gripped weapons.

Another man sat in a chair in front of the door, and I blinked, surprised, wondering if I was seeing things. The man was not wearing a breathing mask. His eyes were closed, but he was definitely alive. He moved his head from side to side, purposefully, but so slowly that it freaked me out. He was an older man, with wispy white hair and a rumpled old suit that looked like it had come from an earlier century. He was holding something long in one hand, maybe a cane. But not a weapon.

"Shit," I whispered after I pulled my head back. Putting a finger to my lips to keep Dorie and Forno quiet, we backed up the passage some more; I suspected we wouldn't be heard with the door between us and them.

"Company," I said quietly. "Behind a glass door, next to the vault."

Forno looked down at me, concerned. "How many?"

"Eight, including three First Clan Helks. All armed except one old man, who's sitting there without a mask."

Dorie breathed in sharply. "Old man?"

"Seems old. Gray suit, white hair."

"Oh no," she said.

"What?" I asked.

"Old and white hair. It must be Joseph."

"Joseph. Who's Joseph?"

"The concierge at the Orion Hotel on Temonus."

It meant nothing to me.

"Well, he's actually *not* the concierge," she said. "The Joseph who helped us was the concierge. This must be the Joseph that Brindos said was Plenko's One."

I felt a little shudder pass through me.

"The same way Landry was Jennifer's One," Forno said. "An actual alien presence inside."

Dorie slipped past me and inched along the passage wall.

"Careful," I said.

She took a quick look herself, then turned back to me and nodded.

Oh, Christ.

I said, "He's one of the Ultras, then."

She nodded. "He's not wearing a mask."

"I noticed."

"And he's alive?" Forno asked.

"He moved a little," Dorie confirmed.

An Ultra, here at the vault. An Ultra like Landry. I swore to myself, because I didn't know what to do next. Seven others surrounding Joseph, all armed. This wasn't going to go down like it had with Landry on Heron Station, even if we did have an extra weapon this time. Now I wished we had Jennifer down here with us and not wounded and stuck up on the station.

"There's too many of them," Dorie said.

Forno took his own look around the corner, then frowned. "Plenko's ass. They're just waiting there." He paused, glancing at Dorie. "And we know what they're waiting for."

Dorie clutched the key tightly to her chest.

I hadn't thought about it until this moment, but if they were waiting there, they weren't waiting for us—they were waiting for Plenko, who might have told them he had procured the key. They might not know we had made it here ourselves. They might not know Plenko *had* the key. Maybe they didn't even know yet what the key looked like.

Could this situation play to our advantage?

Better yet—

I looked at Forno. At Dorie.

"You're getting an idea," Forno said.

"I get them sometimes." I pulled the extra blaster from my pocket, and held it out to Forno. "Take the extra weapon."

"Because?"

"We're going to just walk in there."

Forno scowled. "Not funny."

"Forno, you're a big scary Helk. They might not know all the copies."

Forno's jaw tensed, but I saw a glimmer of understanding in his eyes. I held out the blaster, and he took it.

I turned to Dorie. "They know you. Married to Terl Plenko, and you were copied. The key was given to your copy at your place in Tempest Tower, Jennifer Lisle went undercover, the NIO investigation started, and because your copy died, she couldn't tell anyone about the key, and Brindos and I became involved in the whole thing."

She blinked at me. "How does that help us? They know you too, don't they?"

"They do." I slipped my blaster into my right jacket pocket. Holding my hands out, palms up, I said, "I'm the bad guy. You'll escort me."

Forno shook his head and said, "Plenko could've sent a message to them. The Landry copy could have alerted them somehow. They could know we're coming."

I shrugged. "Maybe."

"They probably know Brindos and I escaped from the Helk district," Dorie said.

Through clenched teeth I said, "Brindos is dead. They don't know how or why and what it might have to do with you."

She nodded. "Okay. It's just that—"

I stopped her. "We have to get in there."

"But seriously," Forno said. "How *are* we going to take out that vault?"

"I'm still working on that part."

"Then tell me the plan that leads up to that part."

Unfortunately, I didn't have even our lead-in planned. In fact, I had only a really thin thought about how to get near them without drawing fire. They outnumbered us seven weapons to our four. Eight weapons on their side if you counted this Joseph, if he could do the same glowing-fingers trick that Landry had used on me.

I told them the plan. My hands would be empty, Forno behind me with his stunner in one hand, blaster in the other, herding me to

them, Dorie another escort, walking on the right side, away from
the left side where the First Clan Helks were. There were more hos-
tiles waiting on the right, but my blaster was in my right pocket,
and when I got the chance to reach for it, I'd aim right, to help
Dorie, while Forno went for the Helks.

"What if that glass partition door is locked?" Forno asked.

"They'll unlock it for us."

"If they don't?"

"*We'll* unlock it by force. If so, we'll come in shooting, so we
won't have much of an advantage. But if at least one of us is standing at the end, we have a chance."

"What about the sculpture?" Forno said.

"Dorie keeps it hidden," I said, watching as she put the sphere
inside her rain jacket. "Leverage if we need it."

"It's not leverage if—"

"Our last resort," I interrupted. "If Plenko didn't know what it
was, none of these at the vault know."

"Unless he got that message to them."

"We'll hope not."

We lined up, me at the front, Forno behind with two weapons
nudged into my back. Dorie on my right, weapon in her left hand,
pointed at my head.

"We get the chance," I said, "we take it. No hesitation. Remember what's at stake. What's already happened to our worlds."

Dorie looked behind her, gazing down the passage we'd traversed
back toward the kiosk entrance. Back there was a ruined planet,
where thousands had died. When she turned back, I caught the glaze
in her eyes I'd seen earlier when she realized she'd lose Brindos and
the last link to her husband.

"Okay, then," Forno said. "Let's go."

"Be rough," I said to him, and we walked around the corner.

I figured at least a couple of the Helks would rush up to the glass
door when we appeared, but they only straightened a little and held
their weapons a bit higher.

The Ultra, the not-Joseph who had been doing the freaky swaying thing earlier, stopped moving completely, but his eyes tracked us as we approached the door.

The glass door was unlocked. Forno grabbed me by the head, his hand covering it completely, and pushed me through. He kept close behind me.

"Move," Forno growled.

No one around the vault came toward us. I kept my eyes on Joseph.

The Ultra now turned his head up, studying us as we approached. I saw no emotion on his face, and I was reminded of Landry's cold, alien presence during the two times I'd been close to her. He was alien, made to look human by the Ultras' technology. To blend in, Plenko had said. To learn from us.

Finally, weapons around us hummed to life, automatic targeting sensors activating.

Black score marks marred the vault's surface near the locking mechanism; they had tried to get the door open. Unless the Ultras had somehow managed to open the door and close it again—and I couldn't imagine they had, judging from the scene before me now— the mortaline was still in there.

What Joseph held in his hand was not a cane but an umbrella, the handle toward the ground, the silver point near his face. I saw dried blood on the tip.

One of the Helks separated himself, closer to Joseph. It was one of the Chinkno copies. One of the other two was a Knox.

"Far enough," Chinkno said through his breather mask, his eyes downturned as he frowned. He looked past me at Forno. "Where's Plenko? Which one are you? Why'd you bring these two here?"

He was buying it so far. I lowered my head; perhaps they'd interpret it as submission, but I was partially relieved, and didn't want to betray anything by the look on my face.

"Plenko's dead," Forno said, ignoring Chinkno's other questions. He slapped the side of my head, the weapon in that hand catching my temple. It stung, and it caused me to stumble a little. "This guy shot him."

That was true.

Seven weapons rose a little higher. Joseph's expression didn't change.

"*Aldast Ozsc*," Chinkno whispered, almost reverently. "But you have the key?"

"No," Forno said. "These two claim to know, but won't say anything."

Joseph's other hand, the one not holding the umbrella, wriggled a little on his lap. Then he looked at me, cocking his head. He moved his mouth as if to speak, but nothing came out, making the whole process spooky as hell. Or maybe he was trying to breathe, even though he didn't seem to need to breathe. Whoever the Ultras were, they had not figured out all the complexities of the human body. They'd been able to control the copies somehow, but maybe not completely.

Sweat trickled down the side of my face.

Chinkno bared his teeth, looming over me like a wave ready to break. "He'll talk," he said. He glanced at Forno. "Or we'll each take an arm and *pull*."

I raised my head and looked at him, then at Joseph, who still didn't move.

A Memor on the right, a female, cleared her throat. It wasn't until then that I recognized her.

It was Lorway, of the Science Consortium. A copy of her, anyway. I didn't imagine the original members of the Consortium were still alive. Her long orange hair hung loose and not in the traditional ponytail; her full lips looked huge on her face, as Memors' lips always did.

Lorway pointed at Dorie. "What about this one?"

"What about her?" Chinkno said. "That's Plenko's mate."

"But how'd she *get* here?"

There was a pause as Chinkno considered this. Then he waved the Memor forward and said, "Search them both."

A search could not happen.

Lorway glided toward Dorie and me, and I acted fast so Forno could react in time. I took a step forward and threw my fist hard into the Memor's soft throat.

She stumbled back, dropping her weapon, hands coming up to her throat, surprise in her eyes.

I wasted a few precious seconds frantically getting my weapon out of my coat pocket as I heard Forno's stunner go off and Dorie's blaster discharge next to my ear. One of the humans went down even as I shot the other Memor in the gut, and I heard Forno yell, "Stay down, snothead!"

Dorie and I pegged the last human at the same time and he fell like a rag doll.

"Cover Lorway," I said to Dorie, turned, and saw Joseph had not moved a muscle.

To the left of him, two of the Helks lay unmoving on the floor; Forno pointed his blaster at the one I didn't know, who was sprawled in the corner, holding his entire arm to his chest in pain. He snarled, trying to get to his feet, but Forno kicked his arm hard, causing the Helk to cry out.

"Hell with this," Forno said, and shot him at point-blank range with the stunner.

Forno then aimed his stunner at Joseph and stood still.

I licked my lips and raised my eyebrows at Forno.

Jesus, we'd done it. Somehow, we'd pulled it off. I focused on Joseph, who looked at me impassively. He didn't look angry. Didn't look amused. Just stared at me with those dead gray eyes.

I wasn't sure if Joseph would understand, but I pointed to the vault door behind him and said, "This is all going to go away. There's nothing more you can do."

Joseph moved his head in a little circle, still imitating mouth movements. He finally lifted the other hand. Forno stepped in closer, aiming his weapon at the Ultra.

"Just stay on him," I said. "Watch his fingers for glow."

The Ultra touched his own face with fingers that trembled slightly. He closed his eyes, shut his mouth tight, and I heard him.

What of Plenko's other?

In my mind, the alien's words found root, and I tried to blink away the odd sensation of hearing a strange voice invade my head. *Plenko's other*. He meant Alan.

"Helk's breath," Forno said. "You hear that?"

"Yeah."

Dorie said, "In my head."

Even though we had our weapons trained on Joseph, I was frightened of him. Soon enough, though, the fear turned to anger. "His name's Alan Brindos," I said aloud. "You made him into a Thin Man, and now he's dead. He was my friend, and now he's dead." I pointed a finger at him. "*Your* fault."

The Ultra's hand trembled some more, trailed down his face, to his neck, and fluttered there. A barely audible cry, like a kitten's, escaped his mouth.

"Who are you, and where are you from?" I asked, even though I didn't figure to get an answer I'd understand.

One of us has already gone beyond the mirror, came the voice in my head. *We are damaged.*

I guessed he meant Landry. Killed on Heron Station.

We cannot hold, came the voice in my head. *We are done here.*

Joseph's hand began to shine white.

"Got glow!" Forno said.

"Wait," I told him.

"Remember what happened to Landry!" he yelled.

"I remember. This is different."

Joseph twisted his mouth around again in odd positions, so much so that his lips didn't even look human. The first true emotion seized his face. Frustration. He couldn't talk.

The glow from his hand spread to his arm.

"Let me shoot him," Forno said.

"No. *Wait.*"

"Back up at least," Forno said, and he grasped my arm and pulled me toward the glass door. "Dorie, back."

The Ultra hadn't given up. The mewling sound came again, modulating in different pitches, and other alien sounds issued from his mouth. Nothing I could understand. The glow rose to his neck, down the other arm, filled in his torso.

Then, clear as a bell, Joseph said aloud, "Dave . . . Crowell."

I stared. I couldn't have been more shocked if I'd found him carrying luggage into the vault and asking for my room number.

The glow spread to his face. In my mind I heard him say, *Sleep now.*

I hoped to hell the Ultra meant himself.

The alien was covered in white from head to foot. It *was* different from the softer glow that had enveloped Landry. Joseph's glow became so bright that we had to look away.

The glow abruptly vanished, and the Ultra's head lolled to his chest. There was that tiny kitten cry again, then his shoulders drooped, the umbrella fell from his hands, and he slipped sidelong to the floor.

He was dead, I was sure.

I stared at Joseph's face. In death, it didn't look much different. Just an old man's, the spirit of life extinguished.

"Now what?" Forno asked.

"What about her?" Dorie said, nodding to Lorway.

"Let her go," I said. I stared hard at Lorway. The Memor pulled and twisted her orange hair, which had fallen forward over her shoulders. "If that's your ship out there, you better get going. As far away as you can."

The Memor scrambled to her feet, glanced nervously at all of us, then ran through the glass door and disappeared down the passage.

"What's that mean?" Forno asked. "Far away?"

"Use Plenko's finger," I said, reaching out to Forno. "Let's hurry. We don't have much time."

"What's going on?" Dorie said.

I pointed at Joseph as Forno unwrapped Plenko's finger.

A white aura had started to surround the Ultra.

"Oh, my God," Dorie said.

"We'll get out of here if we can," I said, "but this is our chance to destroy the mortaline. If I'm right, Joseph's core contains the same antimatter Landry had. The blast should vaporize the metal if we get that door open in time. Get the key out, Dorie. *Now.*"

I didn't know if Landry and Joseph were the only two Ultras hiding in the Union. I figured not, but at least they wouldn't be able to rebuild their Conduits. Not when the last known deposits of mortaline had been vaporized.

I held out my hand to Forno and he handed Plenko's finger to me. I found the key interface on the vault door and touched the sensor plate with the finger. A depression the size of Plenko's sculpture sank in to the door. The indentation glistened with flash membranes and a pink nano-slurry.

Dorie came forward and didn't hesitate to insert the mortaline sculpture into the dent.

The interface clicked and snapped. The depression locked on to the key, which twisted clockwise, then stopped, showing another sensor plate.

I pressed Plenko's finger against it.

The sphere now turned counter-clockwise, gaining speed, until it was all a blur. The interface morphed around the key, swallowing it, and before long the depression was gone, the interface smooth.

"C'mon, c'mon," I whispered.

The vault door opened and there was the mortaline. We all backed away, but I nudged Forno toward the dead Ultra, now awash in glow. We didn't have much time. "Go!"

Effortlessly, Forno picked up the body and flung it into the vault, on top of the mortaline.

"Can we close the door?" Forno asked.

"No time to figure that out," I said. "This is a good time to run like hell. Forno, go ahead of us to the shuttle!"

We fled from the vault chamber, Forno moving with his Helk super speed until he was lost from sight.

I didn't think we were going to make it.

Dorie and I weaved through the underground facility, and it seemed to take forever, like the passage had lengthened since our arrival. Then we saw the ladder, climbed it, and burst from the kiosk. Forno was already in the shuttle's pilot seat, and the thrusters were powering up.

We piled through the door and it whisked shut behind us. The shuttle shot to the sky before we were secure, but I didn't care one goddamn bit. I steadied Dorie with a firm hand and grabbed the bulkhead with my other.

Even inside the shuttle I heard the antimatter detonation clearly. I had a glimpse of the large clearing where we'd first landed and picked out the white of a motionless shuttle just before a massive wall of debris blew across and swept it away.

Our own shuttle shook from the blast's concussive force, but we were clear.

We gained altitude and reached space on our way to Swan Station.

# Epilogue

As it turned out, I didn't get to kick Timothy James's ass.

In death, *he* actually kicked the NIO hard, his own antimatter core detonating and destroying most of the building and killing a number of personnel. Nothing remained of the Ultra Tim Jim.

The Ultra Joseph also vaporized completely, as did all the mortaline in the vault underneath the ghost city of Venasaille. Any evidence to suggest clues about the Ultras and where they came from, if there was any, had been burned away. Theories came and went, but most experts had no way of knowing if they possesed physical bodies. They could be from just about anywhere in the universe, perhaps not laying claim to any actual world or planetary system.

Five other Ultras self-glowed to death, followed by antimatter blasts that obliterated large sections of population centers. An Ultra in the Kenn, an Ultra in the MSA, an Ultra on each world of the Union.

As far as we could tell, all the Ultras were gone.

The Thin Men created by the Transcontinental Conduit—built by the Science Consortium, run by Plenko's Movement, technology provided by the Ultras—had not disappeared. But they'd obviously been left behind. On their own, without the Ultras to guide them, the copies were not especially difficult to corner. Many turned themselves in. Detailed examinations of the copies offered up no evidence about the Ultras either. Most of the copies had been arrested and were being held indefinitely. A few copies died from complications of the copy process, as had happened to Brindos.

Although in the overall scheme of things the number of created copies was minimal, a good number of them had escaped detection and were living among the general population, and many believed they could still do the Union harm somehow, particularly if they teamed up with criminal factions.

The five original members of the Science Consortium had been killed by the Ultras after they had built the first Conduit and the technology behind it was secure. The copies of the Consortium members were among the first to be rooted out and arrested. The Lorway copy from the vault, however, had evaded authorities. President Richard Nguyen ordered a special task force made up of a number of scientists from the eight worlds to study the infrastructure of the remnants of the Conduit towers, but self-destruct mechanisms inside them had melted beyond recognition anything resembling alien technology. No chances were taken with the downed mortaline wire on Temonus, however, and it was destroyed. Shards, bits and pieces, as well as sculptures and other art pieces containing mortaline, were commandeered and secured in undisclosed locations for study by those President Nguyen called the most trustworthy of scientists.

I was nervous about this, but the scraps of mortaline that survived, or remained undiscovered, would never be enough to bring back the Ultra's Thin Man plot. Not that anyone would allow a Conduit to pop up somewhere claiming to be a new weather device: the Union government quickly banned the use of weather control technology on any planet.

The tent city, New Venasaille, was dismantled. Its RuBy-addicted inhabitants were given as much help as possible coming off the drug, but unfortunately, a majority of them died. It was never discovered how so much RuBy ended up at New Venasaille in the first place, but rumors pointed toward several of the underground cartels controlling the larger districts on Helkunntanas. The Union government outlawed RuBy on all planets of the Union except for Helkunntanas, where it was manufactured. The Helk government wouldn't budge on this, but they promised to crack down on the trade of RuBy to the other planets.

In an ironic twist of fate, after the NIO and Temonus Authority finished combing through the wreckage of the *Exeter* and Tower One of the Conduit, investigators gathered enough evidence to prove that Lorway, the Memor from the Science Consortium, had sabotaged the ship. Perhaps during some moment of clarity while working with the Ultras, she realized she needed some insurance. Perhaps she felt doubt about her role. Whatever the reason, she programmed the servo-robot to sabotage the *Exeter* if anything happened to her. The carrier's usual run took it back and forth between Solan Station and East City, and a rather simple but hard to detect DNA-locked telemetry signal in the servo-robot's biomemory activated upon her death, sending the *Exeter* along its final path into the Conduit wire.

Joseph Paul Sando, the Orion Hotel concierge, retired and left Temonus to go back to Detroit. I met him there one weekend, and took him to a baseball game at one of the local high schools. I bought us a couple of hot dogs, even though Joseph craved a good juicy gabobilek.

Paul Melok finished his run of *Stickman* with issue 39, which boasted the final confrontation between Stickman and his archenemy Terl Plenko. He added many of the details I sent to him, including the addition of Plenko's evil master, a nefarious alien that Stickman killed. The alien's body was burned and its ashes were secured forever in a DNA-locked vault. No one but Stickman could ever open it. He was helped at a very key moment by a certain private detective from Seattle.

Melok decided to pull the plug on his business, took the money he had, and went into teaching art and graphic design at a local school. I received a free enhanced flashroll copy of issue 39 signed by Melok and the artist, Tad Anthony, and a little later, Melok sent me a framed cover with a holo-animation of Stickman in peril among the ruins of Ribon.

The new director of the NIO, Aaron Bardsley, asked that I head up a unit created specially to study the Ultras, even though we knew squat about them. At the end of it all, what had we really learned? Not who they really were, or where they came from. Not even *why* they had done it. Dorie told the NIO the drivel she had overheard from Plenko in the shuttle before I killed him. I passed on the conversations Plenko had with me to Bardsley, and let them worry about it. We gained some super tech, but much of it was unusable. What we did know was that their silent invasion had caused a massive loss of life. The Coral Moon disaster on Ribon, the damage to East City when the Conduit came down, the RuBy-addicted refugees at New Venasaille, and the deaths of the Ultras themselves, their antimatter cores killing thousands.

I refused the NIO contract. I'd lost my best friend and partner. I lost Cara. I didn't want anything to do with anything remotely associated with Ultras. Bardsley let me out of my contract early. I packed my bags and headed back to Seattle with a nice little bonus from the NIO and the government for my part in stopping the Ultra invasion. It included an antique Rolex watch I put on my wrist immediately, awed by its craftsmanship. I sat and listened to its ticking for hours at a time.

Jennifer Lisle recovered from the wounds she suffered at Heron Station, but she still favored her left leg. Unlike me, she said yes to the special Ultra unit, and was promoted to Special Ops Director. It put her in line to succeed new NIO Assistant Director Steven Hardy.

I reopened my private-eye business in Seattle. Found an office downtown near the Pioneer District, on the top floor of an old building that used to house an art gallery on the ground level. Most of the rooms above the gallery were rented out as artist studios. The place needed a lot of work, but it was spacious, and I'd be able to use the back half as living quarters. I wasn't sure how well I'd do without Alan around, but I had a few new ideas percolating that might bring me a lot of business.

I took care of the funeral arrangements for Brindos, since he had no family, and a priest from one of the local missions performed a brief ceremony while Dorie, Forno and I attended. The next day, I took his cremated remains to one of my favorite out-of-the-way spots, south of the city to a tiny lake that used to have a few multimillion-dollar homes circling it until 2095, when the last of these houses were boarded up. They were all bulldozed to the ground a few years after that.

Throwing the ashes to the wind, I watched them float out over the lake. "See you on the other side, friend," I said.

Dorie showed up at my place in the morning a few days later, while I was trying to put up a jury-rigged wall to separate the office from the living quarters of the studio. I let it drop and it caught my toe.

I held back a curse, then smiled, thoroughly embarrassed.

"I'm coming to say good-bye," she said.

I nodded, knowing this was coming. "You're off to Ribon?"

"Cruiser leaves tomorrow morning."

I gestured out the large window on the west wall overlooking Elliot Bay. "You want to go have a bite to eat? Out on the pier? There are still a couple of places to get decent seafood."

"You don't even like seafood."

"Well."

She shook her head. "No, I'm going to pass. I have a lot of reading to do about the whole Ribon resettlement project. They estimate the first dome will be finished over the south end of Venasaille in a few months, and I have a lot to learn before then. They want me to hit the ground running once I get there, and I'm still fighting the RuBy withdrawal. I won't be able to get it there." She smiled. "Not legally, of course."

"Of course. But you won't need the RuBy, and you'll be fine. I'm glad you're doing this."

"They're calling the south dome New Venasaille."

"Good choice."

"And they said yes to naming our building after Alan."

"The Brindos Building."

She nodded.

"Good choice."

"I tried to get Terl's name for the north dome, but they didn't go for that. Too many negative connotations."

"Sure."

She fidgeted a little as we stood there facing each other. I wasn't sure what else to say.

"Well," she said. "I better go."

"Dorie," I said, finding my voice.

She turned.

"I'm sorry about Terl's sculpture. Sorry we couldn't get it back after opening the vault. I know how much it meant to you."

She shrugged and tucked a loose strand of her black hair behind her ear. "That's okay. It would've been a nice reminder of him, but instead, I think of it as Terl's gift to the Union. You know? I'm glad it—" She faltered, looked down at the floor.

"Saved the world?"

She smiled, raising her head. "Saved the *Union*."

"And he's helping rebuild a world, through you."

"I'm going to do all I can."

"I *do* hope I can get to Ribon some day for a visit."

She laughed. "Awfully expensive for a P.I."

"I've got plans for private investigator domination."

"That'll be a lot easier with your new partner."

"Jury's out on that, but we'll see." I smiled. "Good-bye, Dorie."

"Good-bye, Dave."

When she left, I went back to my dividing wall, but it wasn't long before Tem Forno came in. He had taken to wearing the gray overcoat Dorie had given to Brindos when they had escaped from Temonus. That didn't stop him from complaining about how cold it was on Earth.

"You just missed Dorie," I said.

He shook his head. "Caught her outside and we talked on the sidewalk. Everyone gave us a wide berth, and I think I can take credit for the car accident halfway down the street. Guy ran into an abandoned vehicle."

I laughed. "Get used to it."

He wrapped the coat tighter around him. "Look, I'm here on your suggestion, and I thank you, but it's going to be difficult fitting in."

"You'll be fine. People will get used to you, and you're already a natural detective with your Kenn background."

"Maybe I should find a fedora to go with this jacket."

"That will be inconspicuous for sure."

"You only love me because I'll be able to scare all the bad guys."

"Don't forget your Helk underworld contacts."

"Yeah, those, too you love."

I patted his shoulder. I almost sprained my own shoulder doing that, but on Helkunntanas, a shoulder grab is a sign of friendship. Hey. I'm learning.

"I'll teach you everything I know," I said.

"And I still won't know nothing."

I grinned, then clapped my hands together. "I've got your first job of the day ready," I said.

He eyed the plywood wall laid out on the floor, then looked at me with amusement. "Helk snot, that is one ugly wall."

"Shut up and lift."